The Girls of Bomber Command

Vicki Beeby writes historical fiction about the friendships and loves of service women brought together by the Second World War. Her first job was as a civil engineer on a sewage treatment project, so things could only improve from there. Since then, she has worked as a maths teacher and education consultant before turning freelance to give herself more time to write. In her free time, when she can drag herself away from reading, she enjoys walking and travelling to far-off places by train. She lives in Shropshire in a house that doesn't contain nearly enough bookshelves.

D1080613

Also by Vicki Beeby

The Women's Auxiliary Air Force

The Ops Room Girls
Christmas with the Ops Room Girls
Victory for the Ops Room Girls

The Wrens

A New Start for the Wrens
A Wrens' Wartime Christmas
Hopeful Hearts for the Wrens

Bomber Command Girls

The Girls of Bomber Command

For my family, as always:

Mum

Duncan, Jana & Emma

Chris, Katka & Elena

Chapter One

October 1941

Pearl paused outside the offices of the *Shrewsbury Mirror* and looked in her handbag. Yes, the buff envelope containing her precious article was still there. It had been there the other two times she had checked during the fifteen-minute walk from home, and every time she had inspected her handbag's contents while getting ready for work. In fact, the article had been securely tucked behind her identity card and her ration book ever since she had placed it there last night. She didn't know what malicious hand could have removed anything from her bag while it had been clamped under her arm, but she wasn't taking any chances.

Drawing a steadying breath, she pushed open the door and walked in.

Wilfred Bottle, the news editor, looked up from his desk, peering at her over the top of his spectacles. 'Ah, there you are, Miss Cooper. Did you type up my report on black-market petrol before you left yesterday?'

'It's all done, Mr Bottle. I put it in your in-tray.' Pearl set her handbag on her desk, slung her gas mask case over the back of her chair and hung her mackintosh on the coat stand. Then, seeing that Wilfred was still rummaging through the papers in the wire tray on his untidy desk, she lifted off the tin lunch box that stood atop the precarious pile and handed him the pages that had been just beneath. 'Here you are.'

'Thank you, my dear.' Wilfred ran his hands through his greying hair. 'I don't know how I'll get on without you.'

Pearl's heart leapt. 'Without me? Has Mr Kingsley already made the announcement?' Surely not – she hadn't even handed in the article he'd asked her to write about the local Spitfire fund. He'd also asked Philip Meadows to submit an article on the same subject. Like Pearl, Philip was a clerk at the *Shrewsbury Mirror*, although he worked for the features editor. As they had both applied to be promoted to the vacant role of junior news reporter, Mr Kingsley, the editor-in-chief, had said he would use their work to make his decision.

Wilfred shook his head. 'Not yet, but you've got it in the bag, you mark my words. I've told Mr Kingsley how you've been helping me write up my reports ever since Mr Collier left, and he'd be a fool not to make you a reporter.'

'That's ever so kind of you.'

'Not at all. You've got a talent for words, anyone with a brain can see that. Why you've been happy to remain a clerk all these years, I'll never know.'

'You know why. Thea needed me.' Despite passing her School Certificate with distinction in all her subjects, Pearl had ignored her teachers' advice and left school to get a job and devote more time to her younger sister. At the time, Thea was ten and already running wild. Several times she had been caught playing by the river when she should have been at school. Their grandmother had been remarkably relaxed about the situation. 'Maybe her attendance would be better if you made the lessons more interesting,' Deedee had told the puce-faced headmistress. Pearl, who had witnessed the interview, had wanted to curl up and die with embarrassment.

Not for the first time, she had wished her grandmother was more like the apple-cheeked, grey-haired women portrayed in her school's storybooks rather than the outspoken free spirit she actually was. Pearl and Thea were by no means the only children at the school being brought up by their grandparents – the Great War and the Spanish influenza epidemic had destroyed more families than just Pearl's – but at least the other grandparents had the decency to look and dress like grandparents and to see to it that their grandchildren did their homework and attended school when they were supposed to. They certainly didn't dye their hair bright red and dress in shapeless tunics in garish tropical shades. Nor did they shrug when their grandchild got a poor school report, and say they were sure the child would pick up the skills she needed when she found an occupation that interested her. Pearl had decided her only option was to free her evenings of schoolwork and get a job instead, and she had been lucky enough to get the position at the *Shrewsbury Mirror* the week after she left school. She had started with high hopes that the clerical role would be a stepping stone to becoming a journalist, her dream for as long as she could remember. Twelve years later, although she was still a clerk, she had never stopped hoping. She could hardly believe she finally had the chance to see her name in print.

Now she gave Mr Bottle a rueful smile. 'I wouldn't say I was exactly *happy* to remain a clerk all this time, but I was too busy supervising Thea in my free time to take on a more responsible job.' Her wry expression became a grimace as she recalled some of the scrapes her sister had managed to get herself into. 'Anyway, I did tell Mr Kingsley I'd like to be a reporter as soon as Thea joined the WAAF and became their responsibility instead.' For, to Pearl's astonishment, Thea had volunteered soon after Britain had declared war on Germany, and had received her call-up papers on her birthday in January 1940. Much of Pearl's surprise had been the realisation that Thea was actually old enough to join. She was twenty-one the day she had left home, and therefore an adult. Not a word Pearl usually associated with Thea. 'It's not my fault there hasn't been a vacancy until now.' Pearl wiped damp palms on her skirt, then picked up the envelope containing her article. 'I'd better hand it in. Wish me luck.'

'You don't need luck. All I ask is that when you've moved on to become news editor of *The Times* or the *Manchester Guardian*, you'll remember old Wilfred Bottle who helped you take your first steps into journalism.'

Feeling a rush of gratitude for the kindly man who had given her so much encouragement in the twelve years since she had joined as an eager sixteen-year-old, Pearl kissed him on the cheek.

'Go on with you,' Wilfred said, looking pleased, 'take your masterpiece to Mr Kingsley before it creases.'

Pearl left the room on trembling legs, the sharp click of her heels on the wooden floor echoing around the corridor. The door to Mr Kingsley's outer office loomed large at the end, and Pearl had to relax her grip on the envelope before opening the door, afraid she would crumple the paper inside. Mrs Norbrook, Mr Kingsley's secretary, occupied her desk, which guarded the door to the editor-in-chief's office. The door was shut, and muffled voices could be heard within.

Pearl gave Mrs Norbrook a cheery greeting, then said, 'I've brought the report Mr Kingsley asked for. Should I leave it with you?'

Mrs Norbrook glanced at the closed door, then back at Pearl. 'It would be best if you waited.'

'All right.' Pearl held out the envelope. 'I suppose you ought to take this.'

An odd expression, too fleeting for Pearl to decipher, crossed Mrs Norbrook's face. 'You hold on to it for now, dear.' She waved Pearl into a seat and glanced back at Mr Kingsley's door, a crease forming between her brows. It seemed to Pearl as though she was wrestling with a problem, and she was about to ask if she needed any help when Mrs Norbrook suddenly gave a small nod, as though making up her mind. She leaned forward across her desk and spoke in a low voice. 'In fact, you ought to know—'

But whatever Mrs Norbrook was about to say was interrupted when the inner door burst open. Philip Meadows emerged, followed by Mr Kingsley. 'Thank you so much, sir,' Philip said. 'You won't regret it.'

Pearl stared at him, unable to take in the meaning of Philip's words. If she hadn't known better, she would have thought he was thanking Mr Kingsley for awarding him the job. She must have misunderstood. Mr Kingsley wouldn't have done that without even reading her report. But Mrs Norbrook's sympathetic glance told its own story.

Mr Kingsley turned his back on Pearl and clapped Philip on the shoulder. 'Glad to have you on board, my boy. With writing like that, I'll be surprised if you're not in the running for news editor when Mr Bottle retires.'

Philip gave a self-deprecating laugh, wheezing a little due to the asthma that had rendered him unfit for military service. 'Oh well, I wouldn't want to presume.'

'Nonsense. I'm only sorry I wasn't able to offer you the job until now. You're destined for great things.'

With dawning dismay, Pearl watched him pump Philip's hand and then usher him into the corridor, saying, 'Just wait until you see your words in print for the first time. There's no feeling like it.'

It was the realisation that Pearl might never see her own words in print that burst the bubble of unreality that had surrounded her while watching the scene play out. Her throat ached as she battled the urge to cry. She rose as Mr Kingsley turned away from the door; he gave a little start, clearly seeing her for the first time. If she hadn't already worked out that he had awarded Philip the job without even doing her the courtesy of reading her article, she would have known from the way he couldn't quite meet her gaze.

'Mr Kingsley, may I speak with you?' Feeling her throat tighten, she swallowed, then drew a steadying breath. Now was not the time to dissolve into tears. If she was doomed to spend her life seeing other people do the job she longed to do herself, the least Mr Kingsley could do was tell her why.

'Ah, Miss Cooper.' Mr Kingsley tugged at his collar as though it was too tight. 'I didn't want you to find out like that.

I'm sure you've gathered that I've given the junior reporter's job to Mr Meadows.'

His gaze flickered towards a memo pad on Mrs Norbrook's desk. Following his gaze, Pearl saw her name, and it hit her that Mr Kingsley had never intended to tell her in person but had asked Mrs Norbrook to type it in a letter. Red-hot anger seethed in her chest, burning away any desire to cry.

Before she could speak, Mr Kingsley gestured towards the door. 'Well, I'm sure you have plenty of work to get on with.'

That did it. 'Not until you've told me why you offered the job to someone else before you even read my work.' Normally she wouldn't dare take that tone with anyone in the office, let alone her boss, but she wasn't going to say goodbye to her dream without a fight. 'I've spent hours of my own time writing this' – she waved the envelope she was still clutching in Mr Kingsley's startled face – 'hours I should have been helping my grandmother. But I did it because you assured me that you would use it to decide who deserved the job.'

She would have gone on, but Mr Kingsley interjected in outraged tones. 'Miss Cooper, calm yourself. I haven't got time to deal with this now. I've got…' he appeared to think for a moment '…I've got a meeting with the printers.'

'That was put back until this afternoon, if you remember, sir,' Mrs Norbrook put in. Although her expression was one of bland helpfulness, Pearl had a strong suspicion she was enjoying seeing him squirm.

The knowledge that she had Mrs Norbrook's sympathy gave her the courage to stand her ground. She tempered her tone, though, knowing that antagonising her boss was hardly the way to win him round. 'Please, sir. All I ask is for you to hear me out. Being a reporter is all I've ever wanted to do.'

Mr Kingsley regarded her from beneath his bushy eyebrows, his mouth turned down. Pearl said nothing more but held her breath. 'Oh, very well,' he said at last. 'Come into my office.'

Pearl released her breath and followed him through the door. 'Thank you, sir.' She waited until Mr Kingsley had settled himself into the large leather chair on his side of the desk, then took a seat in the chair he indicated and placed the envelope on his desk.

Mr Kingsley leaned back in his chair. 'Well?'

She realised then that she would never change his mind, but she pressed on, knowing she would never forgive herself if she didn't at least try. 'I've written a good article,' she said. 'I worked hard to get it right. Won't you at least read it?'

'I'm sure it's a competent piece of writing.' He made no move to pick up her pages, and his tone was so patronising Pearl half expected him to pat her on the head. 'What you have to understand,' he went on, 'is that there are a lot of factors to bear in mind when making an appointment. All you've thought about is writing the piece I asked for, but I also have to take into account who would be the best fit for the team, and there are other considerations as well.'

'I already work for the news editor, and he encouraged me to apply because he wanted me to be his junior. What other considerations can there be?'

Mr Kingsley frowned. 'I don't appreciate your tone, young lady.'

'I'm sorry.' She wasn't. 'But this is something I've wanted for as long as I can remember. I need to understand what I did wrong.'

'How old are you – twenty-five?'

'Twenty-eight.' Pearl stared at him, at a loss to understand what her age could have to do with it.

'Well there you are, then. I'm sure it won't be long before you're coming to me to say you're getting married and you want to stop working here. We all know that journalism can be no more than a diversion or hobby for young ladies, before they settle down to the more appropriate role of keeping a house and bringing up a family. Then I would be left with the task of finding someone else. Why would I want to go through all that when there is a man ready to take on the job? A man, moreover, who has a wife to support and therefore is more in need of the extra income.' Mr Kingsley folded his hands across his expansive belly with an expression of satisfaction as though he was now certain Pearl would be completely happy with the situation.

Pearl gathered her article from the desk with trembling hands. She knew if she didn't remove herself from the office right now she would say something she would regret. 'I'll go and get on with my work.'

'That's the spirit. I knew you'd understand, an obliging girl like you.' He picked up his fountain pen, clearly considering the interview over.

Pearl made it to the door on leaden feet. She was turning the knob, determined to reach the safety of the ladies' room before dissolving into tears, when Mr Kingsley called her back. 'One more thing. Mr Meadows is taking up his new responsibilities today, so I'll need you to pick up some of the clerical work from the features desk until we can find a replacement.'

That did it. It was as though a firework had exploded in her chest. She flung her article at him, the pages fluttering to the floor. Then she stalked to the desk and leaned over it until she was nearly nose to nose with the alarmed editor. 'Do it yourself. I quit.' She felt as though she was standing outside herself, with no control over the words pouring from her mouth. 'If you think I'm going to do the work of two people while that useless, good-for-nothing... *man* takes the job that's rightfully mine then you've got another think coming.'

Mr Kingsley pushed back his chair until he was pinned against the wall. His eyes bulged. 'Miss Cooper, control yourself. You're becoming hysterical.'

'I'm not out of control.' And she wasn't. Not any longer. She knew exactly what she was doing. She wouldn't work a day longer in a place where she wasn't respected. 'But you might find it hard to stay in control when you see you've employed a reporter who wouldn't know a good story if it hit him in the face. Now' – she retrieved her scattered work – 'if you don't mind, I'll take my article to an editor who appreciates good writing above outmoded ideas about women. Goodbye.' She marched into the outer office, resisting the temptation to slam the door, only to stop dead when she saw Mrs Norbrook watching her; the secretary must have heard the whole row.

'I'm sorry, Mrs Norbrook.' Now it was all over, it hit Pearl with full force just how many bridges she had burned. Heat flooded her face.

'Don't be. I thought you were magnificent.'

'You did?'

'Oh yes.' Mrs Norbrook lowered her voice. 'I thought you were by far the better person for the job and I couldn't believe it when Mr Kingsley gave it to Philip Meadows. Well done for standing up to him. It took real strength of character.'

'Strength of character won't put food on the table. Didn't you hear? I quit my job, and no amount of grovelling will get it back.'

'Go on with you. Your talents were wasted here. You won't have any trouble finding another position. Now, don't you worry about a thing. I'll make sure you get paid to the end of the month. That's plenty of time to find something else. Go home and put your feet up for the rest of the day. Goodness knows you've worked hard enough on that article.'

The promise of payment for the rest of the month helped stem Pearl's rising panic. She stammered her thanks and went to gather her things. Much to her relief, neither Mr Bottle nor Philip were at their desks; she would find a way to bid Wilfred goodbye another time, and she couldn't bear to face Philip in his triumph. Then she left the *Shrewsbury Mirror* building for the last time and stumbled up St Mary's Street, wondering how she was going to confess to her grandmother what she had done.

She couldn't go home. Not yet. Not until she had worked out how she was going to fix the mess she had made. She didn't want to burden her grandmother with worry.

Her feet had automatically led her along the route home, down Pride Hill and onto Mardol, but once the riverside came into view she slowed, reluctant to see her grandmother before she had a plan. Far better to tell her that she had resigned from her job if she already knew what she was going to do next. As it happened, she was only a short distance from the Empire cinema. Seeing a handful of women go inside, Pearl followed them, not bothering to read the posters to see what was showing. She bought a ticket for the stalls and settled in her seat, secure in the knowledge that she had bought herself a couple of hours of respite; time to think without being disturbed.

A newsreel was already playing when she arrived; at first she watched the flickering black and white images without really taking them in, letting the knot of tension slowly unwind. After a few minutes, however, an item appeared that made her sit up and take interest. It showed the Duchess of Gloucester inspecting a group of women in the Women's Auxiliary Air Force who were in charge of barrage balloons. From the start, it was clear the WAAFs were doing a responsible job, something vital to Britain's defences. What was more, they weren't being patronised by the men in the picture but were respected for the work they were doing – no matter the somewhat condescending tone of the newsreader.

She had thought of war work before, of course. How could she not when she was surrounded by adverts urging women to 'Join the WAAF and help the RAF' or 'Join the Wrens and free a man for the fleet'? To be honest, she had felt guilty for not making more of a contribution, and had thrown herself into volunteer work, yet had clung to her job because she didn't want to say goodbye to her dream of being a journalist. But now she was out of a job anyway, and she had to admit being a WAAF would be interesting. And when the war was over, she would have plenty of experiences to write about.

She shot to her feet. 'Excuse me. Sorry.' She squeezed along the row, eliciting tuts of annoyance, and then she was racing for the exit. Now she knew what she was going to do, she didn't want to waste any more time. As she raced back up Mardol, making her way to the recruiting office, another advantage of joining the WAAF occurred to her. If she was posted near Thea, she would be able to keep an eye on her.

–

It was early afternoon before Pearl finally crossed Welsh Bridge and made her way to the small but pretty cottage on New Street. She found her grandmother working in the back garden, planting broad beans. Most of the garden had now been turned over to vegetable plots, although her grandmother had left her favourite rose bush growing under the kitchen window. The last of the flowers had bloomed over a month ago, and now the bush had been pruned right back. The only splash of colour in the garden came from the bright pumpkins that were ready to harvest.

'Hello, Deedee.' Pearl and her sister had always called their grandmother Deedee. She had been told it was because Deedee had objected to being called 'Gran' or 'Nan' and had asked to be called instead by her name, Edith. When Pearl had been learning to speak, the closest she could manage was 'Deedee', and the name had stuck.

Deedee looked up. 'You're early, dear. Did you get the job?'

'No, but—'

'No? After all the work you put in?' Deedee sat back on her heels and wiped her grimy hands on her overalls. 'What's that Mr Kingsley thinking? Next time I'm in town, I'm going to give him a piece of my mind.'

At any other time, the threat would have mortified Pearl. Now she wished she could see Mr Kingsley's face when being lectured by a tall, skinny 69-year-old with a mop of flaming red hair. 'Don't worry, I already did that.'

'You did? About time. I hope you told him you were leaving.'

'I… I did.' Pearl knelt beside Deedee, feeling as though the wind had been taken from her sails.

Deedee patted Pearl's hand. 'I'm glad. I always thought you were wasted at the *Mirror*. If you want my advice, what you should do now is volunteer for war work. Everyone says the government is going to bring in conscription for unmarried women soon, so you'd be better off volunteering now, and having a better chance of getting the sort of work you want.'

'Well, I—'

'I know you've got your heart set on journalism, but this would help you see more of the world. Expand your horizons. It would do your writing no end of good.'

'Actually, Deedee—'

'One thing, though. I advise joining the ATS or the WRNS. If you join the WAAF, Thea might think you're trying to wriggle your way into her life.'

Pearl's guilt must have shown in her face, for Deedee's eyes narrowed. 'Out with it, Pearl. What have you done?'

It was pointless trying to hide anything from her grand-mother. She reached into her pocket and pulled out the leaflet she had picked up from the recruiting office. Handing it to Deedee, she said, 'I've already applied for the WAAF. There's still the interview and medical to get through but the recruiting officer didn't seem to think there would be a problem.'

Deedee gave her a long look, then patted her arm. 'Ah well, what's done is done. I dare say you won't be posted anywhere near Thea.'

Pearl took the opportunity to divert the conversation from her hasty decision. 'Has there been a letter from her today?'

Deedee shook her head. 'I don't think it's anything to worry about. She said herself in her last letter how busy she is.'

Busy going to the pub with all the airmen, Pearl thought, although she refrained from saying so. Yet she couldn't resist commenting, 'It only takes a couple of minutes to write a few lines. She knows I worry about her.'

Deedee stood with an ease that belied her age. Handing back the leaflet, she said, 'That's half the trouble. You're her sister yet you act like her mother. You smother her, and it's pushing her away. At some point you're going to have to accept she's an adult and capable of looking after herself.'

'This is Thea we're talking about. The one who nearly drowned when she found that old coracle and decided to test it by taking it out into the Severn.'

'That was ten years ago! She's not a child any more.'

No. She was twenty-two, which gave her far more scope for getting into trouble. Whatever her grandmother might say, Thea was Pearl's responsibility, and Pearl lived in terror of learning that her sister's recklessness had led to an accident. Admittedly Thea seemed to live a charmed life, but surely her luck had to run out one day. It was for that reason that Pearl had asked the recruiting officer if she would be able to request where in the country she would be posted.

'Within reason,' had come the reply. 'You won't find out what trade you'll be doing until you've been assessed at the end of your initial training, and that will have a bearing on where you are posted. But you will be able to request a general area for your posting.'

'So I could request Lincolnshire?'

'You could. It doesn't mean you would be sent there, but we will try to accommodate your wishes. As I said, it depends on your trade. If you want to go to Lincolnshire, it would help if you take up a trade required by a Bomber Command station.'

Of course, Pearl had then asked what they were, and her head was left spinning by the different trades the recruiting officer provided. From clerical work and cook – Pearl was determined she wasn't going to spend the rest of the war in a kitchen – to meteorological observers, parachute packers, radio telephone operators and mechanics, to name but a few. Surely there was something in that list Pearl could do. Because whatever Deedee might advise, she was going to do all in her power to qualify for a posting in Lincolnshire. It was time someone with a sensible head on their shoulders kept an eye on Thea.

Chapter Two

March 1942

'Next stop Lincoln.' The guard's call roused Pearl from the doze she had slipped into, and she lurched forward in her seat as the train began to slow. An odd fluttering in her stomach started as she caught glimpses of a platform through billows of smoke, and saw it was crowded with people wearing uniform in the same grey-blue shade as hers. She scrambled to her feet, heart pounding, and grabbed her kitbag from the overhead luggage rack, terrified the train would leave before she could get out. She finally managed to lower the window and twist the stiff handle, then made an abrupt landing on the platform as the weight of her kitbag made the door swing open before she was prepared. Glancing around, she mentally rehearsed the instructions she had been given together with the travel warrant. *Find the railway transport officer to get information on transport going to RAF Fenthorpe.* Staggering under the weight of her kitbag, helmet and gas mask, she followed the other men and women in uniform, hoping they knew where they were going.

It turned out to be a sensible plan and, after a short wait, the helpful railway transport officer had given her directions. 'Your transport will be along in ten minutes,' he told her. 'It won't be a long journey. Fenthorpe's only about five miles away.'

Pearl nodded and went to stand by the road to wait. It had been a day of waiting: what should have been a short journey from RAF Cranwell had lasted for three hours, her train having stopped in the middle of nowhere for ages with no explanation.

The nerves that she had managed to control during the journey were now getting the better of her, and she twisted her hands as frightening scenarios flitted through her mind. No one at RAF Fenthorpe would be expecting her. Or they would be expecting her but, due to a mix-up, would think she was a mechanic instead of a radio telephone operator. Or she would be in the right place, doing the right job but she would have forgotten everything she had learned during her six-week course at RAF Cranwell—

Stop it! She made a huge effort to pull herself together. *Everything's going to be fine. I got top marks and passed out as an AWC1, for goodness' sake.* She felt a glow of pride, remembering her reward for all her hard work at Cranwell, and her anxiety faded. After an assessment during her initial WAAF training at Bridgnorth, she had been recommended for the trade of radio telephone operator, or R/T operator for short, because of her 'nice voice'. She had then gone to RAF Cranwell to learn her trade and had spent the weeks learning Morse, how to service a wireless and, most importantly for her future role, radio protocols and how to operate a radio telephone. Most of the other WAAFs on the course had passed out with the rank of ACW2 – aircraftwoman, second class. However, thanks to her high marks, Pearl had been one of the select few WAAFs who had graduated as an aircraftwoman, first class.

Much to her disappointment, none of the other WAAFs she had trained with were going to the same place, meaning that for the third time in three months she would have to learn the layout of a new camp alone and make new friends. Still, RAF Fenthorpe was only a few miles from Waddington, where Thea was based, working as an instrument repairer. She had every hope that she would see her sister often and that when she did they would have lots in common now they were both living in Bomber Command stations.

Feeling more relaxed, she was able to smile at the corporal driving the truck that pulled up beside her a short while later.

She had hoped for a chatty driver who could tell her what life was like in Fenthorpe before she got there. Unfortunately he seemed very shy and reluctant to talk, even though he let her sit in the cab, so she looked out of the window in silence as they left behind Lincoln on its hill, and the houses gave way to wide, flat fields, very different from the hills of her native Shropshire. The view looked all the more stark because the trees were still bare after a long hard winter.

Presently, a wooden water tower came into view above the hedgerow lining the road. No sooner had Pearl seen it than she heard the roar of engines. A huge shadow passed overhead, making her shrink in her seat, and the view ahead was filled by a large twin-engined aircraft, its lowered undercarriage seeming to skim the water tower. Remembering her aircraft recognition lectures, she identified it as an Avro Manchester. As she watched, the Manchester glided lower until she could no longer see it, and she guessed it must have landed.

'Is this Fenthorpe?' she asked, craning her neck to see what was beyond the hedge. All she could see was wooden roofs and a vast structure that could only be a hangar.

'That's right. Main gate's just here' – he pointed to the barrier they were passing – 'but I'll drop you by Gate 2, closest to the Waafery.'

The truck bounced over the bumpy road for about a mile before turning down a narrow lane. Over the hedge on her left, Pearl could see buildings, so she expected the gate to be on the same side; but much to her surprise, the driver pulled into an entrance on the right. While he spoke to the guard at the barrier, Pearl looked beyond it and saw a muddy field filled mainly with Nissen huts. Uniformed men and women either strolled around the site or were riding bicycles. Pearl quickly saw the advantage of having a bike, considering that the gate to the main station must be over a mile away, and resolved to write to Deedee to have her bike sent to Lincoln on the train.

'This is where you get out,' the driver told her once the barrier was raised and he had driven through. 'The WAAF guardroom is down there.' He pointed down a path that was gravelled and thankfully free from mud.

A short while later Pearl found herself outside a low hut, laden with her luggage. She fumbled in her pocket for her papers, then walked in.

'So you're the new R/T operator,' the WAAF corporal on duty said when she presented herself in the guardroom. 'We're supposed to be getting a new Met WAAF too, but she hasn't turned up yet. You didn't spot another sprog on your train, did you?'

'Another what?'

The corporal rolled her eyes. 'A new recruit, like you.'

'Oh. No, I didn't notice any others. How can you tell I'm new?'

'Look at your uniform – it's pristine. You look like a child on her first day at school. Anyway, the buttons are a dead giveaway.'

Pearl glanced at the gleaming brass buttons on the corporal's tunic that far outshone those on her own jacket, despite the hours she had put into polishing them.

The corporal gave her a sympathetic smile. 'Keep going with the polish. Another year, and you'll look like an old hand.'

A year? It suddenly hit Pearl what a commitment she had made, joining the WAAF for the duration of the war when she had no idea how long that would be. She made no further comment as she accepted a folded pile of bedding, rough bath towels and a standard-issue packet of sanitary towels from the corporal and then followed her with laden arms along a gravelled path, past a row of identical Nissen huts.

They stopped outside a door with a stencilled number three. 'Here you are,' the corporal said. 'Home sweet home.'

Inside, the layout was much the same as the hut she had slept in during her basic training at Bridgnorth. In the centre was a coke stove with chairs clustered around it. Only one chair was occupied, by a red-haired WAAF who glanced up and swept her with an assessing gaze before returning to the letter she was writing. Iron-framed beds lined the two long sides of the huts. Most were stacked with three 'biscuits' – straw-stuffed mattresses that Pearl had already learned to loathe – and folded bedding. However, the two closest to the door were without bedding, and Pearl realised one of these must be hers. Three hooks were fastened on the wall beside each bed, upon which the occupants had hung their uniforms and coats. Every WAAF had her own shelf, fixed to the wall behind her bedstead; there were also chests of drawers between each bed, and Pearl knew she would be expected to share drawer space with the girl in the bed next to hers.

'This is yours,' the corporal said, pointing to the empty bed on the left. 'You're to be back in the camp by 2230 each night unless you've got a late pass. Breakfast at 0800 and morning parade at 0845. Of course, as you're a shift worker you'll usually be excused from parades, but I expect to see you there tomorrow.'

Pearl could only nod, dazed from the amount of information she had to take in.

'Best get an early night,' the corporal went on. 'You'll be on your feet all day tomorrow, getting your arrival chit signed.'

Once the corporal had left, Pearl made haste to unpack, which didn't take long considering the only clothes she now possessed were those issued by the WAAF. And that included pyjamas and underwear. Once everything was stowed and her kitbag pushed beneath the bed, she made up the bed, thinking to take the corporal's advice. By this time, five more of the hut's occupants had arrived. Although they greeted Pearl with a brief nod and smile, they gathered around the stove without inviting her to join them or even introducing themselves. As she tucked in her sheets, one of the WAAFs called to her. It was the redhead Pearl had noticed earlier. She had a propeller badge on her sleeve proclaiming her to have reached the rank of LACW – leading aircraftwoman, one rung of the ladder above Pearl.

'We're going to the White Horse later. You're welcome to join us.'

'Oh, thanks, erm…'

'It's Blanche. Blanche Dalby.'

'Pearl Cooper.'

'Yes, we know.' Blanche pointed to a card pinned to the wall above Pearl's bed that she hadn't noticed before. Her name was written on it and below it said, 'C of E.' Although what her religion had to do with anything, Pearl didn't know.

'I'd love to come.' Despite her slight embarrassment at missing the name card, Pearl finished making her bed in lighter spirits, glad to find her room-mates were not as stand-offish as they had at first appeared.

She wanted to learn more about life at Fenthorpe but, before she could ask, the door opened to let in the same corporal who had shown Pearl to Hut Three. With her was a very bedraggled-looking WAAF, wearing a uniform as new as Pearl's. Her suspicions that this must be the other new arrival the corporal had mentioned were confirmed when she was pointed towards the remaining empty bed. The newcomer dropped her gear onto her bed, then fumbled with the drawstring on her kitbag, avoiding the gaze of the other WAAFs. Her hair hung over her shoulders in rat-tails, dripping water. The card above her bed proclaimed her to be Jenny Hazleton, also C of E.

'Has it started to rain?' Pearl asked, wondering if that would mean cancelling the visit to the pub.

The newcomer shook her head, pressing her lips tightly together, and didn't reply.

Blanche, however, laughed. Her laughter had a hard, mocking edge. 'I thought even a sprog like you would know what having wet hair means. Darling Jenny here must have arrived with her head crawling with nits.'

The other WAAFs giggled, and comprehension dawned. Pearl had heard tales in Bridgnorth and Cranwell of WAAFs with nits being marched straight to Sick Quarters to have their hair and scalp treated, before being released with dripping wet hair. Pearl opened her mouth to sympathise, but Jenny glared at Blanche, her chin raised. 'At least I know I don't have nits now.' Pearl couldn't quite place her accent but thought she must come from somewhere in the West Country. 'How about you – is your scalp feeling itchy?'

Pearl was standing close enough to see the slight quiver of Jenny's chin that belied her defiant words. She looked very young, and Pearl's heart went out to her.

Blanche regarded Jenny for a moment, her lips curled. Then she shrugged and grabbed her coat from the hook. 'Come on, girls. We'll leave Nitty Nora here to get herself tidied up.' She swept from the room, pausing when she passed Pearl's bed. 'Coming, Pearl?' It was clear Jenny wasn't included in the invitation.

'No thanks,' Pearl replied. 'I'd rather stay here.'

'Suit yourself. Mind you don't catch anything.' Then, laughing at her own hilarity, Blanche was gone, her friends following in her wake.

–

Once the others had left Jenny remained where she was, fixing Pearl with a look that made her think of a wary animal backed into a corner. 'What are you looking at? Never seen someone with nits before?'

'I'm sorry. I didn't mean to stare.' Although Jenny's defensive posture didn't invite conversation, Pearl's heart went out to the girl. She looked so young, Pearl wanted to comfort her, reassure her that she had at least one friend in Hut Three. 'I'm sorry I drew attention to your hair, though. I wasn't thinking. My sister was always coming home with nits, and I caught them from her a few times.' She grimaced at the memory of Deedee attacking her with a fine-toothed comb that threatened to tear out her thick, wavy hair from the roots. 'My grandmother always used to tell Thea – that's my sister – that nits preferred clean hair. I don't know if it's true, but it made us feel better.'

Jenny's sharp features were softened by the faintest hint of a smile. 'My gran always says that, too.' A pause, then: 'I'm Jenny, by the way.'

'Nice to meet you, Jenny. I'm Pearl. This is my first day at Fenthorpe, too.' She pointed at Jenny's kit. 'Need a hand unpacking?'

'No thanks. I don't have much to unpack. Why don't you go to the pub with the others? I'm sure you'll catch them up if you hurry.'

'I'd rather stay here. I hope the other WAAFs are nicer than Blanche because I'd rather stick needles in my eyes than go about with that madam.'

This time Jenny's answering smile lit her whole face. 'Maybe I can find something to make up for missing the pub.' She rummaged in her bag, first extracting three extremely dog-eared books, which she placed on her shelf with the kind of care usually reserved for fragile china. Then she returned to her bag and pulled out a battered tin. 'I got a few days' leave before coming here, so I went home.' She pulled a face. 'Probably where I picked up the lice. Anyway' – she brandished the tin – 'my gran makes the best fruit cake, and she made some especially for me. Fancy a slice?'

'I'd love some. Tell you what, while you finish unpacking, I'll see if I can rustle us up some tea.'

It didn't take long for Pearl to discover a kettle that could be heated on the stove. While she was heating the water, two more WAAFs arrived, one being the corporal in charge of Hut Three, who had a bed screened off from the rest of the room. Corporal Helen Longford was a young woman with dark hair and eyes that brimmed with laughter. Pearl judged her to be about twenty; it was slowly dawning on her that, while she might be a 'sprog' in the eyes of the WAAF, she was among the oldest.

They were still waiting for the water to boil when a noise like thunder shook the hut, making the furniture rattle. It took Pearl a moment to realise a plane had flown low overhead.

'Don't worry – you'll get used to it,' Helen said with a sympathetic smile. 'We're close to the end of the main runway, so that happens a lot.'

Jenny's eyes were wide, making her look like a startled cat. 'How do you sleep with that cacko phoney going on?'

Pearl stared at her in bemusement, wondering if the noise had affected her ears. 'Cacko what?'

Helen's brow, which had wrinkled at Jenny's odd language, suddenly smoothed. 'Oh, you mean cacophony.'

'Is that how it's pronounced?' Jenny's cheeks glowed red. 'I've never heard it said, only ever read it.'

Pearl watched Helen. If she so much as smirked, Pearl would make her regret it.

'Nothing to be ashamed about,' Helen said. 'I'm embarrassed to admit how recently I discovered that Penelope wasn't pronounced Penny-lope.'

Pearl relaxed and laughed along with the others. Clearly Helen was nothing like Blanche. In fact, Helen rose in her estimation when she offered to show Pearl and Jenny around the domestic area of the station the following afternoon. When she heard about Blanche, she wrinkled her nose. 'Don't take any notice of her. She thinks she's a cut above the rest of us because she's a general clerk in Intelligence. Goodness knows how she qualified for that, because she doesn't possess a shred of intelligence as far as I can see.'

Pearl laughed, and Jenny offered her and the other WAAF, who was called Sarah, a slice of cake, but they declined.

'We're spending the evening in Lincoln,' Helen explained. 'We would invite you, but we've arranged to meet a couple of lads from RAF Scampton.' Helen did show them where the hut's supply of tea, cocoa and Ovaltine was kept. 'We take it in turns to replenish our stores,' she told them. 'There's a tin of condensed milk too, but we've given up trying to get sugar.'

Helen and Sarah changed into their 'best blues' – their smartest uniform, mostly reserved for parades and special occasions – and wished Pearl and Jenny a cordial good night. Just before leaving, Helen paused in the doorway and looked back at Jenny. 'You're a Met WAAF, aren't you? If you report to the Met Office at 1100 hours, I'll show you the ropes.'

With that she left. As glad as she was to know that Jenny already had a friend in the Met Office, Pearl wished she could say the same.

With the hut to themselves, and Jenny's possessions neatly put away, the two girls retrieved their enamel mugs, poured the tea and sank into chairs by the stove. The chairs were wicker, with flattened, faded cushions on the seats, and were surprisingly comfortable. The wind must have picked up outside, for it howled down the flue like a banshee; Pearl was very glad to have company on her first night in this strange place. The stove's heat didn't radiate far into the room, and Pearl shovelled more coke into the fire. Seeing the meagre supply in the bucket, she didn't dare heap on as much as she would have liked or the fire wouldn't last the evening. It was a good job spring was on the way; the hut must get bitterly cold in the winter.

While they munched the delicious cake and sipped strong black tea, they discussed their journeys. Jenny had been on leave at her home in the Forest of Dean and had endured a particularly trying journey from Gloucester, as her first train had been full of troops and she'd been forced to sit on the floor.

Once they had cleared away the mugs, Jenny fetched a comb and started to comb out her hair. Now it was dryer, Pearl could see it was the golden colour of ripe wheat. She eyed it enviously; her own mousy brown hair was dull in comparison.

'What's your trade?' Jenny asked.

'I'm an R/T operator – a radio telephone operator. I'll be working in the Watch Office. What about you?'

'I'm a Met WAAF.'

Pearl shook her head. 'I remember the corporal at the guardhouse telling me that but I don't know what it means.'

'A meteorological assistant.'

'That sounds impressive.'

'It's not really, although it's quite interesting. I had to do a special course in London.'

'What does it involve?'

Jenny's face lit up. 'Well, I have to take readings on things like temperature, pressure and wind speed every hour, which we send to Group HQ. Then we have to plot our readings on a chart. It's fascinating.' Her face became more animated as she spoke, and she no longer seemed like an object of pity but a young woman with a true enthusiasm for her work.

'You're lucky getting a job you're so interested in. I hope I enjoy my work as much. What did you do before you joined the WAAF? Have you just left school?'

Jenny's face clouded. 'No, I had to leave school at fourteen. I was desperate to stay on and do my School Certificate but...' Her head drooped. Even by the dim electric light, Pearl could see the blush on Jenny's face. 'Well, we needed the money.'

Pearl's heart twisted with sympathy. 'That's rough. I had to leave school earlier than I would have liked but at least I could stay long enough to get my School Cert. I needed to help my grandmother look after my younger sister and I wanted to start earning too.' She omitted to mention that Deedee had done her best to persuade Pearl to stay on at school, insisting she had enough money to support her through her higher certificate.

'You live with your grandmother?' Jenny asked. 'Are you an orphan too?'

'Yes. My father was killed in the last war, and my mother died of the Spanish flu just after the war, not long after Thea, my sister, was born. What happened to your parents?'

'My mother died having me and my dad was a miner. He got ill from all the coal dust and died when I was ten.'

'How awful. Thank goodness for our grandmothers.'

'It was better than ending up in an orphanage, I suppose.'

This was hardly a ringing endorsement of Jenny's gran, and Pearl's surprise must have shown in her face, for Jenny pulled a face. 'Don't get me wrong, I love my gran, and she's done so much for me. But we don't see eye to eye on a lot of things.'

'Like what?'

'Women's place in society, for one. She thought I should marry her best friend's grandson, settle down and have babies. My grancher was more supportive, but he'd never openly disagree with Gran. It was a relief when I turned eighteen and could join the WAAF.'

Pearl groaned in sympathy. 'Your gran would get on well with my former boss.' She related Mr Kingsley's reasons for giving the coveted reporter's role to Philip Meadows.

Jenny shook her combed locks over her shoulders and gave Pearl a grin. 'Sounds like we both have a lot in common, and I for one intend to make the most of the WAAF. Even though we're bound by regulations, this is more freedom than I've ever had. I think I'm going to like it here.'

'You're right.' Pearl smiled at Jenny. 'And I'm not going to let men like Mr Kingsley wreck my dreams. I'll make the most of my experiences here, and who knows – perhaps I'll find something to write about.'

Chapter Three

The following morning the process of settling in at Fenthorpe began. Pearl and Jenny stuck together for moral support as much as they were able. They had already found the ablutions block the night before, and, from her experiences at Bridgnorth and Cranwell, Pearl knew to rise early so she could get washed before crowds of WAAFs were queueing to get a place at the washbasins. There were also cubicles with baths, although Pearl opted to leave a bath until the evening, when she had more time.

Once they were dressed and their hair pinned up above their collars, they followed the other WAAFs from Hut Three to the mess. Pearl's insides were in a tight knot with worry about her first introduction to Flying Control. Even though she knew she wouldn't be expected to take up her duties that day, she couldn't help worrying about whether she would be up to the task.

Once breakfast was over, and they had endured morning parade, it was time to begin the process of signing in at the various offices that needed to know of their presence in the station. They had both arrived too late the previous day to do anything but report to the WAAF guardroom.

'Where to first?' Jenny asked Pearl as she consulted the list she had jotted down when Helen had told them where they needed to go. Helen had rattled off her instructions so fast, Pearl was very glad she knew shorthand.

'The Orderly Office first, then Pay Accounts. They're both in the administration block.'

Following Helen's directions, Pearl and Jenny set out for the offices, which were situated at the other end of the station. They hadn't walked far along the road that linked the domestic quarters with the rest of the site when engines roared overhead, making Pearl flinch. Before she could work out what was happening, a huge shape blotted out the weak sunshine, and she found herself looking up at the underside of a large twin-engined aircraft. Its lowered wheels threatened to knock the cap off her head. A moment later, and the plane – a Manchester – was climbing swiftly, performing a slow, banking turn. Pearl watched its progress, her heart hammering, for a while before she realised she was clutching Jenny's arm. She let go, embarrassed.

Jenny didn't seem to have noticed. She was gazing upwards, her face pale. 'I thought my heart was about to give out. Come on, let's move before there's another.'

Two more Manchesters flew over before they could get away from the stretch of road that they quickly worked out must run directly along the end of the runway. Although the girls were more prepared now, they still gave them a fright.

'They can't have been flying last night or I wouldn't have got a wink of sleep.' Pearl looked back at the rows of sleeping huts only a few hundred yards away, feeling sorry for anyone trying to sleep after a night on duty.

The road was busy with cyclists and trucks, and Pearl remembered her idea to send home for her bicycle. Without it, she would spend her life tramping along this seemingly endless road. Jenny's face fell when Pearl announced her intention. 'I wish I had a bike.'

'Tell you what. I'll ask my grandmother if she'll send hers. She never uses it any more, so I'm sure she wouldn't mind.'

'You'd really do that?'

'Of course. We girls need to stick together.'

'I'm glad we're in the same hut.' Jenny pulled a face. 'I can't imagine what life would be like if I'd had to face that awful

Blanche alone last night, but I don't feel so bad about having her around now.'

The next couple of hours passed in a blur, and Pearl was very glad of Jenny's company as they followed directions from one office to the next, some helpful, others no more than a vague hand gesture that might mean any one of a number of buildings. At each office, they reported their arrival, signed forms and had their arrival chits stamped and signed. Soon she had repeated her service number so many times she knew it off by heart. The process helped Pearl form a mental image of the huge bomber station, the greatest part of which was taken up by three criss-crossing runways in the centre, forming a somewhat wonky 'A'. A track ran round the edge of the runways, and the offices, workshops and hangars clustered in groups at points outside this enclosing track.

There seemed to be endless personnel on the station, mostly men. Pearl was only just starting to appreciate how many people on the ground it took to support each aircraft that took to the skies. Even so, she had to admit she felt a thrill each time she spotted a man wearing a brevet on his chest that indicated he was an aircrew member.

Jenny evidently felt the same, for as they approached the Watch Office – the building that housed the Met Office and Flying Control – they passed two men deep in conversation. One wore sergeant's stripes and a brevet that proclaimed him a pilot. The other had the rings of a flying officer and an 'N' on his badge. They hastily saluted the officer, who returned the salute without pausing in his stride.

'Bloody Manchesters,' the pilot was saying. 'I don't care how many circuits and bumps they make us do, no amount of practice is going to change the fact they're underpowered. It's like trying to fly a cow.'

Only when the men had gone out of earshot did Pearl realise she had stopped to watch them. To her amusement, she saw Jenny was also regarding them with interest.

It seemed to take an effort for Jenny to drag her attention back to Pearl. 'That officer was good-looking.'

'Was he? I didn't notice. Anyway, I thought he looked very young.' He had looked positively fresh-faced. The pilot had been closer to her age, she thought.

'Ah, so you *did* notice him.'

'I did notice him, I just didn't pay attention to his looks. Believe me, if you'd had the same experience of working with men that I have you would have gone off them too.'

'You can't tar everyone with the same brush as your former boss. Anyway, the officer must be a navigator. I'd love to know more about navigation, wouldn't you?'

'I've never even thought about it.'

'Why? I think it's amazing. Imagine it – you're up in the clouds and can't see anything, yet somehow you have to direct the pilot to the exact location. Or you're on a boat in the middle of the ocean, trying to steer to a tiny island. I'd love to know how it's done.'

Pearl considered it. It might make an interesting feature for a magazine if she could find the right angle. 'Let me know if you ever find out.'

'I will. Maybe I can find a book about navigation.'

Why Jenny would rather teach herself than simply ask one of the navigators, Pearl couldn't ask because they had now arrived at the Watch Office. From the outside it looked like an unprepossessing concrete cube, two storeys high with a flat roof. The upper storey had a balcony wrapping round two sides of the building with a steel staircase leading up to the roof. A bright orange windsock dangled from a pole in one corner of the roof, and another pole stood in the middle, supporting a strange device that whirled in the breeze.

Jenny squinted up at it, holding her cap to stop it sliding off her head. 'An anemometer.'

'An anano…' Pearl gave up trying to wrap her tongue around the word. 'A what?'

'For measuring wind speed.'

'Oh.' For a moment Pearl's innate curiosity toyed with the idea of asking for more information, until her practical side took over. Her head was already buzzing from all the information she had been obliged to take in today, and measuring wind speed would not be part of her duties. She marched to the door. 'Come on. Time to see where we'll be working.'

The door opened onto a narrow corridor with doors on either side and a staircase leading to the upper floor. A low murmur of voices could be heard coming from behind one of the doors, which was ajar. As the girls hesitated, this door swung open and Corporal Longford appeared. Pearl felt a rush of relief at seeing a familiar face.

'Hello, you two,' Helen said. 'I was wondering if you were about to show up. Come with me, Hazleton. Cooper, go upstairs and through the door at the end of the corridor. They're expecting you.'

Her stomach a knot of nerves, Pearl did as she was told.

The first thing she saw walking through the door was a long wooden desk facing the windows, which looked out across the runways. A man with three equally sized rings on his sleeve, proclaiming him to hold the rank of wing commander, was standing, gazing out of the window. Another man sat at one end of the desk, wearing a headset, with what looked like an old-fashioned upright telephone in front of him. There were a pair of chalkboards on the wall next to him, and a cabinet filled with stacks of long cylinders that looked like fireworks.

Pearl hovered by the door, and was on the point of announcing herself when the wing commander looked round. 'Ah, you must be our new R/T operator.'

Pearl raised her arm halfway towards a salute when she remembered she had removed her cap and therefore shouldn't salute. She dropped her arm and stood to attention instead, feeling her face burning. 'Yes, sir. Aircraftwoman Cooper, sir.'

The officer's lips twitched. 'Welcome to the Watch Office, Cooper. At ease. We don't stand on ceremony here. I'm Wing

Commander Fforbes.' He pointed to the man wearing the head-phones. 'This is Corporal Snaith. He'll be taking you under his wing. You'll start off by observing him, then you'll work under his supervision.'

'Yes, sir.' She felt a flood of relief at the news that she would have time to observe an experienced R/T operator at work before having to do it herself.

'We've got a few kites doing circuits and bumps this after-noon. You might as well start now.'

The corporal glanced at her, stony-faced. He jerked his head at the chair. 'Pull up a pew.' He didn't look nearly as welcoming as the wing commander, and Pearl couldn't help wishing it was Fforbes showing her what to do.

Snaith indicated the radio set that was installed under the bench. 'This is a TR9.'

'Yes, I know. I learned all about them at Cranwell.'

From Snaith's scowl, she realised she'd said the wrong thing. 'Really. Well, you'll soon discover there's a whole world of experience you won't have learned on your fancy course. And if I don't think you're up to scratch I'll have you out on your ear faster than you can recite Ohm's Law.'

Pearl resisted the temptation to gabble Ohm's Law at top speed and arranged her features in a serious expression. 'Of course. I'm here to learn.'

'Just make sure you pay attention. Thank goodness there aren't any ops on tonight. I don't want a sprog under my feet with all that going on.'

'Of course.' Pearl wasn't going to let Snaith think she was bothered by his attitude. She would simply show him that she was more than capable of doing any task he cared to throw at her.

'I hope you're a quick learner. Why on earth the RAF decided to send a girl to a busy operational station, I'll never know.'

Pearl bridled. A girl? She was a good five years older than Snaith, if she was any judge. 'I think you'll find I can pick things up as fast as any man.'

'I doubt it. WAAFs should be working in the cookhouse or as waitresses in the officers' mess. Girls just don't have the ability to keep calm in a crisis, and that's what you need for this job.'

Pearl glanced at Fforbes to see what he thought of Snaith's opinions, but he was on the other side of the room, speaking into the telephone. Despite this, something about the tilt of his head gave her the feeling he had heard but was choosing not to interfere, for whatever reason. She was on her own. Squaring her shoulders, she said, 'I'm sorry you feel that way, Corporal, but I can assure you I'll cope.'

What she really wanted to say was: *it's up to you. Either you teach me what I need to know to be a useful member of the team or you can pick up all the work I don't do because I don't know how to do it.* She kept quiet, mostly because she didn't want to find herself on a charge on her very first day but also because she suspected that Snaith would enjoy seeing her fail even if it did make more work for him.

Maybe she was doing him an injustice, though, for he sighed and then said, 'I suppose I've got time to talk you through your duties.' He pointed to the telephone-like object on the desk in front of him that Pearl already knew was a microphone. 'Our main task is to communicate with the pilots of all aircraft approaching the airfield. If more than one arrives at the same time, we need to instruct them to circle, giving them a height, and bring them in one at a time.'

'That makes sense.'

'You'll be expected to learn the correct protocols and phonetic alphabet – all vital to avoid any misunderstanding.'

Pearl forbore to say she already knew them.

Snaith showed her an open notebook on the desk. 'We also have to keep an exact record of every radio conversation in the log. I hope you can write fast.'

'I'll manage.' It was on the tip of her tongue to say she could write in either longhand or shorthand; the only thing that held her back was her conviction that Snaith didn't appear to believe she was capable of anything other than traditional women's work. She would just have to work hard to change his mind.

'At the moment, I'm wearing headphones to listen to the pilots' frequency, but when there's an op on we play it through one of the speakers,' Snaith went on. 'We also keep this board updated, listing all the aircraft on the station.'

Pearl looked where he was pointing and saw a blackboard, propped up by a speaker, divided into columns. In the column on the left, she saw a long list of names such as: '*F-Freddie*' and '*H-Henry*'. Each name had either a red or yellow button next to it. Although most aircraft were marked as being on the ground, three were marked as airborne.

'We have two squadrons at Fenthorpe,' Snaith continued. 'All the aircraft marked with a red button belong to 505 Squadron, and the yellow ones are 642 Squadron. The rest of the board shows the position of all the aircraft, whether on the ground, what height they are at if they are on the circuit, or if they are out of area.'

Pearl quickly saw how useful the board would be. 'So when we come on duty, we can immediately see where all the aircraft are.'

'Correct. Trust me, when the bombers flying ops are returning, you'll need to refer to the board non-stop. I just hope you can—' Just then Pearl heard a tinny voice coming from the headphones he was wearing, although she couldn't hear what was said.

Snaith pressed a lever on the desk microphone and spoke into it. 'Hello *B-Beer*, this is Causeway. Prepare to land, runway three-four.' Then a short while later, in response to something else he'd heard, he said, 'Hello, *B-Beer*, pancake.' He turned to Pearl. 'Pancake is the instruction to land.'

Pearl resisted the urge to roll her eyes. She knew that perfectly well from her course. All the while she had been aware of the growl of approaching engines. Now she looked out of the window and saw a Manchester swoop low and approach the main runway. She caught her breath as one wing dipped at the last moment, threatening to catch on the hedge. Then it levelled out just in time. Seconds later, the wheels struck the ground, and Pearl slowly released her breath as it became clear the Manchester had made a safe landing.

Snaith was adding an entry to the log, so she continued to watch the Manchester as it taxied off the main runway and came to a halt. Men ran towards it, looking no bigger than toy soldiers at this distance, and swarmed around it. She saw a door open in the fuselage, and the crew climbed down using steps the ground crew had carried into position. So many people involved in just one flight. A thrill ran down her spine at the realisation that she was going to play her part. Maybe she would only be a tiny cog in the machine, but she would be here to witness it all and do her part in helping Britain win this terrible war.

'I've shown you all I can for now.' Snaith's voice brought her attention back to the Watch Office. 'You're on duty tomorrow at 0800. Don't be late.'

Chapter Four

'It's funny how quickly we've settled in,' Jenny said. It was a week later and the girls were in Hut Three, getting changed into their best blues for an evening in Lincoln, having both secured a late pass for the night. Two other girls from the hut were going and had invited them when they heard Pearl and Jenny also had the evening off. Pearl had been glad to learn that Blanche was working that evening. Although she had been polite to Pearl, she continued to ignore Jenny. 'I thought I'd never find my way around the station,' Jenny went on, 'but I didn't think twice about making my way back here in the dark last night.'

'I just wish my work was as easy to navigate.' Pearl pulled a face as she dabbed a little of her Evening in Paris perfume behind each ear.

She had long ago worked out that she learned best by doing, and, so far, Corporal Snaith had permitted her to do precisely nothing. 'I'm not letting you anywhere near a TR9 until I can be sure you can handle it,' he had told her on her first day of duty, when he had ordered her to sit beside him and watch what he did. It had been a frustrating few days. How was she to demonstrate her ability without being allowed to handle the equipment?

The job seemed straightforward enough to Pearl. It only really got busy when there was more than one aeroplane returning at the same time. Then the R/T operator had to inform each pilot what height to circle and then bring them down safely one at a time. Although there had been no bombing missions on in the week Pearl had been at Fenthorpe, there had been training flights most days, so she had seen how it all worked. She was sure she wouldn't have a problem if only Snaith would give her a chance. There was little to do when the aircraft were all on the ground or not actually coming in to land, apart from listening in to the speaker tuned to the 'darky' frequency, which was the frequency pilots used if they were lost or in distress.

She still had to study in the evenings, for she would eventually have to sit more exams to be promoted to leading aircraftwoman. She regularly pored over her notebooks and updated them with the new information she had gleaned from a grudging Snaith. In fact, she had originally intended not accompanying the other WAAFs on their trip to Lincoln that night, thinking she ought to revise. Two things had made her change her mind. Firstly, Jenny had pleaded with her to come, telling her it was about time she got her nose out of her books and had some fun. Considering Jenny also spent much of her spare time reading, Pearl thought she really ought to go herself before she gave herself eye-strain. However, she had another reason for wanting to go: the WAAFs were going to the Saracen's Head Hotel, which was popular with personnel from all the RAF stations around Lincoln. Although Pearl had to admit she was interested in meeting the men and women from the other bases, she mainly wanted to go because she hoped she might run into Thea. She remembered Thea mentioning the Saracen's Head in one of her rare letters, and it seemed as good a place to start as any in her attempt to meet her sister. She had, of course, sent a letter as soon as she knew she was being posted so close to Thea, and was irritated, although not surprised, that she hadn't yet received a reply. Despite Deedee warning her not to smother Thea, Pearl still wanted to meet her, to reassure herself Thea was well. Naturally, she couldn't guarantee her sister would be there that night, but at the very least she hoped to meet someone from RAF Waddington who could give her some news of her.

Both Pearl and Jenny had come off duty at four that afternoon so, as neither had visited Lincoln before, they opted to hitch a lift to the city centre in time to have a wander around the cathedral before meeting up with the other WAAFs outside the Saracen's Head. Accordingly, they had dashed back to their hut as soon as they were released from duty to smarten up before going out.

Now Pearl put away her lipstick and gave herself a final inspection in the mirror. She was pleased with her reflection, although she couldn't help shooting an envious glance at Jenny's gleaming blond hair. 'I think we both spruce up very nicely. Are you ready?'

At Jenny's nod, they left and went to sign out at the guardroom. That done, they made their way to the main road to try their luck at flagging down a lift.

Much to their delight, they hadn't been out of the gates more than a couple of minutes before a van trundling along the road pulled up when Pearl and Jenny stuck out their thumbs. A middle-aged woman with greying hair stuck her head out of the window. 'Going into Lincoln?'

Pearl hurried up to the van. 'Yes. Can you give us a lift?'

'Hop in. I can drop you off by the station.'

'Wonderful. Thank you.'

'There's room for you both on the passenger seat. You'll get your uniforms in a mess if you sit in the back.'

Glad to avoid the back of the truck, which bore a distinct aroma of cabbages, Pearl climbed into the passenger seat and squeezed beside Jenny. As an aspiring journalist, she prided herself on being able to quickly draw conclusions about the occupation and character of the new people she met, and, judging by the smell of the van and her weathered face, she decided, this woman must live on a farm.

'Haven't seen you young 'uns around before. Are you new?'

'Yes. We've only been here a week.'

Pearl's surprise that the woman was obviously acquainted with the men and women of RAF Fenthorpe must have shown, for the woman chuckled as she released the clutch and steered the van back onto the road. 'Oh, don't mind me. I know just about everyone in Fenthorpe. That's what comes of being landlady of the village pub. The name's Norah Brumby, by the way.'

Pearl and Jenny introduced themselves and Pearl said, 'You're the pub landlady? I thought you must work on a farm.' So much for her powers of observation.

Norah glanced sideways at Pearl, her eyes twinkling. 'You're a sharp one. My parents were farmers. My brother runs the family farm now, and I still get roped in to help every now and then, especially now they're short-handed. Today I'm collecting a delivery of calomel dust.'

It didn't take long to reach the station at Lincoln and, after Norah had told the girls the best way to the cathedral, she waved them off, extracting promises from them to visit the White Horse soon.

Pearl and Jenny, following Norah's instructions, soon found the high street and followed it across the river. Only a few paces from the bridge, they saw a long white stucco building with a wrought-iron balcony running along the upper level. The lettering above the third-floor windows proclaimed it to be the Saracen's Head Hotel.

'That's useful to know,' Jenny said. 'Now we shouldn't get lost trying to find it later.'

Pearl nodded, noting its location not far from an impressive stone building built across the high street with a huge archway that allowed pedestrians and traffic through. In her head, she started to compose an article describing the essential sights of Lincoln that every tourist should visit.

They walked on, admiring the buildings, which appeared to get older the closer they were to the cathedral. Soon the road started to slope uphill, and, when they reached a steep cobbled street aptly named Steep Hill, Pearl knew a pang of homesickness as she was reminded of Wyle Cop in Shrewsbury.

Above them, at the highest point of the city, the cathedral loomed, gilded in the last of the evening sunshine. As much as Pearl hated getting up in the dark, she was grateful for the double summertime that had been imposed at the start of the war, as it meant they still had enough daylight to enjoy Lincoln.

They puffed and panted to the top of the hill, then stood clutching their sides, taking in the view while they fought to regain their breath. To one side stood the cathedral, and the stone walls of the castle occupied most of the rest of the hilltop. Below, beyond the city's smoky streets, the flat fields and hedgerows of Lincolnshire stretched out as far as Pearl could see. Spring had finally arrived, and the scenery was tinged with the palest green.

'Who'd have thought there'd be a hill like this when it's so flat around Fenthorpe.' Jenny had recovered her breath and gazed out, her eyes reflecting the same sense of wonder Pearl felt.

Pearl opened her mouth to answer but then stopped as her eyes picked out a formation of bombers, some miles distant, heading east. Until then she had almost forgotten the war, and seeing the bombers was a sharp reminder of reality. 'Come on. Let's go and look inside the cathedral. It's not long before we have to get back to the Saracen's Head.'

–

Feeling calmed by the cathedral's magnificent interior, Pearl felt ready to enjoy the pub and make new friends as they set out back down the hill.

'Look, there are the others,' Jenny said as they walked through the stone archway they had admired earlier. She pointed to the group of WAAFs who were approaching from the river and had nearly reached the Saracen's Head. 'Let's go and meet them.'

Pearl took a couple of steps – then froze when she saw another young woman walk round the corner. Although she wore a WAAF greatcoat, she wore no cap and her auburn hair was brushed out in glossy waves that fell over her shoulders in a style that would have earned her a sharp reprimand had any officers been around. She would recognise that hair anywhere, not to mention the slender, upright figure and the pointed chin that was raised in an attitude that seemed to dare anyone to pick a fight with her.

'You go on,' Pearl said to Jenny. 'I'll meet you inside.'

'What?' Jenny turned wide eyes on her. 'Why?'

With a jerk of the head towards the auburn-haired WAAF, Pearl said, 'That's my sister. I need to have a word with her.'

Thankfully, Thea wasn't looking in her direction, or Pearl was sure she would try to evade her. She seemed to be trying to evade someone, though. She darted frequent glances at the doorway of the Saracen's Head as she walked by with rapid steps, and Pearl was sure she was trying to stay in the shadows so she wouldn't be noticed by anyone emerging from the hotel.

Pearl managed to draw level without her sister paying her any attention. She grabbed her arm. 'What do you think you're playing at?'

Thea stared at her blankly, then she blinked and seemed to recover from her shock. 'That's a nice way to greet your long-lost sister. I'm very well, thank you for asking.'

'You wouldn't be long-lost if you'd bothered to answer any of my letters. I've been trying to arrange a meeting with you ever since I got to Lincolnshire.'

'Maybe I didn't want you sticking your nose into my business.'

That stung. 'I'm not sticking my nose anywhere. You're my sister. I've been worried about you. Why don't you write?'

'I do.'

Pearl snorted. 'Yes. Once a month if I'm lucky. And your letters are about as illuminating as a blackout lamp.' She bit her lip and shook her head. What was it about Thea that always brought out the worst in her? They'd barely been together for a minute and they were already bickering like little children.

'Look, I'm sorry,' she hurried on before Thea, her eyes blazing, could add to the argument. 'I don't want to fight.'

'Then don't start one. It wasn't me who nearly jerked your arm out of its socket and demanded to know what you were doing.'

Pearl couldn't help herself. 'Well, look at you. You could get into one hell of a row if an officer spotted you. Where's your cap? And what possessed you to go out with your hair down?' WAAF regulations stated that hair was not to touch the collar, and Pearl had already witnessed how strictly the rule was enforced at Fenthorpe.

Thea raised her eyes to the heavens. 'And you ask why I haven't been in touch.'

At that moment a breeze stirred the hem of her coat, and Pearl caught a glimpse of the clothes she wore underneath. Although she couldn't see the whole outfit, it was clearly made of a close-fitting lightweight fabric in a decidedly non-regulation shade of crimson. 'Good grief, Thea, you're not even in uniform. Are you trying to get yourself thrown out of the WAAF?'

'Don't be so melodramatic. All the girls do it. As long as we're careful, we don't get caught.'

'But you're not being careful. Not with your hair like that.'

'I wasn't born yesterday. I didn't walk out of Waddington like this.'

'But—'

'No.' Thea pulled her arm from Pearl's grip. 'If you think you can swan into Lincolnshire and start bossing me around, you've got another think coming. I'm not a child any more – and, in case you'd forgotten, I've been in the WAAF longer than you. If you want to meet up and hear my advice, drop me a note. Otherwise, leave me alone.' So saying, she stalked away, head held high.

Pearl made no attempt to follow. She knew Thea well enough to know there would be no reasoning with her while she was in this mood. After taking a moment to calm herself and blink away the tears of bewildered hurt, she went in search of Jenny.

'I never asked how you got on with your sister.'

It was the following evening, and Pearl and Jenny were in Hut Three, on their weekly 'domestic' evening. Having swept and dusted all round her bed, Pearl was now polishing her buttons, using Silvo, as advised by several WAAFs, to give her buttons a more silvery sheen, while Jenny was mending a rip in one of her lisle stockings. It was the first opportunity they'd had for a conversation since Pearl had seen Thea.

Pearl applied more polish to each button, rubbing it into every groove, before replying. It had been packed in the Saracen's Head, the bar a sea of airforce blue. At other times, Pearl might have been irritated by the noise, which made conversation difficult; last night she had been grateful that she didn't have the chance to explain what had happened with Thea. Instead she had nursed her glass of lemonade and sat in a corner, watching Jenny hold an enthusiastic shouted conversation with another of the Met WAAFs. She had vaguely recognised a few members of Fenthorpe's bomber crews and had wished she could speak to them, curious to get to know the men who daily flew into danger, but they were sitting at another table, occupied by some obscure game involving beer mats. In particular, her attention had been caught by a man with sergeant's stripes on his sleeves and a pilot's brevet above his left breast pocket. His uniform was a darker shade of blue than most of the other men's, and she wondered why. He had a pleasant, friendly face, too. Approachable, she decided. While the other crewmen were so fresh-faced they looked as though they should still be in school, this man was a little older. In his late twenties or early thirties, Pearl thought.

'Pearl?'

A hand waved in front of her eyes, and she jumped, then saw Jenny grinning at her. 'You were miles away.'

'Sorry.' Pearl gathered her thoughts from her musings on the unknown pilot and turned them back to Thea. 'My sister's fine. Just determined to get herself in trouble, as ever.'

Jenny raised her brows. 'I know I haven't met her, but I thought she looked perfectly capable of taking care of herself.'

'Trust me, she's not. I was always having to get her out of scrapes at home, and she hasn't changed. I mean, there she was, walking through Lincoln as bold as brass with civvies on under her coat without a thought about what would happen if she got caught.'

Jenny's lips twitched. 'It's hardly a hanging offence. Plenty of other WAAFs have pulled that trick.'

'They have?'

'Oh yes. I've heard the Met WAAFs talking about it. I wouldn't dare do it myself, but I can understand the temptation to wear a pretty frock to a special date.'

'A date?' It hadn't even occurred to Pearl that Thea might have been meeting a man. Nightmare scenarios of her sister meeting a disreputable older man in a seedy bar flitted through her mind. The next moment her visions skipped to extortion or Thea being offered strong drink or – heaven forbid – drugs. The *Shrewsbury Mirror* had once run a story on young girls being lured into prostitution by smooth-talking men. What if a similar racket was going on in Lincoln?

Perhaps her horror showed in her expression, for Jenny patted her arm. 'How old is Thea?'

'Twenty-two. No, twenty-three now.'

'That's five years older than me. Do you think *I* need looking after?'

'Of course not.' Admittedly, at their first meeting Pearl's heart had gone out to Jenny because she had thought her vulnerable and in need of a friend, but a week's acquaintance had taught her that Jenny was perfectly capable of looking after herself. 'You might be younger than Thea, but you're much more mature.'

'How do you know? Have you given Thea the chance to prove herself?' Before Pearl could respond, Jenny continued, 'Speaking as the youngest of five, I can tell you how irritating it is to always be treated like a baby by my older brothers.'

'I wouldn't treat her like one if she didn't behave so irresponsibly.' Judging by Jenny's expression, she was never going to agree, so Pearl changed the subject. 'You've got four brothers? That must have been a trial for your grandmother.' She'd remembered just in time that Jenny and, presumably, her brothers had been brought up by their grandparents.

'They were quite a handful.'

'What do they do?'

'They're all miners. They wanted to join up, but couldn't because they're needed in the mines. Can't say I'm sorry.'

Pearl nodded, thinking of the heavy casualties of the war so far. However dangerous working down a pit might be, it must surely be safer than being in the armed forces.

And so the conversation moved on to Jenny's early life in the Forest of Dean and safely away from the trials of being Thea's older sister. Still, after lights out, when Pearl was wriggling in her bunk to avoid slipping into the gaps between her 'biscuits', she couldn't help thinking about what Jenny had said. Had she ever given Thea the chance to prove she was capable of taking care of herself? She had, after all, survived over two years in the WAAF. That had to count for something. Then she recalled how terrified she'd been seeing Thea clinging to that upturned coracle, drifting downstream on the Severn. If Pearl hadn't been there to haul her in, she might not be alive today. Whatever Jenny might say, Thea was a danger to herself and needed to be kept in check.

Pearl shifted again, trying to find a comfortable position. She closed her eyes, willing sleep to come, but her meeting with Thea played itself out on the inside of her eyelids. The replay seemed to get stuck on Thea's parting shot: *I've been in the WAAF longer than you. If you want to meet up and hear my advice, drop me a note. Otherwise, leave me alone.*

But Pearl had no intention of leaving her sister alone. If she was to stop Thea getting into any further trouble, she had to persuade her to agree to a meeting. That left Pearl with no option but to swallow her pride, write a conciliatory note and ask for Thea's advice, much though Pearl scoffed at the thought of her sister ever offering any sensible ideas.

Chapter Five

Pearl went on watch that evening, her pulse racing. Flying Control had been humming with purpose that morning, with the teleprinters chattering and a bustle of aircrew visiting the Met Office on the lower floor.

'We're flying ops tonight, so make sure you're on time and pay attention,' Corporal Snaith had told her.

Now, as she cycled to the Watch Office on the bicycle that had finally arrived by train the day before, together with Deedee's old one for Jenny, she felt a thrill, even though she doubted Snaith would let her speak to any pilots herself. It would be exciting all the same to see their squadrons take to the air for a real mission. She could see the ground crews making last-minute checks to the aircraft in their dispersal points, which were dotted around the runways on hardstanding. Buses carrying the aircrews trundled around the perimeter track, taking them to their machines. She could only imagine the tension they must be feeling, and it put her own nerves into perspective. She pedalled harder, not caring that she would arrive early for her watch. With all that was happening, she didn't want to miss a thing. What aspiring journalist would do otherwise?

Much to her surprise, Snaith was not in position at the desk when she arrived in Flying Control. She had never seen the place without him, and had been starting to wonder if he lived there.

'Is that the time already?' the WAAF she was due to relieve asked. Pearl remembered her name was Vera.

'I'm a little early but I don't mind taking over now.' It was her first opportunity to be in charge of the R/T and she wasn't going to pass it up. No doubt Snaith would turf her from the chair the moment he arrived, but she could at least get the feel of it.

Vera rose, grabbed her jacket from the back of the chair and pulled it on. 'That's good of you. No Snaith? I would have expected him to be here by now.'

'So would I.' Pearl sat down, trying not to let her excitement and nerves show. She didn't want to remind the others that she hadn't done this before, or they might send for another WAAF to take over until Snaith arrived.

'Ah well, I'm sure he'll turn up soon.' Vera pulled a powder compact from her pocket, peered at her face in the tiny mirror and fluffed her blond hair. Then she tilted her head towards the other WAAF sitting at the desk. 'Maggie here will keep an eye on you.'

Maggie, another R/T operator who Pearl recognised but hadn't spoken to before, gave her a reassuring nod and smile. 'I was terrified the first time I was on duty during an op, but you'll be fine.'

'Thanks,' Pearl said, somewhat annoyed at herself for not disguising her nerves as well as she had hoped.

'Anyway,' Vera said, 'there's nothing for us to do at this end of an op. The runway controller directs the take-off. He's based in a caravan down by the runway. We have to stay alert in case there's a boomerang or darky call, but all our hard work is in the early hours when they come back.'

'Boomerang?' Pearl thought she had got to grips with all the Bomber Command slang, but this was a new one.

'It's when an aircraft has to return early, usually because of a technical fault.'

'Oh, I see. Is there anything particular we have to do?'

'No, just direct them to land at the correct runway, same as with any other arrival. The ground crew, ambulances and crash tenders will already be in place, so they'll take over as soon as the plane touches down.' Vera spoke with an assurance that Pearl wondered if she would ever manage. There seemed to be so many things to remember, she didn't know how she would hold it all in her head, let alone recall it at the right moment.

'Anyway, I'm going out to watch our boys take off. Coming?'

Pearl had to glance behind her to reassure herself that Vera's invitation was directed at her. She glanced at Maggie. 'Can I? I mean...'

Maggie waved her away. 'Of course. I'll shout if I need you, but I won't. There's really nothing for us to do yet. Go on, it's quite a sight. You won't want to miss it.'

'Very well, then. Thank you.' Pearl picked up the jacket she had only just draped over the back of her chair and followed Vera out onto the balcony.

The noise of multiple aircraft engines hit her as soon as she stepped outside. She had been aware of the noise while inside, but the full force of it hadn't struck her until now. Even the air around her reverberated, and she could feel the balcony vibrating through the thick soles of her shoes. She could swear her heartbeat had changed to throb in time with the engines. Although the light was fast fading, she could see well enough to make out a line of aircraft – Manchesters and Wellingtons – taxiing towards the runway. At the downwind threshold of the runway was the control caravan. She had hardly laid eyes on it when a green light flashed. The engines of the first Manchester in the line rose to a deafening crescendo, and, slowly at first but rapidly gathering speed, it headed down the runway. Pearl found it hard to believe that the huge craft could possibly attain enough speed to take off. However, at what seemed like the last possible moment the wheels bounced into the air. Pearl held her breath, expecting them to crash back onto the runway, but, after an agonising wait when the Manchester seemed to waver between flight and crashing, it lifted into the air, its wheels barely skimming over the perimeter fence. When the machine banked and climbed steadily, Pearl released her breath. Then another green light came from the caravan and the next Manchester set off down the runway.

'Bloody Manchesters,' Vera yelled into Pearl's ear. 'I've heard the aircrew talking about them. They're a devil to get off the ground, especially when they're weighed down with bombs. We had one crash on take-off last month. The bombs exploded and the heat set off all the ammunition in the magazines. No one could go near it until it had burned out. Horrible way to go. You can still see the scorched crater in the field where it went down.'

Pearl felt sick. In all the excitement, she had barely spared a thought for the crews. How many of them would still be alive at the end of the night? She watched another Manchester heave itself into the air; as soon as it had gained enough height to be sure it wasn't going to crash, she didn't want to see any more. 'I'd better go in,' she told Vera. 'Snaith must have arrived by now, and he'll be wondering where I am.'

But Snaith still wasn't there. Wing Commander Fforbes, looking worried, approached her as soon as she stepped through the French windows and rearranged the voluminous blackout curtains. 'I've just had a message from Sick Quarters. Apparently Corporal Snaith is there. He was knocked off his bicycle on the way here.'

'How awful. Is he all right, sir?'

'He's going to be out of action for a few days with a concussion. Will you manage without him?'

'I'll be fine, sir.' Pearl tried to inject all the confidence she didn't feel into her voice. If Fforbes didn't think she was up to the job, he would be forced to send for an off-duty R/T operator to supervise her. That would hardly make her popular. Besides, hadn't she been champing at the bit to prove herself?

'Jolly good.' Fforbes gave her an encouraging smile. 'By the way, you don't have to keep calling me sir. Save all that nonsense for the parade ground. Just do your job and I'll be happy.'

'Thank you, s——' She caught herself. 'Thank you.'

'He's a good egg,' Maggie said once Fforbes had gone out onto the balcony, a pair of binoculars slung round his neck. 'Don't be afraid to ask for help if you need it. Everyone's very friendly up here. Well, apart from Snaith. I'm glad he wasn't seriously injured, of course, but I can't deny it'll be nice to be without him for a few days.'

Pearl grinned. 'I must say I'm looking forward to actually doing something tonight instead of watching Snaith do it all.'

'I'll be here to help, so ask if you need anything. I'm afraid it's going to be a long wait.'

Another WAAF came in from the balcony and scribbled something on a blackboard. Pearl knew the board was a list of all the aircraft flying ops that night. At the top of the board was the name of the station – Fenthorpe – and below was the station callsign, 'Causeway', and the location of the raid. With the strict secrecy on the base, Pearl hadn't known until this moment that both squadrons were bound for Essen. Below that, the board was divided into two, with the left-hand side being for 505 Squadron and the right for 642 Squadron. There were columns for each aircraft's name, its pilot, take-off and landing times. As Pearl watched, a WAAF picked up a stick of chalk and wrote a take-off time for 505 Squadron's *Q-Queenie*.

'That's my Billy's plane,' Maggie said as she put down the chalk and dusted her fingers. 'He's the tail gunner. Now we have to wait and pray they all come back.'

—

'Target dead ahead, Skipper.' The navigator's voice sounded tinny through Greg's intercom.

Not exactly a necessary observation, for the night sky over Essen was lit with an orange glow from the incendiaries dropped by the first wave of bombers. Flight Sergeant Greg Tallis, pilot of Manchester bomber *F-Freddie*, forced himself to take calming breaths and not grip the control column too tightly. Searchlights stabbed the sky, roving, criss-crossing, and brilliant flashes of flak exploded around them like fireworks. It was vital he kept his head and got in and out of the danger area as quickly as possible. And that meant ensuring the whole crew kept their concentration and did their jobs to the best of their ability.

'Bomb aimer, report,' he said.

'Visibility good,' Jack Murphy replied, from his position lying flat in the nose of the aircraft. 'I can see the target.'

'Thank God for that,' another voice crackled over the intercom. Greg thought he recognised Harry Evans, the mid-upper gunner. 'Just drop the bloody bombs and get us out of here.'

It was what they were all thinking, so Greg didn't waste his breath reprimanding him. Tonight they were aiming for a munitions factory, and no one wanted to have to abort and repeat the run until the clouds cleared over the target, but neither did anyone want to bomb a school or hospital by accident. Not that Greg let himself dwell on the prospect. That was the kind of thinking that would send a pilot mad. When he was on a mission, he didn't think about high-flown notions such as his country or patriotism or even ending the war. He just focused on doing his job to the best of his ability and ensuring the crew did likewise. Right now, it was the bomb aimer's job to guide them to the target, and Greg concentrated on his instructions.

'Bomb doors open, Skipper.'

'Bomb doors open.' Greg pulled the lever, bracing himself for the usual jolt as the doors opened.

'Left, left… steady…'

Greg steered the aircraft repeating the bomb aimer's instructions, but what he really wanted to say was: *Hurry up! Release the damn bombs!* This was always the worst part, trying to hold the plane steady and not lose his nerve when every instinct was screaming at him to turn round and speed for safety.

'Bombs gone.'

Without the weight of the bombs, *F-Freddie* surged upwards, and Greg had a struggle to keep the Manchester under control. There were cheers from the other crew members but Greg didn't relax, nor did he turn the plane round. He had to hold his course until Jack reported that the automatic photographs had been taken, not easy when the explosions on the ground created turbulence that made flying *F-Freddie* feel more like riding a rodeo bull. Greg gritted his teeth, checking the artificial horizon as he fought to keep *F-Freddie* level. Had he thought waiting to release the bombs was the worst part? He was wrong. This was by far the worst part – holding course for another thirty seconds or so. If they didn't get a photograph, the mission would not count as one of their thirty completed missions required to finish a tour of duty.

When Jack finally reported that the photos had been taken, he hadn't even finished speaking before Greg put *F-Freddie*'s nose down to get them out of the melee in the fastest possible time. Simultaneously the navigator shouted out a bearing, giving Greg the course home. Greg knew he would have calculated it in advance, ready to get them on the right route at the earliest opportunity. It was little details like that that made the difference between death and survival.

Flak still exploded around them, and Greg had to school himself not to flinch with each brain-numbing bang. It couldn't be long now before they were out of range. They were going to make it. Another bomb to paint on *F-Freddie*'s fuselage, another mission closer to the end of their tour. Already the glow from the bombed target was well behind them and the sky ahead darker.

That was when a brilliant white light seared through the cockpit, swiftly followed by another.

'We've been coned!' This was from the mid-upper gunner.

Greg immediately threw the machine into a series of manoeuvres, desperate to evade the pair of searchlights that had him pinned where the beams joined. But *F-Freddie* was no nimble fighter, and no sooner had he steered away from the beams than they sliced through the air and found him again. The flak was intensifying. They must be nearing the outer limits of the anti-aircraft fire. If they could just hold on another minute, they would be out of range.

A huge bang deafened him, and the aircraft was flung through the sky like tissue paper in a gale.

'Jesus Christ Almighty!' Again, this was from the mid-upper gunner in his turret.

'Report!' Greg yelled.

'There's a bloody great hole in the port wing.'

'Any fire?' This was the airman's greatest fear.

'No, Skipper. Looks like a piece of shrapnel tore straight through.'

Greg fought to level the plane, and tensed, listening for any change in the note from the port engine that would indicate a problem. 'How's the port engine looking?' He himself twisted to peer at the engine, and released a shaky breath when he could see no sign of smoke or oil.

'It looks undamaged,' Evans confirmed.

By this time they were beyond the range of the searchlights and the anti-aircraft fire. Maybe they were going to make it after all. After checking his compass to make sure he was back on the correct course, Greg settled back in his seat. 'Keep an eye out for fighters,' he told everyone. 'We don't want to get caught out now.'

But they seemed to have got away with it. There was no sign of any enemy fighter aircraft and, by the time the navigator announced they were approaching the coast, Greg allowed himself to contemplate the breakfast of bacon and eggs that would be awaiting him back at Fenthorpe.

They were halfway across the North Sea when a slight roughening in the engine's note jerked Greg from thoughts of food and set his nerves at full stretch. His gaze swept across his instruments, and froze when he saw the port engine temperature was high and the revs were falling.

He spoke into the intercom, struggling to keep his voice calm. 'Bad news, lads. Looks like we've got a coolant leak, and the port engine's running hot. Strap yourselves into your brollies and prepare to bale out.'

There was a chorus of, 'Okay, Skip,' followed by grim silence. He knew everyone else was doing the same as him: listening to the engine, praying it didn't cut out or burst into flames.

He strained his eyes, seeking the dark shape against the night sky that would indicate land ahead. He prayed that the engine wouldn't catch fire before they crossed the coast. As soon as they reached land he could order the crew to bale out, but if the engines caught fire now the crew would likely die of exposure or drowning before rescue came. As for himself, if he could nurse the engine to keep going until they reached land he wouldn't bale out. He couldn't bear the thought of crashing on housing. Instead, he would do his best to either land *F-Freddie* safely or ensure she crashed in an unpopulated area.

He checked the altimeter and his heart sank when he saw they were losing height steadily. Even if the engine didn't catch fire, they might not have enough height to make it to the airfield.

He found himself talking to the plane as one might coax a nervy horse. 'Come on. Keep going. You can do it.'

They couldn't go down now. Not when they had got this far.

–

Pearl caught herself nodding off at her desk. She rubbed her eyes. This would never do. On the point of rising to pace around the office in the hope that it would wake her up, she froze. Was that a distant rumble? She glanced at the clock. Four a.m. From a comment Fforbes had made earlier, it was about the time their squadrons were due to arrive.

The office door flung open and Fforbes stalked in. Grabbing the binoculars, he went straight out onto the balcony. Another officer picked up a phone and gave the order to light the runway flares.

Maggie, looking pale, gave Pearl a smile. 'This is it. Ready?'

No sooner had Pearl nodded than the speakers crackled to life. 'Hello Causeway, this is Gabbro Manchester *E-Easy*. Request permission to land, over.' An instant later: 'Hello Causeway, this is Treacle Wellington *B-Beer*. Request permission to land.'

Pearl drew a deep breath as she pressed the transmit button. She had trained for this and knew what to do. She could cope. 'Hello Gabbro Manchester *E-Easy*, Causeway answering. Permission to land, runway two-two. Hello Treacle Wellington *B-Beer*, Causeway answering. Circle at two thousand feet, is this understood?'

No one snatched the microphone from her hands. No one told her she was doing it all wrong. She was actually guiding Fenthorpe's aircraft in to land!

After that, everything happened so fast she didn't have time to think. She had to 'stack' each returning bomber, instructing them to join the circuit at a different height so there was no danger of a mid-air collision, then bring them in one at a time. Of course, each plane would now be showing their navigation lights, so the pilots should be able to see where they all were. Then, one at a time, she gave the order to pancake. There was also the log to complete for every interaction. She worked furiously, time flying after the long, agonising wait. Eventually there was a lull in the proceedings, and she sat back with a groan and stretched her aching back. She hadn't checked the blackboard for a while and now as she studied it she saw only two aircraft had yet to return, both from 505 Squadron: *F-Freddie* and *Q-Queenie*. Wait, wasn't Maggie's young man flying in *Q-Queenie*?

A glance at Maggie confirmed it. Her face had lost all its colour and, although she was writing an entry in the log with the appearance of great concentration, the deep lines around her eyes and mouth betrayed her anxiety.

'I'm sure they'll be back soon,' Pearl said.

'Yes, yes, I know you're right. Anything could have happened. We often get stray aircraft returning a long time after the main group.' But the haunted expression didn't leave Maggie's face.

The seconds, then minutes, ticked by. Pearl strained her hearing, willing her ears to pick up the distant drone of aero engines. She didn't know anyone on either aircraft, yet at that moment she felt as though she was awaiting the return of a family member.

Another half an hour, then Maggie said, 'They'll be out of fuel soon.'

A glance at the board showed Pearl that Q-Queenie had taken off ten minutes before F-Freddie. So if all had gone to plan, Q-Queenie should be the first of the two aircraft to return. She prayed that both would still make it home.

Two more minutes stretched into eternity. Then a voice came through the speakers, making Pearl jump.

'Hello Causeway, do you read me? Hello Causeway.'

With a pounding heart, Pearl pressed the transmit button on the microphone. Beside her, Maggie leapt to her feet and gripped the back of Pearl's chair. 'Hello, this is Causeway.'

She racked her brains to remember the correct response to an unidentified caller but it proved to be unnecessary, for the caller immediately replied with a complete lack of protocol. 'Thank God. This is Gabbro Manchester F-Freddie. Request immediate landing.'

Maggie gave a little whimper, then clapped her hand to her mouth and slumped back into her seat.

'Hello, F-Freddie, permission to land on runway two–two.'

Fforbes stood with his head cocked to one side as though listening. Pearl listened too and heard the roar of engines, although even to her untrained ears something sounded wrong.

Judging from the grim expression on Fforbes's face, he thought so too.

Another message came through from *F-Freddie*. 'Hello Causeway, this is *F-Freddie*.' Even through the distortion of the speakers, Pearl could detect the strain in the pilot's voice. She thought the man spoke with an odd accent, too, although she couldn't place it. 'It's just me. The rest of the crew baled out when we reached the coast.' There was a burst of static, then: 'Port engine's afire. I don't think—' Another burst of static obscured anything else the pilot might have said.

'*F-Freddie*, do you read me? Are you still there, *F-Freddie*?' She had no idea what to do, but some instinct told her to keep talking to the pilot so he wouldn't feel alone, even if these were to be his last moments.

Wing Commander Fforbes was standing by the window with the curtain drawn back so he could look out, heedless of blackout regulations. Suddenly his back went rigid. 'There. I see him. He's coming in fast. Tell him he's coming in at the wrong angle. He needs to circle until he sees the runway flares.'

Pearl looked up and saw a streak of orange in the distance, and her heart went out to the lonely pilot who was so close to home and yet not close enough. She repeated Fforbes's instructions and then, because she knew that if she were in his position she'd want to keep hearing a friendly voice, she abandoned all attempt at radio protocol and added, 'We can see you, and you're doing so well. Tell me when you see the flares.'

A brief silence, then: 'Right, I've got them now.' Another pause, then he said, 'If you're the last person I speak to in this world, I'd like to know your name.'

Pearl swallowed, fighting against a sudden thickness in her throat. 'I'm Pearl.'

Was that a chuckle? Surely not. No one would laugh if they were facing a fiery death. 'Most appropriate. I'll think of you when I get to the Pearly Gates.'

'Don't say that. You're going to make it.'

'We'll soon find out. I'm coming in. It's now or never.' And from the howl of the engines that shook the building, Pearl could tell it was only too true. She didn't dare reply now, not wanting to distract the pilot when he must be needing all of his concentration to bring the aircraft down safely. However, there was one last transmission from the pilot. 'If I make it in one piece, Pearl, I'm taking you out to celebrate.' Then there was nothing but static.

Chapter Six

Hardly knowing what she was doing, Pearl leapt from her seat and ran to the balcony. Her eyes were immediately drawn to a howling fireball swooping low over the airfield. An instant later she heard the thud of the wheels hitting the ground. She found she was blinking tears from her eyes but, as her vision cleared, she saw the whole aeroplane wasn't yet on fire, although flames were shooting out from one of the engines. Crash tenders and an ambulance sped towards the Manchester, which was still lurching down the runway, losing speed far slower than Pearl would have liked.

Get out! Get out now! Her throat felt raw, as though she had screamed the words, although she knew she hadn't uttered a sound. Never had she felt so helpless as she watched the scene play out below her while knowing there was nothing she could do. When the plane finally lurched to a halt, fingers of flame were already clawing their way along the length of the wing and reaching for the fuselage. The fire crews set to work straight away while other members of the ground crew dragged up a ladder and scrambled up to open the hatch. Pearl pressed a shaking hand to her mouth, willing the pilot to appear. What if he was injured? Would any of the ground crew dare to climb inside a burning plane to free him?

Thankfully this proved unnecessary. By the light of the fire, she saw a man briefly silhouetted in the hatchway before he half climbed, half fell down the ladder. The ambulance crew hurried to assist him. The pilot had barely taken two steps before sharp reports rang out; all the figures gathered around the stricken aircraft flung themselves flat.

'Fire's got into the magazines,' Fforbes said. 'There's no saving *F-Freddie* now.'

Remembering what Vera had said about the plane that had crashed in a neighbouring field, Pearl realised the fire must have got into the ammunition, and the shells were exploding, firing bullets at the crew. She couldn't tear her gaze away from the terrifying scene and prayed that no one would be hit. Finally the explosions stopped and everyone staggered to their feet. The fire crew returned to putting out the blaze, although by this time the Manchester was clearly beyond saving. She looked for the pilot but from this distance she couldn't make him out. Now the excitement had died down, she suddenly remembered she was supposed to be on watch, so she hurried back to her seat.

'Did *F-Freddie* make it down safely?' Maggie asked. Her face was whiter than ever, and her movements were stiff, as though she held herself under tight control.

'Yes. Well, the pilot got out safely. The machine was burned to bits.' Only now did it occur to her to look at the blackboard to see the name of the pilot. Flight Sergeant Tallis. 'Any news on *Q-Queenie*?'

'Not yet.'

Pearl stared at Maggie, wondering what to say. But there was nothing, apart from empty platitudes, and she couldn't bring herself to say she was sure everything would be all right when the most likely reason for *Q-Queenie*'s absence was that it had crashed somewhere between here and the target.

Wing Commander Fforbes came back inside at that moment. He hesitated beside Maggie and then patted her awkwardly on the shoulder. 'You mustn't give up hope, young lady. Apparently there was some fog along the coast. They might have lost their way and been forced to land at another base.'

Maggie brightened. 'Of course. I should have thought of that.'

'I'm on my way to debriefing to see what Tallis has to say, assuming he's unhurt. He might know more.'

'Thank you.'

Pearl and Maggie finished their watch in near-silence. By the time they were relieved, news had filtered in regarding the crewmen of *F-Freddie* who had baled out. All were safe, although the bomb aimer had struck the sloping roof of a farm outhouse on landing and broken his ankle. Everyone else would be issued travel warrants and make the journey back to Fenthorpe the next day. All this they learned from Fforbes, who returned to Flying Control to let them know Tallis had escaped from the wreckage with only minor burns.

'You did well today,' he told Pearl. 'I'll be sure to tell Snaith you're a credit to the training. I'm glad to have you on the team.'

And despite her worries on Maggie's behalf, Pearl couldn't resist a smile at the thought of Snaith being told that a mere woman had performed well at a job he'd believed she would be unable to manage. It was good to know that there were some men at Fenthorpe who appreciated her contribution.

But of *Q-Queenie* there was no news. Finally, about half an hour before the end of their watch, Fforbes announced, 'I'm sorry but I'm going to have to inform Group that *Q-Queenie*'s crew are officially missing. And the Committee of Adjustment will need to be informed.'

Maggie simply nodded and gazed down at her hands with blank eyes.

'It doesn't necessarily mean they're dead,' Fforbes went on in a gentle voice. 'If any baled out over enemy territory and were captured, it will take some time before the news filters through to us. And if I know *Q-Queenie*'s crew, they're not going to let themselves be captured easily. They may yet make their way back home.'

Maggie made no reply, and Pearl knew that the likelihood was that they were all dead. Pearl couldn't decide what would be worse – knowing they were dead or enduring weeks of false hope before finally learning the truth, if ever. She knew that in the case of aircraft that crashed into the sea, for example, some families never knew for sure what had happened to their loved ones.

–

Even though Fforbes had told Maggie she could leave early, she declared she was able to finish her watch.

'It will probably be weeks before we get any firm news,' she said. 'I'd much rather be working than fretting. It's his family I feel sorry for. At least I have the comfort of working where he did, so I'll hear as soon as there's any news.' At the end of their watch, she hastened away without waiting for Pearl to pull on her coat, saying she needed to write to Billy's parents.

Full of pity for Maggie, yet also admiring her strength, Pearl left the Watch Office alone and pushed her bike towards the cookhouse, deciding to get breakfast before going to catch up on her sleep.

She hadn't gone far when a rather unkempt man approached, his right sleeve torn and blackened. She thought he was on his way to the Watch Office but when he saw her he veered from the path and approached. 'Excuse me, you don't happen to know if a young lady named Pearl is still in Flying Control?'

His voice was unmistakable – it was the pilot of *F-Freddie*. And now she recognised the accent as Australian. In fact, she also recognised his face – this was the same man she had noticed at the Saracen's Head. The darker uniform must be the uniform of the Royal Australian Air Force.

She smiled. 'I'm afraid she's left.'

'Any idea where she went?'

'That depends why you want to see her.'

The corner of his mouth twitched as she spoke, and Pearl know that he had recognised her voice too. 'I was going to invite her for a no-expense-spared evening out, but if you won't tell me...' He made an exaggerated show of turning away with a hangdog expression.

Pearl knew when she was beaten. 'Oh very well, as you already know, I'm Pearl. I—'

She had been about to say how glad she was to see him in one piece, but her words were cut off in a muffled squeak when the pilot stooped and planted a kiss right on her lips. When he drew back, he looked very pleased with himself. 'Greg Tallis. I'm very pleased to meet you this side of the Pearly Gates.'

There was no way she was going to let him get away with taking liberties, narrow escape or not. 'I don't know how you do things in Australia, but here it's usual to shake hands.' Despite herself, she was unable to suppress a smile, and it took all her willpower not to press her fingers to her lips, which tingled from the kiss.

'Sorry about that.' Yet his eyes twinkled, and he sounded utterly unrepentant. He indicated his singed sleeve; Pearl caught glimpses of a dressing beneath the torn fabric. 'Right arm's a bit sore, but if you insist.' He stuck out his left hand.

Now Pearl regretted sounding like a total prude. 'I forgot you'd been burned,' she said ruefully.

'Moral of the story – never try putting out a fire with your flying suit if you happen to be wearing it at the time.'

Pearl stared at him, shocked that he could be so casual about the narrowness of his escape. In her mind's eye, she saw him struggling to reach the Manchester's escape hatch, warding off the fire with his right arm. Then, recollecting herself, she shook his left hand with her right, which should have been awkward but the feel of his warm fingers, strong yet gentle round the back of her hand, was oddly pleasant. 'I'm very pleased to meet you,' she said, then was instantly annoyed with herself for sounding so formal. She couldn't think of their radio exchange without feeling they had made a real connection, so surely there was no need to sound so stiff and British. Or maybe it was just hearing her voice in comparison with Greg's assured Australian drawl. 'I don't know if you've heard, but your crew are all safe.'

'Yeah, they're going to be annoyed with me when they learn I landed without a hitch after making them find their own way home. But anyway,' he added before she could comment that she didn't think landing in a ball of flame counted as 'without a hitch', 'I didn't come looking for you to talk about my crew. I want to thank you for talking me down.'

'I was just doing my job.'

'No, you kept me going when I thought I didn't have a hope. I can't tell you how good it felt to hear a friendly voice. Now, let's not forget I promised to take you out to celebrate, and I know you won't turn me down, because that would mean forcing me to break my word.'

'Well, if you put it like that.' Pearl had, in fact, intended to turn him down. Being so new to the station and with so much to learn, she didn't really have the time. But there was something about Greg that drew her, although she couldn't adequately explain it to herself. Maybe it was because although he seemed to be trying to hide it now, there had been that moment of vulnerability when he had thought he was going to die. And he hadn't patronised her as so many men had in her experience, but had reached out to her and been grateful for her help. 'I suppose it wouldn't hurt. There's so little to celebrate these days, after all.'

'That's the spirit. When are you free?'

'I'm free tonight, actually. Oh, but maybe you don't feel up to going out this evening.'

'I'm right as rain. My arm's a bit singed but not too bad.'

And so Pearl found herself contemplating an evening with a man she hardly knew, instead of testing herself on her latest lessons as originally planned. She comforted herself with the thought that a journalist would always seize the opportunity to meet new people. And it wasn't as if Greg was asking her on a date. When they had been speaking over the radio, he had probably pictured a beautiful young woman like Thea, not someone pushing thirty and dull-looking. After all, hadn't he told her the only reason he was repeating his invitation made on the spur of the moment was because he didn't want to break his word? In the end she arranged to meet him in the NAAFI at seven that evening, certain he wouldn't be interested in seeing her again after that.

–

Pearl dressed with greater care than usual when she rose from her nap that afternoon, opting to wear her best blues. By the time she had arranged her hair in a neat roll in the nape of her neck and applied a little lipstick, it was nearly five o'clock. Having slept through lunch, she decided to make her way to the NAAFI now and see if she could grab a bite to eat. She took one of her exercise books with her, intending to test herself on Morse to kill time before she met Greg.

Helen had already been out to collect the post for Hut Three, and Pearl was disappointed not to get anything from Thea, although she had been happy to see a letter from Deedee. As intended, she had sent a note to Thea the morning after seeing her in Lincoln, doing her best not to sound judgemental and taking her sister up on her offer of advice on life in the WAAF. So far, nearly two weeks later, Thea had failed to answer. Pearl was trying to give Thea the benefit of the doubt, telling herself the post might have been delayed, or Thea could be too busy to reply, but as the days passed with no news these excuses were getting harder to believe.

Once in the NAAFI and armed with a tray bearing a mug of tea and a sticky bun, Pearl went to look for a quiet table where she could enjoy the news from Deedee. However, she had to grip the tray to stop it slipping from her hands when she saw her sister sitting alone at a table in the far corner. She dashed up to Thea, placing the tray on the table so carelessly that tea slopped from her mug. 'Why are you here? Is something wrong? What's happened?' Her first thought was that something must have happened to Deedee, and Thea had been given leave to visit Fenthorpe to break the news to Pearl.

Thea, who had been scowling into her mug as though it contained slimy pond water, glanced up. 'Oh, it's you.'

'Yes of course it's me. Who else were you expecting to see?'

'You're the last person I want to meet.'

Pearl pulled out a chair and sat down feeling bewildered. Not to mention hurt. 'What brings you here, then?'

Thea's scowl deepened. 'I didn't exactly have a choice. I've been transferred.'

'Here?'

'No, Timbuktu. Yes of course here. Why else would I be in this miserable pit?'

But Pearl could give as good as she got where Thea was concerned. 'Oh, I don't know. You might have had a day off and decided to visit your wonderful, caring sister who's been worried sick because you never answer any of her letters. You never know, she might even treat you to a cake if you asked nicely enough.'

The corners of Thea's mouth curved upwards. 'The ginger cake does look tasty.'

Pearl pulled out her purse and rose. 'And when I come back, you can tell me all about your transfer.'

Thea sighed theatrically, then called after her, 'I'll have a cup of tea, too. I don't know what this is, but it's definitely not coffee.'

When Pearl returned a couple of minutes later with the tea and ginger cake, she added a lump of sugar to her own tea, deciding she was going to need to extra sweetness to deal with whatever scrape Thea had got herself into now. 'Come on then,' she prompted, once Thea had stirred two lumps of sugar into her own cup, 'tell me what you did to get yourself transferred.'

'Well, that's charming. You make it sound like I'm in disgrace. Why do you always assume the worst?'

Bitter experience. But Pearl couldn't bring herself to say it. 'Fine. I'm sorry. Did you request a transfer, then?'

Thea stirred her tea again before replying. She seemed to be taking great care not to slop a single drop over the rim. 'No. And before you ask why I didn't reply to your letter, I did, but I only just sent it. I'd run out of paper and I couldn't buy any more because I was on jankers.'

Although there was still a lot of air force slang Pearl was unfamiliar with, she knew what jankers meant. It referred to punishment duties carried out while confined to base. 'Why am I not surprised? Don't tell me – you were caught wearing civvies.'

'I would have got away with it if some busybody hadn't reported the hole in the fence some of us used to get in and out of the camp. When I got back it had been blocked up, so I had no choice but to use the gate.'

'You mean you regularly go out without permission?'

'Everyone does. It's not as if it's a crime. We're not doing any harm.'

'But it's against regulations. If you didn't think you could abide by strict rules, why did you join the WAAF?' This was something that had always puzzled Pearl. Thea had volunteered almost as soon as war had broken out, and Pearl had never understood why – if she had been so keen to do war work – she hadn't applied for factory work instead, which was better paid and would have allowed her greater freedom and probably more leisure time.

Thea shrugged, not meeting Pearl's gaze. 'Why did *you* join? I thought you were all set to become a star journalist.'

'So did I. But apparently there was a man who needed the job more than me.' Perhaps if she hadn't been so frustrated with Thea, she wouldn't have let slip about her disappointment, but she blurted it out before she could stop herself. When she had written to tell Thea she was joining the WAAF, she hadn't revealed what had happened at the *Shrewsbury Mirror*, choosing to frame her decision as a positive move, saying she wanted to serve her country. Now she waited for Thea's delight at her plans going awry.

Much to her surprise, Thea simply said, 'I'm sorry. I know how much that meant to you.'

'It did.' Pearl was too taken aback to say anything else. 'But it's probably for the best. Now conscription for women has started I'd have been called up anyway. At least this way I got more choice over where I was sent.'

They sat in silence for a while, eating their cakes. Then, when Thea was dabbing the crumbs from her plate, she said, 'I thought you would give me an earful when you found out I'd got into trouble.'

Pearl sighed. 'I would if I thought it would make any difference.'

Thea grinned. 'You're learning at last. Well, as a reward for your restraint, I'll tell you that I think I got transferred because the officer in charge of our Waafery wanted to get rid of a troublemaker and pass me on to someone else to deal with.'

'Just your bad luck you ended up in the same place as your big sister.'

'Luck had nothing to do with it,' Thea said darkly. 'I made the mistake of letting slip that I have a sister here. I think I was transferred here in the hope you would keep an eye on me.'

'Well, they're in for a shock when they discover how little influence I have on you.'

'Oh, I wouldn't say that. I did survive my childhood, after all.'

If that was the most positive comment Thea could think of for Pearl's childcare abilities, Pearl wondered why she had bothered. 'Thanks a bundle. All those years I spent making sure you ate properly, had nice manners and did your homework on time, and the best you can manage is that I didn't kill you.'

'And I didn't kill myself by my own stupidity, and I didn't drive the neighbours to murder. That has to count for something.' Thea did, at least, look more cheerful now.

Pearl glanced at her watch. 'What do you want to do now? I could show you around if you like.' If she hurried, she could be back at the NAAFI in time for Greg.

But Thea was shaking her head. 'I'm not your responsibility any more. Don't you understand? I joined up to get out from under your thumb.' For a brief instant Thea's eyes widened, and Pearl knew she hadn't meant to say that. It didn't stop it from hurting, though.

'You wanted to get away from me?' She had known Thea wanted her independence, but never dreamed that it was more personal than that, that Thea had wanted to escape her.

'Not you as such, but your interference. I needed to be in a place where people treated me like an adult and weren't always waiting for me to make a mistake.'

Pearl snorted. 'I don't call sneaking out without permission acting like an adult.'

Thea rose. 'I knew you would be like this. Look, I don't want to be here, but I don't have any choice. Still, we don't have to spend time in one another's company. I suggest that as long as we're both in Fenthorpe, I do my thing and you do yours and we'll avoid each other as much as we can. How does that sound?'

It sounded awful. On the other hand, if she didn't agree then Thea would actively avoid her. At least if she gave Thea some space she might relent later on. 'I suppose I can do that.'

'Good.' Thea glanced at the clock. 'Anyway, I must go and get ready. I met a very good-looking tail gunner earlier, and he's taking me out later.'

'Who——?' Pearl bit off her question, seeing the warning glint in Thea's eyes. Keeping this not-interfering promise was going to be difficult. 'Have a nice time,' she said instead; what she really wanted to do was warn her not to let the man take any liberties.

'Oh, I will.' And Thea's smile did nothing to allay Pearl's fears. Pearl watched her sister take her cups and plate to the counter with a growing sense of worry. How was she supposed to sit back and do nothing while her sister dived head-first into trouble?

Chapter Seven

Pearl had already been nervous about seeing Greg again, so after her conversation with Thea she didn't feel at all like going out for the evening. Once Thea had swept out of the NAAFI – quite an achievement considering how stiff the door to the wooden hut was – Pearl ordered another cup of tea and tried to calm down by reading Deedee's letter. An impossible task when she kept hearing Thea's voice over and over again, telling her she had joined the WAAF to escape Pearl's interference. It was a bit rich considering that, if she hadn't interfered multiple times over the years and extricated her sister from all sorts of accidents that her impulsive, wild behaviour had got her into, who knew where Thea would be today? Either in the grave or prison, Pearl thought grimly.

'Are you going to drink that tea or are you trying to create a whirlpool?'

Pearl jumped, and stopped stirring her tea, dropping her teaspoon with a clatter. She looked up into Greg Tallis's grinning face. 'Oh gosh, is that the time already? I was miles away.'

'Not exactly what a bloke wants to hear. You could at least pretend to have been counting down the minutes.'

Pearl folded away her letter and tried to put on her coat, but had trouble finding her left sleeve. 'I was looking forward to seeing you.'

'Here. Let me help with that.' Greg leaned across her to straighten her coat and hold it up so she could slide her arm into the sleeve. This resulted in his face being so close to hers, they could almost be dancing the waltz. He smelled of a blend of coal tar soap, cigarettes and engine oil. Pearl backed away hastily, suddenly aware of how broad his shoulders were and the warmth of his body. She was taken aback by the wave of attraction that hit her. It must be the danger he had been in when she had first heard his voice; it lent him an air of glamour. She needed to remind herself that she didn't know him at all. She wasn't attracted to Greg Tallis but to the image of the brave pilot. So what if he was good-looking? She wasn't Thea. She was cautious Pearl, who knew how men didn't think twice about trampling over a woman's hopes and dreams in order to achieve their own.

Remembering that helped her overcome her attraction and give Greg a cool smile once she had her coat on. 'Thank you. Where are we going?'

'How about the Piebald Pony?'

'Where?'

'Sorry – I forgot you were new here. The White Horse pub in the village.'

Until arriving in Fenthorpe, Pearl had never set foot in a pub in her life, and now she was going into her second one in two weeks. She might have objected had she not still been stinging from Thea's remarks. What better way to show her sister that she wasn't the same old cautious Pearl than to be seen in the local pub? 'That sounds fine. I haven't got a late pass though.'

'Don't worry – I'll deliver you to the WAAF guardroom well before ten thirty.' And his lack of dismay at having to leave the pub before closing time reinforced her belief that he was treating her out of gratitude and not because he had any romantic designs on her.

They signed out at the guardroom and strolled down the lane towards the village. It was cloudy and a fresh wind made the hedgerows rustle. Pearl pulled her coat around her more tightly, glad of its warmth. Even though the weather had her worried that winter might be making a return, the birds sang of spring. Their song was so cheerful, it was hard to believe a savage war was raging and enemy bombers might even now be heading for Britain's cities, preparing to unleash fire, destruction and death. She nearly spoke the thought aloud, then remembered in the nick of time that Greg had been involved in just such a raid last night. Doubting he would want to talk or even think about his part in the raids, she tried to think of a safer topic of conversation.

'Why did you call the pub the Piebald Pony?' Pearl glanced sideways at Greg and saw he was smiling.

'It's a bit of a joke. You'll understand when you see the sign.'

By this time they had entered the village, and Pearl admired the buildings lining the high street. Most were built from a pale limestone, with a few painted houses standing out a brilliant white among the creamy stone. 'This is the first time I've been into the village,' Pearl said. 'I'd have come sooner if I'd known it was so nice.'

'It's a pretty place. There's a tea room as well as the pub. It's a good place to go if you want a change from the NAAFI.'

Pearl resolved to visit with Jenny the next time they had an afternoon off. 'Where's the pub?'

'Not far. Right in the middle of the high street.' He pointed to a long white building with tall chimneys and a roof of varying heights. Pearl was charmed by its higgledy-piggledy appearance.

The main door was set into a porch that jutted out into the street. When they got there, Greg opened the door for her. Before walking in, she glanced up at the sign that creaked above them and immediately saw how the pub had earned its unofficial name. For the sign had clearly not been repainted in several years and the paint was peeling in places, most notably in three large patches on the back of the white horse itself, revealing the dark wood beneath.

Pearl gave a little laugh. 'It's definitely a piebald.'

When she went in, she caught a brief glimpse of a crowded and rowdy public bar before Greg steered her towards a glass-panelled door on the right. Most of the occupants wore RAF uniform, she noticed.

'We'll sit in the snug,' Greg said. 'More chance to hear each other in there.'

Before they went through the door, Pearl caught sight of two airmen, each with a beer glass balanced on his head. The men surrounding them were counting and cheering. Before she could work out what they were trying to achieve, she was inside a smaller, cosy room. The door closed behind them, blocking out most of the noise from next door. The snug had a curved bar in one corner, linked to the bar in the other room by a door. The rest of the room was filled with highly polished tables and cushioned chairs. There was a large fireplace on the far side of the room, and the glowing coals in the hearth provided welcome warmth. Greg steered Pearl to a table placed in a bay window with thick dark-red curtains that made it feel secluded from the rest of the room.

'I'll get us some drinks,' Greg said. 'What will you have?'

Pearl opted for ginger beer and watched Greg as he walked to the bar. While he might not have movie-star good looks, Pearl had to admit she found his pleasant, open face attractive. Maybe it was the way his light brown hair was carelessly tousled, showing he didn't pay a lot of attention to his appearance, or perhaps it was the laughter lines creasing the corners of his eyes, but she liked how he exuded confidence. Of course, as she herself was older than many of the crewmen on the base, it could be that she enjoyed seeing someone who must have experienced something of life before the war rather than joining up straight from school.

The thought made her curious about his background, and so when he returned with their drinks she asked, 'Are you from Australia? I've been trying to place your accent.'

'That's right. Aussie born and bred, that's me.'

'What did you do before the war?'

'I was still a pilot. A commercial one, though, working for a charter company. Flying's the only thing I've ever wanted to do.'

'You owned your own plane?' Pearl was stunned. Greg hadn't struck her as wealthy.

He laughed, showing white teeth. 'Strewth, no. I got a small legacy from an uncle, and I used every penny to pay for flying lessons. I could never hope to own my own machine, let alone a charter company. I'm just an employee.'

'Did you enjoy it?'

Greg's eyes lost focus. 'It's the best job in the world. I wouldn't want to deal with all the paperwork involved in running my own charter company. All I've ever wanted to do is fly. I'm counting the days until I can go home and go back to flying without being shot at or having to drop bombs.'

'When did you come to England?'

'I volunteered for the air force as soon as war was declared.' His mouth twisted. 'I wasn't going to miss the excitement.'

Excitement? Pearl thought back to the previous night and Greg's brush with death. That was the kind of excitement she could do without. 'How long have you been in Fenthorpe?' Fenthorpe had only become operational a few months ago. It was one of many bomber stations that Bomber Command was building in eastern England.

'Not long. I started out as an instructor, because they were short of experienced pilots at first, but I quickly got browned off with that, and after a lot of work persuading the powers that be I was finally able to retrain for bombers. The mission you helped me land from was my fifth.'

Only his fifth mission. Pearl supposed his earlier work as a pilot instructor must explain his air of confidence, for she had imagined him to be one of the more experienced bomber pilots. If he had only completed five missions, he still had another twenty-five to go before finishing his tour. While she hadn't been on a Bomber Command station for long, she already knew that not many crews survived to the end of a tour.

Greg took a sip from his beer glass, then said, 'What about you? I know you must be new here because I would have noticed you if you'd been here before. Where have you come from?'

Pearl tried to ignore the little flutter she felt in her stomach, not only at his insistence that he would have noticed her but also at the gleam in his eyes as he regarded her over the rim of his glass. He was simply trying to flirt with her, and it was a long time since she had been a foolish teenager and young enough for her head to be turned by a handsome man's passing interest. 'This is my first posting,' she replied. 'I used to work on a regional newspaper.'

'A journalist? That explains why I feel like I've just been interviewed.'

She blushed a little at that. 'No, just a clerk.'

'I can't imagine you as *just* anything. If you handled your work at the newspaper with the same skill you used to talk me onto the runway in one piece then you must have had the whole office perfectly organised.'

After a month with Corporal Snaith, it felt wonderful to be praised for her work. 'Thank you. I can't take any of the credit for you getting down safely, though. You would have managed it without me.'

'Not likely. I thought I was a goner. If it hadn't been for your calm voice, making me believe I was going to be all right, I don't know how I would have held it together. If I'm ever in the same fix again, it's your voice I want to hear.'

Pearl wasn't usually lost for words but she struggled now to think of an adequate response. 'I'm sure anyone else would have done the same,' she said finally. 'I'm really glad I helped, though.' She felt a little uncomfortable at the intense turn the conversation had taken and tried to change the subject. 'How's your arm?'

'It's fine. But don't think you can turn the conversation back on me. It's my turn to interview you.'

Greg took another gulp of beer, racking his brains for a question to distract her. Although it had been important to him to express his gratitude for her part in his safe landing, he wanted to move the conversation away from his narrow squeak. He didn't want to think about how close he had come to a sudden and violent death. If he let himself dwell on it, he would have a struggle climbing into the pilot's seat for his next mission. The excitement of flying, the thrill of handling a heavy Manchester while it was buffeted by the wind – that was what he liked to think of. Not to mention the heady relief at seeing Lincoln Cathedral at the end of a mission, the high tower on its hill telling him he was almost home. He would think of the excitement and not let himself contemplate pain or death.

Something in Pearl's expression when she had told him she was 'just' a clerk made him curious, and he seized on that. 'Tell me about your work at the newspaper. How long were you there?' Now he came to look at her properly, he decided she was a few years older than most of the other WAAFs, maybe in her late twenties. Most women her age would be married with children, and he wondered why she was still single.

'I was there twelve years, from when I left school at sixteen.' There was a definite light of challenge in her eyes. Many women over twenty tended to be coy about revealing their age.

Greg did a quick calculation. 'That makes you twenty-eight.' He wondered if she had given the information needed to calculate her age as a test. Perhaps she wanted to put him off; he had sensed a reluctance to accept his invitation. It was the first time he had had to use all his powers of persuasion when asking out a pretty WAAF.

'Twenty-nine, actually. It was my birthday a couple of weeks ago but I was too occupied with the move here to celebrate.'

He raised his glass in a toast. 'Belated happy birthday. Twenty-nine's a good age. I should know – that's how old I am.' After they clinked glasses he went on, 'You must have liked the work to stay in the same job so long.'

'I did enjoy it but I really wanted to be a reporter.' Suddenly her features were animated, and he saw in her expression the same passion that he felt for flying.

He couldn't help but be drawn in by her enthusiasm. Leaning across the table, he asked, 'Then why join the WAAF?'

The corners of her mouth turned down. 'When the editor gave the job I wanted to someone else who was far less suited to the role, I knew it was time to leave.'

'Let me guess. The person who got the job was a man?'

She raised her eyebrows. 'That's right. How did you know?'

'My mother's a vet, and she's always having her judgement questioned or having her services refused because people want to see the "real vet".'

'A vet? That's amazing. She must be a remarkable woman.'

'She certainly is. But we were talking about you and your total drongo of an editor.'

She snorted. 'Drongo. I'll have to remember that one. Well, he told me the man who got the job instead of me had a family to support. It was nothing to do with who was the best writer. He even had the cheek to tell me I would only get married and leave.'

'Why – are you engaged?' Greg couldn't deny the lurch of disappointment. While other men might not object to dating women who were already in a relationship, especially when the war had turned so many lives upside-down, it wasn't something he would contemplate.

'No.' The relief was short-lived; she continued, 'To be honest, I'm fed up with men. I can't see myself ever wanting to tie myself down to one.'

Greg had heard other women say something similar but, whereas they were speaking out of frustration after disappointments in love, he sensed Pearl had a different reason. 'Why? Just because one man treated you like that, it's no reason to tar us all with the same brush.'

'I know that. There was a lovely man in my office who was ever so supportive. But most men seem to think women should stick to domestic work.'

'Well, women like you must be changing their minds. Look at you all – R/T operators, mechanics, parachute packers and even pilots.'

'Oh yes, you want us now there's a shortage of men to do those tasks. The same thing happened in the Great War but as soon as it was over all the women were expected to give up their jobs to the men again. The same thing will happen when this is all over.'

Greg couldn't argue with that, having grown up witnessing the struggles of his mother to be taken seriously. 'Are you going to try and get a job as a reporter after the war?'

Pearl looked pensive. 'I want to. It's the only thing I've ever wanted to do. But who knows how long the war is going to last? There's no sign of it ending, is there?'

Greg shook his head. There was no need to answer. The situation looked so desperate; it almost seemed to be tempting fate to think about what they might do after the war when there was no guarantee they would survive or even if the Allies would be victorious.

'And look at me,' Pearl went on. 'I'm twenty-nine now. Who knows how old I'll be after the war? And we'll all be fighting for the same jobs.' Then her mouth set in determined lines. 'Doesn't mean I won't try, though.'

'That's the spirit. If it's that important to you, you should hold on to your dreams. If we don't have hope, what is there to fight for?' This earned him a smile that made his insides perform a loop-the-loop. It was a long time since he had enjoyed a simple conversation so much, and he didn't want it to end. Propping his elbows on the table, he asked, 'Why is journalism so important to you?'

'It's something I've wanted to do ever since I learned to read. My father was in the army in the last war, and I remember scouring the newspapers with my mother for any reports concerning his regiment. I was only about five or six, but it made me want to be a journalist so I could tell people about the important things happening in the world.'

'And to think I was still reading picture books at the same age.'

She grinned. 'It helped to have an incentive.' Then her smile faded. 'Even after my father was killed, right at the end of the war, it didn't stop me dreaming. I wanted my writing to change the world.'

A faint blush tinged her cheeks. 'And yet I couldn't even get a job reporting local news, and you can hardly call writing about church fetes world-changing.'

'I bet it was important to the people organising them, though. And they raised money for good causes. Don't knock it just because it wasn't writing about earth-shattering events. Anyway, it would have been a start.'

'That's what I thought.' And now Pearl's eyes were shining again. 'I know I couldn't have started writing for a national paper, not without a degree, but this would have been a step in the right direction.'

Her enthusiasm was infectious, and Greg found himself hoping with all of his heart that Pearl would get her dream one day. He had thought her pretty when he had first seen her but now, with her eyes outshining the sparks of fire upon the hearth, he thought she looked beautiful. What a pity she had vowed not to become involved with any men.

Funny. He had invited her to the pub partly as a thank-you but also because he found the prospect of an evening with a pretty WAAF appealing. He had taken other WAAFs out, although never more than once, not wanting to become too attached to anyone when he knew every evening could be his last. Yet here he was, wishing he could spend more time with the one woman who he already knew wouldn't want to go out with him.

At least, not as a boyfriend. But maybe as a friend? And then an idea occurred to him. 'Have you ever thought of starting up a newspaper for RAF Fenthorpe? I'm sure plenty of people would be interested in it.'

Pearl's eyes widened. 'Start one of my own? I wouldn't know how.'

'I bet you would. What do you think it would involve?'

'Well, it would need volunteers to write for it to start. I couldn't write everything myself. And then there would have to be someone to lay it out and edit the articles. And of course it would need to be printed. Goodness knows where we would find the money for that.'

'But apart from the finance and organising a printer, you could do it?'

'Well, yes, if I had enough volunteers.' Pearl leaned across the table. 'It would be rather fun. Let's see, we could have news about what was going on at the base of course, and maybe even news from other RAF stations nearby. A crossword and puzzles page might be fun. Oh, and what if we could find an artist who could draw a cartoon?' Her ideas were coming thick and fast and as she spoke her hands weaved pictures in the air. She wasn't looking at Greg and he knew she was seeing herself as a journalist, writing about life at Fenthorpe.

Then her face fell. 'I don't suppose we could ever make it happen though.'

'I don't see why not. I'd pay good money for news relevant to me instead of all the farming news we get in the local newspaper here, and I'm sure most people at Fenthorpe feel the same way. I'll help.'

'You will?' The blazing smile was all the reward Greg needed.

Chapter Eight

Once Greg had said goodbye to Pearl at the entrance to the Waafery, he wandered to his own hut, unable to keep himself from whistling a merry tune. His head was full of Pearl, of her smile, the way her eyes shone with enthusiasm. He wouldn't begrudge evenings spent working on the paper instead of being out on the town. Not if it meant spending more time with Pearl.

The whistling died on his lips when he pushed open the door to his hut. Knowing the crew of *F-Freddie* were not coming back until tomorrow, he'd expected to see their empty beds. What he hadn't expected was the empty beds on the other side of the hut. The ones occupied by *Q-Queenie*'s crew. The only person there was Flight Sergeant James Fitzgerald, who was *Q-Queenie*'s bomb aimer. He hadn't flown with the rest of his crew the night before, having sustained an injury to his shoulder from flak a week earlier, and still hadn't been cleared to fly. He was sitting on his bed, his writing case open on his knees and his pen in his hand. But from where Greg was standing, it looked like there was nothing on the notepaper but several ink blots.

'Evening, Fitz,' Greg said, 'where is everyone?'

But he knew the answer even before Fitz looked up at him with empty eyes. The room wasn't merely lacking the rest of *Q-Queenie*'s crew but had been stripped of their belongings.

'Someone from the Committee of Adjustment came in not long after you left this evening. *Q-Queenie* didn't return last night.' Fitz indicated the blotted sheet of paper. 'I'm trying to write a letter to David's parents but I've no idea what to say.'

David was *Q-Queenie*'s pilot, and Greg knew they had been close friends.

Greg slumped onto his bed. 'I'm so sorry, mate. Did anyone see what happened?'

Fitz shook his head. 'I'd hoped you might have more news.'

'Afraid not. The flak was a nightmare. It was all I could do to hold it together long enough to get us to the target and safely away.' Greg shuddered, remembering the strain of keeping *F-Freddie* on course while being buffeted by the violent firestorm all around. 'Then we developed engine trouble on the way back and dropped a long way behind the main stream.'

Fitz gave him a weak smile. 'I heard you had a narrow squeak. How's your arm?'

Greg flexed it experimentally, wincing at the painful tug of blistered flesh. 'Not too bad. Nothing to stop me flying. Not that I've got anything to fly now *F-Freddie* is nothing but a charred skeleton.'

'What do you think will happen to us?'

'No idea. I suppose my crew will be split up to fill gaps in other crews. Pity. We were just starting to work well together. Saying that, most of them were near the end of their tour, so I'd have been looking for a new crew soon, anyway.' Instead of forming a crew with other newly qualified men, Greg had been drafted into an existing crew when their pilot had been killed. 'I'd always assumed I'd carry on in *F-Freddie,* though.'

'Do you reckon you'll get another Manchester?'

Greg snorted. 'I hope not. Bloody things are underpowered and a bugger to get off the ground. I'm holding out for a Lancaster.' The new Avro Lancasters had started to be distributed to squadrons in Bomber Command, and Greg had heard that the huge four-engined machines were a joy to fly.

'Who knows? Maybe you'll get lucky. And let me know if you need a bomb aimer.'

'I do. I heard mine has broken his ankle. I'll make a request for you if that's what you want.'

'It is.' Fitz sighed, glancing down at his writing case. 'I wish writing this letter was as easy as getting a new crew.' He grimaced. 'I can't bear to think what David's family will have to endure.'

'Yeah. The not knowing must be awful.' Greg knew the procedure. The crew of Q-Queenie would be posted as missing, and enquiries would be made through the International Red Cross to find out if they had been captured or if their remains had been found. It could be months before there was any news. All too often there was no news, and the endless waiting must be pure agony for families. Greg could only pray that when his time came, there would be witnesses who could confirm his end so his parents wouldn't be forced to endure the anguish of never knowing what had happened to their only son.

He unlaced his boots and placed them under his bed, painfully aware of the emptiness under most of the other beds. There were no operations on that night, so there was little noise outside, apart from the muffled sound of talking coming from the other huts, and from one of them came the tinny sound of 'Over the Rainbow' being played on an ancient gramophone. Inside the hut all was quiet aside from the scratch of Fitz's pen and the creak of bedsprings when one of them shifted. Greg swung his feet up onto his bed and leaned back, shifting to find a comfortable position against the metal headrest.

He gave his head a little shake, trying to shake off his sombre mood. 'What we need,' he announced to Fitz, 'is a night out. Tomorrow night we're going to go to the Piebald Pony and raise a glass to the crew of Q-Queenie.'

'Sounds like a good plan.'

They would drink to the memory of their lost room-mates, then they would do their best to forget them. It might sound cold, but Greg knew it was the only way they could continue to function.

He couldn't shake off thoughts of his own parents, though, and how worried they must be for him. Knowing he wouldn't be able to relax for some time, he took out his own writing case from his locker and dashed out a letter to them. He didn't mention anything about his near miss or the loss of *Q-Queenie*, instead writing a cheery letter full of the gossip from Fenthorpe and recent trips to Lincoln. He even mentioned Pearl, saying she was thinking of starting up a newspaper, and he would post one to them if it ever got off the ground.

He had thought writing home would ease his restlessness but, when he had finished it and addressed the envelope, he still couldn't settle. He couldn't get Pearl or, oddly, the newspaper out of his mind. Maybe Pearl's enthusiasm for journalism was infectious, for he felt the need to write down his thoughts and feelings even though he barely knew what they were. The feeling was compelling, and, knowing he wouldn't get any rest until he had at least tried, he smoothed out a fresh piece of notepaper and took up a pencil to save ink. He hadn't written any compositions since school, so he was rusty. Without any conscious attempt to order his words, he simply wrote down each thought as it occurred. For the first time in his life, he wished he could write poetry, because the plain sentences he wrote down failed to convey what it was like to lose six friends in a single day. Nevertheless, he couldn't deny his sudden need to write *something*; and, if this was all he could manage, it would have to do.

The Empty Beds

Six beds in my hut are empty tonight. The bedding has been stripped, the shelves and drawers emptied. Even the pinned photographs and the names above each bedstead are gone, leaving bare walls and a few pinholes.

Three nights ago the hut was full. We played cards, wrote letters, polished buttons, darned socks, just as we had every night since we arrived. We teased a lad who had just got engaged. Now those pinholes on the wall are the only things that show they were ever here. Tomorrow

*– if I have a tomorrow – I will raise a glass in their
honour. Then, gradually, they will fade from memory.
Other men will take their beds, put up their own photographs, and the hut will once again be full of conversation,
card games, mending and polishing. For a while.*

The words dried up, and Greg read what he had written. It was
clumsy and unpolished but he felt that even if he tried to edit
it he would never find the perfect words. He tucked the piece
away in his writing case, suddenly too tired to decide what to
do with it. Maybe he would give it to Pearl to see if she thought
it good enough to include in her paper. If he did, he wouldn't
reveal he had written it. That would be far too embarrassing.

Odd that he was thinking about seeing Pearl again as though
he could be certain it would happen. Until today, he had deliberately not allowed himself to plan ahead. He had simply done
all he could each day to ensure he and his crew were alive at
the end of it.

Meeting Pearl seemed to have changed that. Now he was
looking further ahead, hoping he would live long enough to see
her again. He had even offered to help her with the newspaper,
as though he expected to be alive long enough to see the first
edition. For the first time in ages, despite the fate of *Q-Queenie's*
crew, he had hope, and he didn't know if that was a good or a
bad thing.

–

Early the next afternoon, Pearl hurried to the cookhouse,
desperate to talk to Jenny. She had been bursting to tell her
about the newspaper idea when she got back to Hut Three
but Jenny had already been asleep. Mornings were always too
busy for much chatter, what with getting washed and dressed,
stacking their biscuits and bedding and tidying the area around
their beds, and Jenny had had to rush off to start duty before
they had time to go for breakfast.

Pearl had gone on to pass a dull morning in Flying Control. There hadn't been much to do, besides keep an eye on a couple of training flights, but at least Snaith had allowed her to do more than observe. 'I suppose you can be trusted,' he had told her when he had directed her to sit in the chair at the desk rather than stand behind his. Coming from him, this was high praise. She knew she wouldn't have any more trouble with him.

She had just collected a dollop of potatoes and some vegetable pie when she saw Jenny sitting alone at one of the smaller tables to one side of the hut. She was holding a book in one hand and her fork in the other.

Pearl set her tray down opposite her friend with a crash and dropped onto the bench. 'Put that book down,' she said. 'I've got something to tell you.'

Jenny placed a bookmark between the pages and set the book down on the table with a reverence that made Pearl think of someone closing the Bible in church after reading the lesson. Despite her impatience to share her news, she couldn't resist glancing at the title to see what had Jenny so enthralled. '*The Geology of Arran*,' she read aloud. 'Seriously?' Then, seeing the look of hurt on Jenny's face, she modulated her tone. 'Is it interesting?'

'Oh yes. Did you know the Highland Boundary Fault runs through the island, so it's the best place to study Lowland and Highland geology? I'd love to go there.'

Despite her excitement about the paper, Pearl was intrigued by Jenny's choice of reading, even if she wasn't particularly interested in the subject. 'I didn't know you were interested in rocks. Are all your books about geology, then? I assumed they were novels.' Until now she had never thought to ask about the books that Jenny kept with such great care.

'I would love more novels. I don't get much choice about what books I have, you see.'

'Why?'

A faint blush coloured Jenny's cheeks. 'My family never had enough money to spend on books. Or *waste* on books, as my grandmother would say. Nearly every penny I earned had to go towards the household costs.'

'That's a shame.' While Deedee wasn't rich, she had never struggled to provide for her granddaughters, and she had always regarded books as essentials, never luxuries. 'Where did you work?'

'At the local mine. I was an office junior.'

'Is that where you picked up your interest in geology?'

'No, my books are on all sorts of subjects. I wanted to keep on learning after I left school, but I lived a long way from the nearest library, so I could never get there. I got all my books from jumble sales, and you'd never believe the odd assortment of titles you can find there.'

'I think I've got an idea.' Pearl glanced at *The Geology of Arran* with a grin. 'Well, if you want more novels, you're welcome to borrow any of mine. I brought a couple with me, and I'm sure Deedee – that's my grandmother – will be happy to post more.'

'Do you really mean that? It would be wonderful.'

'Of course.' Pearl swallowed. As Jenny had also been brought up by her grandmother, Pearl had pictured them having very similar home lives. More and more, Pearl was realising that her upbringing had been far more privileged than Jenny's. Deedee had enough money to get by, having apparently been left a small inheritance from her late husband's family, although Pearl had never met any of them. In fact, she had never even known her grandfather. All she knew was what Deedee had told her: that she had lost him when she had still been very young.

Jenny's face fell. 'I wish there was something I could do in return.'

'Funny you should say that. How do you fancy helping produce a newspaper?'

'What? I wouldn't know how!'

'I'm not asking you to run it, but I need volunteers willing to contribute items.' Pearl outlined the ideas she had discussed with Greg. 'What do you think?' she asked in conclusion. 'Do you think we could produce something of interest to people on the base? I think it would be fun.'

'It's a wonderful idea. You've been wanting to be a journalist all your life, so it would be a terrible shame if being in the WAAF meant saying goodbye to all your dreams. And I know people on the base would like to read news relevant to them. Do you really think I can help?'

'I wouldn't have asked if I didn't. You obviously read widely, and that's a great start for any writer.'

Jenny looked pleased. 'No one's ever praised me for reading a lot before. My gran was always telling me to get my nose out of my book and help out.'

'That's settled, then. We can think more about the sort of things you want to contribute later. So that's you, me and Greg we've got lined up so far. I wonder who else we can ask? I suppose some of the other girls in our hut might want to help.'

'Help with what? Why don't you ask me?' A tray slammed down next to Pearl's; she glanced up, startled, to see her sister taking a seat beside her.

'Thea, I didn't think you'd be joining us.'

'Evidently not.' Thea's hurt expression took Pearl by surprise. After all, the last time they'd met she'd said they should each do their own thing.

'It's lovely to see you, though.' Pearl turned to Jenny. 'This is my sister, Thea. She's just been posted here.' Then to Thea, 'This is my friend Jenny Hazleton. She's in the same hut as me and we arrived the same day. What hut are you in, by the way?'

'Four.'

Jenny brightened. 'That's right next to ours. How long have you been here? Pearl never mentioned you'd arrived.'

Thea turned a significant gaze on Pearl but said nothing. Pearl answered for her. 'She only arrived yesterday. I was going to tell you but I hadn't had a chance.'

'I think it's wonderful you're here,' Jenny said to Thea, seemingly oblivious to the atmosphere between the two sisters. 'And you can help with the newspaper too.'

'What newspaper?'

'Pearl's thinking of starting a paper for RAF Fenthorpe.'

'That's not a bad idea. There are enough people on the base to populate a small town, so why not create a paper especially for them?'

'That's what we thought.'

And Pearl found herself watching Jenny and Thea talking together far more naturally than she and her sister had done for years. Thea looked positively animated, a far cry from the young woman who always seemed to go out of her way to challenge anything Pearl might say. It was odd to see her look so friendly.

After a while the conversation dried up, and Jenny smiled at Pearl. 'That's wonderful. Now we've got Thea too.'

Pearl forced a smile. 'Welcome on board, Thea. That is, if you're sure you want to join in?'

The eager expression faded from Thea's face. 'Why wouldn't I? It sounds fun.'

'It won't be just fun. It will be hard work, fitting it in around our duties.'

Thea rolled her eyes, looking far more like the sister Pearl knew. 'I do realise that. I can be responsible sometimes.'

Pearl, on the verge of retorting that she found that hard to believe, considering she had been punished for leaving Waddington without permission, noticed Jenny casting worried looks between the two sisters. She bit back her acid retort and made an effort to be conciliatory. 'Of course, I'm sorry. I'd love to have you on the team.'

Thea nodded, then arched her brow. 'Now, what I really want to know is – who is this mysterious Greg?'

'Oh, he's one of the bomber pilots.' Pearl did her best to sound offhand.

'Haven't you heard?' Jenny asked. 'Pearl was on duty when he had to make an emergency landing. He took her out for a drink last night to thank her.'

'Well done, big sis. Maybe you do know how to live after all. I can't wait to meet him.' Before Pearl could correct her, Thea

89

glanced at her watch and gave a theatrical sigh. 'Sorry but I have to go. I'm supposed to report to Hangar Three to meet my new sergeant. I can't wait to actually start work. Getting my arrival chitty signed has been a bore.' She picked up her tray and rose. 'We should meet later to discuss your newspaper idea though, Pearl. Why don't we go to the pub this evening? I'll drop by your hut at 1800 to collect you.' Then she sailed out, leaving Pearl to reflect that it was a good thing neither she nor Jenny were on duty that evening.

Chapter Nine

'So,' Thea began once the three girls were sat round a table in the snug of the Piebald Pony, drinks at their elbows. 'You're the boss, Pearl, where should we start?'

Pearl pulled an exercise book from her pocket. She opened it at the back page and took out a pencil. She felt a little guilty for not including Greg in the discussion, considering it had been his idea in the first place, but she didn't know how to get hold of him. 'I've made a list of things we need to think about,' she said. She read it out, counting each item off on her fingers. 'In no particular order, we need to think of a name for the paper, decide how often we'll produce an edition, how much we'll charge, how to find the money to produce it in the first place. Later, when we know how many volunteers we've got, we can decide how to distribute the tasks.' She sipped her ginger beer, then carried on. 'Where was I? Oh yes. What items to include, finding a printer, how many copies to produce, how many pages and who we approach to get permission for the paper in the first place.' She glanced sideways at Thea, deciding this was the perfect opportunity to start healing the rift between them. 'You've been in the WAAF longer than either of us. Do you know who we need to get permission from?'

Thea's brow wrinkled. 'I've never been involved in starting up a club, if that's what this is. I sang in the choir for a while but I don't know who gave permission to start it up.'

'I never knew you were in the choir.' Pearl refrained from asking why she had stopped. Probably because she'd been unreliable. One of Pearl's fears about involving Thea in the paper was that she would fail to deliver promised articles and leave Pearl to sort it all out.

Thea just grinned. 'My life at Waddington wasn't all hard work, you know.'

No. That's what Pearl had been afraid of. With a heroic effort, she didn't rise to the bait. 'I wondered about approaching Section Officer Blatchford.' This was the WAAF officer in charge of the Waafery who was therefore responsible for the WAAFs' welfare.

Thea's brow cleared. 'Yes, she should be able to point you in the right direction.'

'Fine.' Pearl made a note next to that item. 'I'll speak to her tomorrow.'

Jenny craned her neck to read Pearl's list. 'That's a lot to cover.'

'I know. I'm not suggesting we solve everything this evening. I just wrote things down as I thought of them. We won't be able to sort out a printer yet, so we can ignore that for now.' Pearl studied her list again. 'I think the name is important. It needs to say who it's for and let everyone know what to expect. How about the *Fenthorpe Mirror*?'

Thea pulled a face. 'That sounds dull.'

'No, go on. Say what you think, don't try and break it to me gently.' But Pearl was laughing. 'Sorry, I know that was a feeble idea. What do you two think?'

'The *Fenthorpe Grapevine*?' Thea suggested, although she didn't sound convinced.

'If we have Fenthorpe in the title, it sounds like it's for the village,' Jenny said. 'But Pearl, you said the title should tell everyone who it's for.'

'That's true,' Pearl said. 'Fenthorpe is out, then. How about simply calling it the *Grapevine*? I quite like that.'

'But that sounds like a paper for wine makers,' Thea said.

They tried out some other names but nothing seemed quite right. 'Right. We'll leave it there,' Pearl said in the end. 'We could carry on with this all night and get nowhere. Let's all think about it and come up with suggestions to discuss at our next meeting. We don't need a name yet, anyway.' She consulted her list. 'There's some basic stuff we ought to decide upon before I take the idea to Section Officer Blatchford. Like what kind of subjects we're going to cover, how many pages to print, how many copies to print and how much to charge.'

'Let's start with what the paper's going to contain,' Jenny said. 'That's what Blatchford's going to want to know when we ask permission.'

'All right.' Pearl turned to a new page, her pencil poised. 'Obviously we want to write about what's happening on the base – news, social events and so on. What else?' Secretly, she wished there was a real news story to investigate, but she knew that would be too much to hope for. She should just be happy that she was going to keep her journalism skills honed so that if this war ever did end, her experience might make her stand out among all the other hopefuls applying for jobs.

'How about a focus on a different trade in each issue?' Jenny suggested. 'I mean, I know we've got parachute packers, fitters, drivers and so forth, but I don't really know what a lot of them do or what their day is like.'

'That's a great idea. We could do a regular "Day in the Life" feature.' Pearl scribbled it down. 'What else?'

'We need something that's a bit of fun, too,' Thea said. 'I was chatting to one of the ground crew in the NAAFI last night, and it turns out he worked as an illustrator in an advertising company before the war. How about I approach him to do a cartoon strip?'

Pearl stared at Thea. 'You've hardly been here a day and you already know more people than me.'

'Oh, I don't know. You're the one who's been out with a pilot. When are we going to meet him?'

'Soon, I hope. He is supposed to be helping us with the paper, after all. But I wasn't *going out* with him. He was just being nice.' Pearl was already wondering if he had really meant it when he had offered his help with the newspaper.

'I wouldn't mind if a few good-looking pilots wanted to be nice to me.' Thea waggled her eyebrows.

'Thea, honestly! It wasn't like that. Anyway, let's get on with what we're supposed to be doing. I like your idea about the cartoon, by the way, so do ask your friend if he'd like to do it.' Pearl gave Thea an anxious glance, wondering just how friendly she had got with this man she hardly knew.

Thea gave a wicked grin. 'I can't wait.' Then she shook her head. 'I can read your face like a book, Pearl. Would you feel any better if I told you that Corporal Yates is happily married with a young family?' Then, in an aside to Jenny, 'She's so easy to tease, you know. I can't resist. It was so obvious she thought I'd spent the evening in a passionate clinch with an oily Lothario.'

'I was thinking nothing of the sort.' Pearl could only hope her relief didn't show in her face.

'Glad to hear it. Although in the interests of complete honesty, I should say that Corporal Yates *was* oily, although that's only because he works on engines all day.'

'Can we get on?' Pearl could feel her control over this meeting slipping. Something she should have expected with Thea being there. She dreaded to think what editorial meetings would be like when they had more volunteers, if she couldn't even keep the three of them on task.

'I always enjoy crosswords,' Jenny said.

Pearl gave her a grateful smile. 'Me too. And maybe we could ask people to contribute poems or short stories once we get going.'

She added the suggestions to her list. 'That's probably enough for a start, unless either of you can think of anything important we've missed.'

'There is something,' Thea said, and Pearl was surprised to see the laughter had faded from her expression. 'You haven't been here long, so you won't know the worst thing about working on a bomber station.' She waved a hand at Pearl's list. 'Correct me if I'm wrong, but your idea is to cover the latest news while keeping the tone fairly light-hearted.'

'I think so, don't you?' Pearl looked at Thea and Jenny in turn.

They both nodded, and Thea went on, 'The thing is, the biggest news on the station is something we try not to talk about. At least, it is if Fenthorpe is anything like Waddington.'

With a sinking sensation in the pit of her stomach, Pearl realised what Thea meant. Glancing at Jenny, she saw dawning realisation in her face. 'You're talking about the bomber crews that don't come back.'

'That's a really good point, Thea.' Jenny's face was grave. 'We need to think carefully about how we report it.'

'If we do at all,' Thea finished. 'What do you think?'

Pearl was silent for a moment. She watched the bubbles rising in her glass, knowing that the wrong decision could make or break the unnamed newspaper. Furthermore, a small portion of her thoughts was occupied with surprise that it was Thea of all people who had introduced such a serious subject. 'We can't ignore it,' she said finally. 'If we're reporting news we have to report all of it, good and bad.'

'But no one's going to want to shell out for a paper that's full of reports of aircraft shot down or gone missing,' Thea pointed out. 'Because some editions, that's all it will be. Don't look at me like that,' she added, with a scowl at Pearl, who had, admittedly, been about to scold her for being callous. 'You wait until four, five or even more of our planes don't come back. You wait till you feel like you're walking through a ghost town the day after a large op. You wait till you can't sleep because your hut is full of girls crying themselves to sleep after their young men failed to return. You wait till you meet a fresh-faced new gunner in the NAAFI, and your only reaction is to wonder whether he'll still be around this time next week.'

Pearl couldn't answer. She had no words. All she could do was stare at Thea, wondering in horror what else her sister had experienced since she had joined the WAAF. Whatever it was, maybe it explained why she never said much in her letters.

It was Jenny who broke the heavy silence. 'You're both right. We can't ignore our losses. It would be like lying or pretending the lost crews didn't exist. But we can't let it dominate the newspaper either. We haven't really discussed what the whole point of the paper is, but I think it's something to bring us all together. Give everyone something to talk about, something to smile about but without forgetting those we've lost. We can acknowledge the crews we've lost in a quiet way. We could have a column that simply names those lost since the last edition, with maybe a short Bible verse or a suitable quote.'

Pearl found her voice at last. 'Well said. Both of you.' She couldn't bring herself to look Thea in the eye, though, still wondering what other changes her time in the WAAF had wrought. 'I like your suggestion, Jenny. We could have an In Memoriam column and outline it in black. If we put it on the back page, that gives it a prominent position without dominating the news. What do you think, Thea?' She finally managed to look at her sister.

But Thea's expression revealed no trace of the impassioned speech she had just delivered. 'I think it's the best solution. There's someone else you should run it by, though.'

'Who?'

'Your pilot friend. Greg.'

And yet again, Pearl knew Thea was right, notwithstanding the distinct glint of mischief in her eyes that told Pearl the sister she knew hadn't changed *that* much. The bomber crews would surely be those most closely affected by an In Memoriam column. 'I'll be sure to ask him when I see him.'

'And when will that be?' There was no mistaking the teasing tone.

'I don't know. I've only met him the once, and I don't know how to contact him.'

'You could always leave him a message at the sergeants' mess.'

The answer was so obvious that Pearl was cross with herself for not thinking of it. More proof that, while she was the elder by some years, Thea had far more experience of life in the WAAF. 'Yes of course.' She hid her irritation by making a note. 'I'll do that tomorrow, along with going to see Blatchford.'

'We're getting along nicely,' Jenny observed. 'What else do we need to decide tonight?'

'Not much,' Pearl replied. 'I suppose we ought to decide how big the paper is going to be, because that will affect how many items we need to write for each edition. Also how often we're going to produce an edition.'

'You're the one who's worked on a paper,' Thea said. 'That makes you the expert. What do you think?'

Pearl couldn't deny the warm glow she felt at Thea's acknowledgement of her expertise. It was good to know her sister still thought she was better than her at some things. 'I think we should keep it fairly small, at least at first while we're learning the ropes. The smallest paper would be two pages – in other words, printing on two sides of one sheet of paper.'

'Oh, but that wouldn't look like a proper newspaper.' Jenny looked disappointed.

'It's all right – I wasn't suggesting we only do two pages. I was just explaining how it works. The next size up would be four pages. That's still a single sheet of paper, although using bigger paper than for the two-page edition, but it's folded in half to make the four pages. The next size up would be eight pages – two sheets folded into four pages each. I suggest we opt for a four-page layout. With the paper shortage I don't think we can justify more.'

'Sounds good,' Thea said. 'Two pages looks a bit feeble and I'm sure we can easily write enough to fill four. How often are we going to produce it?'

'Considering we all have jobs to do and exams to study for, I'd say it should be monthly. We can always change it if we get enough volunteers.'

Thea nodded, and Jenny said, 'That sounds fine to me.' Then after a pause she said, 'We're really going to do this!'

Thea rose. 'This calls for a celebration. I'll get us some more drinks. Same again?' When she returned with the drinks, she raised her port and lemon. 'Here's to the birth of our newspaper, whatever it's called!'

Pearl and Jenny raised their glasses and they all clinked glasses.

Then Thea added, 'And here's to the mysterious Greg, wherever he's got to!'

Pearl laughed despite herself, and drank.

—

Another half an hour passed with the girls talking through ideas for the first few news items to include. Although Pearl joined in, she found she was distracted by thoughts of Greg. Had he been waiting for a message? Would he be disappointed when he discovered that they'd had the first meeting without him? It was odd that he should occupy so much of her thoughts when they hardly knew one another.

At half past nine Thea reminded them they needed to start back if they were to sign in at the guardroom on time. Seeing Pearl's startled look, she gave a wry smile. 'I don't want to end up on jankers on my first week here. Give me another fortnight and I'll have discovered all the sneaky ways in and out of the base.'

Pearl refused to rise to the bait.

She opened the door of the snug, pulling on her coat, and was hit by a wall of noise from the public bar. It was even louder than it had been the last time she had visited the pub. Everyone was chanting, pointing at something or someone out of Pearl's line of sight. It took her a moment to realise they were chanting a name: 'Tallis! Tallis!'

Wasn't that Greg's surname? Overcome with curiosity, she edged inside so she could see round the corner. Her eyes smarting as she gazed through the fog of cigarette smoke, she saw a crowd gathered around three men. Two of them stood side by side while the third was precariously balanced with a foot on one of each of the lower men's shoulders. The top of his head skimmed the high ceiling.

'Tallis! Tallis!' the crowd chanted. And now her eyes had become accustomed to the haze, Pearl could see the balancing man was indeed Greg. He wobbled, one hand flailing. Pearl caught her breath. What on earth was he playing at? An instant later, he regained his balance. Now she could see that in the hand he hadn't been using to balance he held a brimming beer mug. As she watched, he brought it to his mouth and drained it without pausing for breath. When it was empty, he flourished it at the cheering men gathered around and tossed it down into their waiting hands. Surely now he would jump down safely? But instead he groped behind his ear and produced a pencil. Reaching above his head, twisting into an impossible position, he wrote something on the white plaster. His legs were trembling from the effort to balance, and Pearl couldn't tear away her gaze, terrified he would crash to the floor and break his neck.

A hand fell on her shoulder, making her jump. She glanced round to see Thea.

'What's going on?' her sister asked, shouting to make her voice heard. Then her gaze slid past Pearl to the scene beyond, and she grinned. 'They must be aircrew. They're always pulling some stunt or other.'

Pearl looked back at Greg in time to see him stick the pencil back behind his ear and salute the crowd. His moment of triumph was short-lived, however, for he suddenly wobbled, his expression changing from glee to alarm. Then the pyramid collapsed, and all three men crashed to the floor. Pearl cried out and took a step towards them, but stopped when they scrambled to their feet, presumably unhurt – although surely they would have bruises.

There was a tug on her arm and Jenny was shouting in her ear. 'Come on, or we'll be late.'

Pearl turned away and followed Jenny and Thea outside. Once the heavy blackout curtain and the door were closed behind them, they shut out most of the noise from the bar.

'Golly, it was total chows in there.' Jenny was shaking her head as though trying to rid her ears of the ringing. Pearl blinked at her, trying to work out what she had just said.

'I'm sorry – what?' Thea asked.

But Pearl had already worked it out. 'I think you mean *chaos*, Jenny.'

'Do I? I've never actually heard it said before. Chaos. I'll have to remember that.'

'Oh, I don't know,' Thea remarked. 'I think chows sounds much better. That's how I'm going to pronounce it from now on.'

They all laughed and set off for the station at a brisk walk. Pearl listened to the others' chatter in silence. What had possessed Greg to do something so reckless? She had thought that with him being a few years older than average for a bomber pilot he would be more sensible, but obviously she had got it wrong.

It was a good thing that thanks to British Double Summer Time there was still lingering light in the sky, because her head was too full of Greg's dangerous antics to concentrate too hard on where she was going.

Thea hadn't been surprised. Had she meant that all airmen behaved like that? What would it be like, being friends with a man who acted without a thought of the consequences to himself or others? She already had enough on her plate making sure Thea didn't get herself into any more trouble. She didn't think she wanted another reckless person on her hands.

Chapter Ten

Greg stumbled into the operations block, wishing he hadn't stayed up so late the night before. A hand slapped him on the back and he turned to see Fitz, puffy-eyed but grinning. 'Great send-off last night. We did the crew proud.'

'Yeah. Probably a good thing I haven't got a kite to fly today, because I'm still feeling the bruises.' Even so, Greg went to join the huddle of crewmen by the noticeboard, knowing there was a chance he would be required to fill in for a sick or injured pilot. His own burnt arm hadn't been serious enough to get him passed unfit, and a late night wasn't a good enough excuse. Mindful of that, he had limited his drinking, as he always did on a night out. He could never forget that his crew relied on him being fully alert.

Word had gone round after breakfast that ops were on, so now all members of the bomber crews needed to check the noticeboard to see if they were slated to fly. From the attitudes of the men already running their fingers down the lists, Greg gathered that wherever they were going – and that wouldn't be revealed until the briefing that afternoon – the operation required the squadron's full strength. He strolled up to the board, waiting for the men in front to move out of the way so he could see who was flying. Finally he prodded a man between the shoulder blades. 'Come on, mate. It's hardly *War and Peace*. Move aside.'

The man turned and Greg saw it was his wireless operator, Max Turner. The crew of *F-Freddie* had arrived back in Fenthorpe yesterday evening, in time to join in the revelries at the Piebald Pony. Max gave him a smile that looked strained. 'Morning, Skip. We're both flying today.'

'What? You're having me on. I didn't think there were any spare kites.'

'There aren't. We're in *T-Tommy*. Their pilot and wireless operator were injured the other day and haven't been passed fit.'

Greg groaned, waving a mental goodbye to his plan of riding his motorcycle up to Lincoln. He had even hoped to find Pearl and persuade her to join him if she was free. He wasn't happy about flying with a different crew, either. After five missions, the crew of *F-Freddie* had started to gel and had developed a routine together that Greg knew he could depend upon. He didn't know any of *T-Tommy*'s crew, and they didn't know him. For the sake of everyone concerned, he hoped that night's mission would be an easy one.

'Let's go,' he said to Max. 'Time to round up the crew and get our test flight over with.'

'So much for a quiet day,' Max remarked. 'I was hoping to see Thea. Did you know she's been transferred here?'

'No. That's good news. Maybe she'll succumb to your charms now you'll see more of each other.' Thea was a WAAF from another RAF base who Max had met in Lincoln and rapidly become smitten with. Although she hadn't returned his feelings, she had been kind to Max and had gone out with him a few times, even accompanying him to a dance when the rest of their crew had teased him about not having a date.

'I can hope,' Max replied, looking more cheerful.

Greg slapped his shoulder. 'Come on, then. Let's see if *T-Tommy*'s crew are up to scratch.'

Pushing through the crowd, Max had the misfortune to bump into Flying Officer Sheldrick, the station adjutant. 'Sorry, sir.' He sidestepped to move past, but Sheldrick stopped him, forcing Greg to wait as well.

'You might think being a member of a bomber crew excuses you from showing respect to an officer but you'd be wrong.' Sheldrick glared at Max. 'Have you forgotten how to salute?'

Max, his face beetroot red, saluted. 'Sorry, sir,' he said again. The poor lad looked mortified.

As soon as they were out of earshot, Greg tried to comfort him. 'Don't mind Sheldrick. Rumour has it he washed out of pilot training and resents the bomber crews.'

Max nodded, although he remained subdued as they went to prepare for their test flight. The only positive thing about the encounter was that Greg's anger acted on him like strong coffee and gave him the jolt he needed to fully wake up. Sheldrick could have reminded Max to salute without humiliating him. While any other crew member would have shaken off the reprimand with a laugh, Max took things to heart. If he ever got the chance to teach Sheldrick a lesson, Greg would take it.

By the time he was taking *T-Tommy* out on its test flight, he had brushed off his anger and was able to pay his full attention to the task at hand. In addition to the usual tests of guns, oxygen, instruments and the aircraft's systems, the flight also gave Greg the opportunity to assess his temporary crew, and he knew they would be doing the same with him and Max. The crew of *T-Tommy* had already successfully completed eleven operations, and worked well together. No one grumbled about having a different pilot or wireless operator for this mission and, by the time he headed on a bearing that would return them to Fenthorpe, he had no worries about working with this new crew. When the airfield appeared ahead, it was Pearl's voice that gave him permission to land, and he took that as a good omen.

His thoughts remained with Pearl for the rest of the day, remembering how much he had enjoyed their evening together. It was only when it was time for the briefing that he made an effort to clear his mind of anything that didn't involve the mission. The usual signs of heightened security were obvious as the group of pilots and navigators approached the briefing hut; there was already a large padlock on the phone box outside the NAAFI, and two members of the RAF police stood outside the briefing room doors, ready to stand guard once everyone was inside. Greg knew the whole camp would now be closed to all but vital traffic. All precautions were taken to prevent any unauthorised person from discovering the location of that night's target or from leaking that information. Should the Germans hear where the bombers were heading, they would send their deadly night fighters to intercept them before they reached the target.

Walking inside, Greg saw *T-Tommy*'s navigator at a table in the second row back from the stage. He went to join him, casting a glance at the blackboards arranged around the stage. 'G'day, Pat. Care to take a bet on the target? Ten bob says we're going to Happy Valley.'

'No fear. I bumped into Fitz earlier, and he warned me never to bet against you. I hope you're wrong, though.'

Greg did, too, if he was honest. Happy Valley was the name the aircrews had given to the Ruhr Valley, and a trip there was anything but happy. It was a popular target, being a vital industrial centre, and it was always heavily protected with anti-aircraft fire and night fighters. Greg glanced again at the red curtain concealing the back wall of the stage. Behind it would be the map marked with that night's route and target. All the crews had their ways of guessing the target before it was announced, and Greg had grown rather good at it. Once he completed the morning's flight, he would loiter by the machine while the erks – the ground crew – moved in to prepare it for the mission and make note of any faults that had been observed during the test flight. Watching how much fuel they put into the machine gave Greg a good idea of the distance he would be flying and was therefore a clue to the location.

More men filed into the hut, and it was soon filled with an expectant buzz. Greg watched the senior officers as they took their places at the front. The hum of conversation died as Squadron Leader Laurie Price, 505 Squadron's CO, cleared his throat.

'Good afternoon, gentlemen.' Price reached for the curtain cord and pulled it to open the curtains. Greg held his breath as a map was gradually revealed. He quickly picked out a red cord pinned to the map that showed the route, and followed it as it crossed the coast at Mablethorpe, then ran across the North Sea, before turning in a dog-leg at a point on the Danish coast. From there it crossed Denmark and skimmed the east coast of Jutland until it ended at a point on Germany's Baltic coast with a red circle drawn round it. Not Happy Valley, then. This was a part of Germany Greg hadn't flown over before, and he had no idea what kind of opposition they would be likely to meet.

'Today's target is Rostock,' Price said. 'This is a vital mission.'

Greg resisted the urge to roll his eyes. The CO never failed to state that a mission was vital. They could be dropping leaflets, and he would still say it was vital to the war effort.

'Your target will be the Heinkel factory here' – Price tapped the map – 'and the aim is to disrupt production of the aircraft.'

The CO then handed over to the intelligence officer, who went into more detail about the target and the reasons for the mission. Next came briefings from the navigation officer, who described the precise route and bearings for each course change. Next to Greg, Pat took detailed notes, and Greg also jotted down the course outline, not wanting to be entirely dependent on the navigator in case Pat was incapacitated. He also paid close attention to the Met Officer, who gave them information about the cloud cover, risk of icing and projected wind speeds. Again, this last information was of most interest to the navigator, who would need to factor in wind vectors when guiding them to the target and home again, but Greg noted them down too. Following this came briefings from the gunnery officer and armaments officer.

When the briefing finished, Greg headed with the other pilots to the flight office. He was just passing the sergeants' mess when he saw a familiar figure heading away, and his heart sped up. Pearl. He had hoped to see her the day before, but he'd needed to catch up with his crew when they returned and then give Fitz's lost crewmates the send-off they deserved. Now he hurried to catch her up.

'G'day, Pearl. Dare I hope you were looking for me?'

Pearl jumped and turned, facing him with an expression that briefly echoed the look of startled excitement she had had just after he had kissed her. It didn't last long before her expression became more guarded. 'Oh, hello. I wasn't expecting to see you.' There was a coolness to her tone that had never been there before, not even when she was scolding him for taking liberties. 'I left a message for you at the sergeants' mess.'

'I haven't been there since breakfast,' Greg told her. 'I've been busy. I'm flying tonight.'

'Tonight? But I thought you didn't have a plane.' Her voice held a note of genuine anxiety. And although Greg didn't want to cause her worry, he couldn't deny the comfort of knowing that she wasn't entirely uncaring.

'*T-Tommy* was short of a pilot, so I'm standing in for him.'

'*T-Tommy*,' she repeated, as though committing the name to memory. 'I'll be sure to look out for you.'

'And I'll listen for your voice when we get back.' Disconcerted when she didn't smile in response, he hurriedly groped for another subject. 'Did you say you were looking for me at the sergeants' mess?'

'Oh, I wasn't looking for you.' Her brief display of anxiety was completely gone now, and the coolness was back. 'I just left you a message in case you were still interested in helping with the newspaper after all.'

She seemed to be implying that he had changed his mind. 'I said I would and I meant it.'

'That's good then.' Her tone and expression implied otherwise.

He didn't have time for this. He needed sleep, and there were things he needed to attend to before it was time to leave. But he couldn't leave Pearl until he had got to the bottom of her inexplicable standoffishness. 'I really did mean it. Listen, Pearl, I don't know what I've done. I thought you wanted to be friends, but now I get the feeling you don't want me around.'

She shook her head. 'It isn't that.' She paused and chewed her lip as though listening to an inner debate. 'I just... I saw you in the pub last night. You were fooling around.'

'Ah. You saw me writing on the ceiling.'

'Yes. Why would you risk your neck like that?'

'Well, I need some excitement after spending all day doing my dull job.'

She had the grace to smile at that. 'I know. It's not my place to tell you how to live your life. I just—' She broke off with a shake of the head. 'Sorry. I know you must have things to do. This isn't the time and place for this.'

'No. I do want to explain, though, if you'll listen.'

'Of course. I'm free tomorrow afternoon.'

'I should have the day off tomorrow.' *No. Stop it. Don't tempt fate.* 'Shall I look for you in the NAAFI?' *If I'm still here.*

Judging from the tightening of her mouth, she was thinking the same thing. 'I'll be there.' She didn't need to add *I hope you'll still be alive.* The unspoken words hung in the air between them.

'Good. I'll see you tomorrow, then.' What was he doing, making plans? He never made plans. He lived from one moment to the next, never thinking too far ahead. That was the only way he could retain his sanity. 'Are you on watch tonight?'

She shook her head. 'I've got to go back on in a few minutes but I'm off tonight. I'll look out for *T-Tommy*, though.'

Taking him by surprise, she suddenly leaned towards him and kissed his cheek. 'Take care.' Then she darted away as though she had been burned.

—

Idiot, idiot, idiot! Pearl could feel her cheeks burning as she dashed away. What had possessed her to kiss him? All right, so she had kissed him on the cheek rather than full on the mouth... Her face burned even hotter as she relived *that* kiss. But she shouldn't have done it at all. She was supposed to be keeping him at arm's length, for goodness' sake.

Even as she chided herself, she tried to block out the heavy words tolling in the back of her mind. He could die. This time tomorrow, he might be dead. She couldn't understand how he appeared so carefree when he knew he was flying into danger. Yet deep down, she knew that was why she had kissed him. She was cross with herself for being distant towards him when he was facing death, so she'd wanted to show him she cared. Sending him off without letting him know would have been cruel. And she could never live with herself if he died and her last words to him had been so cold.

She still had half an hour before returning to Flying Control, so she decided to see if she could find Section Officer Blatchford to ask about the newspaper. She straightened her tie and cap, checked no hair had escaped from the neat roll at the nape of her neck and went to see if she could find her.

She was in luck. As she approached the WAAF guardroom, Blatchford was just leaving. After saluting, Pearl said, 'I was hoping to ask you about something, ma'am.' She wondered if she would ever get used to deferring to a girl who must be several years younger than her. Surely no older than Thea.

'What about? Cooper, isn't it?'

'Yes, ma'am. Well, I got together with a few friends, and we thought it would be a good idea to start a newspaper for everyone on the base.'

'An interesting idea. What did you need my help with?'

Encouraged not to get an outright rejection, Pearl said, 'I suppose we'll need permission, but I don't know who to ask. And we'll need a place to meet and help with other things such as printing and funds to get started. I worked on a newspaper before I joined up, so I've got some experience of the work involved.'

'Well, I'm not in a position to give permission myself but I'll do what I can.'

'Thank you.'

'I'll need a list of your requirements and an outline of your plans for the paper. Let me have them by 1700 tomorrow.' Before Pearl could thank her, she strode away, leaving Pearl with a whirling head, weak with relief.

Pearl hurried into her hut to collect the exercise book she had used to jot down her ideas at the pub and a sheet of writing paper. If she was quick, she could copy out the list for Blatchford and hand it in before going back on duty. Then later... Her stomach knotted. Later, the two squadrons would be leaving on their mission, Greg with them. Last time she had been exhilarated by the sight and sound of so many bombers taking off. Would she feel the same way now she knew one of the pilots?

Chapter Eleven

The remainder of the afternoon flew by, and before he knew it Greg was in the locker room, getting into his flying kit. He already had his thermal underwear on beneath his uniform and a warm sweater over his shirt, and now he pulled on his Sidcot flying suit over the top of everything. There were several posters on the walls reminding them to empty their pockets, and Greg obediently checked that his were empty, removing the letter he had written earlier that afternoon to his parents and putting it in his locker. He had got into the habit of writing a letter to his parents every time he was flying ops. Other airmen were also checking they had their lucky charms with them – something they *were* able to bring with them, as they couldn't carry anything containing any information that would be of use to the Germans should they be captured. Even things like old bus tickets had to be left behind. Greg supposed the letters to his parents were part of his ritual, although he had vowed never to start depending upon a talisman. What if he forgot it? Would he start to believe he wasn't going to survive the mission? There was a chance it would affect his flying and make his fears a self-fulfilling prophecy.

No. He would never risk it, nor the lives of the crew who depended on him. Instead, he tried to empty his mind of his fears before leaving, telling himself that he would fly to the best of his ability and, if they were shot down, then it was meant to be. He tried never to think beyond each day. The letters to his parents were part of his process of making peace with his fate. Every letter was pretty much the same. He told them he had no regrets, whatever happened. He said he wasn't frightened and that he had reconciled himself to whatever might happen. He told them that he loved them and he hoped the knowledge that he had been proud to serve his country would help them come to terms with his death. The part about not being frightened was a lie, but there was no point in upsetting them by revealing that.

With his letter securely stowed in his locker, he joined the queue to collect a Mae West and parachute. Along with the rest of the crew, he was also issued foreign money in case they were forced to bale out over Europe. Then, wearing the life jacket and with his parachute fastened behind him, he headed out to find the bus that would take them out to *T-Tommy*. Seeing Max and the rest of the crew ahead, he pushed through the crowd to join them. 'G'day everyone,' he said, grinning at them. 'Nice day for a jaunt.'

It didn't deserve to be called a joke, but the crew laughed. Greg's comment had achieved its purpose, which was to break the ice and help relieve the tension. Before he had the chance to say anything else, one of the WAAF drivers called for the crew of *T-Tommy* and *G-Giraffe*, so they hurried to board the bus. Another young WAAF was waiting beside the truck to hand them each a flask. 'Soup or tea?' she asked each crew member in turn. Greg asked for soup, then scrambled on board, hampered by his heavy parachute, which bumped against the backs of his thighs.

A drive around the airfield's perimeter track brought them to *T-Tommy*, where the ground crew were still doing last-minute checks. As well as missing his usual aircrew, Greg also missed his usual ground crew. He could only pray this bunch were as competent as the team he was accustomed to. Once the hatch was opened and the ladder dragged into place, the crew climbed aboard, although some elected to relieve themselves against one of *T-Tommy*'s huge wheels before taking their positions. It was, after all, a long flight, with only the most rudimentary of toilets on board. One of the erks handed Greg an empty flask with a wink, and Greg accepted it, knowing that the cold and the low pressure could cause havoc with his bladder. Even though he knew the ground crew would already have done this, he checked the engine cowlings and tyres, then followed the crew inside and inspected items such as the escape hatches and oxygen. He then squeezed forward, climbing over the main spar and into the cockpit, and strapped himself into his seat harness. After stowing his flasks, fervently hoping he wouldn't mix them up, he began his pre-flight checks. The process of checking instruments and flipping the correct switches in the right sequence helped settle his nerves. He always found his nerves were the worst just before he strapped himself into his seat but, once there, he was fully occupied and all other concerns faded into the background.

Finally he called out of the window, 'Contact port.' Once the port engine had roared into life, its propeller whirling, he repeated the process with the starboard engine. Now all there was left to do was wait for his turn to take off. He watched G-Giraffe, for it needed to taxi to the runway before T-Tommy. Each bomber had a set order of take-off and a set height to climb to when in the air. Any mistake could result in a mid-air collision. In the dark, it was nearly impossible to see the other bombers in the group; you could fly a complete mission without seeing the planes that you knew couldn't be far away.

After a wait, G-Giraffe taxied out of its dispersal point. Once it was clear, Greg followed, feeling the vibrations through the cockpit increase, his heart pumping not from nerves but excitement. Flying was the only thing he had ever wanted to do, and nothing could compare with the thrill he got from easing an aircraft into the skies. Not that he had ever been carrying over ten thousand pounds of explosives when he had flown with the charter company back home. And now he was waiting at the top of the runway, holding the aircraft against the brakes, waiting for the signal to take off, and he felt another frisson of fear. Any mistake on take-off would very likely cost the whole crew their lives, because of the risk of the payload exploding.

Then came the flash of green light, and he opened the throttles completely and released the brakes, concentrating on nothing but getting this beast of a Manchester safely into the air. At full revs and with maximum boost, the engines howled and the control column vibrated, making his palms itch. He followed the flare path that marked out the runway, checking his airspeed indicator, and when it told him he had finally achieved take-off speed he eased back the column. When the wheels left the runway the vibrations also calmed.

A tinny voice reached him over the intercom, and he recognised Pat. 'Nice take-off, Skipper.'

'Yeah,' came another voice, although he didn't recognise it. Probably one of the gunners. 'Last mission, we hit a crosswind just after take-off, and I swear the port wing tip nearly knocked off the station commander's cap.'

At least it seemed as though the crew didn't object to him being their pilot. Just as he had been reluctant to fly with a crew he didn't know, he supposed they had felt the same way. More so, as their lives on this trip depended upon how well he could fly. With the familiar banter starting over the intercom, it looked as though they had decided they could trust him.

'Navigator, bearing,' he said. Then, once he had adjusted to follow the correct course supplied by Pat, he said, 'Stay alert, everyone.' Although they were unlikely to encounter enemy fighters this close to home, it wasn't impossible.

Satisfied he had stamped his authority on the crew, he settled in for the long flight.

–

'Crossing the Danish coast now, Skip,' the navigator called. 'New course bearing one-one-zero.'

Greg complied, tensing. The North Sea crossing had been uneventful, but now they were close to Germany there was a greater risk of being intercepted by night fighters. 'Keep a sharp lookout for enemy aircraft, everyone,' he ordered. 'Sing out if you spot anything.' He followed his own instructions, constantly turning his head this way and that, straining to look into the darkness for any sign of movement.

The navigator had just announced they were over the Baltic coast when there came a frantic shout across the intercom. 'Skip, night fighter on our tail. Corkscrew starboard!' This was followed by a burst of machine gun fire.

Greg didn't wait to hear if the tail gunner had scored a hit but immediately plunged *T-Tommy* into a corkscrew – the best manoeuvre for evading fighters. As he dived and banked first one way and then the other, he heard more gunfire.

'I think he's gone, Skip.' This was Max's voice, shaking a little. 'I'm sure I saw him go—' His voice broke off with a cry and simultaneously there came further gunfire. It wasn't until *T-Tommy* lurched that it dawned on Greg that they were still being shot at. Worse, they had been hit. There was nothing he could do but corkscrew again and pray they finally succeeded in shaking off their pursuer.

'Any damage?' he called. 'Report!'

'The fuselage has been holed, Skipper, but I don't see...' The voice tailed off.

'Who was that – mid-upper gunner? Report!' Greg twisted round in his seat, but he couldn't see further behind him than the navigator's position. Why the sudden silence? What had happened?

He was about to order the bomb aimer back to see what was going on when the voice spoke again, this time sounding oddly flat. 'Skipper, this is the mid-upper gunner. The wireless operator has been hit.'

Greg's stomach clenched. Max! 'How bad?'

'Bad.'

'All right. Give him first aid and let me know how he's doing. Bomb Aimer, go back and help.'

'On it, Skipper.'

'And someone tell me if we've lost that bloody fighter!'

There was another burst of gunfire, making Greg tense, waiting for the bullets to strike. But then someone crowed over the intercom and there was a triumphant shout in a distinct Welsh accent. 'Skipper, Tail Gunner. I got him! He's going down.'

Greg fought to pull the machine out of its controlled dive, blowing out a shaky breath. 'Nice one, Tail Gunner. Anyone else see it?'

'Mid-upper gunner here, Skipper. I saw it. Preece hit him head on, and it's going down in flames.' And now Greg could see it, a ball of flame in the darkness, spinning earthwards.

About to congratulate Preece, the words died on his lips, for he had just glanced at the instrument panel and seen the number one fuel tank on the port wing was nearly on empty. He tapped the dial as though by some miracle this would magically refill the tank. Then he recollected himself and switched to the number two tank.

'Bad news, lads. The fighter must have holed one of our fuel tanks. We don't have enough to get us to the target, let alone there and back. I'm going to have to turn us round.'

He waited for the protests, for they had gone this far and Max had been injured, and now their flight wouldn't count as a successful mission, meaning they were no closer to reaching the end of the tour. But none came.

'What's going on back there? Bomb Aimer, how's Max?'

As soon as the bomb aimer spoke, Greg knew it was bad news. 'Bomb Aimer here, Skipper. Max is dead.'

Greg swallowed. It was inevitable that he would lose members of his crew. But Max… he was so young and there was an earnestness to him that immediately endeared him to Greg and the rest of the crew. Eager to learn and prove himself, he had quickly become a favourite with the crew. And now he was gone.

'Skipper? Did you get that?'

Greg pulled himself together. Now was not the time to indulge in reminiscence. The rest of the crew were depending on getting them home in one piece. 'I got it. Navigator, give me a course home. One that avoids the worst of the flak.'

The navigator replied so quickly, Greg knew he must have already had a course prepared. 'Bearing two six zero, Skip.'

Greg wasted no time in altering course. 'Let me know when we cross the coast, Navigator. I'll jettison the bombs once we're over the sea.' Landing with a full payload was dangerous and to be avoided at all costs. 'The rest of you, stay alert for fighters.'

'Okay, Skipper,' came the response from all the men. All except Max. Greg did his best to put Max's loss out of his mind and gave his full attention to surviving the flight home.

Chapter Twelve

In the event, the North Sea remained mercifully clear of enemy fighters, and Greg felt some of his tension drain away when Pat informed him that they were now above the Lincolnshire coast. From there it was a short journey to RAF Fenthorpe. As they had been forced to abort their mission early, there were no other returning aircraft, so *T-Tommy* was given immediate clearance to land.

There was none of the usual elation once he had taxied *T-Tommy* to the assigned dispersal point and shut down the engines. While the rest of the crew waited outside in sombre silence for their transport back to the operations block, Greg remained inside, crouched beside Max, not wanting him to lie there alone like forgotten baggage while they waited for the ambulance crew to carry him away.

It was strange to see Max so still. Someone had closed his eyes and straightened his body as best they could in the cramped space. A line of bullet holes had been drilled through the fuselage, and the wireless was in ruins, destroyed by the same attack that had ended Max's life. All around him lay the signs of the frantic struggle to save his life: the contents of the first-aid box were scattered around him, lying in a pool of congealed blood. Max's flying suit was open to the waist, and his battledress beneath appeared to have been torn open. Bloodstained bandages swathed his chest. Greg took a brief look and shuddered, then hastily arranged Max's clothes to cover the wound.

He laid a hand over Max's chilled forehead. 'See you on the other side, mate. Save me a place at the bar.'

Movement behind him made him turn. The ambulance crew had arrived. One of them peered through the hatch. 'We'll take him from here, Skipper. Go and get yourself a cuppa to warm up.'

With nothing more he could do for Max, Greg climbed out and stood with the rest of *T-Tommy*'s crew to watch while the ambulance men carried him out, nothing more now than a shape under a blanket. Already the ground crew were moving in, and Greg knew he needed to tell them about the holed fuel tank.

'Any problems with the instruments, Skipper?' a woman's voice asked.

Greg spun round, convinced it was Pearl who had spoken, although what she would be doing out here he had no idea. The WAAF who'd addressed him wasn't Pearl, though. It was too dark to make out her colouring, but she was taller and wearing battledress – the trousers and short jacket worn by RAF and WAAF personnel alike who had duties out of doors. The shock of Max's death must have affected him more deeply than he'd realised, making him imagine he heard Pearl. He realised he'd been staring at the WAAF for several seconds, so he hastened to answer. 'The wireless got pranged, but the rest are fine. The number one fuel tank in the port wing is holed, though.'

'Righto. I'll be sure to tell the flight mechanic.'

Greg wandered over to join the rest of the crew, who lingered while the drivers loaded Max's body into the ambulance. All talk ceased and they watched until the doors closed, hiding the blanketed figure from sight, and the ambulance trundled away at a sedate rate. Still silent, they scrambled into the waiting truck, which took them on the reverse journey to the one they had taken earlier that night. They hastily shed their parachutes, Mae Wests and overalls, accepted steaming mugs of tea from a few sympathetic-looking WAAFs, then made their way to be debriefed.

Typically by this stage, Greg would be barely able to keep his eyes open after the strain of handling the heavy bomber and staying alert for the duration of a long flight. This time they hadn't been much farther than the coast of Denmark, so Greg was more awake than usual and better able to recall the events of the night. Ironic, considering they didn't have much to report besides Max's death. They were usually asked if they had had a clear view of the target, if they had shot down any enemy aircraft and if they had seen any of their own aircraft go down. In that instance, they would then be asked if they had seen any parachutes. Now there was little to report besides the heavy flak they had seen at the coast, although it had affected the bombers ahead of them in the stream more than it had them.

'I shot down an ME 109,' the tail gunner announced.

Greg gave a start of surprise, having forgotten their brief moment of triumph.

'Anyone else see it?' the WAAF intelligence officer asked. A lock of hair escaped her severe bun, dangling across her cheek and catching the light. It was the same soft brown colour as Pearl's hair.

'I saw it go down,' Greg said, making an effort to pull himself together. First the WAAF fitter and now the intelligence officer – he was seeing Pearl everywhere. What was wrong with him? This was not the time to indulge in pleasant daydreams about Pearl. 'It was in flames and in a spin. No doubt it was a goner. I couldn't identify it though.'

There wasn't anything more they could report apart from going over the circumstances of Max's death. Greg followed the others out of the room, still clutching his untouched tea. It was only one in the morning, so far too early for the traditional post-mission breakfast of bacon and eggs, and he didn't think he'd be able to sleep. There was still one thing he had to do, though – his own personal post-mission ritual. Returning to his locker, he wrenched it open and removed the letter to his parents. Taking out his cigarette lighter, he lit the flimsy paper and held it, watching the flames consume the unneeded farewell. Before the flames reached his fingers, he dropped it to the floor and stamped out the fire, leaving little more than a black smear on the polished concrete. Then he turned to leave and head back to his billet. He had the unpleasant duty of informing his own crew that Max was dead. And the even more unpleasant task of writing to Max's parents. He had flown the mission on which Max had died, so the least he could do was tell them that their son had been brave and hadn't suffered. Greg had no idea if Max had suffered or not, but he wasn't going to let that stop him doing his best to give the grieving parents whatever peace of mind he could offer.

He'd just reached the locker room door when the sound of a locker door opening made him glance back. An officer he didn't recognise was standing at the open door of Max's locker.

The man glanced up. 'Committee of Adjustment,' he said.

Greg gave a curt nod and marched out, seething. He knew Max's personal effects needed to be returned to his family, but did they have to be quite so cold, stripping Max's locker before the poor lad was even in the mortuary?

'Excuse me!'

What now? Greg gritted his teeth and did his best not to snarl at the WAAF who had just called to him. She looked familiar. 'Didn't I just see you with *T-Tommy*'s ground crew?'

She nodded. 'I'm Thea. I just wanted to ask...' She swallowed and glanced down at her hands, which were knotted together in front of her stomach. 'A friend of mine was flying with *T-Tommy*'s crew tonight. I saw them take out the body.'

It was clear what she was trying to ask, so Greg took pity on her. 'It was Max Turner. We were attacked by an enemy fighter and he was hit.'

He braced himself for hysterics but none came. Thea just looked up at him. He could just make out her white face in the darkness. 'Oh. I'm sorry. He was a sweet boy.'

And now it dawned on him who she must be. 'Are you the Thea who used to be based at Waddington? I remember now that Max mentioned you'd just been transferred here.' Although Max had spoken constantly of Thea, Greg had never actually met her, not having been with Max when he had met her.

'Yes, that was me. I was very fond of him. As a friend. I was always clear about that. I hope he didn't—'

'He understood. Don't worry.' Then, feeling the need to explain how he knew Max so well, he added, 'I'm Greg Tallis, *F-Freddie*'s skipper. Or I was until it blew up. We were both on *T-Tommy* tonight to fill for injured crew.'

If he hadn't expected Thea's calm reaction to the news of Max's death, he was completely unprepared for what followed. Thea gave an incredulous laugh. 'Greg? *The* Greg?'

'I don't know about that.'

'The mysterious Greg who's starting a newspaper with my sister?' The way Thea said it made *starting a newspaper* sound the same as having an affair.

Now Greg understood why Thea's voice had reminded him of Pearl's. 'If your sister is Pearl Cooper, then that's me.'

Thea stuck out her hand. 'Thea Cooper. I've been dying to meet you. I just wish it was under happier circumstances.'

Greg shook her hand. 'Nice to meet you, Thea. I really must go, though.'

'Yes, of course. It's rude of me to keep you standing when you must be exhausted. Pearl would never forgive me.'

Greg heard her grin more than saw it and couldn't resist a smile in return despite himself. And as he made his way to his sleeping hut, the knowledge that Pearl had spoken to her sister about him was a balm to his sore heart.

–

Pearl woke, bleary-eyed after a restless night. It definitely made her uneasy to know a friend of hers was flying ops. Although she knew some WAAFs went to stand on the edge of the airfield to watch the departing planes, she had resisted the urge to join them, as she wanted to write to Deedee, to thank her for sending some novels for Jenny. She had collected the parcel from the camp post office the day before, and Jenny had been overjoyed.

However, once she had finished the letter, she found she couldn't concentrate on her studies as intended but found her thoughts drifting to Greg and what he would be doing at that moment. When the sound of aero engines started, she gave up all pretence of study and put her books aside. She would have loved some company, but Jenny was on duty late that evening and the other WAAFs of Hut Three were either also on duty or had gone to wave the crews off. Blanche, Pearl had been amused to note, had made up her face carefully before setting out for the airfield, even though it was so dark outside that no one would have noticed if she had given herself a clown's face.

Then the engine revs increased until they hit howling point. The next moment, the whole hut shook as a plane roared overhead. Then another. Pearl had counted them all. Twenty-six. She had lain awake, unable to let her mind relax and drift off into sleep. Not when, for all she knew, their boys were fighting a desperate battle in the skies over Europe. One plane had arrived back long before the others. She had no way of knowing how many minutes or hours had passed before the others returned, but every second of that time was filled with dread. Had only one of their aircraft made it back safely? But later she had heard a distant rumble that had swelled into the blissful sound of aero engines, and she had counted them in one at a time until she reached twenty-six. Only then had her exhausted mind drifted into sleep.

She was still muzzy-headed as she made her way to the cookhouse for breakfast. As she had left Jenny sleeping off her night duty, she took her exercise book with her and a pencil, for she had woken with an idea for an article about how those left behind at RAF Fenthorpe passed the time when the aircrews were flying ops. Seeing Thea hunched over her table, her hair so carelessly arranged that several strands were already uncoiling themselves and heading dangerously close to her collar, Pearl went to join her.

'For goodness' sake, Thea. Put your hair up before you end up on a charge.'

Thea gave a start and sat up straight. Only now Pearl was standing in front of her did she catch a glimpse of something gold and green she was holding in her hand. Thea shoved it in her pocket before Pearl could get a proper look at it.

Then she put her hands to her hair and tucked the offending strands back round the ribbon that she had tied round her head. 'Good morning to you, too, *Mother*.' But there was less bite than usual in her tone, as though her heart wasn't in it, and, now Pearl came to look at her face rather than just her hair, she thought Thea looked subdued, her eyes red-rimmed.

She sank onto the bench opposite her sister and leaned across the table. 'Are you all right? What's happened?'

'Why? Afraid I'm going to get myself into trouble and make you look bad?'

'That's unfair! I'm worried about you. You look awful.'

'Gosh, thanks.'

Pearl said nothing more but treated Thea to a level stare. She was all too familiar with her sister's deflection techniques when upset. Finally, Thea's shoulders slumped, and she rubbed her eyes. 'Fine. If you must know, a friend of mine was killed last night.'

Pearl's thoughts flew to Greg. 'Who?' Then, after a pause when Thea did nothing but stir her porridge, Pearl frowned. 'Hang on. You've only been here a few days. I didn't think you knew any of the aircrews.'

'I met him in Lincoln at the Saracen's Head, when I was still at Waddington. I don't think you knew him. His name was Max.'

'Oh. I'm sorry.' Pearl gazed at Thea, feeling helpless. She had never been so aware of how little she really knew her sister. 'Were you close?' She really wanted to ask if Thea had been in love with this Max. If only Thea didn't close herself off.

'I wasn't in love with him, if that's what you mean.' Again the accusing tone.

'No.' But her protest sounded feeble even to her own ears, and Thea simply gave her a look, one eyebrow raised. Pearl gave in. 'Oh well, maybe I did wonder.'

'Really? And you'd hidden it so well.'

Pearl grinned despite herself. Although it was on the tip of her tongue to tell Thea that if she would simply be more open, Pearl wouldn't have to subject her to the third degree all the time, she refrained. Thea was understandably upset about her friend, and Pearl should be offering her comfort, not criticising her. 'I am sorry about your friend, really. If you feel like telling me about him, I'd love to hear.'

'Really?' Thea's surprise seemed genuine, not like the sarcastic retorts Pearl had grown so accustomed to.

'Yes, really.' On the point of pressing Thea to confide in her, she paused, all of a sudden remembering what Deedee had said on hearing she'd joined the WAAF. *You smother her, and it's pushing her away.* Maybe it was time she listened to Deedee. Making a supreme effort, she held her tongue, picked up her spoon and made a start on her own porridge.

The sisters ate in silence for a while. It was only when Pearl was scraping up the last of her cold, lumpy porridge that Thea spoke in a low voice. 'Max was a sweet kid. Only eighteen, and he acted and looked even younger.' She gave a little laugh. 'I've never felt so old. He had a crush on me, although I always told him I didn't feel the same way. But I enjoyed his company and liked being like an older sister to him.' She gave Pearl a significant look. 'Maybe we're more alike than I'd ever realised.' But she carried on before Pearl could answer. 'Anyway, his crew were all as fond of him as I was, but when he told them about me they teased him so unmercifully that I told him I'd go to a dance with him, so he could show them a photo of the two of us together. That was the night you saw me in Lincoln.'

'He left you there all alone?' Pearl was so indignant she quite forgot Max was dead.

'Of course not. He was very considerate. He'd arranged a lift with an officer who had his own car. He offered to drop me at Waddington but... well, I didn't want to get into trouble if the officer noticed I wasn't in uniform, so I said I'd get the bus. Only, as you know, I missed it.'

Pearl hardly knew how she was feeling. There was relief that Thea hadn't been up to anything immoral or dishonest that time in Lincoln. But how could she say that without it sounding like she had a low opinion of Thea? It was dawning on Pearl that she really needed to reassess the way she treated her sister and her opinion of her. Whenever she thought of Thea, she thought of the girl who was always getting herself into trouble, who needed her older sister to look out for her. Was it really the same girl who regarded a member of a bomber crew as too young for her? Who had looked out for him and cared for him enough to accompany him to a dance to protect him from his crewmates' teasing? Pearl could hardly reconcile the two versions of Thea.

As much as she hated to admit she was wrong, especially to Thea, her sense of justice wouldn't allow her to remain silent. 'I'm sorry. About jumping to conclusions in Lincoln, I mean.'

'Apology accepted. And will you promise to listen to me next time instead of jumping down my throat?'

'I'll try. Wait. Next time? I hope there isn't going to be a next time.'

Thea rolled her eyes. 'I'm not twelve any more but I haven't magically transformed into you, either.'

'I never tried to turn you into someone like me. I just wanted you to think more carefully about the consequences of your actions.'

'Pearl, please. I don't want to argue with you. Not now.'

'I didn't mean to argue. I just—' Pearl bit her lip. She really did need to try to stop using every conversation with Thea as an opportunity to lecture her. 'Never mind. I *am* sorry about your friend.'

'Thank you.'

'Is there anything I can do?'

Thea shook her head. 'No. This isn't the first friend I've lost to the war and it won't be the last. The only thing I can do is carry on with my work to the best of my ability.'

There was a pause while they both finished their tea, then Pearl asked, 'How did you find out about your friend, anyway? The aircrews aren't even up and about yet.'

Thea grimaced. 'He was flying in *T-Tommy* last night. That's the Manchester I'm assigned to, and I was there when they got back.'

'*T-Tommy*? I think that was the plane Greg was flying last night.' In fact Pearl *knew* it was but she didn't want Thea to know she had committed the name to memory and was alert for any news of *T-Tommy*'s crew.

A futile hope, as it turned out. Thea's lip curled. 'I know. I met him.'

'He's all right, then?'

'Relax. He came out without a scratch, although *T-Tommy* was damaged and couldn't complete the mission.'

Pearl's relief was mingled with a nagging sense of embarrassment. She didn't like the thought of Thea meeting Greg without her knowledge. 'Did you speak for long?'

'If that's your way of asking if I mentioned you, then yes I did.'

Please don't let Thea have implied I fancied him. 'What did you say?'

'Admit it – what you really want to know is what he said about you.'

'Thea!'

'Oh, all right. Honestly, you should trust me more. All I asked is if he was the same Greg who was working on the newspaper with you.'

'Is that all?'

'Yes! What did you think I was going to say? Anyway, he was tired and had just lost a member of his crew.'

'Of course. I'm sorry.' Pearl swallowed, unsure what the strange pang in her chest could mean.

–

Pearl left the cookhouse with Thea and hadn't gone more than a few yards when an imperious voice said, 'Cooper!' It was Section Officer Blatchford.

Both girls turned and saluted. Pearl could swear she heard Thea mutter under her breath, 'What have I done now?' Out loud and in unison they said, 'Yes, ma'am?'

Blatchford looked from one to the other, a small furrow between her brows, then her face cleared. 'I forgot you two were sisters. It's Pearl Cooper I want to speak to.'

Pearl sensed Thea relax beside her. She waited for Blatchford to speak while running through her mind any misdemeanour she might have unintentionally committed.

'At ease, and don't look so worried. I merely wanted to let you know I've spoken to my superiors about your newspaper scheme. To cut a long story short, everyone thinks it's a good idea and the station commander himself has approved it.'

Glowing with pride, Pearl said, 'That's wonderful news. Thank you, ma'am.'

'You can use one of the classrooms for your meetings. Come and see me later so I can show you the booking forms. The best news is that the station commander has agreed to release funds to cover the costs of printing the first three issues, and we'll discuss further funding once we've seen how much you can raise from sales. He expects to see the first issue at the start of June, so get to work.'

'We will. Thank you.'

As soon as Blatchford was out of sight, Pearl turned to Thea. 'You heard her – we've got work to do. Are you free for our first meeting this evening? I'm pretty sure Jenny is.'

'I should be. Even if they're flying ops tonight, I should be able to get some time off. I'll let you know.' Thea looked almost as pleased as Pearl felt, and there was no sign of their earlier disagreement. It was one of the things Pearl valued in her sister – she didn't hold grudges.

'Great. I'll go and see Blatchford when I come off duty, and book a room. I'll send you a message when I know when and where.'

'And will you invite Greg too?'

'Of course.' Pearl refused to rise to the bait. 'It was his idea in the first place. It would be rude to exclude him.' She could only hope Thea didn't try to embarrass her in front of Greg, although she wouldn't put it past her.

'Well, I'd better be off. I have to be on duty soon. See you later.' Thea set off, but she had only gone a few yards when she paused and looked back. 'Thanks for listening. About Max, I mean.' And then she was gone. Pearl, who had been too taken aback to answer, watched her sister until she disappeared round the corner of the NAAFI. She was starting to realise that she didn't understand Thea nearly as well as she had always supposed.

Chapter Thirteen

Thea, Jenny and Greg were all available that evening, there not being any ops on. Thanks to Section Officer Blatchford's help, there had been no difficulty in booking a classroom, and now the core members of the editorial team sat round four desks that they had pushed together. For Greg's benefit, Pearl outlined the ideas that they had discussed last time, and then she told them the news about the station commander funding the first three editions. 'But that's not all,' she said, raising her voice over the others' exclamations of delight. 'In return, we need to have the first edition out at the beginning of June.'

'But that only gives us just over a month,' Jenny said. 'And we haven't even found a printer yet.'

'I know. It's not going to be easy, but a tight deadline will make us buckle down to work.'

'And everyone could use a morale booster,' Greg added. 'Let's put together a paper that will make everyone smile.'

'Well said.' Thea raised an imaginary glass in Greg's direction.

'We still haven't thought of a name, though,' Pearl put in, trying to ignore the sudden stab of irritation she felt at seeing Thea behave with such familiarity towards Greg. 'That's really important now, because we can't design our masthead until we know what it's called. I was thinking of something along the lines of the *Bulletin Board*.'

'That's a great idea if we want to send everyone to sleep. It sounds like something full of announcements about the next kit inspection and the best way to polish buttons. Who wants to pay for that? No, I've got a better idea.' Now Thea's eyes were sparkling. 'What do you think about the *Bombshell*? It makes it sound exciting and surprising and it's also a connection to us being a Bomber Command station.'

Jenny frowned. 'Doesn't "bombshell" mean shocking or unwelcome news?'

Thea shrugged. 'I think it sounds more like exciting news.'

'You would,' Pearl said. She was still smarting over being told her idea was boring. While she had lain awake the night before, listening out for the returning bombers, she had run several ideas for titles through her mind and had thought the *Bulletin Board* was a good one. 'What do you think, Greg?'

'I think the *Bombshell* is a great title. It will make people sit up and take notice.' He looked slightly apologetic. In other words, he thought her idea was boring too. Did he think *she* was boring? 'You're the one with newspaper experience, though, so you get the casting vote. We'll go along with whatever you think best.' Greg glanced at the other two girls. 'Won't we?'

'Of course,' Jenny replied straight away. Pearl found her obvious confidence heartening.

Thea nodded, although something in her expression made Pearl's heart twist. It reminded her of the day ten-year-old Thea had raced home from school, pigtails flying, her face alight.

I won the school prize for my story about a flying horse!

That's wonderful, well done.

The headmistress said it was so good, she's going to display it on the wall outside her office. Will you collect me from school tomorrow so I can show you?

Of course.

And Thea had been so delighted she had clapped her hands. But Pearl had ruined it all the next day. She had gone to the school as promised and read the story written in Thea's very best handwriting while Thea stood beside her, bouncing on her toes. It had been an entertaining story about a girl who had made friends with a flying horse that had flown her up to a magical city in the clouds.

'It's very good,' Pearl had said. 'But I think the girl should have asked her parents before going off on all those adventures.' Thea was always running off without telling Pearl or Deedee where she was going. It had seemed a good opportunity to remind her sister that she always needed to ask permission and tell one of them where she was going. It had been the wrong thing to say, though. She'd realised too late that Thea had wanted praise from her older sister who had just started an exciting job on a newspaper. Praise from Pearl would have been praise indeed. Instead, Pearl had chosen to use the moment as a learning opportunity. All the light had faded from Thea's face, and she had walked home with dragging feet, all her bounce gone.

Thea had the same look now. It wasn't even disappointment. It was resignation. As though Thea had been foolish to ever expect wholehearted praise from her sister. Or for her ever to think one of Thea's ideas was good. And really, when she thought about it, she could see the sense in what Greg had said. It was a name that would make people sit up and take notice. She thought about the servicemen and women at Fenthorpe, talking about the new paper that had just come out. The *Bombshell* was a name everyone would remember, that would get everyone talking. The *Bulletin Board* sounded like a way for the officers to give information out to the station personnel.

'You're right, Thea. The *Bombshell* is a good name. It will make people expect something that's a bit fun but also relevant to them. I vote for the *Bombshell*.'

'You mean it?' Thea's face lit up.

'Course I do. Right. We've got a name. We're going to need an artist to design our masthead for us. Thea, didn't you say something about approaching an artist to draw a cartoon?'

'Corporal Yates. I already asked him, and he said he'd love to do it.'

'Great news. We must invite him to our next meeting.'

'I'll ask him. I'm sure he'll want to join in. He says he's looking forward to doing something creative again.'

'Wonderful.' Pearl made a note of Corporal Yates's name. 'Now, we've got four pages to fill. I should write a "welcome" piece, letting readers know what to expect and what's coming up. I'll pull together some news items about what's happened on the base and what's coming up in June. Jenny, you had the idea of a "Day in the Life" feature. Do you think you could write a piece about the Met WAAFs? I've seen you out and about with your clipboards around the station, but I don't really know what you do.'

'Do you think people would really be interested?'

'Yes,' Thea put in. 'I always feel sorry for the Met WAAFs when they have to go out in a storm or high winds, and I'm sure plenty of others feel the same.'

Pearl nodded. 'Exactly. It would be good to know why it's so important. As long as it's not classified information, of course.'

'Well, if you really think I can do it.'

'No one better,' Pearl told her. 'What else?' She leafed through her notes from the last meeting. 'We said something about asking people to submit stories, didn't we? We ought to put the word out to encourage people to get writing stories of around fifteen hundred words.'

Thea drew breath as though about to say something, but subsided. A moment later she said, 'I've always fancied trying my hand at compiling a crossword. Do you think I can be trusted with that?'

Pearl stared at her, wondering at the bite in her tone. 'Of course. That's a great idea.'

'You're too kind.'

If they'd been alone Pearl would have tried to get to the root of Thea's sarcasm. As it was, she could only hope it was another of her passing moods that would be quickly forgotten. 'Greg, what about you?' Then she remembered she hadn't consulted him about the In Memoriam column. She quickly caught him up with their discussion.

'I agree. I think we need to acknowledge those we've lost without going to the length of obituaries. I can collate the names each month if you like.'

'Are you sure?' It seemed painfully close to home for someone whose own name could soon be included in the list.

'It's fine. Honestly. And I used to help with my school magazine, so I can help with organising the layout if you like.'

'That would be a great help. Thanks.'

'Mmm… cosy,' Thea murmured in her ear.

Pearl felt her face grow hot and hoped Greg hadn't heard. 'Well, I think that's plenty to get started with. I've got the afternoon free tomorrow, so I'll head into Lincoln to make enquiries about a suitable printer. Anyone else free to come along?'

Thea and Jenny both shook their heads but Greg said, 'I probably won't be flying tomorrow. I'll know for sure tomorrow morning. We usually find out if we're stood down in the late morning.'

Pearl took great care not to look at Thea as she said, 'That would be lovely.'

Greg grinned. 'Wrap up warm – I'll give you a lift on my motorbike.'

A motorbike? Pearl didn't know if she liked the sound of that. Far too fast and dangerous. It was too late to back out now, though, and they really did need to sort out a printer urgently. She just hoped Greg didn't like riding at high speed.

–

Pearl pressed her cap tightly to her head as the wind threatened to whip it off. The road, alarmingly close, rushed towards her, the hedgerows on either side nothing but a pale green blur. Her eyes were streaming. She fiddled with the borrowed goggles, but they seemed to have been made for a larger head than hers and she couldn't stop the wind from sneaking in at the corners.

'How are you doing down there?' Greg yelled.

Pearl craned her neck to look up at him where he sat astride the motorcycle. At that moment the sidecar hit a bump in the road, and she clutched the edge in alarm. 'I'm fine,' she lied, trying to force her face into a smile instead of the rictus of stark terror that was its natural expression at the moment. When Greg had told her they would go by motorbike, she had imagined riding pillion, her arms daringly wrapped round his waist. It had been a pleasant daydream, and one that had made her admit she *did* find Greg attractive. Her only worry had been how to manage sitting astride the saddle without showing her knickers to all and sundry. When Greg had proudly showed her the sidecar, she had actually thought it was a good idea, despite the slight twinge of disappointment that she wouldn't get to wrap her arms round him. He had even provided a thick tartan travel rug to drape over her knees. What she hadn't counted on was how frightening it was to be only inches from the road while it sped beneath her. Before the war she had seen pictures at the cinema of the Big Dipper at Blackpool Pleasure Beach. Who would be mad enough to ride something so terrifying, so completely out of their control? she had asked herself. Now she knew the answer – it was the same people brave enough to sit in a sidecar while a daredevil pilot rode the motorbike it was fastened to.

Greg, on the other hand, looked exultant. 'This is the nearest thing to flying while remaining on the ground!' he shouted.

If flying was worse than this, you would never get her on a plane. 'Wonderful!' she yelled, trying to keep the fear out of her voice.

Maybe she hadn't succeeded, though, for Greg frowned and throttled back. The scenery no longer rushed by at such an alarming rate. 'Sorry,' Greg called down to her. 'I keep forgetting that not everyone likes speed as much as I do. Is that better?'

'Much. Thanks.' Going at a more sedate rate, she found she could breathe freely and didn't feel the need to grip the edge of the little car quite so tightly, able instead to look about her and enjoy the scenery. Now they were in the last week of April, cow parsley flowers danced upon their tall stems at the roadside, and the grass verges were studded with golden dandelions. Ahead of them, the buildings of Lincoln drew closer, the cathedral on top of the hill clearest of all, its tower skimming the clouds.

'Where shall we start?' Greg asked.

Pearl had already thought about this and had looked at some of the local newspapers lying around the NAAFI that morning. The *Fenthorpe Gazette*, she noticed, had its office in Lincoln. She gave the address to Greg. 'I thought we might ask if they could recommend their printer. It's such a small paper, I doubt they have their own press.'

But when they arrived at the address, they found the *Fenthorpe Gazette* was sited in the same offices as a whole host of newspapers, including the *Lincoln Daily,* the *Lincolnshire Bugle* and the *Eastern Express.* Pearl gazed up at the vast office building in dismay. She would have had no hesitation in walking into what she had imagined to be the *Fenthorpe Gazette's* tiny, single-room office and chatting with whoever happened to be there. But this… She gazed at the vast offices of what was clearly one of the biggest newspaper groups in the country, and her heart quailed.

Pull yourself together, Cooper, she told herself. *You've dreamed of working in a place like this all your life. It's never going to happen if you're too scared to step inside a proper newspaper office.* And deep inside, she couldn't deny a little thrill of excitement. This was exactly the kind of place she had dreamed of working, somewhere she could report real news. She would never be able to forgive herself if she didn't take a look inside.

She gave Greg a wry smile. 'We might as well start big and work our way down. Coming?'

Greg straightened his tie and opened the door for her. 'After you.'

Pearl gazed around in awe as she walked inside, into a spacious entrance hall. The walls were covered in oak panelling, with framed newspaper front pages hanging here and there. On the back wall was a lift with a large brass plate on the wall beside it. It was too far to make out, but Pearl presumed this was a list of the various departments and which floor they were on. To the right of the doorway was an imposing desk occupied by a smart middle-aged woman. Behind her was a gilt-framed oil painting of a Victorian gentleman with bushy whiskers and a stern expression.

The lift pinged as Greg closed the door behind them; several people emerged, but they walked past Pearl and Greg without seeming to notice them.

'Let's see what it says on that list over there.' Pearl pointed at the brass plaque. 'It might give us a clue where we should try.'

'You never know,' Greg commented. 'There might be a department for RAF personnel wanting to start their own newspaper.'

However, they had only taken a few steps when the woman at the desk called to them. 'Excuse me. Can I help you?' Her tone suggested that she would gladly help them out of the door.

Pearl approached the desk. 'Thank you. Yes.' She did her best to sound like an efficient reporter who wasn't at all over-awed by her surroundings. 'We're starting a newspaper at RAF Fenthorpe and we're looking for somewhere that would print it for us. I thought if we came here, we'd find someone who could point us in the right direction.'

The receptionist looked her up and down with the most supercilious expression. 'I'm afraid we won't be able to help you. The Haughton Newspaper Group doesn't concern itself with local newsletters.'

'No. Of course.' Pearl had never felt so humiliated in her life. 'We were hoping someone could recommend—'

'Excuse me. I couldn't help overhearing. Can I offer my assistance?'

Pearl spun round to see a tall, lean gentleman at her elbow. He appeared to be in his sixties and wore an immaculately tailored suit that screamed Savile Row. He had an overcoat draped over his arm and held a walking stick in his free hand. Bright blue eyes twinkled beneath bushy grey eyebrows. Pearl took an instant liking to him. 'That's very kind of you. Do you work here?' Maybe he was one of the editors, in which case he could probably advise her on a good printer.

'I do indeed. Did I hear correctly – you are starting a newspaper for RAF Fenthorpe?' The man's accent was cultured, sounding more like it belonged in a London club than a provincial office.

'That's right. I'm Pearl Cooper and this' – she tilted her head towards Greg – 'is Flight Sergeant Greg Tallis.'

'A pilot.' The man was eyeing the pilot's brevet on Greg's uniform. A fleeting expression of wistfulness crossed his face and he swallowed, appearing overcome. Then he made a visible effort to control himself. 'Why don't you both come up to my office? I can spare you a quarter of an hour, and I'd like to do what I can to help the men and women of RAF Fenthorpe.' He led the way to the lift. Pearl, following him, had to bite back a smile at the disapproving look on the receptionist's face. She hoped the kind man wouldn't get into trouble with his superiors for this, but she was far too eager to see more of the offices of Haughton Newspaper Group to turn down his offer. The lift doors opened, and he stepped inside. 'I live just outside Fenthorpe,' he said, nodding at the lift boy, who evidently recognised the man and pressed the button for the right floor without needing to be told. 'That's why what you said caught my attention. Anything I can do to help my neighbours.'

The lift came to a smooth halt, and the boy opened the doors. They stepped into a corridor that rang with the clatter of frantic typing and the ringing of telephones. Drifting from many of the offices came the sound of people talking in urgent tones. Pearl felt a sudden thrill, knowing that all around her people were going about the business of gathering and writing news. There was no opportunity to explore, though, for their benefactor led them straight into the room opposite the lift. This was a large, airy office, giving the impression that the man must occupy a senior position in the company. There was already a woman at the desk, however. She looked up with a bright smile when they all trooped in, and didn't seem at all cross to have her office invaded. 'Good afternoon, Mr Haughton,' she said. 'Did you enjoy your lunch?'

'It was delicious, thank you, Hilda. Please see I'm not disturbed for the next fifteen minutes. This young lady and gentleman are going to tell me all about their plans for a newspaper. Would you be so kind as to bring us all some tea?'

Mr Haughton. Pearl frowned as she followed him through another door. Surely not the same Haughton as the Haughton Newspaper Group? But when she saw the office they had now entered, there could be no doubt. A vast oak desk stood beside a wide window that gave views of the river and the countryside beyond. The desk alone was hardly smaller than Mr Kingsley's office back in Shrewsbury. The walls were lined with bookcases, filled with reference books. It took all of Pearl's strength of will to resist the temptation to peruse the shelves. She couldn't wait to tell Jenny all about it.

Mr Haughton took a seat at his desk and invited Pearl and Greg to sit down. 'Now, tell me all about your newspaper.' He addressed his question more to Greg than Pearl.

Greg gave a small shake of the head. 'Pearl's the one with the plan. It's best coming from her.'

'Of course. Do forgive me, Miss Cooper.'

Scarcely believing that she was in the office of the man who must surely be the owner of several newspapers, Pearl gathered her courage and described their plans. Mr Haughton listened with every sign of interest, jotting notes down as she spoke, not interrupting unless he wanted her to clarify anything. She was in the middle of her speech when Mr Haughton's secretary, Hilda, brought them all tea in fine, bone china cups. Pearl left hers untouched on the desk, afraid the cup would rattle in the saucer and give away how much her hands were shaking. 'So you see,' she concluded, relieved to have got through it all without becoming tongue-tied, 'we need to find a printer quite soon and I thought it would be worth asking at the offices of the *Fenthorpe Gazette*. I had no idea it was part of such a large group.'

'Yes, the *Fenthorpe Gazette* has a very small circulation compared with our other newspapers, but I wanted to do something for my own neighbourhood, even if it does usually operate at a loss. And for the same reason, I'd like to offer you help with your venture. Please bear with me while I consult our printing schedule.' He opened a large ledger and made more rapid notes. Pearl and Greg exchanged glances. Pearl took a sip of tea, grateful to be able to moisten her dry lips. She had no idea what Mr Haughton might mean by 'help', but it almost sounded like he was going to agree to print the *Bombshell*. It seemed too good to be true. She hoped the cost wouldn't be too high.

Finally Mr Haughton closed the ledger. The heavy book shut with a thud that made Pearl jump. 'Yes, I have room for a small print run on the last day of each month. How many copies would you like?'

'Thank you.' Pearl refused to get too enthusiastic until she had heard what the cost would be. The station commander might have offered funding, but she couldn't dream of asking him for an extortionate amount. She knew it was part of her role as editor to keep the costs minimal. Although she had done all the calculations, her mind now went blank; she needed to consult her notes before giving Mr Haughton a number. As she leafed through her exercise book, frantically looking for the page where she had jotted her proposed printing run, she spoke her thoughts aloud. 'We've decided to stick with a simple four-page edition for the first run because we're learning everything as we go along.'

'Very sensible. You don't want to run before you can walk.'

'Exactly! Once we're more experienced we can add more pages if necessary.' Pearl finally found the right page. 'Here we are. Right. Well, there are about two thousand people at RAF Fenthorpe. We can't expect everyone to buy a copy, and those that do will probably share it with their friends, so I decided upon two hundred copies for the first edition, and we'll see how they sell.'

'I think you might be underestimating the *Bombshell*'s popularity,' Mr Haughton said. 'I expect plenty of your young men and women will want a copy of their own, especially if you're including puzzles like a crossword. They might want to send a copy home to their families, too. I think we should double your estimate and print four hundred. In fact, that's a number that cries out to be rounded up to five hundred.'

Pearl swallowed. She had thought Mr Haughton had wanted to be kind, but now she worried that he was trying to swindle her. 'How much would that cost? I'm not sure we can afford—'

'Cost? My dear young lady, you've misunderstood me. I thought I made it clear. I'm offering to print the *Bombshell* for free.'

Chapter Fourteen

'For free? Why?' In her shock, Pearl blurted out the question, unable to frame it in a politer fashion.

'Like I said – I live not far from RAF Fenthorpe, and I have the greatest admiration for all of you young people who have sacrificed so much to serve your country. This is something I can do to help brighten your lives.'

'It's very generous but I can't—'

'You can and you will. I won't take "no" for an answer.'

'Gosh. I don't know what to say.'

Mr Haughton smiled. 'Say "yes". I hasten to add, I didn't ask you to describe your plans for no reason. I wouldn't be offering to print the *Bombshell* if I didn't have the greatest confidence in its editor. I can tell you've thought long and hard about how you're going to make it work, and your ideas are sound.'

Pearl's heart squeezed at the praise. 'That's very kind. It means a lot coming from someone who clearly knows as much about running a newspaper as you do.'

The remainder of the meeting was spent going over the practicalities. Pearl agreed to get all the articles typed up and send everything, together with dummy sheets showing the layout of each page, to the office for typesetting and printing. Mr Haughton had questioned her closely about her knowledge of marking up articles with instructions for different type sizes and weights, leaving Pearl feeling as though she were sitting an exam.

Eventually Mr Haughton had leaned back in his chair. 'You've got your head screwed on right. There's no doubt you paid attention to all the details when you were at the *Shrewsbury Mirror*. I predict the *Bombshell* is going to be a great success.'

Then he excused himself, saying he had another meeting. 'I'll see you down,' he offered.

Pearl followed him into the lift in a daze. She'd never dreamed they might find a benefactor who would take interest in their tiny newspaper.

'I very much look forward to reading your first edition,' Mr Haughton told them as he ushered them through the foyer. 'And do let me know if you would like any help or advice. In fact, why don't you and your team join me for a little celebration after it's published?'

'Oh, that would be lovely. If we know in advance, most of us should be able to organise our duties around it.' Pearl glanced at Greg and saw that he looked pleased by the invitation.

'Very well, I'll write and let you know the date once I've consulted with my housekeeper.' He handed her a card. Then he frowned. 'You know, my dear, you do remind me of someone but I can't place you at all. We haven't met before, have we?'

Pearl shook her head. 'No. I'm sure I'd have remembered you.'

'Ah well. The perils of getting old.'

—

Once they were back outside the building, Pearl turned shining eyes to Greg. 'Isn't that marvellous? What a lovely man.'

'It's certainly a bit of luck that he lives close to Fenthorpe.' In truth, Greg had felt totally unnecessary at the meeting. 'You'd better believe what he said about him not supporting us unless he'd been convinced we could do a good job. That was all down to you. You were very impressive.'

Pearl's glowing smile made the whole trip worthwhile. 'I don't think he'd have heard me out if it hadn't been for you, though. Didn't you see his face when he saw your pilot's brevet?'

'No. Why?'

'He seemed lost in thought for a moment. And sad. If you ask me, he's lost someone close to him who was a pilot. I think he stopped to hear us out because of you.'

Greg smiled at her. 'Good to know I was more use than just someone to give you a lift into Lincoln.' And he was cross with himself for forgetting how alarming it could be to ride in the sidecar. She had gamely endured most of the journey without complaint. If he hadn't noticed her terrified expression he would never have known he was scaring the living daylights out of her. He had been saving his fuel for some time and so it was ages since he had taken the bike out. Navigating the bends and dips in the Lincolnshire roads always helped him forget the stress of his duties, and he had missed it. That was no excuse for frightening Pearl, though, and he would have to take especial care not to go too fast on the return journey, or she would refuse to go out with him again. And he sincerely hoped there would be other days out together.

He glanced at his watch. 'What would you like to do now? We sorted the printing out far faster than I'd thought. How about a drink to celebrate?'

'That'd be nice. I don't know Lincoln all that well. Where shall we go?'

'I'm not sure. I only really know the pubs, and they won't be open yet.'

Pearl's mouth tightened, giving him the feeling he'd said the wrong thing, although for the life of him he couldn't think what. She went to pubs, after all, so it wasn't as if she'd signed the pledge. Then he remembered overhearing some WAAFs saying something about a place run by the Women's Voluntary Service. 'There's the Bishop's Pal – a WVS canteen up at the Bishop's Palace.'

Pearl's expression cleared. 'That sounds perfect. I haven't been there yet.'

After a quick ride up the steep road on his bike, they soon found themselves in the peaceful surroundings of the Bishop's

Palace. Perhaps influenced by its location, the canteen had a hushed atmosphere even though most tables were occupied. Luckily a couple rose to leave just as Pearl and Greg arrived, and Greg was quick to claim their table.

Pearl sank into her comfortable armchair with a sigh. 'This is wonderful. I can see I'll be spending a lot of my free time here.' The waitresses were friendly, and Pearl seemed to unwind under the influence of her tea and a generous date slice. She chattered enthusiastically about their wonderful luck. Greg enjoyed seeing how animated she had become now she was talking about a subject so close to her heart. It was this passion that drew him in, made him want to learn more about journalism, even though he had never given it a second thought before he'd met Pearl. He was glad he had suggested producing a newspaper and glad he had volunteered to help. And not just because it gave him the excuse to spend more time with her, although that was a strong incentive.

'Do you think we should still charge for the *Bombshell*?'

Greg had been so lost in admiration, it took him a moment to register what Pearl had said. 'I think we should because there are bound to be unexpected expenses.' He congratulated himself for his fast recovery. 'We could donate any profits to the RAF Benevolent Fund.'

'That's a good idea. It'll give people an incentive to buy a copy, too.'

There was a pause while they sipped their tea, then the conversation moved to Mr Haughton's generosity and his invitation. 'I wonder where he lives?' Greg said. 'I know the area pretty well.'

Pearl drew out the card Mr Haughton had given her. 'This is his personal address, not the office one,' she said. She read it out. 'Thomas Haughton, Fenthorpe Hall.' Her eyebrows shot up. 'That sounds imposing.'

'Fenthorpe Hall – are you sure? That's where our officers are billeted.' He wasn't too comfortable at the prospect of a gathering under the eye of the station commander.

'Wait.' Pearl had flipped the card over and now studied something handwritten on the reverse. 'It says here he's moved to the gatehouse.'

'Ah that makes sense. I've been past Fenthorpe Hall several times, although I never knew who owned it. It's huge. The grounds are lovely. It must have been quite a place before the war. Even the gatehouse is bigger than your average house.'

'I can't wait to see it then. Imagine Jenny and Thea's faces when we tell them where we're going.'

The afternoon passed quickly. All too quickly. Greg found he was dreading the return to Fenthorpe. Not because he didn't want to be there but because it would mark the end of this interlude with Pearl. He had only known her a few days, so how was it that his thoughts were becoming dominated by her? Working together on the newspaper wasn't enough; he wanted to spend all the time he could alone with her.

He plucked up the courage as they were strolling back to where they had left the motorcycle. 'I've really enjoyed today,' he told her.

'Me too.' Her happy smile gave him the encouragement to continue. He had no idea why he was so nervous, for he had asked women out before.

'I'd like us to spend more time together if that sounds like fun to you.'

'Well, we'll see each other at *Bombshell* meetings.'

'That's not exactly what I meant. I'd like to take you out to dinner. Just the two of us,' he added, in case he found himself taking out Jenny and Thea as well.

Her frozen expression gave him his answer before she spoke a single word. 'That's very flattering, of course.' Her tone had lost all its warmth, and he braced himself for her excuse. 'I'm not looking for more than friendship at the moment. I do hope you understand.'

'Of course. You can't blame a bloke for trying.' He grinned to show her his feelings were unhurt. He must have been convincing, for her expression relaxed.

This wasn't the first time he'd been turned down, either, but it was the first time it had hurt. What had he done wrong? He had been fairly certain she enjoyed his company, and a few times when their eyes had met she had coloured, making him believe she was as attracted to him as he was to her. He would never have asked if he hadn't thought she would welcome it.

The momentary coolness had disappeared from Pearl's expression. 'I'm sorry,' she said. 'But I did so want to be friends with you. Please say we can still be friends.'

'Of course we can. Like I said, you can't blame me for trying, a pretty girl like you. But I promised to work on the newspaper, and I want that even more now I've heard all your ideas.'

Even so, he found the return journey awkward. Every slow, painful mile.

Chapter Fifteen

After the successful trip to Lincoln, Pearl threw herself into her work, both in Flying Control and for the *Bombshell*. Although she had always taken her duties seriously, now she had the added incentive that hard work helped her forget her awkwardness at turning down Greg.

She knew she must have encouraged him. That she found him attractive was impossible to deny. Yet even had she not been put off men in general by Mr Kingsley's actions at the *Shrewsbury Mirror*, she had good reason for not wishing to become deeply involved with Greg. First, she couldn't forget seeing his antics at the pub. The human pyramid stunt had risked not only his own neck but those of his friends. Maybe if that had been an isolated incident she could have dismissed it, but she couldn't forget his exultant expression when he had been speeding along the lanes to Lincoln. This was a man who enjoyed the thrill of risk-taking. Even though he had noticed her unease and had slowed down, he hadn't thought twice about endangering her until that moment. No. While she was happy to be his friend, she didn't trust him with her heart. Another reason was that his free time seemed to revolve around pubs. When he had suggested going for a drink to celebrate in Lincoln, he had confessed that the only places he knew in the city were pubs. While Pearl had nothing against them, she wanted to visit other places too. Going out with Greg, it seemed, would involve high-speed motorcycle rides and drinking in bars.

Anyway, Greg didn't appear to be upset by her rejection. He had taken it cheerfully enough, and had even asked her out twice since then – when she had turned him down again, he had responded with the casual, 'Can't blame me for trying', and left it at that. She was sure he would soon turn his attention elsewhere, although she sincerely hoped he wouldn't ask out Thea. Her sister already took too many risks for her own good, and Pearl dreaded to think what would happen if those two got together. She also couldn't deny that, despite having turned Greg down, she couldn't bear the thought of seeing him with her sister of all people.

With two weeks to go before she needed to collate the articles for printing, Pearl called a meeting of the *Bombshell* team. The permanent volunteers had expanded slightly, with the addition of Corporal Geoff Yates, who had agreed to contribute the artwork, a young WAAF working as a parachute packer who had offered to report on the various sports matches going on between Fenthorpe and nearby RAF stations, and also two girls from the admin section who had enthusiastically signed up, saying that, although they didn't feel confident enough to write any articles, they could help with typing and proofreading.

The main point of the meeting was to look at the masthead Geoff had designed. It was important to get it right, as it would be used for all future editions.

'What do you think?' Geoff asked, placing the design on the table.

Pearl felt a sudden thrill to see the name of the paper emblazoned in a bold font across the banner. On either side of the newspaper's name was a whirring propeller and below it was a bomb falling through clouds. The drawings were done with finer lines than the letters, making the name stand out. 'I think it's perfect,' she said, glancing at the others, who all nodded in agreement.

'It's starting to feel real, isn't it?' Jenny said.

'It is. Especially now we've got articles coming in to fill up the space.' Pearl had already started to draw up the dummy sheets, thankful for her years of experience on the *Shrewsbury Mirror*, which had given her the skill to estimate how much column space each item would occupy. There was a column for news from the various clubs and societies on the base; Olive Jackson, the sports reporter, had already contributed an entertaining account of the netball match between RAF Fenthorpe and RAF Scampton, and was now working on a report of a cricket match that had been held the day before. In addition to designing the banner, Geoff had produced a cartoon strip called 'Bert the Erk', featuring the hapless Bert, a fitter who was constantly getting into scrapes. Pearl had written her introduction, which took up the central spot on the first page, and also an article on local houses that had been requisitioned. She had done a bit of digging around the neighbourhood and discovered where the families who owned the houses had moved to and written a bit about their backgrounds.

'How's your "Day in the Life" feature coming along, Jenny?' Pearl tapped the empty space on page two where she had decided to place it.

'I've nearly finished. Would you read it through for me before I get it typed up? I want to be sure I'm doing the right thing.'

'Of course. I'm sure it'll be good, though.' Pearl turned to Thea. 'What about the crossword?'

'I'm nearly there. You can have the grid if that would help. I've got that all worked out. I'm still trying to come up with good clues for a couple of words in it but that's all. I was thinking, though. Now we don't have any printing costs, why not make it a prize crossword? We could offer a prize of, say, five shillings. It might encourage more people to buy their own.'

'Good idea.' Pearl scribbled a note. 'I'll mention it in my welcome article. You'll need to add an entry form to the bottom of the crossword and instructions on where to return it to.'

Pearl consulted her notes again. 'That's nearly everything sorted out, then. There's only one problem – so far, we haven't had a single entry for our story, and I'd set aside half of page three for it.'

'I've had several of my friends say they want to write something,' Fiona, one of the admin WAAFs, said. 'But they all say they need more time.'

'I suppose that would be a problem, although I did hope getting a story published in the very first edition would be a good incentive, not to mention the payment.' Pearl tapped her pencil against her teeth, thinking. The day after meeting Mr Haughton, she had put up notices around the base, telling everyone that the *Bombshell* would be coming out next month. As well as asking for volunteers to contact her, she had asked for contributions of short stories and poems, offering five shillings for each short story published and two shillings for poems. 'The trouble is,' she went on, 'we can't wait much longer for a suitable contribution. We've got to give Fiona and Kate time to type everything up, and it'll take me at least a day to get the dummy sheet right. But I can understand that we've really not allowed enough time for people to write a good story. What do you think we should do?'

'Why not give it another week?' Greg suggested. 'Those of us who know anyone planning to write something can chivvy them along.'

'But what if no one comes forward? No one's going to buy the second edition if the first one had a load of blank space on page three.'

'There you go, always thinking the worst,' Thea said. 'I used to be a dab hand at limericks. I'll write a selection featuring some of the senior officers – enough to fill your half-page. Or I could make up some more puzzles.'

'Better do the puzzles,' Pearl told her. 'I don't want you getting court-martialled.'

'Always the protective sister.'

'That's got nothing to do with it. Who's going to compile the crossword if you get kicked out?'

Thea gave her a wicked grin. 'Just for that I'll write a limerick about the illustrious editor of the *Bombshell*.'

Pearl ignored her and addressed Greg. 'Fine. We'll do what you suggest, then, and leave it another week. If no one's sent anything suitable by then, we'll use Thea's... contributions.'

They wrapped up the meeting soon afterwards. Jenny was going straight on duty, so Pearl returned to Hut Three alone.

She hadn't gone far, though, when Greg caught her up. 'Hold on a minute.'

Pearl faced him, resisting the urge to roll her eyes. No doubt he was going to ask her out again. Was he ever going to get the message she wasn't interested? 'What is it?'

'I just remembered something that might be suitable if we don't get any fiction,' he said.

Pearl, who had been mentally rehearsing a polite but firm refusal, was momentarily taken aback. 'Oh. Well let's hear it. Why didn't you mention it in the meeting?' She wasn't disappointed. Really.

'I didn't know whether it was the sort of thing you were after, so I thought I'd ask you first.' He shuffled his feet a little. 'You see, a... a friend of mine showed me something he'd written. It's not a story. More a journal of sorts. Thoughts of a crew member. Would you like to see it?'

If she didn't know any better, Pearl would have thought Greg was hiding something. He wouldn't meet her eyes. He looked almost embarrassed. But she knew Greg well enough to know he was straightforward and never embarrassed about anything, so she dismissed the notion. 'Of course. Anything's got to be better than Thea's limericks.'

He flashed her a grin, looking more like his usual self. 'Great. I'll dig it out tomorrow— That is, I'll ask my friend if he's still got it.'

Pearl had already turned back towards the Waafery when Greg called her back. 'I don't suppose you fancy coming to the cinema with me tomorrow?'

She laughed. Now that was definitely more like the Greg she knew. 'No thanks. I'm on duty.'

'One of these days I'll stop asking. You should really say yes before you miss out.'

—

The next day, Pearl found herself hailed by Greg as she was on her way to the cookhouse. He waved a piece of paper as he jogged towards her.

'Here's the article I told you about. The one my friend wrote.' He didn't meet her eyes as he said it, making Pearl wonder if the friend had been killed. 'It might be useful if no one subs a story in time. Anyway, must dash. Rumour has it we're flying ops tonight, and I need to go and check.' He ran off with a wave, leaving Pearl clutching the page. No matter how much he wanted to get back in the air, she couldn't help hoping he remained grounded. While his wildness made him unsuitable as a boyfriend, she enjoyed his company and found that she looked forward to newspaper meetings knowing he would be there.

An image formed in her mind's eye of going to a meeting and seeing an empty chair where he usually sat, and it gave her an almost physical pain. How would it feel to be on duty in Flying Control, waiting in vain for Greg's return? How would it feel to see his name in that sombre box on the back page of the *Bombshell*, outlined with a thick black border? She shuddered, feeling suddenly cold despite the warm sunshine. It didn't bear thinking about.

She hurried to the cookhouse to get her breakfast. She had hoped Jenny or Thea might be there but, as she could see no sign of them, she took her breakfast tray to an empty table and started to read the article.

> *The Empty Beds*
> *Six beds in my hut are empty tonight…*

'What have you got there – a love letter from some handsome admirer?'

Thea's voice made Pearl jump. She realised her eyes were brimming with tears and hastily wiped them away while Thea placed her tray on the table and took her place on the opposite bench. 'Don't be an idiot.' She showed the page to her sister. 'It's something Greg gave me, written by one of his friends.'

'Is it any good?'

'Yes. I don't think I can print it, though. I'll have Section Officer Blatchford on my back, telling me I'm damaging morale. Look.' She gave it to Thea, then made a start on her porridge while she waited for Thea to finish. As she ate, one phrase hammered through her mind: *if I have a tomorrow.* How did it feel to live day after day, knowing it could be your last? Oh, she knew that no one could truly know what would happen to them from one day to the next, but for a member of a bomber crew death was a very real presence, not simply a distant possibility. What did that do to your mind? Pearl didn't think she could face it without going mad – yet that was reality for all the crewmen.

Reality. 'You know what? Hang Blatchford, I'm jolly well going to print it. We should be reporting what life is really like here, starting with this.'

'Good for you.' Thea slid the paper back across the table to Pearl. 'It makes you think, doesn't it? I'd stake my life on it being written by a crew member. The bit about him raising a glass in their honour, then slowly forgetting them… that's how they acted at Waddington, and I'm sure it's the same here. It seems harsh, but it's how they cope. You can't blame them.'

A sudden thought struck Pearl. 'Thea, that night we went to the pub… I saw Greg in the public bar, and he was horsing around with his friends, pulling some reckless stunt, writing something on the ceiling.' She tapped the place where the writer mentioned raising a glass in honour of his departed friends. 'Is that what he was doing?'

'I expect so. Every squadron has its own rituals, but they're all a way of coping, of not cracking up under the horror of it all.' Thea dropped her voice. 'Not long after I arrived at Waddington, I saw something awful. A plane caught fire on landing. Most of the crew escaped, but the tail gunner was trapped; the mechanism must have jammed. I wasn't far away, and I saw it all. The crew were trying to break him free while inside the gunner was hammering at the perspex, screaming.' Thea shut her eyes briefly. When she opened them, Pearl could almost see the horrific scene in their depths, of a trapped man, visible to all through the clear tail gunner's turret, burning to death in front of Thea's eyes. 'In the end the crew had to abandon him or risk being burned to death themselves. We all had to run away before the fire reached the magazines. I'll never forget how it felt, knowing we were dooming the poor man to die. That night our flight sergeant took us to the pub and we basically had a party.' Thea gave a twisted smile. 'I don't think I've laughed so much in my life. He knew what he was doing – if I'd stayed in, I would have spent the whole evening playing the scene over and over in my mind. I'll never forget what happened, but going out like that helped me to put the horror behind me. It helped me carry on. If I thought too much about all the men who've died I could never carry on, harsh as it sounds.'

'How terrible.' Pearl would have given Thea a hug had she not known Thea would object to being hugged in front of everyone in the cookhouse. 'I wish I'd known.'

'Why – what good would it have done?'

Pearl shrugged. 'None, I suppose. I would have liked to have supported you, though.'

Thea's expression softened. 'You can't mother me for ever. Besides, if that had happened to you, would you have told Deedee?'

'Of course not. I wouldn't want to...' Pearl tailed off, finally getting Thea's point.

'Exactly. You wouldn't want to worry her,' Thea finished for her. 'There's another reason, too. Seeing… what I saw… I felt tainted. Like it had ruined my view of the world for ever. I didn't want to ruin it for you as well.'

Pearl gave her sister a wry smile. 'Looks like I'm not the only one who feels protective towards her sister. I really need to stop thinking of you as a mischievous ten-year-old, don't I?'

They continued their breakfast after that, and the conversation moved on to happier subjects. Pearl didn't know when she'd enjoyed Thea's company so much. Just as she rose to leave, Thea said, 'Oh, I nearly forgot.' She pulled a couple of folded sheets of paper from her pocket. 'I wrote this story last week but couldn't pluck up the courage to submit it. But if you don't think Greg's friend's piece is suitable, have a read and see if this will do.'

'I didn't know you liked to write.'

'I've always jotted little stories down, since school, but I've never shown them to anyone else. This is something I wrote a while ago and I reread it last week and thought it wasn't too bad. I've edited it a bit. Anyway, see what you think.'

Pearl had never seen Thea look so hesitant before. 'I will. Thank you. I look forward to reading it.' Thea's flush of pleasure made Pearl hope it was good enough to print, because she'd hate to have to criticise her after the progress they had made. She recalled Thea's acid tones when Pearl had complained that no one had submitted any stories, and it dawned on her that Thea was probably irritated that Pearl hadn't asked her.

–

For the rest of the day, Pearl couldn't forget what her sister had told her. Ever since Thea had joined the WAAF, Pearl had been hurt by her sister's brief, offhand letters that gave little or no information about her life. Now Pearl was starting to understand. If she had witnessed the horror of a man being burned alive, she wouldn't have told Thea about it either, so she couldn't blame Thea for doing exactly as Pearl would have done. Even so, it pained her to know that Thea had been burdened by an experience she couldn't share. At least now they were serving in the same place, Pearl could try to be more supportive. Thea, as a fitter working on the bombers, must get to know the crewmen even better than Pearl did. Pearl only heard the pilots. Thea would see them all.

Neither could Pearl forget what 'The Empty Beds' revealed about Greg. Yes, he was somewhat wild and reckless; but was that his actual personality or was it his way of coping, as Thea had suggested? When she thought about how Greg acted when he was with her, all she could recall was his kindness and attentiveness. He had taken her journalism ambition seriously, to the extent that he had suggested the idea of starting a newspaper. Come to think of it, hadn't he refused to take credit for her ideas about the *Bombshell* when Mr Haughton had initially directed his questions to Greg? She couldn't imagine any of the reporters at the *Shrewsbury Mirror* doing that. Now she had started thinking along these lines, she thought again about riding with Greg in the sidecar. True, he had gone too fast for her comfort at first, but as soon as he had noticed her fear he had slowed down. And he hadn't needed reminding to go slow on the ride back but had ridden at a sedate speed the whole way.

Some journalist she was. She had made assumptions about him early in their acquaintance and let those assumptions colour her observations ever since.

She was also surprised and a little humbled at the faith Thea had shown in her. She doubted Thea had ever forgotten the time Pearl had criticised her prize-winning school story, and so she hoped Thea's confession that she had never stopped writing was a sign that she was coming to trust Pearl again.

Pearl was working in Flying Control that morning. As there was no flying while she was there, all she had to do was listen out for emergency calls. With no one to object, she unfolded

Thea's story on the desk in front of her and read it. She ended up reading it twice through, enjoying it thoroughly. It was an entertaining and spooky tale of a young woman inheriting a haunted house on a deserted moor. Even though Pearl didn't usually choose to read ghost stories, she was so absorbed in it that she didn't notice when Maggie arrived to relieve her.

'What are you reading – a love letter?' Maggie asked, looking more cheerful than she had since her fiancé had gone missing.

Pearl folded away the pages. 'It's a blood-chilling story that you'll be able to read if you buy the *Bombshell* when it comes out.'

'Ooh, I definitely will then. I love the kind of tale that makes my hair stand on end.'

Happy that there was at least one promised sale, Pearl went to see if she could find Thea to tell her that she would be printing her story. Luckily there would be enough space to print both that and 'The Empty Beds', and Pearl couldn't wait to see how both items would be received.

But when she got to the NAAFI, it wasn't Thea she found, but Greg. He was drinking tea, writing a letter.

'Writing home?' Pearl asked, taking a seat opposite him.

Greg nodded. 'I might be bored out of my mind without a kite of my own, but I think it makes my parents happy to hear from me more regularly than usual.' Then he pushed the letter aside. 'Did you get a chance to read the article from my friend?'

'Yes. It was really good. It made me cry my eyes out, which was embarrassing because I read it in the cookhouse. I've decided to print it. What's your friend's name?'

A crease formed between Greg's eyes. 'He prefers to remain anonymous.'

'I don't blame him. All right, I'll call him "Anon" then. To be honest, I hesitated to include it in case the senior staff thought it was bad for morale.'

'What changed your mind?'

'It helped me understand the experience of the bomber crews. I mean, I'm sure no one who hasn't flown a mission can really understand how it feels, but anything that can give us some idea has to be important.' She paused to take a sip of tea, studying Greg over the rim of her cup. 'Is that how *you* feel?'

'Absolutely.'

'I wish I'd known before.'

'Why – would you have accepted one of my many offers of a date?'

'Yes.' The reply slipped out before she could think better of it.

'So—' the corners of Greg's mouth tilted upwards '—if I were to ask you out again, would you say yes?'

Pearl was unable to keep a straight face. 'There's only one way to find out.'

'Pearl Cooper, you tease!'

'Well – are you going to ask me or not?' She had no idea what possessed her to be so bold. Maybe it was her talk with Thea that had made her realise she needed to start living her own life instead of trying to be a substitute mother for someone who clearly resented her taking that role.

Greg leaned across the table and held her gaze. 'Pearl, would you like to come to the cinema with me on your next free evening?'

Strange how she hadn't noticed the gold flecks in his blue eyes before, like sunlight dancing on the sea. 'I'm free tomorrow evening,' she said.

'Is that a "yes I'm free tomorrow evening and I'd like nothing better than to go out with you" or "I'm free tomorrow evening and I fully intend to spend it polishing my buttons"? Just to be clear, you understand.'

Pearl made a show of examining the gleaming buttons on her tunic. 'Well, they're not as shiny as I would like.' But she couldn't keep up the pretence any longer. 'Of course I'll go out with you. What's on?'

'Why – would it make a difference to your answer?' Greg still gazed intently at her, and she swallowed, imagining sitting close beside him for the duration of a film. She doubted she'd be able to pay much attention to the plot.

'I suppose not.'

'Good. Then, assuming I'm not flying tomorrow night, I'll meet you here at 1800.'

'Why? Do you think you might be flying?'

Greg scowled. 'I still don't have a plane, so I'm left to kick my heels most days. I don't understand why we haven't received a replacement yet.'

Pearl couldn't be sorry. Every day without a replacement for *F-Freddie* was another day she didn't have to worry about him. 'I'm sure it will arrive soon enough,' she said. 'And in the meantime, I look forward to tomorrow evening.'

'Excellent. I'll see you then if not before, and we'll take a gamble on the film.'

Chapter Sixteen

The next morning, the news that there were no operations on left Greg more cheerful than usual. While other crew members took the opportunity to go for a jaunt into Lincoln, he contented himself by settling down in the sergeants' mess to write another letter to his parents. Although he chafed at the inactivity, one thing he didn't miss about flying ops was the necessity of writing his usual farewell letter. Now he could take his time and write the kind of chatty letter he knew his parents would enjoy. Once he had responded to the news his mother had told him about a cousin's wedding and his uncle's promotion at work, he wrote:

> There is plenty to do here, and some of us, myself included, have started up a newspaper for the base. We plan to publish the first edition next month, and I will try to send you a copy so you can see all the work we have been doing.

Somehow it seemed wrong to write about the *Bombshell* without mentioning Pearl. Before he knew it, he had drifted from writing about the paper to writing about her.

> You would like Pearl. She's the editor. She worked on a newspaper before she joined the WAAF and it's her ambition to be a journalist. I've been seeing a lot of her in the last couple of weeks. In fact, I heard her voice before I ever met her because she—

Cursing his thoughtlessness, he crossed out the last sentence heavily. He had been about to mention losing *F-Freddie*, and the censor would never allow that. Now he had wasted some of the precious space on his aerogramme.

> *We're going to the cinema together this evening. I wish you could meet her. I can just imagine how you would both react. Dad would go all bashful, because she's very pretty, and Mum would be impressed by her determination to prove herself. I remember Mum saying that women have to work twice as hard as men to get on in a man's world, and I think Pearl would agree with her.*

Greg paused and looked at the letter. How had that happened – nearly a third of the sheet of paper was about Pearl. He toyed with the idea of discarding the letter and starting again on a fresh bluey, but that would have been a shocking waste of paper when they were being encouraged to save every scrap. He would just have to carry on and expect a whole lot of questions in his next letter from home. He had never mentioned any women in his letters before and now he hadn't seemed to be able to stop describing Pearl.

He picked up his pen again and dipped it in the ink bottle. However, before he could write more, he heard the rumble of aero engines approaching. The noise increased the closer the aircraft came until it was a roar that sounded like a whole squadron approaching, which was strange because he was positive none of Fenthorpe's aircraft were in the air today. For a horrible moment he thought it must be enemy bombers, and he ran to the door to look out. Even when common sense told him the sirens would be sounding the alarm if enemy aircraft were approaching, he couldn't stop himself from running outside to look into the sky.

The sight that met his eyes made his spirits soar. Three huge aircraft were circling the airfield and, even as he watched, one turned into the wind and approached the runway. It was the most magnificent bomber he had ever seen, with a vast wingspan and four engines. He instantly recognised it as one of the new Avro Lancasters.

The Lancaster touched down in a perfect landing; the other two soon followed. Scarcely knowing what he was doing, Greg started to run across to the airfield, eager to see the machines at close quarters. What he wouldn't give to fly one of them!

Several other men from the aircrews were dashing towards the new arrivals, and Greg feared there would be such a crowd he wouldn't be able to get anywhere near the Lancasters. Therefore, he was profoundly grateful when a car pulled up beside him and the station commander stuck his head out of the window. 'Fancy a lift, Tallis? You'll be wanting to be introduced to your new kite.'

Greg scrambled into a seat behind the WAAF driver, scarcely able to believe his luck. 'Thank you, sir. Am I really getting one of those beauts?'

'Absolutely. The whole squadron is getting them eventually. Your crew is getting one of the first ones, but we're phasing out the Manchesters, you'll be glad to hear.'

'Good riddance to them, too.'

The station commander chuckled. 'I thought you'd say that.'

Greg craned his neck to get a better view of the Lancasters as they drove round the perimeter track. All three were on the ground now and each was being guided to the hardstanding by a member of the ground crew. He thrilled at the evident power of the engines, their roar drowning the sound of the motor car he was in. By the time the car pulled up, one of the Lancasters was already stationary, and ground crew were running towards it, evidently as keen to get a close look as he was.

Greg scrambled out of the car in time to see the last of the four huge propellers swish to a stop. A short while later the fuselage hatch opened and a figure appeared in the opening, lowering a ladder. Only one person climbed down: a slight lad who seemed swamped by his overalls. It was only when the pilot removed his cap, allowing shoulder-length red hair to escape, that Greg realised his mistake. The pilot was not a man but a woman. He had heard that the Air Transport Auxiliary had been obliged to take on women but this was the first time he had seen a female pilot in Britain, although he had met a few in Australia.

The corporal who had been standing by the hatch when the pilot had emerged was still peering into the Lancaster's interior. 'You're having me on,' he was saying. 'A slip of a girl like you couldn't handle a Lancaster.'

'Why not?' a hard voice asked him. It was Thea. Greg hadn't noticed her standing with the rest of the ground crew until then. 'Next you'll be saying a woman couldn't repair instruments.'

'Be careful,' another erk said to the corporal. 'Remember Cooper had to fix the mistake you made with *T-Tommy*'s compass the other day.'

The corporal scowled. 'I was having a bad day, that's all.'

Other members of the ground crew had now surrounded the pilot and were asking her questions about the Lancaster's performance. A hand slapped Greg on the shoulder, and Greg turned to see Fitz. 'Wouldn't be bad, eh, being piloted by a pretty girl like that.' Fitz gave a jerk of the head towards the pilot.

'Was she pretty? I didn't notice.' Greg only had eyes for the Lancaster.

Thea, who had finished arguing with the corporal, was now gazing up at the enormous propellers, her eyes wide. She had evidently overheard Greg's comment, for she sauntered over and smiled. 'Full marks to you, Greg. I shall have to tell Pearl you walked right past a stunning redhead without a second glance. Or even a first. You must be looking forward to your date.'

'I am,' he said simply, not bothering to ask how she knew about it. Gossip seemed to fly around Fenthorpe faster than radio waves. 'But I have to admit, I'm looking forward to getting my hands on my own Lanc.'

'Why?' Fitz's eyes had narrowed. 'Are you getting one of these?'

'That's right. Station commander himself told me.'

'Has the rest of your crew been allocated yet?'

Greg shrugged. This was a sore point. After he'd put a lot of work into getting his old crew working well as a team, it looked like he had lost them. Max had gone for ever, of course, but he had hoped to keep the rest of the group together; but, annoyingly, in the time since *F-Freddie* had been destroyed the remaining members of his crew had been absorbed into other teams. 'I don't think so,' he said. 'I'll probably have to take on survivors from other crews. I'll definitely ask for you.' Fitz had a reputation as one of the best bomb aimers and he couldn't think of anyone he'd rather have steering the way to the target. 'Let me know if you hear of a decent navigator, too.' A good navigator could make all the difference between directing his pilot on a route that would skirt the worst of the flak and making an error that would send the plane right through the centre of the storm.

'I'll have a think,' Fitz said.

Greg hardly heard, though. He was too busy drinking in the sight of the Lancasters and wondering which one he would fly. He wished he could climb inside one, but the ground crew were busy working on them and he would only get in the way. Instead, he had to satisfy himself by walking right round them to familiarise himself with the exterior. With any luck, if he could get a crew together, they would be able to take his Lancaster on a training flight the next day.

All in all, things were looking up. He had one of the famous new Lancasters and he was going on a date with Pearl later. Did life get any better than that?

—

Pearl had to laugh. They had been in the cafe at the Regal Cinema for half an hour and so far Greg had yet to stop talking about his new Avro Lancaster. She found his enthusiasm endearing and wasn't at all offended by him not holding hands and gazing at her dreamily, like the couple on the next table. She would far rather talk about something he was interested in; this gave her a far better idea of what he was like than she would gain by holding his hand.

'Does it mean you'll be back to flying ops?' she asked when he paused to drink his tea.

'Not yet. The whole squadron's being stood down while we do training flights. I spent most of the day sorting out the other members of the crew, but I think we're going to be doing our first test flights tomorrow.' Greg's eyes shone, and Pearl couldn't help but feel a little of the eagerness that seemed to light him up from the inside.

'I'll listen out for you tomorrow,' she said. 'I was on duty when the Lancasters arrived, and they created quite a stir in Flying Control, I can tell you. And the noise! They shook the whole building.' She wouldn't let him see her anxiety about his starting to fly again. She already knew him well enough to understand that he could never be happy in a safe job while others risked their lives. If she was going to be in a relationship with him, she had to accept it and pray he survived unscathed.

'I can't wait to fly *C-Charlie*,' he told her for about the hundredth time – *C-Charlie* was the designation of his new Lancaster. 'She's a real beaut. Four Merlin engines!' And he was off again.

She chuckled. 'A pity you can't write us an article about the workings of a Lancaster, but the censors would never let us get away with it.' For one of the conditions the station commander had stated was that the *Bombshell* had to be read by a senior officer before going to print.

Greg looked instantly contrite. 'Am I going on about it too much? I'm sorry. Let's talk about something else.'

As tempting as it was to discuss the *Bombshell*, Pearl resisted, deciding that if Greg could hold back from talking about his beloved Lancaster then she could avoid talking shop as well. 'Tell me about your home,' she said instead. 'I know you come from Sydney but I don't really know what that's like.'

'Well, I grew up in a small town in the Blue Mountains, and my folks still live there. But the charter airline I work for is based just outside Sydney, and I live in a small town on the coast not far away. It's the best of both worlds – a short train ride to the city centre and an even shorter walk to the beach.'

'Oh, I'd love to live by the sea. I live in Shropshire, which doesn't have a coast, but Deedee, my grandmother, used to take us on the train to Llandudno every summer. I love it there, although it probably wasn't anywhere near as warm as your home.'

'Yeah, it does get pretty hot in the summer compared with here, and not nearly so cold in the winter, although it can get icy up in the mountains. The cold Christmases here feel really strange. We always spend Christmas outdoors at home, so it was funny seeing all the frost and snow.'

'I can't imagine a summer Christmas. For me it's a day to stay inside by the fire.'

'Well, once I started my job I didn't get much time off over Christmas either to stay in or enjoy the beach. It was always a busy time for me.'

'Why? What sort of work did your company do – taking passengers?'

'Sometimes. More often we were hired to transport goods to the farms and townships further inland.'

'Why did they fly the goods in? I'd have thought that would be very expensive.'

Greg's eyes twinkled. 'You're forgetting how vast Australia is. It can take days to reach some places by train or road. Far easier to fly.'

'Golly.' Pearl stared at him in awe. 'I can't imagine living somewhere so huge. What's the farthest inland you've flown?'

'I regularly fly supplies out to Alice Springs. That's right in the centre of Australia, over twelve hundred miles.' He grinned. 'That's about the same as going from Land's End to John O'Groats there and back. Or it would be if driving from end to end through Britain involved driving over endless dust roads through the desert.'

'I can see why you wouldn't want to drive then.' Pearl was filled with a longing to visit some of the places Greg had described. 'I'm starting to realise there are so many places I've never seen. I wish I could go there. Maybe after the war.' If the world wasn't so changed by then that no one would be able to travel. It didn't bear thinking about.

Greg looked pensive. 'I can't really think about life after the war. I'm glad I took the opportunity to travel before it all started.'

Pearl swallowed, knowing what he had left unsaid. He couldn't think about life after the war because there was a good chance he would no longer be in the world by then. Making an effort to brighten the mood, she said, 'At any rate, we'll be seeing Hawaii tonight. The film is set in Honolulu, and I'm going to try imagining I'm actually there.'

'Hawaii. Now there's a place I'd love to visit. I like your thinking.'

In the event, Pearl had trouble imagining she was in an exotic paradise even though the temperature in the Regal was approaching tropical. While the film, *Navy Blues,* was an enjoyable musical comedy, she found sitting pressed close to Greg's side made it hard to think of anything apart from his closeness. As the lights went down in the auditorium and the main presentation started, her thoughts kept drifting from the action on screen to his hand lying next to hers on the armrest. Her feelings towards him had changed so much that now she longed for him to hold her hand.

As though he had read her mind, he slid his hand over hers and clasped it in his warm, comforting grip. A thrill of exultation coursed through her and she felt so light-headed she could almost believe she was floating. She returned his grip with a squeeze of the hand to show him she approved, then she dared to rest her head on his shoulder. Maybe she wasn't in Honolulu or a beach near Sydney, but she was with Greg. The man for whom, she was rapidly coming to realise, she had more than friendly feelings.

When Greg leaned closer and kissed her cheek, she had no hesitation in turning her head and seeking out his mouth with her own. When their lips met, she thought the pounding of her heart must be drowning out the drums in the musical number playing out on screen.

The evening passed by in a blur. Between kisses, she hugged his arm close, leaning her head against his chest. She deliberately shut out the sensible voice in her head telling her they had no future. As far as she was concerned, that was the whole point. No one knew what the future held, so, while such a thing as a 'now' existed for them both, she would seize it with an open heart.

Chapter Seventeen

'It's here! It's here!'

Pearl had been dreaming of lying on a warm beach, soaking up the sunshine with Greg at her side. Inexplicably, an earthquake had rocked the shore, shaking her from side to side. She cracked open her eyelids and squinted up at Jenny, who was shaking her shoulder. 'What? What's here?'

'The *Bombshell*, you chump. Mr Haughton's just delivered them.' Jenny waved a copy in Pearl's face. 'Most of them were sent to the NAAFI but I managed to grab us a copy each. Look!'

Pearl snatched the newspaper from Jenny's hand and perused it eagerly. 'Oh, this is perfect.' She ran her fingers over the title, taking pride in how professional all the articles looked in their columns. She read the main item on the front page with its bold headline: *News to surprise and entertain.*

She grinned at Jenny. 'Pinch me! Did I really write this?'

'I know! I got goosebumps all over when I saw my Day in the Life article.'

Seeing how black the ink had made her fingers, Pearl wrinkled her nose. 'I'd better get up and wash before I ruin the bedding.' She glanced at the clock and saw it was nearly midday. She'd come off night duty that morning and hoped to get a nap in before the *Bombshell* copies arrived. Clearly she had been more tired than she had thought. Nevertheless, she had the rest of the day free, and she intended to celebrate the first publication day. 'Coming to the NAAFI? I want to see how well it's selling.'

'Try and stop me.'

Pearl went to the ablutions block for a hurried wash and then changed into her uniform. Then she and Jenny grabbed their bicycles and made their way to the NAAFI. A roar overhead made her flinch, then the sun was blotted out by the shadow of a Lancaster as it flew overhead. She wondered if it was *C-Charlie*. The thought of Greg at the controls made her smile. If anything, Greg had been even more passionate about the new Lancasters after his first flight. He seemed happy with his new crew, too, which also made Pearl happy. Or as happy as she could be, knowing they were all training to fly dangerous missions. They were both careful not to speak of the inevitability of Greg starting operational flying again soon, or of the future. Pearl was simply making the most of the fact that she could see him any evening she wasn't on watch. She was grateful for this interlude, knowing their time together would be limited once the squadron was deemed ready for missions. No matter what happened, she would cherish these long summer evenings spent walking hand in hand through Lincoln or along leafy lanes, talking of their homes or family holidays before the war. Anything but what might happen in days to come.

'Get a move on, daydreamer!'

Pearl realised she had stopped cycling and was taking the weight of her bike on one leg, gazing up at the now empty sky. Jenny had stopped a few yards ahead and was looking back at her, grinning. 'Wipe that soppy smile off your face and get pedalling. I want to see if we've sold any yet.'

'Sorry. I was thinking about Greg.' Pearl caught up with Jenny, then put on a burst of speed to overtake her. 'What are you waiting for?' she yelled.

They were both hot and dishevelled by the time they entered the NAAFI, and walked up to the counter, looking for copies of the *Bombshell*. The staff in the NAAFI had agreed to take charge of selling the paper, setting the money aside for the Benevolent Fund.

'I don't understand,' Pearl said, looking at the tiny pile of newspapers on the counter. She spoke to the girl who was making their tea. 'Why haven't you put more copies out?'

The girl placed the teapot on a tray and said, 'We did. These are all we have left.'

'You're joking.'

'No. They're selling faster than our carrot cake, and that's saying something. Take a look around.'

Pearl's attention had been so fixed on the pile of newspapers, she hadn't looked at the customers sitting at the tables. Now she saw that at nearly every table, men and women were leaning over a copy, either busy reading or talking about it with their friends.

Jenny grinned at her. 'Looks like we'll need to order more copies next time.'

'I can't believe it. And to think I was worried they wouldn't sell.'

—

True to his word, Mr Haughton had sent a formal invitation to the editorial team to join him for a celebration of the *Bombshell*'s first edition. It was to be on June the third, and most of the team had been able to arrange for free time to attend. The only person who couldn't be sure was Greg, who had to wait until the morning of the party before he could be sure he wouldn't be needed on a mission.

When the day of the party dawned clear and sunny, Pearl experienced considerable qualms as she waited to hear if any operations were on that night. Although he and his crew were only making training flights with *C-Charlie*, not all the Manchesters had been replaced yet, and there was a chance he would be required to pilot one. Bomber Command was throwing all its might against Germany, and only three nights ago it had launched what it called a 'thousand-bomber raid' on Cologne. In order to achieve this number of bombers, even inexperienced crews from operational training units had been pulled into service, although most had been flown by experienced pilots. *C-Charlie* had been required to fly, accompanied by an extra pilot who had more experience with Lancasters. Miraculously, all of Fenthorpe's crews had returned safely, although *C-Charlie* had sustained severe damage from flak and was rendered unserviceable for the next night's thousand-bomber raid on Essen. Pearl couldn't even pretend to be sorry, and now she prayed *C-Charlie* wouldn't be needed that night. She endured an anxious wait until she received a scribbled note from Greg telling her the crew was returning to training and, as *C-Charlie* was still being repaired, he was free for the day.

Pearl was still overwhelmed with relief and happiness when the group met at the guardhouse and walked along the lanes to Fenthorpe Hall, eagerly discussing ideas for the next edition of the *Bombshell*. Another popular topic of conversation was the identity of the anonymous author of 'The Empty Beds'. It was all anyone seemed to be talking about on the base, and she had heard several names suggested, from the tail gunner of *B-Beer* all the way up to Squadron Leader Price. Blanche Dalby had even offered her a precious pair of nylon stockings in return for his name and had refused to believe Pearl's declaration that she didn't know. Whatever disagreements people might have over the mysterious author's identity, though, everyone was united in praise for the article, much to Pearl's relief. She had been braced for a reprimand for publishing something that could damage morale, and was grateful that it had clearly had a positive impact.

For the most part, Pearl kept quiet during the walk, content to listen to the others. She and Greg walked hand in hand and, when Pearl heard a skylark, its joyous song seemed to express her feelings perfectly.

The gatehouse of Fenthorpe Hall was, as its name suggested, beside the entrance to the imposing hall. The gatehouse itself looked substantial enough to comfortably accommodate a large family, making Pearl quite nervous as the group climbed the steps into the porch.

'Should we go to the back door, do you think?' Jenny asked, looking up at the stone building with wide eyes. But before anyone could answer, Corporal Geoff Yates reached up and rang the little bell dangling from the wall.

A tiny woman whose dark hair was streaked with grey answered the door. Pearl wondered if she was Mr Haughton's wife, but she said, 'Come in, all of you. Mr Haughton's been looking forward to your visit. I'm Mrs Stockwell, his house-keeper. Come on through to the drawing room.'

They walked through a spacious hallway with a polished wood floor and walls covered in paintings of horses. A grand-father clock stood near the bottom of the stairs, solemnly ticking out the seconds. The whole place smelled of beeswax.

'Gosh,' Jenny muttered, looking up at the grand wooden staircase, 'my whole house would fit in this hall. If this is the gatehouse, Fenthorpe Hall must be huge.'

Then Mrs Stockwell opened a set of double doors and they were shown into a light, airy drawing room. Mr Haughton rose from a large wingbacked armchair and came to greet them. 'Welcome, do come in. It's lovely to meet you all. Now, I know you, Miss Cooper, and you, Mr Tallis. Perhaps you would be kind enough to introduce me to everyone else?'

Once the introductions were made, Mr Haughton led them to a table laden with sandwiches and cakes. 'Do help yourselves. Mrs Stockwell is a genius at making rations stretch. If we were in Fenthorpe Hall, I'd entertain you in the garden as it's such a lovely day. Perhaps you would care for a tour while we're here? Much of it has been turned over to vegetable beds, of course, but it's still very pretty. The officers very kindly let me visit the gardens even though they're living there now.'

Pearl helped herself to food, wondering how many weeks Mr Haughton and his housekeeper had had to starve them-selves to put on such a magnificent spread. It would have been considered lavish even before the war.

There was a bookcase near the table, and when Jenny wandered over to it, eyes alight, Mr Haughton asked her, 'Are you fond of books?'

'I love them.' All Jenny's awe had disappeared in her enthusiasm. 'You can never have too many books.'

'A sentiment I entirely agree with. Feel free to borrow anything that takes your fancy. A pity I can't show you my library up at the Hall, but most of my books are now packed away in the attics. I only have a few of my old favourites here.'

'Oh, I wouldn't want to take any if these are your favourites.'

'Nonsense. I know most of them off by heart. It would make me very happy to see them enjoyed by someone else. To be honest, the print is generally too small for me to manage nowadays. But some of these belonged to my late wife, and I just couldn't bear to see them locked away in the attic for heaven knows how long.'

So Mr Haughton was alone apart from his housekeeper. As Pearl watched him point out some books Jenny might enjoy, she wondered if he had invited the group because he felt lonely. This suspicion grew when she noticed a framed photograph on a table beside the open French windows. She paused to look at it. A sepia-tinted photo of a young man in uniform, it was too old to be a recent photograph, so she guessed it was from the Great War. The man looked very serious; Pearl thought the photograph must have been taken just after he had joined up. Although she didn't recognise the uniform, the wings on the man's chest revealed him to be a pilot in the Royal Flying Corps.

'I see you have made the acquaintance of Tom junior.'

Pearl jumped a little, not having noticed Mr Haughton approach. Jenny stood a little behind him, clutching three books to her chest. 'Oh, is this your son?'

Mr Haughton nodded. 'He was so proud to earn his wings. This was taken the day before he left to join his unit in France.'

'What does he do now?'

From the sudden stillness in Mr Haughton's expression, Pearl immediately knew the answer. 'Oh, I'm so sorry.'

Mr Haughton patted her shoulder. 'It was a long time ago. At least, I suppose it must seem a long time to you. It feels like only yesterday to me. Poor Tom was killed just three days after he arrived in France, shot down while he was on patrol.'

'How awful.'

'He died doing what he loved. I comfort myself with that. And it's why I like to take an interest in what you're all doing at RAF Fenthorpe. It feels like keeping Tom alive. He was fascinated by everything to do with aviation. In fact, one of the books this young lady has borrowed is one of his books about the theory of flight.'

Pearl resisted the urge to roll her eyes at Jenny. She had assumed Jenny had borrowed some novels, but she might have known she would choose some technical tome as well. 'You'll have to watch out for Jenny,' she said. 'She'll be a walking encyclopaedia before long if she carries on like this.'

They joined the others outside, and soon Mr Haughton seemed to have shaken off the melancholy caused by remembering his son and was praising their work on the *Bombshell*, telling them all they would be a credit to any newspaper. A little later, Mrs Stockwell joined them, carrying yet another cake. This one had a lit candle in the centre.

'Is it your birthday, Mr Haughton?' Pearl asked him.

'Yes, although you'll have to forgive me if I don't reveal my age. And please, call me Thomas.' Mr Haughton turned to his housekeeper. 'Really, Mrs Stockwell, I told you I didn't want to make a fuss.'

'Nonsense. Everyone deserves to be spoiled on their birthday.'

'Absolutely,' Pearl said. 'I wish you'd told us.' It was now becoming clear that the little party to celebrate the newspaper's success had, in fact, been an excuse to gather some company around him on his birthday. 'We would have brought you a gift.'

'And that's why I didn't tell you. Your delightful company is all the gift I need. If I'd told you, you'd have felt obliged to get me something, and I really have everything I need.'

Apart from company. Pearl's heart went out to him. He had lost his wife and his son. No wonder he threw himself into his work. 'Well, thank you for inviting us. We're having a lovely time, and it's an honour to celebrate your birthday with you.'

They all sang 'Happy Birthday' and watched Mr Haughton blow out the candle.

'Now,' Mr Haughton said, once they had eaten a slice of the delicious fruit cake, 'I hope no one is in a hurry to get back, because it would be my pleasure to show you around the grounds.' His eyes twinkled. 'I promise to keep you away from the house. I'm sure you're not in a hurry to bump into any of your officers.'

None of them needed to get back, and all confessed to a curiosity to see the gardens. True to his word, Mr Haughton kept them well away from the house. He also avoided the large vegetable plots, taking them instead to a secluded area beyond an orchard. He led them through an archway through a high yew hedge. 'There used to be a fine wrought-iron gate here, but it had to be melted down at the start of the war,' he told them.

The scent of roses hit Pearl before she saw where she was. They were in a compact garden, completely surrounded by the yew hedge. Gravelled pathways twisted through the garden, making it seem larger than it was, and every flower bed was filled with roses.

'Oh, how beautiful,' Pearl said, and the others murmured their agreement. She drew a deep breath. 'What a divine scent.' She bent down to smell the flower closest to her, a full Old English variety, with yellow petals streaked with a deep, fiery orange.

'I see you've found my favourite,' Mr Haughton said. 'The variety is called Heart of Hope, created in honour of one of the finest actresses of her day.' Mr Haughton's eyes were focused on a distant point. 'It was a great relief to me when I discovered the rose garden would not be dug up. It was painful to see the main garden dug up, of course, but I'll be able to replant when I get the house back. But there are some irreplaceable roses here, and I would have been devastated to lose them.'

'It's such a peaceful place.' She pointed at a bench placed opposite the yellow and orange rose. 'I could sit here for ever, smelling the roses and listening to the hum of the bees.'

'That's my favourite bench. And on days like this, when I'm not at the office, I allow myself half an hour to do just that.' Mr Haughton sat on the bench and beckoned for Pearl to join him.

Pearl hesitated, looking for Greg. A beautiful garden like this with lots of quiet nooks would be the perfect place to get him to herself for a while. However, Greg had walked on ahead with Geoff and appeared to be deep in conversation. She went to join Mr Haughton, trying not to show her dismay at Greg's apparent lack of desire to spend time alone with her.

'You seem lost in thought,' Mr Haughton said.

She gave a small shake of the head. 'Just thinking some things over,' she said. 'I'm sure you know how it is.'

'Indeed. Well, if the "things" you need to think over include your young pilot' – he inclined his head in Greg's direction – 'I don't think you have too much to worry about. I would say he's smitten with you.'

'Oh, I don't think… I mean, it's early days.'

Mr Haughton just smiled. 'I'm sure you know best.' Then he patted her arm, levered himself to his feet and went to join Jenny and Thea, brushing his fingers over his favourite rose as he went past.

Pearl watched him go, feeling too flustered to join the others just yet. Instead, she settled back on the bench, enjoying the warmth and the sweet scent of roses. Surely Mr Haughton was mistaken? While Greg had persisted in asking her out despite her initial refusals, he had never seemed downhearted, so she couldn't believe his feelings ran deep. As for her own heart, she would take a leaf out of Thea's book and take each day as it came. At least, that was her aim. Whether she could forget all worries about the future remained to be seen.

Chapter Eighteen

'I've got a great idea for your paper.'

Pearl put down her spoon and exchanged the briefest of glances with Jenny before nodding at the WAAF who had interrupted her breakfast. 'We've actually got a meeting at 1800. You'd be very welcome to come along and tell us about it.'

'Oh. I'd love to but I've arranged to do something else.'

'Not a problem. Just write down your idea and hand it in to one of the team. You'll find our names on the front page of the latest issue. If we like it, we'll be in touch to let you know how many words we'd like and the deadline.'

The girl blinked. 'Sure. Right. I'll do that, then.' She hurried away to join her friends on another table.

'And that's the last we'll hear from her,' Jenny said once the WAAF was out of earshot.

Pearl couldn't argue with that. It wasn't that she didn't welcome ideas, and she would have greeted a new member of the team with open arms, but she had learned the hard way that all too many people wanted to tell her about a brilliant idea they had for an article or story but far fewer of them were prepared to do the research and actually sit down to write it. 'It's like they think we just snap our fingers and the words magically appear on the page.'

It wasn't the first time she had said this, and Jenny simply acknowledged her complaint with a sympathetic tilt of the head. 'That's the price you pay for success.'

Pearl cheered up. She grinned across the table at her friend. 'We are a success, aren't we.'

'We certainly are.'

They had now released three issues, printing more copies each time and selling out. And, although there were plenty of people like the WAAF who had just approached Pearl, there were enough people who had been eager to contribute, either by joining the team or by offering to write an item. All in all, things were going well for Pearl. Not only was she seeing her journalism dreams coming true, albeit for a volunteer newspaper, she was enjoying her work in Flying Control and was earning praise from her seniors. Even Snaith had grudgingly admitted that she could be trusted to stand watch unsupervised. Above all, she was enjoying her time with Greg and was beginning to think she was falling in love with him. The only cloud on the horizon was the knowledge that he would begin operational flying any day now. Her consolation was that, now August had arrived, the nights were getting longer, which meant better cover for the aircraft as they crossed into Europe. She had dreaded operations resuming during the light summer nights when the enemy would have found it much easier to see them coming.

All in all, Pearl reflected as she finished her cereal, life in Fenthorpe was going well. She could even socialise with Thea without the evening ending in an argument.

When she climbed the stairs to Flying Control a few minutes later, however, she heard a hum of expectation, the rapid tapping of Morse keys and the chatter of teleprinters. Even before she walked into the room, she knew what that meant. The squadrons were flying ops that night. Her thoughts flitted briefly to the piece Greg's friend had written – she still didn't know his identity. How many empty beds would there be after this night's work? She settled at her desk, put on the headset and made an effort to concentrate. The best way she could help Greg and all the crews was to do her job to the best of her ability. Still, she couldn't resist studying the senior officers whenever they came into the office, and straining to hear in case they let slip that night's destination. None of them ever did, although tonight they didn't appear too grave, giving her hope Greg's mission would be straightforward.

When she got a short break a couple of hours later, she went up onto the roof to watch one of the Lancasters take off on its night flying test. Greg and his new crew had already completed theirs with no problems, so Pearl felt quite relaxed as she watched *D-Donald* soar into the air, covering her ears as it zoomed over the control tower. No matter how many times she saw it, she marvelled every time at the apparent ease with which the giant aircraft left the ground. Maybe it was Greg's enthusiasm rubbing off on her, but she couldn't watch a Lancaster take to the skies without admiring its elegant lines. Once you got over the sheer size, you couldn't deny the plane's beauty. Seeing them flying in formation like a flock of geese never failed to bring a lump to her throat.

'Feeling nervous?'

Pearl spun round, pressing a hand to her chest, only to relax when she saw Jenny. Her friend held a clipboard and was evidently on her way to take the readings from the rooftop weather station. 'I wasn't until you crept up on me. Trying to give me a heart attack?'

'Well, you didn't hear when I called your name.'

'I wouldn't have heard a foghorn over the racket of those engines. In answer to your original question, though, of course I'm nervous. Do you blame me?'

'Course not. I'm nervous too. Greg's crew is starting to feel like a family.'

'Oh? Anyone in particular?'

'For the last time – I like Edwin. I think we're going to be good friends. But I'm not ready for a relationship. There's so much to learn. I don't want to tie myself down too young.'

Pearl raised her hands in mock surrender. 'I know, I know. Sorry!' In the past few weeks, Pearl had started to wonder about Jenny's feelings for Edwin Holland, a new arrival to Fenthorpe, who was *C-Charlie*'s navigator. He had been keen to help out with the *Bombshell*, contributing some mathematical and logic puzzles, as well as writing an interesting guide to the night sky, telling readers what constellations and planets to look out for that month. Jenny, always eager for new books, had devoured the text on astronomy he had lent her. Pearl had thought the bookish Edwin would be a good match for Jenny, but Jenny had declared she had no desire to end up married with twenty children – her words – before she had had a chance to see more of the world. Although Jenny had never spoken much of her home life, Pearl wondered if it had coloured her view of marriage. Anyway, Jenny *was* very young, having joined the WAAF as soon as she turned eighteen. Pearl couldn't blame her for wanting to learn all she could in the WAAF to make up for the formal education she'd been denied.

Jenny leaned against the rail beside her. 'It's fine. I know you were only teasing. Anyway, I've got some news that should comfort you.'

'Oh yes?'

'I don't know where tonight's target is, but I overheard the Met Officer say there should be clear skies.'

'And that's good news? Doesn't that mean all the enemy fighters and anti-aircraft batteries will be able to see them?'

'It *is* good news. It means they'll have a clear view of the target with less likelihood of their bombing run going orey.'

'Going what?' By this time, Pearl was used to Jenny's occasional mispronunciations and could usually work out what she meant. She thought about it for a few seconds and then understood. 'Oh. You mean *awry*.'

'No! Don't tell me I've been saying it wrong all this time.' Jenny suddenly cringed. 'Oh no – I think I said it to Edwin the other day, and he didn't correct me. He must have thought I was an idiot.'

'No he doesn't. He must think you're really intelligent, or he wouldn't lend you all those technical books.'

Jenny's face cleared. 'You really think so?'

'I know it. Anyway' – Pearl brought the conversation back to Jenny's information about the clear skies – 'thanks for telling me the forecast. Let's hope *C-Charlie* has an easy run.'

Having listened to discussions among Greg's crew for some weeks now, she knew enough about bombing runs to know that if the bomb aimer couldn't get a clear view of the target, the pilot would be forced to circle the area and repeat the approach. Although she knew some bomb aimers dropped the bombs anyway, to get them clear of the flak at the earliest opportunity, she already knew enough of Fitz, *C-Charlie*'s bomb aimer, to know he would only release the bombs when he could see they were over the target and not a nearby school or hospital. While she would never dare to ask him how he felt about releasing destruction, she could tell it bothered him.

Greg had always been clear. 'We're all responsible,' he would say. 'The whole crew, including the scrambled eggs who send us there, the ground crews who keep our machines in working order, everyone. Our successes are everyone's successes, as are our failures.'

Pearl chuckled, remembering her reaction the first time she had heard of the senior officers being referred to as 'scrambled eggs' – owing, Greg told her, to the fancy gold braid decorating their caps. It was just like Greg, though, to see the bigger picture. At a time when bomber pilots were receiving the medals and not the rest of the crew, Pearl had come to deeply appreciate Greg's innate sense of fairness in refusing to accept all the praise just because he had piloted the plane. Although *C-Charlie*'s crew had only been together for a couple of months, Pearl had been moved by the level of trust they all had in their skipper. Of course, that could also be because Greg was the oldest by some years, earning him the affectionate nickname of 'Gramps'. But, having seen the team together, Pearl had faith that they would all do their jobs and obey Greg without question on a mission. Even Edwin, who, as a newly gazetted pilot officer, was actually the highest-ranked member of the crew.

Jenny pushed herself back from the railing where she'd been leaning. 'Anyway, I must get on, or I'll get in a row for being late with the readings.' She patted Pearl on the shoulder. 'Try not to worry about Greg. I'm sure he'll be fine.'

—

'Causeway to *C-Charlie*, pancake.'

'Now that's a welcome voice to hear.' Greg smiled as he put *C-Charlie*'s nose down and lined her up with the runway flares. He was careful not to let his concentration slip as he levelled out, and a second later felt the wheels touch down in a perfect landing.

'Nice one, Skipper,' Fitz said. 'I can't tell you how good it feels to have got our first successful mission under our belts.'

'Hear hear,' came Edwin's voice over the intercom. The other members of the crew joined in with their own congratulations along the lines of, 'Thanks, Gramps.' Finally, from Jack Knight, the tail gunner, came, 'Well done for evading that night fighter, Skipper. I nearly peed my pants when I saw it heading right for me.'

Greg was too busy concentrating on following directions into the correct dispersal pen to answer but, as soon as he had cut the engines, he released his seat harness with a relieved sigh and let the tension of the night drain from his muscles. 'Nice job, everyone,' he said. 'First round's on me in the Piebald Pony tomorrow.' Pearl would understand why he couldn't spend the evening alone with her.

Once he'd fully shut down the engines and spoken to the flight mechanic, telling him to check the tail for damage after it had picked up a line of bullet holes as they were making their escape from the target, he dragged himself onto the waiting bus with the rest of the crew. He nearly nodded off as it bounced over the rough perimeter track, and had to make an effort to rouse himself enough to scramble out and hand back his parachute and Mae West.

As he was standing by his locker, burning the letter to his parents, Fitz appeared at his shoulder. He handed him an envelope. 'Sorry, Skip,' he said. 'I picked this up by accident this morning but it's yours. I chucked it in my locker and forgot all about it. Hope it's nothing important.'

Greg looked at the handwriting but didn't recognise it. 'Thanks,' he said, stuffing it in his pocket. 'I doubt it's anything special. Come on, let's get debriefing over and done with.'

Exhaustion was well and truly setting in by the time the crew stumbled into the debriefing room, clutching the mugs of tea some WAAF volunteers had handed them. Looking round, Greg was relieved to see many of the other crews were already there.

He hated debriefing. For a start, it was depressing when it became clear that other crews had not made it back. But also, by this time he just wanted to fling himself into bed and sleep; instead he had to force his muzzy brain to recall details of a mission he often wanted to forget. At least this time the operation had been relatively straightforward and all had gone to plan.

He and his crew went to sit round a table just vacated by another crew. The intelligence officer, a brisk but kind young woman, handed them all cigarettes and waited while they lit them. Then by gentle but persistent questioning she coaxed the important details from them. The bomb aimer had had a clear view of the target and the munitions factory had already been ablaze by the time their bombs joined the inferno. They hadn't seen any friendly bombers go down, but the tail gunner was sure he had hit an enemy fighter, although none of the other crew could confirm it. Finally, when she was satisfied there was no more information to be squeezed from them, the intelligence officer released them, and they headed for their billets – Edwin to find a car to take him to Fenthorpe Hall and the others to their hut.

The trouble was, by the time Greg was in bed he found himself unable to sleep. Every muscle in his body ached from hours of handling the heavy controls and his eyes burned in their sockets, but his mind was suddenly alert. Knowing sleep would be impossible until he could coax his brain away from flying an imaginary plane, he slipped out of bed, quietly so as not to disturb the others, and groped for his battledress jacket, which he had draped over a chair. Feeling inside his pocket until he heard the faint crackle of paper, he pulled out the envelope Fitz had handed him. Then he picked up his torch from atop the bedside cabinet and slipped back into bed. Then, angling the torch so that it didn't shine into the faces of his hut-mates, he opened the letter and read.

Dear Flight Sergeant Tallis,

First I would like to thank you for the kind letter you sent to my parents after my brother, Max, was killed in action. As you can imagine, his death was a terrible blow to us all and we will always miss him. However, your thoughtful words at least reassured us that he didn't die alone and didn't suffer. Max was proud to be in the RAF and the day he was accepted as a crewman was one of the happiest of his life. His electrician's qualifications meant he could have accepted a safer trade as a member of the ground crew, but he always longed to fly and said he would never forgive himself if he passed up the opportunity for a trade that would take him into the air. Although it is small comfort, it helps to know he died serving his country and doing a job he loved.

He always spoke highly of you, saying he had complete faith in you as his skipper. Therefore, although this is difficult to write, I have decided to trust you with a problem. A few weeks ago, my parents finally received Max's personal effects. As sad as it was, it helped them to get his books and family photographs, and I know they will always treasure them. Max didn't own much yet he did have an item that was of great sentimental as well as monetary value. This was a gold pocket watch that had once belonged to our grandfather. Our father gave it to Max when he joined the RAF, and it was intended to be a family heirloom. You can imagine our dismay, then, when it was not returned with his other belongings. There was also a decorative gold tiepin that we couldn't find, although Max was always losing this so it might well have been mislaid before his death. It was in the shape of a four-leaf clover set with tiny emeralds and Max used to wear it as a lucky charm during his missions, so it's also possible it fell off when he was injured and is lost on the aeroplane he died in.

We are not so concerned about the tiepin, but the pocket watch is of great importance to my family. Last year I had a baby boy, and Max always said that, if anything happened to him, he would like his little nephew to have the watch. It is bad enough that he will grow up not knowing his uncle, and now it looks like he won't even have the pocket watch to remember him by. If there is anything you can do to help locate it, I would be very grateful. I enclose a photograph of Max holding it, to help you with identification. Although the photograph doesn't show it, the initials G.M.P.T. are engraved on the inside of the lid.

I do hope you will be able to help us.
Yours sincerely,
Beatrice Little

Greg pulled the photo from the envelope and stared at it. Already Max seemed like a distant memory, someone he had met years ago instead of a crewmate he had lost only a few months back. The photograph showed Max looking proud in his smartest RAF uniform, which looked so new it was clear that the photo was taken not long after he had joined, probably on his first leave. In his hand he held a large watch with the cover opened to show the watch inside. The watch fitted neatly into his palm, and it was on a chain that dangled from his fingers. He remembered seeing Max with it. The young radio operator could often be found in the evenings lovingly polishing it, turning it this way and that to admire the engraved fern pattern on the outer case. He also vaguely recalled the tiepin, having seen Max fasten it beneath his lapel before an operation. Try as he might, though, he couldn't remember Max putting it on before the mission that had resulted in his death. He might very well have lost it – Max was frequently losing things, always borrowing another's button stick or darning needle because he had mislaid his own. But while Max was careless with many of his possessions, he only let the watch out of his sight when flying, and Greg knew that he had stowed it in his locker before setting out on the fatal mission to Rostock. It was as though knowing of his tendency to lose items made him extra careful of something so precious.

Like Max's sister, Greg could dismiss the loss of the tiepin as a mishap or it falling into some joint in *T-Tommy*'s interior when his crewmates were fighting to save his life. Greg would talk to *T-Tommy*'s old crew, but he doubted it would turn up. Anyway, *T-Tommy*, along with all the other Manchesters in the squadron, had been taken away when the replacement Lancasters arrived. They had probably been stripped for spare parts by now, so, if the tiepin had lain unnoticed inside the plane, it was lost for ever.

The watch – now, that was more serious. Greg knew without a doubt it had been in Max's locker, and all Max's belongings from there would have been taken away by the Committee of Adjustment. In fact, now he thought back, he could remember seeing someone from the committee at the locker. It was clear that none of the other items in Max's locker, including money, had gone missing, so what had happened to the watch was a mystery. He would have to find a member of the committee and ask who had been responsible for clearing Max's belongings. But as all of his other valuables had been returned, Greg very much feared someone must have gone into the locker room and broken into Max's locker at some point during the night while the crews had been away. Everyone who knew Max knew about the watch. Greg would have to keep his ear to the ground to see if anyone had more money than usual.

He put the letter away, sleep even further away than when he had opened it. He sincerely hoped they wouldn't be flying another mission tomorrow. Or, rather, later that day, as it was already near dawn. Giving up on sleep completely, he rolled out of bed, collected his towel and wash kit, and went to the ablutions block for a shower.

Chapter Nineteen

'You look worried.' Pearl studied Greg's face anxiously. Usually you couldn't get him to stop waxing lyrical about the joys of flying Lancasters, and, when he had met her that afternoon and asked her to come for a walk with him, she had expected him to tell her what it had been like flying *C-Charlie* on its first bombing operation. Not that he would have been able to tell her any of the important details of the mission, but she had thought he would say how it had felt to fly *C-Charlie* in earnest.

Greg didn't reply at first, although she could see he was mulling over his answer. She weaved her arm round his, pressing herself to his side. They were walking along one of the lanes that wound around the outskirts of Fenthorpe. The leaves rustling on the hedgerows were now the dark green of high summer, and the sun was out, lighting the ripe wheat fields with a golden glow. Pearl tightened her grip on Greg's arm, grateful that the powers that be had decided RAF Fenthorpe would not be flying ops on the same day she had off, thus allowing her to share it with him.

Finally Greg sighed. 'I'm sorry. I've not been very good company.'

'Don't say that. You've been quiet, but that's understandable seeing as you're so tired. I'm still happy to be with you. If you don't feel like talking that's fine, but I thought you looked like something's weighing on your mind. If it would help to speak of it, I'm happy to listen.'

'There *is* something. I got a letter yesterday from the sister of my old wireless operator. The one who was killed in action when I flew *T-Tommy*. Max Turner.'

Max. The name was familiar and it took Pearl a moment to realise where she had heard it. 'Wait a minute. Isn't that the young man Thea went out with a few times?'

'You're right. I keep forgetting it was Thea poor old Max was besotted with. She was very kind to him.'

'Thea told me about him.' Pearl gave a little laugh. 'She said he was too young for her but she enjoyed his company and went out with him to stop his crewmates teasing him. I keep forgetting Thea's in her twenties and older than so many of the bomber crews. I always think of her as my baby sister.'

'Well, Max was very young. I mean, he acted young. There were other men on the crew no older than him in years but much more worldly wise. Max always seemed very young and innocent compared to the others.'

'What did his sister say?'

'Max had a pocket watch, a family heirloom, that didn't get returned with the rest of his belongings. He always put it in his locker before flying, even when doing training flights, but no one seems to know what happened to it. I had a word with someone on the Committee of Adjustment and he showed me the inventory of Max's possessions, but the watch wasn't mentioned.'

'What's the Committee of Adjustment?'

'Oh, it's horrible but necessary. They're the ones responsible for going through the lockers and quarters of those killed or missing and returning belongings to the families.'

Pearl thought of the article by Greg's mysterious friend – she was still no closer to learning his identity. 'That's what that "Empty Beds" piece was about. I think about that a lot. It really haunts me.'

'I know. One minute you're living in a hut full of men, the next it's been stripped bare. Then in no time at all it's full again with new crewmen.'

Pearl hugged his arm more tightly, not knowing what to say. She wouldn't be able to bear to live like that. She thought of life in Hut Three and tried to imagine returning to find it empty because everyone else had been killed that day or gone missing in action. How would it feel to see all of Jenny's books gone from her shelf and nothing but bare walls and a stark metal bed frame where she had created her little home away from home? And, although she wasn't so close with the other girls in the hut, she had grown to like them all – or at least tolerate, in Blanche's case. Domestic evenings, when they stayed in to clean the hut, mend their clothes and polish shoes and buttons, had become a time for cosy chatter. Losing them would be unthinkable.

Wishing she hadn't asked about the Committee of Adjustment, she said, 'Do you think someone's stolen Max's watch, then?'

'It's the only explanation. Someone must have gone through his locker while the crews were out on the mission.' Greg pressed his free hand to his temple. 'I've asked everyone I can think of today but, although several men saw Max put his watch in his locker, no one saw anyone remove it. Someone's stolen it, and I have no idea who. And the watch is probably long gone by now, sold to some unscrupulous dealer for a tidy sum.'

Greg's anger and bewilderment were obvious, and she completely understood why he felt that way. While the bomber crews were risking their lives, some nasty individual had taken advantage of their absence for his own gain. However, Pearl could immediately see the flaws in Greg's reasoning. For instance, no one else had reported any missing items, so it looked like only Max's locker had been broken into. But the thief would have had no way of knowing that Max was going to be killed that night, so why only target that locker? She would have liked to discuss it more but, seeing how upset Greg was, she decided not to add to his worry. 'Tell you what,' she said. 'The next afternoon we both have free, we'll go for a wander around Lincoln and look around any likely antiques dealers. Would you recognise the watch if you saw it?'

'I think so. And I could definitely identify it if I could see the initials inside the case.' A pause, then: 'Would you really do that?'

'Absolutely. I didn't know Max, but it makes my blood boil to think of someone stealing his things. It's like grave-robbing.'

'That was my reaction. It's been weighing on my mind all day. I've reported it to the RAF police, of course, but they didn't seem that interested in investigating.'

'But if we find the watch in Lincoln, they'll have to take notice.'

'Absolutely. Anyway, I can tell Max's sister we're looking into it. I really didn't want to have to tell her there was nothing we could do.'

'Good. Then we'll go to Lincoln as soon as possible.' Quite apart from wanting to help in any way she could, she found herself eagerly anticipating the chance to carry out a real investigation.

–

It was another week before they were both free to make the trip to Lincoln. Greg awoke to find Fenthorpe fog-bound. Knowing Pearl had come off night watch that morning, he wandered impatiently around the operations block, waiting for the news that would surely soon be forthcoming – that there would be no flying that day.

On what must have been his tenth circuit of the block, he met Flying Officer Ian Sheldrick, the station adjutant. Recalling Max's run-in with the adjutant, Greg made haste to salute, expecting it to be returned with no comment, and was therefore surprised when Sheldrick stopped. 'Word's reached me that you're asking after some missing items.'

'Yes, sir.' Greg explained about the letter he had received from Beatrice Little. 'I feel responsible,' he concluded. 'Max was a member of my crew, after all.'

'Very commendable, I'm sure,' Sheldrick said. 'Nevertheless, do bear in mind that this sort of thing isn't good for station morale. We can't have you accusing the ground crews of theft.'

'I haven't accused anyone of theft. I *did* ask *T-Tommy*'s ground crew if they had seen Max's tiepin but I don't for one minute think any of them stole it. I just wondered if it had fallen off Max when he was hit. I saw him wear it as a lucky charm sometimes, and I thought it might have dropped onto the floor when the lads were trying to save his life.'

'I suppose that's a possibility. What about this watch, though? Stolen from his locker, did you say? That's very serious. I'll ask around about it and see if anyone was seen hanging around the lockers that night. And the pin. An emerald four-leaf clover, did you say?'

'That's right, sir.'

'I'm sure I saw one of the WAAFs with something like that in church the other day. I can't remember her name but she's a pretty thing. Auburn hair. Arrived under a bit of a cloud as far as I remember. Not too fond of regulations. I'll mention it to the WAAF squadron officer.'

The stab of excitement Greg felt at a possible lead turned to dismay. Sheldrick seemed to be describing Thea. But it must be coincidence. Thea wasn't the only auburn-haired WAAF, and plenty of them had a reputation for testing the limits of what were, after all, very restrictive regulations. He hated to think Pearl's sister might have anything to do with Max's missing valuables.

But once he'd thanked the adjutant and returned to the operations block to find that operations were, indeed, off, he couldn't forget that Max had been out with Thea a few times, so if anyone knew of the valuable items he possessed it would be her. He went to find Pearl with a heavy heart.

Pearl had already applied for a late pass that day, and had arranged to meet Jenny and Thea at the Saracen's Head in the evening. When she woke after a short sleep following her night watch, her spirits lifted in contrast to the fog, knowing Greg was bound to be grounded. She had hardly seen him all week, so she eagerly anticipated a whole afternoon in his company.

Sure enough, when she reached the NAAFI he was already there and confirmed he was free to make the trip to Lincoln. 'Let's go now,' he said. 'I'll buy you lunch in Lincoln as an advance thank you. I still can't believe you're willing to spend a damp, foggy day traipsing around antiques dealers.' He seemed to be in a gloomy mood, but it was probably just a reflection of the weather.

'It's because I care about you.' More than care. The strength of her feelings for Greg was frightening, considering she had no idea where it was going. Greg had not spoken of love, and, remembering how cheerfully he had taken her earlier rejections, she found it hard to believe he felt as deeply about her. She had started going out with him as a bit of fun. Her feelings hadn't been supposed to turn this serious so quickly, and even telling him she cared seemed too much. He looked taken aback and awkward, so to lighten the moment she laughed and added, 'Plus I get to look at lots of shiny jewellery and pretend I have enough money to buy something. Do you think the dealers would let me try anything on? I fancy myself in a diamond necklace.'

Greg's expression cleared. 'I'd like to see you in a tiara. Are we going to use assumed names? You can be Lady Esmerelda Ponsonby-Smythe.'

'Good grief. That makes me sound about ninety. Anyway, I don't think I can carry off a title. How about Lucinda Makepeace, whose father made a fortune from the brewery trade?'

'Perfect. What about me? And don't try making me the Earl of anywhere. I can't be anything other than Australian with this accent.'

Pearl regarded him while she thought, pleased to see him looking more cheerful. 'Actually, you ought to give your real name in case any dealers offer to get in touch. But there's no reason you can't have a made-up background. You could be the owner of Tallis Airways.'

'I like it. Very well, Miss Makepeace, shall we go?'

They took Greg's motorbike – Pearl being more used to travelling in the sidecar by this time – and were soon in Lincoln, which was swathed even more deeply in fog than Fenthorpe had been. The mist swirled through the streets, adding to the air of mystery and intrigue Pearl was already associating with their visit. After a quick lunch at the Bishop's Pal, they ventured outside into the murk and began their search for jewellery shops and antiques dealers.

It didn't take long to find their first one, on a side street near the top of Steep Hill. Pearl, pleasantly full after a huge bowl of a tasty vegetable and pearl barley soup, was keen to get started.

The moment they walked into Fortescue and Sons Fine Antiques, Pearl sincerely hoped this wasn't the right place, because they were greeted by a portly elderly man with fluffy white hair and beard. She would have hated to think badly of anyone who looked like Father Christmas. She glanced around the dimly lit interior, half expecting to see elves hard at work making toys. There were no elves, only rank after rank of glass cabinets with gleaming windows, displaying fine bone china, glass ornaments, jewellery and, yes, clocks and watches. All the timepieces were working, the constant ticking adding to the sense that, somewhere out of sight, toymakers were busy creating clockwork marvels.

'Good afternoon,' the man said. 'I'm Mr Fortescue junior. How can I help you?'

Pearl was tongue-tied, trying not to wonder how old Mr Fortescue senior was. Thankfully Greg launched into the story they had rehearsed over lunch. 'G'day. We're just looking.'

Pearl recovered her voice and took Greg's arm. 'Now, don't be shy, darling.' She smiled at Mr Fortescue, hoping she wasn't overacting. 'I promised Greg a present for his birthday. He's going to be thirty. Such a sober-sounding age. I want to get him something special, and Daddy says he's just paid me my allowance. What do you think, darling – cufflinks? Or a lucky charm maybe?' She said in an aside to the proprietor, 'He's a pilot, you know. I'm so proud of him.'

Greg choked, and, fearing he would give the game away by laughing, she steered him away from Mr Fortescue to look into the cabinets. She pointed at the first likely objects she could see. 'These tiepins are pretty. How about one of these?'

Greg appeared to examine them intently for a moment, then shook his head. 'No point,' he said. 'I can't wear one with my uniform. Same goes for cufflinks.'

They walked around the shop admiring everything they looked at, having agreed beforehand that making a beeline straight for the watches might look suspicious to a guilty dealer. Everything was beautifully polished and cared for, and Pearl would have loved to spend longer looking at everything. She couldn't forget the real reason they were there, though, so she finally paused by the cabinet containing pocket watches. 'How about a watch? You would look very distinguished carrying a watch on a chain.' She peered into the cabinet. None of them looked like the one in the photo Greg had shown her but she waited for him to join her.

'That's a good idea.' He studied the contents of the shelves. Pearl could tell by the minute relaxation in his features that Max's watch wasn't on display. 'These are all in silver cases, though. I'd prefer gold.' He turned to Mr Fortescue. 'Do you have any gold ones?'

'I'm afraid not, sir.' He tried to persuade Greg that one of his silver watches was the finest example of its type, but Greg was having none of it. 'It's got to be gold. A man of my standing needs to be seen with the very best.' He told Mr Fortescue how to contact him, then, after asking him to let him know if he got any gold watches in, he took Pearl's arm and they left.

They visited two more antique dealers, with similar results. The second shop did actually have a very fine gold pocket watch, and, although Pearl could immediately see it wasn't Max's, the persistent salesman took it out of the cabinet for Greg to examine. As Greg had already announced he wanted a gold watch, Pearl was starting to worry they would end up having to buy it, although she had no idea how they would be able to afford the hefty price tag. Thankfully, Greg spotted a minute scratch on the back and declared it substandard.

Pearl burst into a fit of giggles the moment they were out of sight of the shop. 'Oh my goodness, I thought I was going to have to buy it. Well done for spotting the scratch or I'd have been forced to admit I was penniless.'

'It would have made an entertaining scene for the proprietor. You'd have had to break down and confess your father had cut off your allowance.'

'And then you'd have raged at me, saying you'd never have got involved with me if you'd known I didn't have any money.'

'Good thing we're not rich, then. At least you know I'm not going out with you for your money.'

No. But Pearl was starting to wonder why he still wanted to go out with her. It couldn't still be gratitude for the time she had talked him down to a safe landing. The trouble was, the more she saw of him the stronger her affection for him was becoming. The wild behaviour that had put her off at first had turned out to be a way of coping with the danger he faced daily and the frequent loss of his friends. Now she knew him better she saw his kindness and thoughtfulness. And his passion for flying was attractive. But although Greg clearly enjoyed her company, she couldn't help comparing herself with the other girls on the station, many of whom were prettier than her and much more fun company.

By this time they were on The Strait, the narrow lane linking the bottom of Steep Hill with the high street. The section they were in was barely wider than an alley. Seeing a poky shop selling second-hand jewellery, Pearl took Greg's arm, not wanting to think too much about why he still wanted to go out with her. 'Let's look in here. We don't have long before the shops shut, so we mustn't waste time.'

She didn't hold out much hope for this shop, though. Its windows were grimy and the sign hanging above the door was peeling, making it hard to make out the name in the dim light of the alley.

Greg squinted up at it. 'Keyes's Emporium. A grand name for a dingy shop. Still, since we're looking for stolen property, maybe it's a better bet than the others.'

They were greeted by a young woman who looked to be in her mid-thirties. She was dressed in an elegant navy blue costume, with glimpses of gold at her wrist and throat revealing that business must once have been good, even if the war was making things hard for everyone. She introduced herself as Mrs Keyes, the wife of the owner.

Pearl and Greg went through the same routine as before, gradually homing in on the small display of watches. Pearl immediately felt her heart fall, for none of the pieces on display resembled Max's.

'Are these the only ones you have?' she asked Mrs Keyes, once they had examined and dismissed the available timepieces.

'I'm afraid so. If you leave me your address, I'd be happy to contact you if we get anything suitable in.'

As Greg had wandered to the rear of the shop, Pearl took it upon herself to give Mrs Keyes his details. Then she called to Greg, 'Come along, darling. We might have time to look in one more place.' She was making the most of calling him 'darling' that day, as she wouldn't dream of addressing him with such an endearment usually. It presumed a greater depth of feeling than she was prepared to admit.

Greg's voice came in reply, although she couldn't see him. Keyes's Emporium was one of those old-fashioned shops that was larger than its exterior suggested, being far longer than it was wide. Greg's muffled voice seemed to come from the remotest depths of the shop. 'Come here. I think I've found something.' His voice held a tone of suppressed excitement that set Pearl's pulse racing. She ventured into the shadowy recesses of the shop with Mrs Keyes on her heels.

'It would be wonderful if your young man has found something he likes. I do like to support our men in uniform. My husband's in the army, you know.'

They found Greg not in the main shop, but peering through a doorway into the room beyond. The door was ajar and, following his gaze, Pearl could see a table with several items upon it. One was clearly a gold watch and, certainly at first glance, bore a close resemblance to the missing one. Its case was open, and she craned her neck, trying to see if there were any initials engraved on the inside of the lid, but from the angle she was at the reflection from the overhead light made it impossible.

'Are you preparing that watch for sale?' he asked. 'It does look like exactly the thing I'm after.'

'Oh dear.' Mrs Keyes pressed a beringed hand to her chest, looking distressed. 'I will, of course, be offering it for sale later, but I'm waiting for it to be valued. You see, I'm just running the shop for my husband while he's away with the army. He used to deal with valuing the items we get. I have a brother who knows about antiques, and he visits every now and again to help out with that side of the business. I do have an assistant who does the buying, but I always like to get my brother to take a proper look at everything before I put it up for sale. I'm not terribly good with numbers, you see.' She gave a self-deprecating laugh. 'My assistant, Mr Bright, does the bookkeeping for me, and I get my brother to run an eye over it when he visits. Between you and me, I don't know how honest Mr Bright is, and my brother offered to keep an eye on him. I wouldn't want to accuse him of anything without evidence, and my husband trusted him. Anyway, it's so difficult to get good workers these days.'

'Can I take a look?' Greg asked. 'If I like it, perhaps you would reserve it for me until you can get it valued?'

Mrs Keyes appeared to hesitate, then said, 'I suppose it wouldn't hurt.' She went into the room and brought the watch out to Greg. He examined it carefully and, when he looked at the inside of the case, his mouth tightened. Glancing up at Pearl, he gave a barely perceptible nod. 'Where did you get this?'

'Actually I'm not sure. I wasn't here the day it was brought in. It was Mr Bright who was working in the shop that day.'

'Didn't he tell you anything about the man who sold it to him?'

Mrs Keyes frowned 'What business is it of yours, anyway?'

Greg chewed his lip, and Pearl knew he was wondering what to tell Mrs Keyes. Pearl couldn't see any option but to tell her the watch was stolen. If her assistant had bought it, she could be completely innocent. Greg had evidently reached the same conclusion, for he said, 'I'm afraid we haven't been completely honest with you, Mrs Keyes. You see, we've been looking for this very watch. It was stolen from a member of my crew at RAF Fenthorpe.'

Mrs Keyes's hand flew to her mouth. 'Oh my goodness, how dreadful. I had no idea. What are you going to do?'

'I'm afraid I'm going to have to hand this to the police. They'll want to question Mr Bright.'

'I suppose your crewman will be pleased to have it back, but it's going to be a real blow for my business.' Mrs Keyes sank onto a chair and dabbed her eyes with a handkerchief. 'Oh dear, what will my husband say? I was so sure I could manage the business in his absence but I've made such a mess of things.'

Pearl was moved to pity. She patted the woman's shoulder. 'Don't worry, Mrs Keyes. If the police can catch the thief, they might be able to reclaim the money your assistant paid for it.' A thought occurred to her. 'You said you weren't sure of Mr Bright's honesty. What if he knew he was dealing in stolen goods?'

'Do you really think so?'

Pearl threw Greg a helpless look.

Greg closed the watch case with a snap and came to stand beside Pearl. 'That's for the police to decide. It's in their hands now.'

'Yes, I suppose it is.' Mrs Keyes turned pleading eyes onto Greg. 'Please tell your crewman I had no idea the watch was stolen.'

'I wish I could. He was killed in action.' Seeing Mrs Keyes clutch her chest, Greg evidently repented of his harsh words, for he said, 'His family will be very happy to have it back. I'll be sure to pass on your message.'

'Oh, thank you. And do pass on my condolences, too.' Mrs Keyes dabbed her eyes again, and looked on the verge of hysterics. She made no objection to Greg taking the watch away with him, even though Pearl had worried she might suspect she was being conned.

'I need to hand this straight to the police,' Greg told Pearl when they left the shop a short while later. 'Do you want to come with me, or would you prefer to wait for me at the Saracen's Head? The others should be there by now.'

Pearl elected to go straight to the Saracen's Head, so Greg went off alone to make his report, promising to meet her at the bar as soon as possible. She felt sorry for Mrs Keyes, who was clearly horrified at what had happened. Pearl wasn't clear on the law regarding handling stolen goods, but she hoped the poor woman wouldn't get into trouble.

However, once the excitement was over, Pearl couldn't help thinking how the afternoon's events would make a good report for the *Bombshell*. Now, that would be serious reporting, better than just writing about the news of the various sports and clubs at RAF Fenthorpe. As she wandered down the high street to the Saracen's Head, she was already drafting the report in her head.

Chapter Twenty

Once the police had finished with the watch, Max's sister was delighted to get it back, and she wrote Greg a letter brimming with gratitude. The police did what he considered to be a shamefully lacking investigation into how the watch had found its way to the shop in Lincoln and concluded that Max must have lost it before his last flight. They refused to believe Greg when he insisted that Max always left it in his locker when flying, and, as Greg couldn't swear to seeing the watch in the days before the fateful mission, concluded Max must have had his pockets picked while on a night out in Lincoln. The only person who was punished was Mrs Keyes's assistant, who received a fine and was dismissed from his job. The police did investigate Mrs Keyes's shop but could find no other evidence that they had been dealing in stolen goods, so the investigation was left there.

'It's as though no one wants to believe anyone could have stolen something from a crew member's locker,' Greg complained to Pearl two weeks later when it was clear the case had been closed. 'It's like they're refusing to investigate in case they discover the unthinkable – that there really is a thief in Fenthorpe.'

'What are you going to do?' Pearl reached across the table and squeezed his hand. They were once more in the cafe in the Regal Cinema, overlooking the high street in Lincoln.

Seeing the care and concern in Pearl's face eased the tight knot that had formed in his stomach when he had heard the news earlier that day. He was coming to depend on Pearl more and more as each day passed. He had first been attracted to her by the sound of her voice and her calmness and then, when he had seen her for the first time, he had admired her good looks. But the more he came to know her and her determination to succeed, combined with her deep desire to support and nurture the lucky few she was close to, the deeper his feelings had grown. In fact, he knew he was falling in love with her. The only thing that stopped him shouting his feelings from the rooftops was the knowledge that his odds of survival were poor. This gave him two reasons to hesitate. Firstly, he thought it was unfair to draw her into a deeper relationship because he hated to think of her grieving for him should he be killed. The second reason was more selfish. If he asked her to marry him – something he was starting to long for – how could he be sure that, if she agreed, it was out of love and not just pity that he was likely to die soon? If they did marry, he wanted to be certain she came to the marriage with a whole heart.

'There's nothing I can do but remain vigilant,' he said. 'I made it clear I wasn't happy with the case being closed, and if I hear about anything else going missing I'll make sure they take it seriously.'

'I wish I hadn't published that story now,' Pearl said. In the edition of the *Bombshell* that followed the prosecution of Mrs Keyes's assistant, she had reported it, taking the angle that the bomber crews could be assured that nothing had been taken from the lockers.

'I don't know. It might be for the best.'

'Why?'

Greg stirred his tea while marshalling his thoughts. 'It's like this,' he said eventually. 'If we acted as though we thought there really *was* a thief in Fenthorpe, it would put him on his guard. But since everyone's acting like the matter is closed, he might be more careless. Rest assured if anything else goes missing, I'm going to catch him. He'll wish he'd never been born.'

Pearl gave him a little smile. 'Just promise to give me an exclusive for the *Bombshell*.'

'You can count on it.'

Although Greg remained vigilant, weeks passed and he heard not as much as a whisper that anything else had gone missing. At the end of November, he and his crew got a week's leave, and Pearl managed to wangle a forty-eight-hour pass for the final weekend. He had hoped she might invite him to stay with her in Shrewsbury, but she seemed reluctant and suggested they meet in Llandudno instead, saying she wanted to show him the seaside town she had loved as a child. On a whim, he spent the first part of his leave in Criccieth in North Wales, having seen a picture of the castle and thinking it looked an interesting place to visit. He had enjoyed a few days of long walks by the sea, admiring the dramatic mountain scenery across the bay, then caught the train to Llandudno on the Friday to meet Pearl.

They spent the weekend strolling along the seafront and climbing the Great Orme. Standing atop the high headland with Pearl's hand in his, gazing at the tiny streets and buildings far below, he felt as though the war was nothing but a distant dream. But once they climbed back down, he became increasingly aware that their time alone was slipping away. From then on, every moment together was bittersweet as he became ever more certain he was in love with her, but the uncertainty of his life still made him hold his tongue. Yet he couldn't prevent his mind drifting to the future, thinking how much he looked forward to more weekends like that one. When they returned to Fenthorpe, however, reality kicked in and he ruthlessly suppressed those thoughts. But where before he had almost resigned himself to the prospect of death, now he felt fear. Fear that a beautiful future could be torn from him.

Returning to operational flying was almost a relief. When he was at the Lancaster's controls, he was able to push his anxiety to the back of his mind, needing all his concentration to get *C-Charlie* to the target and back. It was only on the days when they were stood down that the fear gnawed at him from the inside, making him indulge in high-jinks when he was out with his crewmates. Because he had to show the world he wasn't afraid.

The day after the December edition of the *Bombshell* arrived in Fenthorpe, he went to the Piebald Pony with Pearl, Thea and the rest of the editorial team. It had become their custom to go out together to celebrate another successful edition. This time they had something extra to celebrate, for Pearl had passed her boards and been promoted to leading aircraftwoman. She proudly displayed her new propeller badge on her sleeve and her face glowed as everyone drank a toast in her honour.

After everyone had drained their glasses, Greg went to the bar to buy another drink for himself and Pearl. As he waited to be served, he couldn't help overhearing the conversation between Trevor Banks, a young gunner from Jamaica, and Norah, the landlady.

'Where's Steve this evening?' Norah was saying as she pulled a pint. 'The pair of you are usually joined at the hip.'

'He's... he didn't make it.'

Norah slopped beer over the counter, but ignored it as she stared at Trevor in dismay. 'I'm so sorry, duck.' She finally noticed the pool of beer and wiped it up, shaking her head sadly. 'I don't think I'll ever get used to it. Seeing someone as right as rain one day and gone the next. You will let me know if there's anything I can do, won't you? I was fond of Steve.'

'We all were.' Trevor pulled some coins from his pocket and handed Norah a shilling. 'Actually I could do with some advice,' he said while Norah opened the cash register to get his change.

'Ask away. There you are, duck – tuppence change. You don't mind if I serve Flight Sergeant Tallis, here, do you?'

And while she got Greg's drinks, Greg listened as Trevor explained his problem. 'You see, Steve always made me promise to take care of his fiancée if anything happened to him. He showed me where he kept his savings – in a box in his locker – and said I was to take it for his girl in Jamaica. He even left a letter to me with those instructions so there would be no argument about me taking the money. She doesn't have any close family, and his mother doesn't like her, so he couldn't depend on her to look out for her. But when I went to his locker, it had already been emptied.'

Here Greg couldn't help but interrupt. 'Sorry to butt in but did you speak to anyone on the Committee of Adjustment? They'd understand if you showed them the letter.'

'I did. But they said no money was there. The box was in his locker, but it was empty. The man I spoke to said Steve must have spent it and didn't believe me when I said he wouldn't have done that.'

There was nothing Greg could do apart from give Trevor a sympathetic look. He paid Norah, collected his drinks and returned to his table.

Pearl was occupied in an argument with Jenny over how to pronounce hyperbole. 'You're pulling my leg,' Jenny was saying as he took his seat. 'It has to be hyper bowl.'

'I promise I'm not joking.'

'But why?' Jenny's voice was almost a wail.

'I'm with you, Jenny,' Thea put in. 'I'm convinced English spellings were made up by people who want to make themselves feel superior to ordinary people.'

While the conversation carried on around him, Greg brooded over his drink. Was it possible that someone had broken into Trevor's friend's locker? If so, was it the same person who had taken Max's watch, or mere coincidence? Even if it was the same person, what could he do about it? The RAF police had apparently dismissed Trevor's report, but Greg had no reason to doubt it. Trevor and Steve had been close friends, as Norah had said; you hardly saw one without the other. If Steve had spent or moved the money, Trevor would have known.

'Penny for your thoughts.'

'What?' Only now did Greg realise that there was a lull in the conversation, and Pearl was regarding him with raised eyebrows. 'Sorry. I was miles away.'

'I could see. Anything the matter?'

'Nothing really. I was just—' But after all, Pearl had gone out of her way to help find Max's watch. Leaving her in the dark would be unfair. 'Ah well, I suppose it won't hurt to tell you.' And he filled her in on what he had heard at the bar.

A pucker formed between Pearl's brows as he spoke. 'Do you think the same thief is still breaking into the lockers?'

'I don't know what to think. Anyway, it's not like looking for a stolen watch. I can't see any way of finding stolen money.'

'Not unless we see someone throwing money around all of a sudden.'

'I expect any thief would have more sense than that. He wouldn't want to draw attention to himself.'

Pearl's eyes opened wide. 'That's a good point. What if the thief decided to stop stealing valuables like watches because they're too easy to trace? I mean, if he's been stealing money instead, maybe no one would notice. Trevor only noticed Steve's money had gone because he'd promised to send it to Steve's fiancée.'

'Speak for yourself. I'd notice if someone had stolen my money. I haven't got that much to spare.'

Pearl sat up suddenly. 'Unless the thief is only targeting the lockers of dead crewmen.'

Greg felt sick. He was convinced Pearl was right.

But Thea, who had also been listening intently, shook her head. 'I don't see how it could be done. By the time anyone on the ground hears that someone's bought it, the bombers have started to return, and the crews are filing in and out of the locker rooms. The thief would never be able to break into a locker without someone seeing.'

Greg couldn't dispute that, although he couldn't shake off the feeling that Pearl was right and he was missing something. Making an effort to shake off his misgivings, he changed the subject to the content of the next edition of the *Bombshell*, something they all had strong opinions about, meaning that everyone soon forgot about the missing money.

Later on, after they had left the pub, Thea stopped halfway down the street. 'Bother. I've forgotten my jacket. It's my best one, too.'

'I'll get it,' Greg offered. 'Don't wait for me. I'll catch you up.'

He jogged back into the pub and straight away saw Thea's forgotten tunic, hanging over the back of her chair. He grabbed it by the lapels, and gave it a jerk when one of the sleeves got caught. The action made him grip the lapel tighter, and something pricked his index finger.

Uttering an oath, he dropped the jacket and examined his finger, cursing all the more when he saw a bead of bright blood welling up. He dabbed it with his handkerchief, then picked up the jacket, more carefully this time, and examined it to see what he had caught his finger on.

A green and gold glint beneath the lapel caught his eye. Turning it back, he froze when he saw what was unmistakeably a tiepin, stuck into its underside where it would be concealed. The tiepin was gold with a four-leaf clover at its head. Each leaf held a tiny emerald.

The noise of the pub faded as he gazed at the pin, feeling sick. This looked exactly like the tiepin Max's sister had described. Greg had forgotten about it, as Beatrice Little had been more bothered about the missing watch, but surely there couldn't be two identical pins on the same bomber station. How had Thea got it?

Movement returned to his limbs. Without knowing what he was going to do or say, he marched out of the pub and then once outside broke into a run, straining to catch up with Pearl, Thea and Jenny. They had been joined by another group of WAAFs, who he vaguely recognised and knew lived in the same hut as Pearl. He didn't let the audience stop him, though. The girls, obviously hearing his footsteps rapidly gaining on them, turned to look as he ran up.

'What on earth—?' Pearl began.

He didn't wait for her to finish. Waving the pin dangerously close to Thea's face, he demanded, 'Where did you get this?'

Thea's face turned crimson. 'Oh, I' – she darted a shifty glance at Pearl – 'I got it from a friend.'

To Greg, that glance was an admission of guilt. 'Who from?' He held on to the hope that someone else had given it to her and she had accepted the stolen item unwittingly.

'I don't want to say.' If anything, Thea's face burned an even brighter red.

'You stole it.'

'Greg!' Pearl looked horrified. 'Take that back this instant.'

Thea shot Pearl an exasperated glare. 'I can stand up for myself, thank you very much.' Then to Greg: 'I think you owe me an apology.'

'I will if you explain how you come to be wearing Max Turner's tiepin. Something, I might add, that his sister reported as missing along with a watch that turned up in a shop in Lincoln. Did you have anything to do with that as well?'

'What do you mean, "as well"?' Thea's arms were ramrod straight at her sides, her fists clenched. 'If you think I'm a thief, go ahead and say it.'

The other girls from Pearl's hut were listening, saucer-eyed. One of them – an elegant redhead Greg recognised from the administration section – turned to her friends. 'Well! I would never have spoken to her if I'd known she was a thief. Come on. We don't want to mix with the likes of *her*.' She stalked off with her nose in the air, followed by her friends, leaving only Pearl, Jenny and Thea with Greg. All three were staring daggers at him.

'Look, I was taken by surprise and I spoke hastily,' he said to Thea. 'I'm sorry I didn't give you a chance to explain. But this pin should have been returned to Max's family, and I do need to know who gave it to you.'

'Fine. Max gave it to me.' Thea turned to Pearl. 'That night you saw me in Lincoln.'

'Oh Thea. I thought you said you hadn't led him on.'

'I didn't.' Thea's voice was high with indignation. Turning her back on her sister, she said to Greg. 'If you must know, this is how it happened. Max said he wanted to give me a gift to remember him by if anything should happen to him. He was a sweet boy and I liked him' – here she raised her voice, her next words clearly aimed at Pearl – 'and even though I'd made it clear I would never love him, he insisted he wanted to give me something.' She modulated her tone and carried on in a more even voice. 'And he gave me this.' She pointed at the tiepin still in Greg's hand. 'He said he knew I didn't love him, but that didn't stop him loving me. And he made me promise to wear it always. And I always have. I had to wear it under my lapel because I didn't want to get in a row over my uniform. I've spent enough time in jankers.'

'I'll say,' Pearl muttered.

Thea turned a fierce glare on her. 'And you can stay out of it too.' She turned back to Greg and, just for a moment, before she schooled her features, her chin wobbled, and he thought she looked like a lost little girl. 'If I'd known his sister had missed it, I'd have explained about it when I wrote to his parents. I thought they'd have known but I suppose he was fed up of being teased about me. I liked having it because he was my friend. The only person who didn't try to change me or lecture me every time I made a mistake.' Here Greg saw Pearl wince. 'But anyway,' Thea continued, 'keep the bloody thing for all I care. I don't want it if everyone believes I'm a thief.'

Dashing a hand across her eyes, she stumbled away.

There was silence for a moment. Jenny cast glances at Greg and Pearl, biting her lip. Finally she said, 'I'd better go after her,' and ran to catch Thea up.

Now it was just him and Pearl, and he didn't like the way Pearl was looking at him. He doubted there were any kisses coming his way.

'You never mentioned a missing tiepin,' she said.

'Max's sister didn't think it was so important. She thought it likely he had lost it. Either that or he'd worn it as a lucky charm and it had dropped off when he'd been hit and it was lost in the bomber's fuselage.'

'Yet the moment you found it, you immediately accused Thea of being a thief.' Pearl's voice was cold.

'I made a mistake. I should have asked her about it instead of accusing her, I know.'

'I'll say.'

Greg had never seen Pearl this angry. Had never guessed she could *get* this angry. 'I'm sorry. What more can I say?' He bitterly regretted not thinking it through before storming after Thea. He could explain to Pearl that he hadn't slept well and was still exhausted after a mission that he had, after all, only returned from in the early hours of that morning. But that sounded too much like he was making excuses for his behaviour. Pearl was often tired after a night watch, yet she didn't storm around the station accusing people of being thieves.

'I don't know if there's anything you *can* say. You called my sister a thief. How do you think I feel?'

'Look, I know you're upset, and it's only natural you'd want to defend your sister. But none of this reflects on you. Thea could rob every bank in Lincoln, and it wouldn't change how I feel about you.'

He thought this sounded like a huge romantic gesture, so couldn't understand the flare of rage in her eyes.

'I don't believe it. You still don't trust her.'

'What? No. That's not what I said.'

'I brought her up, you know. If you think Thea could steal, what do you think of me?'

Greg couldn't understand. Hadn't he just said his opinion of Pearl was unaffected by his opinion of Thea? He was starting to think he shouldn't have had that second pint of bitter. Trying to make sense of Pearl was like trying to see a landing strip when it was blanketed in thick fog. 'I don't think Thea stole the pin. I told you. I jumped the gun. Thea's explanation was reasonable.' But even as he said it, he remembered Thea's guilty glance in Pearl's direction when he had confronted her.

His expression must have betrayed him, for Pearl put her hands on her hips, scowling. 'I don't believe this. You're still not entirely convinced of her innocence, are you? I can't face you at the moment. I'm going back to my hut.'

And without waiting for him to say anything else, she stalked up the road after the others. Greg toyed with the idea of catching her up and trying to get her to listen, but he seemed to keep saying the wrong thing. It was probably best to wait until he saw her again before trying to explain himself. Instead he contented himself with following her at a distance, keeping an eye on her to make sure she reached the WAAF guardroom safely. Only when she was safely there did he make his way to his own billet.

—

Pearl stormed into Hut Three and flung her things down on her bed. Jenny wasn't there, although Pearl could see her uniform already hanging neatly on the little rail by her bed. She had probably gone to the ablutions block.

The others were there, though, and Pearl could guess what they had been talking about by the way conversation stopped when she arrived.

After an awkward minute or two of silence, Blanche, who had been brushing her hair, approached. 'I just want you to know that whatever your sister has done, we don't hold it against you.'

Pearl bristled. 'Thea hasn't done anything. She's not a thief.'

Blanche gave her a look that could only be described as pitying. 'You don't know that for sure. It's no secret she was transferred from Waddington because she was always getting into trouble.'

'Not for theft! Yes, she's been on jankers for being late, but she's hardly the only one. She's got a good heart.'

And had she ever said that to Thea? Shame twisted deep inside when she thought of all the times she had lectured her sister about her behaviour, yet she could barely remember a time she had praised her. Or told her how much she loved and valued her. No wonder she always seemed to put Thea on the defensive.

Blanche curled her lip. 'Oh come on. I heard what your Australian chap said – she was wearing a pin that had been stolen from a dead crewman's locker. You can't deny it. Unless you think your boyfriend planted it on her?'

'Of course he didn't. I admit she had the pin but that was because she was friends with Max, whose it was, and he gave it to her.'

'And you believe her?'

'Yes.'

'So do I.' Pearl hadn't seen Jenny come in, but now she stood at her shoulder, looking for all the world like she was prepared to take on Blanche in a fight. And anyone else who dared upset Pearl. This was a side to Jenny Pearl hadn't seen before. 'Thea's my friend,' Jenny said. 'I know she would never steal from anyone, let alone one of the bomber crews. If you bothered to get to know her instead of judging her from rumours, you'd trust her too.'

Blanche shook her head and sneered, but whatever she might have been about to say was interrupted when the door swung open and Helen walked in. 'Get a move on, you lot. Lights out in ten minutes.'

In the scramble to get ready for bed, no more was said on the subject. Pearl did murmur a heartfelt thank you to Jenny before dashing out to the ablutions block. Before she left, though, Jenny grabbed her arm. 'Greg believes Thea too, you know. You have to believe it. You know how he treats his crew – like they're his younger brothers – and I think he feels responsible for losing Max. That's why he overreacted when he saw

Thea had the tiepin. But he calmed down when he heard her explanation.'

Pearl only nodded before hurrying out. By the time she got back, Jenny was already in bed, no more than a lump under her covers, so there was no more chance to speak to her that night. Sleep being impossible, she tried to sort out the events of the evening in her mind. As much as she wanted to believe Jenny, she couldn't get past the fact that Greg's first response had been to accuse Thea. She could forgive him and even remain friends with him. But could she ever love him? She didn't know.

Chapter Twenty-One

The first thing Pearl did when she and Jenny walked into the cookhouse the next morning was look for Thea. It didn't take long to find her, scowling into her porridge, surrounded by a ring of empty space.

She glanced up when Pearl plonked her tray down in the place opposite. 'Oh, it's you. Come to lecture me?'

It took Jenny's warning glare to remind Pearl to bite back the rebuke on the tip of her tongue. After drawing a steadying breath, she offered her sister a pleasant smile and sat. 'Not today. How are you? I was furious at Greg for accusing you like that.' Then she remembered she owed Thea an apology. 'And I'm sorry I scolded you about leading Max on. I should have trusted you to do the right thing.'

The defiance left Thea's expression, replaced by wariness. 'Yes, you should. Anyway, whether or not you trust me doesn't make a whole lot of difference, because no one else seems to. Have you heard the whispers doing the rounds about me? I think Greg must have told someone else about me having Max's tiepin because I've heard more than one person say they're not going to sit with a thief.'

'So that explains the quarantine zone. It's not Greg, though.' She was still angry with him, but she knew he would never spread gossip.

'Who is it, then?'

'Blanche. When I got back to Hut Three last night, she had the gall to tell me that she didn't think your being a thief was any reflection on me. What a cheek! I gave her a piece of my mind, and Jenny looked like she was ready to go five rounds with her in the ring.'

Thea's expression cleared. 'I'd forgotten Blanche was there. I'm glad it wasn't Greg, even if he did look ready to haul me in front of the authorities. Do you think he believed me?'

'He saw sense eventually. I'm not happy with him, though.'

Thea frowned. 'Promise me you won't fight with him on my behalf? I can fight my own battles, and he's good for you. It's been a refreshing change seeing you enjoying yourself for once and not always taking the world on your shoulders. You're actually starting to act like a young woman in her twenties instead of a harassed forty-year-old.'

'I'm not like that.' Pearl looked to Jenny for confirmation and was annoyed to see her fighting a smile. 'Don't tell me you agree with Thea?'

'Well, the night I arrived, there was a moment when I thought you were going to offer to tuck me into bed and tell me a bedtime story.'

Thea choked and set her drink down hurriedly. 'That's Pearl through and through! She thinks she has to mother everyone.'

'I do not!'

'Not any more,' Jenny assured her. 'As Thea says, I think Greg's been good for you. And there's nothing wrong with being responsible. I mean, we're all doing responsible jobs. But it's good to see you having fun, too.'

'That's rich coming from you. You've always got your nose in a book. Where's the fun in that?'

'Reading *is* fun. Anyway, don't try to deflect this onto me. We were talking about you and Greg.'

'I know.' And Pearl could no longer avoid confronting the worry she'd pushed aside last night. 'I like him and I *was* having fun going out with him. But yesterday he accused Thea without even waiting to hear her side of the story.'

Thea raised her eyebrows. 'As did you.'

'I never! I didn't for one minute believe you had stolen anything.'

'I'm not talking about that. But when you heard I had accepted it from Max, you immediately told me off for leading him on. Without, I might add, waiting to hear my side of the story.'

Pearl looked down at her hands. 'You're right. I did do that.' And if she could genuinely be sorry and determined to treat Thea better in future, surely she had to trust Greg to do the same. He had, after all, apologised to Thea for not giving her a chance to explain.

Thea sat back, looking satisfied. 'And so are you going to make it up with Greg as soon as you see him?'

'Which one of us is supposed to be the older sister?' When Thea said nothing but simply folded her arms and raised her eyebrows, Pearl relented. 'Oh, very well. Yes – I'll try.'

—

Although there was another lull in operations, Pearl was too busy with her own duties to see Greg that day, leaving her with the feeling of uneasiness at not being able to clear the air between them. She was on watch that afternoon while *C-Charlie* was on a training flight, and she felt jittery for the entire time the Lancaster was in the air, knowing that even apparent routine flights could end in tragedy. She couldn't bear the thought of Greg flying again until she had had a chance to speak to him.

In the event, the flight went smoothly and made a perfect landing. She took comfort from hearing his cheerful voice over the radio, and thought that, if he was feeling resentful towards her, he hid it well.

At the end of her shift she went to the NAAFI, hoping to see him before she had to return for the night watch. Unfortunately he wasn't there, so she had to content herself with the thought that, as there were no operations on that night, he would at least be safe. Now December had arrived, she wished with all her heart for a heavy fall of snow to ground the aircraft and keep everyone safe. So far her prayers had gone unanswered; the weather had become mild and drizzly, with not even a good ground fog to keep the squadrons from flying.

About half an hour before she had to return to duty, she checked her mail to see she had a letter from Mr Haughton, written in an elegant copperplate hand.

> *Dear Miss Cooper,*
>
> *I'm delighted to see how well the* Bombshell *is going, and I am impressed with the sterling work by you and your team. As we are approaching Christmas, I wondered if you and Flight Sergeant Tallis would care to join me for tea at the gatehouse on Saturday afternoon? You will be welcome any time after three o'clock.*
>
> *Yours sincerely,*
> *Thos. Haughton*

The rest of Pearl's free time was spent writing a hurried note of acceptance to Mr Haughton, where she explained that although she would be free to come she wouldn't know if Greg would be available until late morning, but she was sure he would be delighted to accept if he was free. She also thought, although she didn't put this in her letter, that the walk to the gatehouse would give her and Greg a chance to talk. Because tea with Mr Haughton if she and Greg didn't clear the air promised to be very awkward indeed.

In the event, although there were ops on Saturday night, Greg was available because *C-Charlie* had developed an engine fault. However, her quiet walk was spoiled when some of the other girls in Hut Three declared it was a lovely afternoon for a walk and they would accompany Pearl and Greg as far as the turning to a footpath that led back through the fields to Fenthorpe. As the turning was within sight of the gatehouse, this didn't allow

Pearl any opportunity for a private conversation with Greg. He held her hand as they walked, however, giving her hope that he didn't harbour any resentment.

Once the others had climbed the stile onto the footpath and were hidden from view by the tall hedgerow, Greg tugged her hand to pull her closer. 'I'm sorry we haven't had a chance to speak since the other night. Are you still angry with me?'

'No. But I was upset that you immediately suspected the worst with Thea. You don't really think she stole that pin, do you?'

'No.' But the pause before his reply was a shade too long to set Pearl's mind completely at rest. She couldn't help thinking Greg had lost his faith in Thea and therefore Pearl herself. Because Pearl refused to believe Thea would have stolen anything.

Greg spoke again, interrupting her musings. 'What do you think I should do with the pin? If Max gave it to Thea, he'd want her to keep it.'

She couldn't help herself. '*If* Max gave it to her?' Maybe it was something to do with his accent, but he didn't sound convinced.

'Just a turn of phrase,' Greg told her. 'I didn't mean it to sound like I doubted her.'

Pearl wished she could have talked it through properly with Greg, because she still felt as though he harboured doubts. Frustratingly, though, they were out of time, as they had arrived at the gatehouse.

Mrs Stockwell must have been looking out for them, for she opened the door before they even reached the porch. 'Do come in. Mr Haughton has been so looking forward to your visit.' She took their coats and hats, then ushered them into the drawing room, saying Mr Haughton was in his study. 'He's taking a phone call, but he'll be with you in a moment.'

Greg and Pearl sat in silence on a leather sofa. Pearl gazed into the fire, struggling to think of any subject other than

Thea, Max and that bloody tiepin. An impossibility when it was the only thing she wanted to talk about. Greg evidently felt the same, for he didn't speak either and instead studied a painted landscape on the chimney with all the concentration of an art connoisseur. Pearl found herself comparing the rapid ticking of the elaborate gold mantel clock with the stately *tock-tock* coming from the grandfather clock in the hall and was nearly driven to distraction when the rhythms wouldn't match. Although it wasn't long before she heard Mr Haughton's footsteps approaching, it felt like an eternity.

She sprang up as soon as Mr Haughton entered the drawing room, barely hearing his greeting in the rush of relief. 'It's so good of you to invite us,' she said, shaking his hand.

'Not at all. It's always a pleasure to see you both.'

After they had exchanged the initial courtesies, Mr Haughton soon steered the conversation to the *Bombshell*, and Pearl relaxed, feeling on safer ground. By the time Mrs Stockwell wheeled in a trolley laden with cups, plates and a selection of cakes and sandwiches, she and Greg were conversing almost normally. Almost. She was constantly aware of the space between them on the sofa and the fact that they never touched except by accident. Still, she thought they both put on a good show, smiling and talking to Mr Haughton as though nothing was wrong.

Not that the topic of conversation itself was relaxing. Mr Haughton questioned Pearl closely on how well the *Bombshell* had been received and ideas for future editions.

'I can't believe how enthusiastic everyone is about it,' she said in conclusion. 'It always sells out, and lots of people have told me how much they look forward to each new edition.'

'It's all anyone can talk about in the sergeants' mess on the day it comes out,' Greg added.

'I'm not at all surprised,' Mr Haughton told her. 'I knew the day we met that you had the gumption to make a success of it. I would never have given you my support if I hadn't been convinced you were the right person for the job. We shall have to see about increasing the print run next year.'

'Oh, that's very kind but you're already doing so much for us.' Pearl was torn between delight at Mr Haughton's praise and embarrassment that he was going to considerable expense and trouble for the paper when she could offer nothing in return.

'Nonsense. I consider it an investment in the future, and we should always think ahead.'

Beside her, Greg shifted as though he was suffering discomfort. She couldn't ask if he was all right, however, for Mr Haughton was still talking. 'The war won't last for ever, however much it might feel that way. Seeing the success you and your team have made of the *Bombshell* gives me hope that, once all this is over, there will be men and women like you who will be the journalists of the future. The kind of journalists who will strive to make the world a better place.' Mr Haughton paused to take a bite of crumbly fruit cake, then said, 'So tell me, Pearl, if you had one dream for the *Bombshell*, what would it be?'

At first, Pearl was thrown, unsure what to say. She ran ideas through her mind such as increasing the number of pages, or publishing fortnightly or even weekly, but they seemed too practical to be described as 'dreams'. Then she remembered an idea she'd had at the very first meeting. 'Well, I don't know if it would be possible with our small team, but it would be marvellous to see it expand beyond RAF Fenthorpe and include the other bomber stations nearby. Possibly even extend to the whole of 5 Group. We all work very closely, so a newspaper to cover the whole area would make us feel more united, don't you think?'

Mr Haughton raised his teacup in salute. 'I applaud your vision and ambition. Well, who can tell what will happen in the days to come? I—'

But he was interrupted as Greg knocked his teacup over, slopping the remains of his tea down his jacket.

Greg leapt up, dabbing at the stains with his handkerchief. 'I'm such a galoot. Please excuse me.'

'You'll find Mrs Stockwell in the kitchen,' Mr Haughton told him. 'She'll sort you out.'

Once Greg had left the room, Mr Haughton cleared his throat. 'I hope you won't think I'm interfering, but I can't help noticing a distance between you and Mr Tallis. A distance I didn't notice last time we met. Have you had an argument?'

Pearl gave a self-deprecating laugh. 'And I thought I had hidden it so well.'

'I won't pry, of course, but I don't like to see a rift between two young people who are so well suited.'

'It's not a rift as such. More that we both said some thoughtless things the other day and there hasn't been a chance to clear it up.'

'Well, if you want my advice, you should make every effort to talk it over with him at the earliest opportunity. I—' but then he waved his hand as though batting away the comment he had been about to make. 'Suffice it to say, I've had my share of heartbreak. Some of it was unavoidable but some was down to my own foolishness. Don't let a good thing slip through your fingers.'

—

Thanks to Mrs Stockwell's ministrations, Greg reappeared after a few minutes with his tunic looking as good as new. The visit didn't last long after that, and Pearl resolved to take Mr Haughton's excellent advice on the walk home. It was dark by this time and, there being no moon, they needed their torches to show them where to put their feet. Pearl was very glad to accept Greg's arm, and even then they both stumbled frequently over unseen obstacles. When Pearl stepped into a pothole and lurched sideways, Greg steadied her, then pulled her closer, wrapping an arm round her waist.

Pearl leaned into the embrace, feeling safe and cocooned. Their connection was strong enough to overcome their disagreement, and she should speak up now rather than let it fester any longer.

While she was still working out how to open the conversation, Greg murmured in her ear, 'Are you still angry with me?'

'No. Not angry.'

'Then what is it? I can tell you're not happy.'

'I was angry at first,' she said. Somehow it was easier to speak her thoughts into the darkness than if she was looking into his face. 'Your first reaction when you saw the tiepin was that she had stolen it.'

'I know. Thea bore the brunt of my pent-up frustration, and I'm sorry. What happened to Max's watch has been preying on my mind and I didn't realise the stress it had put me under until I snapped at Thea. But you reacted like it was an attack on you, and I couldn't understand that. My suspicion of Thea had nothing to do with how I feel about you.'

What *did* he feel about her? She didn't dare ask in case his feelings didn't run as deep as hers. 'It did feel like you were accusing me. Thea was only a baby when our mother died, and I've always felt responsible for her. When you accused her, it felt like you didn't trust me or my judgement.'

'I've always trusted your judgement, ever since I heard your voice telling me I would make it to the ground safely. And I can understand how you feel about Thea, I really do. I feel the same about my crew. They all seem so young, and whenever we fly they're utterly dependent on me to get them back in one piece. Yet I mustn't forget that I depend on them too. Every one of them has to perform their job to the best of their ability or the chances of a safe return are greatly reduced. I'm only just starting to realise that.'

Pearl thought about that. 'Are you saying I need to let myself depend upon Thea more?'

'Any of your friends, really. Why do you think you have to take the responsibility for everything and everyone upon your own shoulders? Didn't you notice the way Thea resented you immediately speaking up for her?'

'Of course I did. She nearly bit my head off.'

'Well, as she said, she can fight her own battles. How much do *you* trust Thea?'

Pearl was immediately up in arms. 'I know she'd never steal anything. If you're telling me I should suspect her, then you don't know her or me at all.' A lump in her throat suddenly made speaking difficult. In Greg she had thought she had found someone who valued and understood her, and now she felt like their relationship was on shaky ground.

'That's not what I mean at all.' Greg's arm squeezed her close, and he kissed her on the cheek, his lips chilly from the cold air. 'You're certain Thea didn't steal anything, and, as I've been trying to explain, I *do* trust your judgement. Anyway, I know how keen Max was on Thea, and it makes perfect sense that he would give her his tiepin.'

'Then what do you mean?'

'You don't have to do everything yourself. You don't trust Thea not to get into trouble or to do things properly, and I can see how much that's hurting her.'

This wasn't what Pearl wanted to hear. Whenever Greg or Jenny or Thea herself said something of the sort, it felt like an attack on everything she had done to take care of her sister.

'Pearl? Say something. I hope I haven't upset you.'

Pearl drew a deep breath. 'It's hard not to get upset when you tell me that I shouldn't be concerned for my own sister.'

'That's not what I'm saying. Of course you want to look out for her. Haven't I just said that's how I feel about my crew? But she's an adult and she's trying to prove to you that she can cope on her own.'

Finally understanding dawned. 'And every time I leap to her defence, it looks as though I don't trust her to sort things out herself.'

'Exactly. I'm not saying she won't ever need help, but you need to step back and let her handle things, while being there in case she decides she does need your advice. The times you've given her responsibility for something on the newspaper, haven't you noticed how pleased she was?'

'I suppose so. I *have* been trying. Jenny's been telling me the same thing. It's hard, though, to let go when I've taken care of her for about as long as I can remember.'

'Why is that, anyway?'

'I thought I told you. My father died during the last war, before Thea was born, and my mother died soon after she had Thea.'

'Yes, but you had your grandmother, and from what you say she's not all that old. You were only six. Why did you feel you had to take sole responsibility?'

'You've never met Deedee.' Pearl chuckled, then went on to explain. 'Honestly, you would understand if you met her. She's unconventional to say the least. She lost my grandfather years and years ago, before my mother was born, I think, and I suppose having to cope for so long on her own meant she wasn't like the other women I know. All my friends had grandmothers who kept their houses spotless and loved to bake treats for their grandchildren.'

'Did she neglect you?'

Hearing the worry in Greg's voice made Pearl hasten to explain. 'Oh no. Not at all. She clearly loves us very much but she's… I don't know, it's like her head's in the clouds most of the time. While I would be trying to persuade Thea to do her homework, Deedee would tell us we should make the most of a sunny afternoon and go for a walk. Or play in the snow. She was never serious.'

'But she looked after you. Fed and clothed you. You were only six when your mother died, so she must have taken care of you.'

'Well, yes. She just wasn't like—'

'Other grandmothers. Yes, you said.'

'Oh, I knew you wouldn't understand.' The trouble was, Pearl was finding it hard to put into words why she had felt the need to look after Thea. Because now she came to explain it, she didn't understand what had driven her to take on so much responsibility at a young age.

'I'm trying. And you're right – I don't know your grand-mother. I hope I can meet her one day.'

'You do?' Pearl wished there was enough light to see his face so she could see if he was serious. He'd not spoken of the future before.

'Yes, really. She's special to you and you're special to me.'

'I am?' Was this the moment that he was finally going to declare his love? Pearl's mouth went dry.

'Of course. Why do you think I want to spend so much time with you?'

'I-I thought…' What – that he simply enjoyed going out with her because it took his mind off the horrors he experienced on bombing missions? She swallowed. 'I mean, you enjoy my company, don't you?' There had been times when they were alone in Llandudno that she had thought – hoped – he was going to say he loved her. He never had, though.

'Yes. And I carried on going out with you because the more I was with you, the more I've grown to like you. Why are you still going out with me?'

Like. Not love. She could only respond by muttering, 'The same.' Her love for him had weighed on her heart for some time now and the pressure to speak of it was becoming unbearable. Yet she didn't feel able to say it in case he didn't return her feelings.

Greg stopped walking and, his arm still round her waist, pulled her to a halt. He wrapped both arms round her and pulled her close. Staring up at him, she saw the dark outline of his face silhouetted against the starry sky. One of his hands came up and traced the line of her cheek, down to the corner of her mouth. 'I wish I could say more, but I can't. Not when I'm still not halfway through my tour. Please be patient with me.'

She had to cling on to hope that this meant he really did love her. She nodded, then, remembering he probably couldn't see that, she said, 'Of course.'

Which one of them initiated the kiss she didn't know, but she knew she didn't want to stop. She wound her arms round his neck, pulling him closer, saying in the kiss what she couldn't say in words. Her heart pounded furiously against her ribs, so hard she was sure he must feel it.

Finally, reluctantly, Pearl pulled away from Greg and laughed. 'Come on, we'd better get back. I heard there's going to be a kit inspection tomorrow, and I need to check I haven't lost anything.'

Holding hands, they made their way back to the station. Pearl felt happier than when they had set out, glad that she and Greg had taken a tentative step forward, yet she wished with all her heart to know if he loved her.

Chapter Twenty-Two

Why hadn't he told Pearl he loved her? That was the thought hammering in Greg's mind when he woke up the next morning. But when the lists went up on the noticeboard a few hours later, informing him that all serviceable Lancasters would be flying ops that night, he knew why. Walking with Pearl in the dark, he had been swept away by the feel of her in his arms, but he knew that until he had completed his tour he couldn't promise her anything.

Later, in the briefing, he groaned along with everyone else when the station commander pulled back the curtain to reveal a route marked out in red string heading for Mannheim, deep in enemy territory. This meant a long crossing over land, leaving them vulnerable to flak and night fighters.

He paid attention to the briefing as the Met Officer promised light winds but the possibility of cloud cover over the target. Next to him, Edwin Holland, his navigator, was scribbling notes about the wind speeds. 'I don't know why I bother,' Edwin muttered in an aside in the pause in the briefing while the Met Officer moved to another board. 'Last time they promised us light winds, we were nearly blown off course by vicious high-level winds.'

'I'm sure you'll find time to go to the Met Office to see what Jenny thinks.' For Greg had noticed Edwin seemed rather keen on Jenny, and wondered why he had never asked her out. But he didn't know Edwin well enough to ask him, the main reason being that Edwin was an officer and therefore not billeted with the rest of the crew. Greg often wondered if Edwin felt lonely, and made a note to include him in the general invitation to the pub that had become his habit on the day after a mission.

There he was, allowing himself to think ahead again. He had caught himself at it several times recently, most notably when he had been at Mr Haughton's. When Pearl had been outlining her vision for the future of the *Bombshell*, he had pictured being there at her side. Mr Haughton's comment that nobody knew what would happen in days to come had brought him back to reality with a nasty jolt, making him spill his tea.

Looking too far ahead was a dangerous habit to slip into. Greg turned his focus to the briefing. Not that he was superstitious, but he felt that the moment he took having a tomorrow for granted, he would stop concentrating on the job at hand. And even a test flight could be dangerous if he didn't keep his whole mind on the job.

He managed to stick to his resolution for the remainder of the day, even resisting the temptation to seek out Pearl in the NAAFI in the afternoon lull when there was nothing more to do but wait until it was time to kit up. However, after he had written his letter to his parents, he still had a lot of time on his hands. So, picking up his pencil again and finding a fresh sheet of paper, he tried to put down in words what he wished he could say. He wrote from the heart, not taking the time to find the right word but letting them pour out onto the page.

He was reading it through when the call came round that it was time to head out to the Lancasters. He folded the letter to Pearl away carefully, then pocketed the letter to his parents and made his way to the lockers, following the crowd of airmen all heading in the same direction. It was funny how alone it was possible to feel even in a crowd.

Once he had put his parents' letter in his locker along with his valuables, he glanced around the room to see if there was anyone present who shouldn't be there, or anyone who seemed to be taking particular note of what the men were stowing away. But he couldn't see anything that struck him as odd, so he made an effort to put his worries out of his mind. For him, leaving the locker room was the start of the process of forgetting his personal life and closing his mind to everything but the mission. By the time he had collected his Mae West and parachute, he was only thinking of *C-Charlie* and his crew.

–

'Did you check our forecast with Jenny?' Greg dropped into a seat on the crew bus next to Edwin. Thankfully, Edwin had never pulled rank and always deferred to him when they were in the air.

Edwin nodded. 'She said she thought the forecast for low winds was optimistic, but she also pointed out that, as she only collects and plots the data and has nothing to do with forecasting, I shouldn't take her word for it.'

'What are you going to do?'

'Are you kidding? She's more widely read than I am. If she thinks there are going to be strong winds at high levels, I'm going to factor them in.'

'Wise man.'

Time seemed to speed up then. One minute they were scrambling out of the bus at *C-Charlie*'s dispersal pen, the next moment Greg was strapping himself into the pilot's seat, the next he was opening up the engines and speeding down the runway. Then they were in the air, climbing steeply.

'Nice take-off, Skip,' called out one of the gunners; Greg wasn't sure which one.

'All right, concentrate, everyone. Navigator, course.'

Edwin called out the bearing, and they were on their way, joining a stream of bombers they couldn't see but knew they must be close to. Greg took his own advice and concentrated on his instruments, taking care to stay at his designated height.

The moment they crossed the Dutch coast, Greg's fears of heavy flak were borne out. Brilliant flashes burst close to the aircraft, buffeting them wildly, and searchlights scanned the skies. 'Navigator,' he called over the intercom, meaning to ask for a course that would take them round the worst of the explosions, but at that moment a cry came from one of the gunners.

'Lanc going down to port!'

Even as the words tore across the intercom, Greg saw a streak of scarlet plummet only yards from the tip of *C-Charlie*'s port wing. He instinctively banked, and doing so probably saved their lives, for a fighter appeared out of nowhere, spitting glowing streams of tracer fire at the point where *C-Charlie*'s tail would have been if Greg hadn't made his sudden manoeuvre. It shot below his line of sight; simultaneously, several of the crew yelled out belated warnings. Greg didn't wait for it to come back but threw the machine into a series of violent manoeuvres. He heard the rattle of gunfire, then Sid Eccles, the mid-upper gunner, saying, 'I think I got it, Skip.'

Greg returned to his designated altitude and levelled out, holding his breath, expecting at any moment to feel the craft judder as bullets struck. But apart from the turbulence from the flak storm, nothing impeded *C-Charlie*'s flight. 'Did anyone else see it go down?' he asked the crew.

There was a chorus of, 'No, Skip,' and, 'Sorry Gramps,' and a groan from the unfortunate Sid, who would be unable to claim his 'kill'.

'Keep your eyes peeled,' he told them. 'We can't count on luck like that again.' Then, to Edwin, 'Navigator, bearing.'

After only the briefest of pauses, indicating that Edwin had already anticipated the request and was working on it, Edwin said, 'One six niner, Skip.' Once Greg had completed his course correction, eyes straining all the while for any sign of more enemy fighters, Edwin added, 'The wind speed's much stronger than forecast. Good thing I paid attention to Jenny. I'll have to tell her next time I see her.'

This was far too much like forward planning for Greg's liking. 'Keep your mind on your task. Get us to the target and have a return course ready for the moment the photo flash goes off. And that applies to all of you,' he said for the benefit of the rest of the crew. 'I want your minds alert and your eyes keeping a sharp lookout.'

There was a chorus of assent, and they flew on.

Although they saw more flak as they crossed into Germany, the defences seemed to be concentrating on the aircraft ahead of *C-Charlie*. Greg wouldn't let himself or anyone relax, though, and reminded the crew to keep a lookout for enemy fighters. This was one of the longest missions he had flown, and the strain was beginning to tell. Lancasters were huge aircraft, and each manoeuvre took an effort. He could feel his mental and physical reserves draining, so for the first time, he took one of the 'wakey wakey' Benzedrine pills pilots were routinely provided with. As the minutes ticked by, he found it had an odd effect, making him feel simultaneously weary and wide awake.

It was a profound relief when Holland announced they were four minutes from the target. Greg sat a little straighter and started looking for signs of the raid – flashes of flak, the glow of fires and the coloured flares the Pathfinders should have used to mark the target. Without needing to be told, Fitz slid down into the bomb aimer's compartment. Most men would have had a scramble to get into the cramped space, but Fitz had a catlike knack of fitting into the most unlikely nooks and crannies.

'Over to you, Bomb Aimer,' Greg said.

'Right, Skip.' Then a moment later Fitz muttered something inaudible followed by: 'Target's completely obscured by cloud, Skip. No sign of any marker flares.'

The words had barely reached Greg's ears when a loud explosion rocked *C-Charlie*, throwing Greg against his harness.

'Bugger me, that was close!'

Greg thought it was Sid. 'Report – any damage?'

'Nothing, Skip. We got lucky there.'

More flak was exploding around them, orange flashes lighting the cockpit. Greg knew their luck could fail at any moment. 'Navigator, confirm we're on course.'

'We're spot-on, Gramps. One minute to target.'

Greg thought rapidly. He could repeat the bomb run and hope the cloud cover cleared, or continue by dead reckoning and release the bombs when Edwin said they were over the target.

Then Fitz cried, 'Skipper, I can see the marker flares. We're nearly there.'

Greg relaxed. A recent development in Bomber Command had been the introduction of the elite Pathfinder squadrons. They were the first aircraft at the destination and dropped coloured flares onto the targets. This gave the following bombers a clear site to place their bombs. The Pathfinder squadrons had started up while the squadrons at Fenthorpe had been on training missions with their new Avro Lancasters. Now they were back on operational duty, it made finding the target much easier. Even Greg, who didn't have the clear view that Fitz had, looking as he did through a glass panel in the nose, could see the red flares a little way ahead with ease.

'Left, left, steady,' Fitz called. Then, 'Bombs gone.'

The moment the photo flash came, Edwin called out the new bearing without being asked. Greg banked immediately, willing them out of the danger zone before they were hit by flak or another fighter plane. He had barely completed the manoeuvre when there came a loud crash, and the Lancaster rocked violently. Greg felt the shock through the control column and had to fight to stay on course.

'Report!' he yelled.

There was a lengthy pause, long enough for Greg to fear the worst. Then came: 'Tail gunner here, Skip. There's a hole in the fuselage the size of Lincoln Cathedral. Sid and George are down.'

'How bad?' Greg ran a quick eye over the instrument panel but couldn't see any sign of any systems failure. It was a blow to have both the mid-upper gunner and the wireless operator out of action, though.

'I can't tell,' came the reply. 'My hydraulics have jammed and I can't get out to see them.'

'You'd better get back to see what's happening,' Greg told Allan Doughty, the flight engineer, who was already unbuckling his harness. 'See if you can get Knight free and tell him to man the turret.' They would be hopelessly vulnerable to attack if all their gunners were out of action. 'Fitz, get back there and give first aid. Then man Sid's gun if he's not able to.'

He immediately addressed the helpless tail gunner. 'Help's on the way, Knight. Hang on.'

'I don't have much bleeding choice, do I?' came the reply.

Greg winced at the fear in Jack Knight's voice and could only imagine what it must be like to be trapped in that exposed perspex bubble with flak exploding all around him. 'I bet you anything you like we'll get you out safe and sound.'

'Anything?'

'Anything at all.'

'Okay. If I make it back, you have to hang the adjutant's cap in a tree.'

'Deal.' Greg had no idea how he was to get hold of Sheldrick's cap, but he'd agree to anything at the moment if it took Knight's mind off his predicament.

By this time Doughty had reached the tail gunner's position, and Greg fell silent as he waited for a report. All he could do was continue along the course Edwin had given him and pray they weren't coned by the searchlights. Even as the thought crossed his mind, he saw three searchlights home in on an unfortunate Lancaster, pinning it in full view while flak converged on the area. Then two fighters came into view, both making for the helpless Lancaster that couldn't shake itself free from the cone of light no matter how much it turned and dived. Greg watched with his heart full of pity as it caught fire, then plummeted into a steep spinning dive. He saw no parachutes, nor did he expect to, knowing it would be impossible for the crew to extricate themselves once the Lancaster had started to spin, as they would be pinned by centrifugal force.

Along with pity, he also felt guilt. Guilt at the relief he felt that the defences had focused on another Lancaster, leaving them free to escape. He put *C-Charlie*'s nose down, sacrificing height for more speed in his bid to reach the coast and get away from the flak batteries and searchlights before their luck ran out.

It was some time before Doughty returned. 'I managed to get Jack free, and he's now manning the mid-upper turret. The hydraulics on the tail gunner's turret have seized up, so we've lost that position. His shoulder took a hit from shrapnel, but it's not too bad. I managed to stop the bleeding and he insists he's well enough.'

'How about George and Sid?'

'Not good but I think they'll make it. Sid got a nasty wound to the side, and George burned his hands putting out a fire where the shrapnel hit. He'll be okay but his hands are too badly burned to operate the wireless. Fitz is still giving Sid first aid.'

'Just great.' Greg addressed the rest of the crew. 'Everyone who can stay on his feet, I need you to keep a sharp lookout. We don't have a hope shooting back at any fighters, so we'll need to evade them. Sing out if you see anything.'

Taking his own advice, Greg stared out into the night sky, looking for the slightest movement against the stars that would reveal a night fighter. The return flight was going to be a long, tense journey.

—

Pearl couldn't sleep. She had stood outside, watching the Lancasters take off on their mission and listening to the fading growl of their engines. Then she had returned to her hut. But sleep eluded her. She wished she was on duty. At least then she would know when the first Lancasters returned, and she would know when *C-Charlie* arrived. But here in her narrow bed, all she could do was toss and turn, trying to get comfortable, clutching the thin blankets around her as, once the stove had gone out, the heat faded. Although she knew it would be hours before the planes returned, she couldn't help but strain her ears, listening for the first sound of Merlin engines.

Minutes stretched into hours until finally she could bear it no longer. She scrambled out of bed and groped for her uniform. She would go and volunteer with the WAAFs who made tea for the returning crews. At least then she would see Greg the minute he arrived. Or be among the first to know if he didn't make it. As awful as that would be, it was preferable to hearing it from someone else, seeing the bad news in their eyes before they even said the words.

As she crept to the door, pulling on her coat, a sleepy voice spoke from the darkness. 'Where are you going?' It was Jenny, thankfully.

'The operations block. To help with making the tea.'

'Hang on. I'm coming with you.'

A short while later, they were on their bikes, heading for the place outside the operations block where the buses would unload the returning crews. A small huddle of WAAFs had already gathered, bundled in their coats and stamping their feet to stay warm. Pearl was surprised to see Thea there, for she had been on duty that day and would have been working on *C-Charlie*, her assigned Lancaster, until the crew had boarded. 'Couldn't you sleep, either?' she asked.

Thea shook her head. 'The crew are like family. I often stay up when they're flying ops.'

'You do?' Why had she never known? An uncomfortable thought occurred: maybe Thea was right. Maybe she still hadn't learned to listen to her sister.

Then an even more unwelcome thought struck. If Thea regularly volunteered to meet the returning crews, she would be around the lockers at night when they were unattended. And no one had reported any valuables missing until after Thea had arrived at Fenthorpe.

Pearl scarcely heard Thea's reply over the ringing in her ears. No. She refused to believe it. Her gut reaction when Greg had accused Thea had been to defend her, and she stood by that decision. Hadn't Greg himself admitted that it would have been just like Max to give Thea his tiepin? She had known Thea since the day her sister was born and, although she had often despaired that she would never stop getting herself into trouble, that trouble had always been down to mischievousness and lack of common sense. She had never done anything criminal.

'Do you know where tonight's target is?' she asked Thea now, more for the sake of dispelling the unwanted suspicion than for any real interest. If she'd been on duty that night she would have known, but the location was kept a closely guarded secret from anyone who didn't need to know.

'Mannheim,' Thea told her. 'I heard the crews talking about it when they were boarding the plane.'

Mannheim. Pearl dredged up the memory of the maps pinned up around the Watch Office. That was well inland. Greg didn't often speak of his missions, but he had said that the further over enemy territory they had to fly, the more trouble the anti-aircraft defences were. She gazed up at the sky, wishing she could hear the sound of the returning Lancasters.

She wasn't sure how long she stood craning her neck, but her focus was jolted back to ground level when someone patted her arm. It was Jenny. 'They'll be fine. It's too soon to expect anyone back – Mannheim's a long flight.'

'I know. I'm sure you're right. I can't bear this waiting though. My mind seems to run away with itself and picture all sorts of horrors.' She turned to Thea to make a comment, only to see a space where she had stood. 'Jenny, did you see where Thea went?'

Jenny shook her head. 'No idea. Wait. Is that her?'

Pearl looked and saw Thea's dim shape emerging from the door of the operations block. 'Sorry,' she said when she got back to Pearl's side. 'I was bursting for the loo. This cold wind is playing havoc with my bladder. I had a good idea, though.'

'While you were on the loo?'

Then it struck Pearl that there wasn't a ladies' lavatory in any of the buildings Thea could have come from. But before she could say anything, Thea laughed and said, 'I get all my best ideas there, don't you? Anyway, I thought this might make a good article for the *Bombshell*. Instead of A Day in the Life, we could write A Night in the Life and describe what it's like to wait for the bombers to come back.'

'That's not a bad idea. Do you want to write it?' And Pearl pushed aside her glimmer of suspicion in her eagerness to occupy her mind with the newspaper.

It was a good hour before Jenny suddenly said, 'Quiet! Can you hear engines?'

Her heart racing, Pearl held her breath and listened. It took a moment but then she heard it too: a distant throb, more felt than heard. A hush fell over the group, and Pearl wondered how many girls, like her, were silently praying that their sweethearts were returning safely. The distant noise resolved itself into a hum and then a roar.

'It's them!' Jenny cried.

Soon the dark shapes appeared in the sky, and the runway flares were lit. As the Lancasters descended one at a time and made their landings, Pearl wished more than ever that she was in Flying Control, listening to the voices of the pilots as they requested their landing instructions. Greg might have already landed, but she wouldn't know until the buses returned, bringing the crews back to be debriefed.

The first buses set out for the dispersal points, and the WAAFs hurried into the small kitchen to make the tea. Even though she was now occupied, Pearl continued to count the returning bombers. Thirty had taken off earlier – she had counted every one as it roared overhead. Now she kept a mental tally as they returned. Four so far, the ear-splitting noise as each landed and then taxied to the dispersal points drowning out the noise of any others that might be approaching. Then the buses started to roll up to the huts, and the WAAFs hurried to meet them as the crewmen climbed out, making sure each one was given a mug of tea.

'Thanks, love,' the man said who took Pearl's offering. He wrapped his hands round the mug and grinned at her. 'Perishing cold up there tonight.'

Pearl eyed all the emerging men intently and her heart fell when she didn't see any faces she recognised. But already the air was filled with the drone of more engines. Surely *C-Charlie* would be among them.

The men filed off towards the locker room and then on to the debriefing hut. Pearl had been tempted to ask them if anyone knew if *C-Charlie* was safe, but she remembered Greg telling her that they usually didn't know of the fate of any of the other members of their squadron until they were back on the ground and could see for themselves who was there. So with each man she greeted him with a smile as she handed him his tea and said, 'Welcome back,' and let him move on. Some of the men were gabbling and laughing ten to the dozen, slapping each other on the back and discussing their next trip to the pub. Pearl thought they were probably feeling the effects of an adrenaline surge now that they knew they had survived another dangerous mission. Other men seemed to be so tired they could barely hold up their heads. She watched them file past, all the while counting the next group of Lancasters coming in to land. Eight... nine... ten. It was only with a great effort that she continued filling more mugs and handing them out and stopped herself from running all the way to Flying Control to consult the board and find out which Lancasters were back and which were still unaccounted for.

The main group of Lancasters seemed to be arriving now, and for some time they circled the airfield, waiting for their turn to land; and, as time went on, Pearl's tally slowly but steadily increased to twenty. Each time a bus rolled up she would start forward eagerly, only to be disappointed when none of Greg's crew emerged, although she did her best to hide her disappointment and welcome each man back with a friendly smile.

There was another lull in the arrivals when the count reached twenty-five. Pearl, who had fought back her anxiety throughout the early arrivals, now felt sick. But many of the crews were still with their Lancasters, waiting for buses, so she tried to comfort herself by telling herself: *He'll be on the next one. He's got to be here. Just wait. I'll see him get out of the next bus, and imagine how glad he will be to see me.*

The buses were bringing the last of the crews that had so far arrived when Jenny grabbed her arm.

'Can you hear it – more Lancasters!'

She looked almost as fraught as Pearl felt, and she was reminded that Jenny was friends with Greg too. And Edwin. The reminder that she wasn't alone in her fears prompted her to offer Jenny a reassuring smile. 'I'm sure *C-Charlie* will be in this group.'

'She'd better be,' Thea said, appearing as if by magic at Pearl's side. Pearl had noticed that many of the ground crew and aircrews referred to the Lancasters in the feminine, in the same way that sailors referred to their ships. 'If Greg doesn't bring her back in one piece, I'll give him an earful for giving the crew more work.'

Pearl chuckled, although she didn't feel much like laughing. 'And I'll tell him off for giving us a scare. Come on, that's the next bus arriving.'

But *C-Charlie*'s crew wasn't on that one, either. Finally, twenty-eight Lancasters were back, their crews all transported to the operations block and given their tea, while *C-Charlie*'s crew was conspicuous by its absence. Although Pearl stared at the sky, willing the darkness to lift so she could gaze to the horizon and search for the two final Lancasters, the sun stubbornly refused to rise. And two Lancasters remained unaccounted for: *C-Charlie* and *P-Peter*.

The WAAFs in the kitchen started to pack up. 'Might as well face it, that's all we're getting back tonight.'

'Oh, please wait a little longer,' Pearl begged. 'I'm sure they'll be back in a minute, and they'll be desperate for a hot drink.'

The woman in charge relented. 'I'll give them another fifteen minutes.'

'Thank you. They'll be here soon, I'm sure of it.' But she wasn't sure at all. She kept telling herself that just because Greg hadn't got back to Fenthorpe, it didn't mean he wasn't safe – he might have made an emergency landing at another airfield. But as the minutes ticked by, she felt her faith draining away.

Then, ten minutes into the fifteen-minute extension, Pearl heard the unmistakable sound of Merlin engines. 'This is them, it has to be.' The wait while the Lancaster came in to land and taxied to its dispersal point was unbearable. A bus set off to meet the crew, and then Thea announced in a low voice, 'They've sent ambulances.'

'Oh, God.' A layer of ice seemed to be constricting Pearl's heart. There came another agonising wait until the bus returned.

When it jerked to a halt with a squeal of brakes, Pearl grabbed a cup of tea, marvelling that she had strength enough to hold it. She approached the bus, fighting to drag air into her lungs.

When the door opened and Greg stepped out, Pearl thought her legs would fold up under her. She did her best to put on a bright smile, knowing he must be exhausted and not wanting to let him see her fear. 'Welcome back,' she said, handing him the mug.

There was definitely light in the sky now, enough to see that he looked tired, but he brightened when he saw her. 'Now there's a sight for sore eyes. Sorry if we gave you a scare. We were dodging enemy fighters over the North Sea and took a roundabout route home as a result.'

'I'm just glad to see you back. I heard they'd sent ambulances to your crew.'

'Nothing too bad, thank God. Some shrapnel wounds. The wireless operator and mid-upper gunner will be out of action for a few days but should be okay.'

Knowing Greg was exhausted and still had to endure the debriefing, she gave him a little push. 'Go on. I'm sure you're anxious to finish up and get to bed.'

He nodded. 'I'll come and look for you in the NAAFI tomorrow afternoon if you're around?'

'I'll be there some time after two.'

He gave her a jaunty wave and strode off after the rest of his crew.

Pearl knew she should return to her hut to grab what sleep she could, but found she was shaking so much she had to lean against the nearest wall. How many more times would she have to do this? How many more anxious waits could she bear? *Maybe I should request a transfer. It might not be so bad if I didn't know for sure which nights he was on ops.*

Then a tap on the arm roused her from her musings. 'Come on, Pearl, you look exhausted,' Jenny said.

Pearl levered herself off the wall and followed Jenny to fetch their bikes.

'Awful about *P-Peter*, isn't it?' Jenny said in a low voice as she picked up her bicycle.

'Is there any definite news?' Pearl felt terrible for forgetting about the other late bomber.

'No. Just listed as missing.'

Pearl stepped onto her pedals, thinking of the families of *P-Peter*'s crew who now faced an agony of uncertainty. At least she had the comfort of knowing Greg had arrived safely. This time.

Chapter Twenty-Three

When Pearl went on duty the next morning, she discovered that *P-Peter* was confirmed lost. It had made a darky call and been picked up by the R/T operator at RAF Scampton but then contact had been abruptly lost. A short while later, reports had arrived of a Lancaster crashed just outside Scampton, and the aircraft had quickly been identified as *P-Peter*. None of the crew had escaped. It was a cruel reminder that a bomber crew could make it all the way back to England, only to crash a few miles from their destination.

Her watch was uneventful, but Pearl fretted over the fate of *P-Peter* to such an extent that she wished she had more to occupy her. She was haunted by the awful wait of the previous night. Could she really go through that every time Greg was flying ops? Added to this was the very real possibility that another night might end without the same happy result. It could very easily have been *C-Charlie* failing to return instead of *P-Peter*.

As such, by the time she had finished duty and had her dinner, she was longing to see Greg, to assure herself that he was well and had escaped last night's mission unscathed.

She was about to go into the NAAFI when she noticed a group of men gathered behind the hut, around a tall elm tree that had been left undisturbed when RAF Fenthorpe had been built. Her gaze immediately landed on Greg, and she also recognised Fitz and one of *C-Charlie*'s gunners. The other men she didn't recognise, although from the brevets on their uniforms they were also aircrew.

On the point of turning away, she paused when Jack Knight, *C-Charlie's* tail gunner, ran past and joined the men under the tree. He held an officer's cap, which he waved in Greg's face. 'And you bet I couldn't do it!'

Fitz whistled. 'That's never the adjutant's cap.'

'Are you calling me a liar? Take a look.' Jack tossed it to Fitz.

Fitz examined it and gave a grudging nod. 'Definitely Sheldrick's. How did you manage it?'

'I snatched it off his head when he was walking out of the admin block. I did it at a run, so I'm pretty sure he didn't see my face.'

The other men laughed and clapped.

'Go on, Gramps,' the gunner said to Greg. 'Now it's time to live up to your side of the bargain.'

Fitz was starting to look uncomfortable. 'No one will think any worse of you for backing out. Personally, I prefer it when my pilot doesn't have concussion.'

At first it had been curiosity that had kept Pearl listening to the conversation. Now dread kept her rooted to the spot. Remembering Greg's stunt in the pub and his obvious love of riding his motorbike at high speed, she knew he must have accepted some kind of outrageous dare. She was tempted to march up to the group and demand Greg accompany her to the NAAFI that instant, but remembering Jenny and Thea's remarks about her propensity for mothering those she loved, she held back, knowing Greg would object to her telling him what to do in front of his friends. All she could do was watch and pray that Fitz's common sense would win the day.

Jack snatched the cap from Fitz's hands and tossed it to Greg. 'Or are you going to chicken out?'

Greg spun the cap on his finger. 'Course not. I'm a man of my word.'

So saying, he removed his own cap and dropped it on the ground. Then, placing the stolen cap on his head, he leapt up and scrambled up the thick ivy surrounding the elm's trunk until he could catch hold of the lowest branch. Pearl watched in horror as he swung himself up into the boughs and began to climb. Now she wished she *had* marched in and stopped the crazy stunt, but it was too late now. If she called out, his attention might waver, causing him to lose his hold.

The elm was nearly bare of foliage, with only a few withered yellow leaves clinging here and there. This made Greg's antics clear for all to see. The men shouted encouragement as he climbed higher. They clearly didn't share her concerns over startling Greg from his perch. From their shouts, Pearl soon gathered that Greg had been dared to place the cap at the highest possible point in the tree. She watched with her heart in her mouth as he climbed ever upwards. At first each branch bore his weight easily, but the branches were thinner the higher he climbed, and they bent under his weight.

He was about two-thirds of the way up when Fitz shouted, 'That's high enough. Don't be an idiot!'

But the men not in Greg's crew still cheered at him to go higher. And higher he went. Pearl couldn't hold back a cry when his foot slipped, but the shouts from the other men drowned out her voice. She watched in horror as he clutched the branch above his head and scrabbled to regain his footing. It only took a matter of seconds before he was secure again and climbing once more, this time keeping closer to the trunk where the branches didn't bend so much. But Pearl didn't think her heart would ever recover. She pressed a hand to her chest, blinking away tears of fear and anger as she watched. Why did he have to be so reckless? Wasn't it enough that he risked his life every time he flew on a mission? What possessed him to gamble with his life on a day like today?

Finally, he reached a place where the branches were too thin for him to climb higher. He removed the cap, which had miraculously remained on his head throughout the climb. Pearl watched, dry-mouthed, as he leaned out, clearly attempting to dangle the cap some distance from the safety of the trunk. For several horrifying seconds, his position seemed more and more precarious as he clung with only one hand to a fragile branch and stretched, the hand holding the cap flailing as he struggled to hook it around the end of a twig. Then he finally managed it. The cap dangled from its branch and Greg eased himself back against the trunk, acknowledging the men's cheers with a jaunty wave.

'Told you I'd do it!' he shouted.

Then his foot slipped and he lost his hold and crashed down through the branches.

–

Greg flung out his arms, scrabbling for a hold, too scared to cry out or even breathe. Thin twigs lashed his face and then he felt a sharp blow across his ribs. He had just enough sense to realise he had struck the branch below, and he gripped it tightly before he could fall again. For some time he couldn't do anything but wrap both arms round the branch and wait for his pounding heart to steady. The cheers on the ground had stopped. It took him a moment to realise he had closed his eyes. When he opened them, he found himself gazing down at a group of upturned faces, all wearing expressions of shock.

'Are you all right, Gramps?' Fitz called.

Greg's questing feet found a branch, and he gingerly tested it to see if it would take his weight. When it didn't give, he raised his chest off the branch that had saved him and dragged air into his lungs. 'Never better.' He made the rest of the descent without incident, necessarily moving more slowly to protect his bruised and aching ribs.

What had possessed him to agree to such a ridiculous dare? Just because Jack was prepared to risk a dressing-down for stealing the adjutant's cap, that didn't mean he had to risk his neck. The trouble was, the adrenaline had been fizzing through his veins all morning and he had felt in need of an outlet. Still, he could have gone for a walk or something.

When his feet landed on the ground, he wanted to collapse to his knees and kiss it. Instead, reluctant to show weakness in front of the others, he picked up his discarded cap, placed it on his head and turned to face the adjutant's hat, which swayed in the breeze but showed no sign of falling. 'Salute, lads,' he said and gave the cap an exaggerated salute. Then he remembered Sheldrick dressing Max down for not saluting on the same day the lad had been killed, and knew why he'd accepted this particular dare. *This is for you, Max*, he thought as he completed the salute.

The others saluted and clapped him on the back. 'You had me worried there, Skip,' Fitz told him.

'Oh, you know me. I live a charmed life.'

'I hope your luck lasts a little longer, then.'

'Why?' But then Greg saw Fitz give a jerk of the head towards the NAAFI hut, and he froze. For Pearl stood there, her face set in a scowl.

'How much did she see?' Greg asked.

'No idea. Better not put it off.' Fitz wandered up to the others and said, 'Come on, we'd better get out of here before Sheldrick spots his cap.'

They dispersed, leaving Greg staring at Pearl. Now his bruised ribs were the least of his problems. Although they had cleared the air after he'd accused Thea, he knew he hadn't completely regained Pearl's trust. And now she had seen this, when he knew exactly how she felt about his risk-taking.

Squaring his shoulders, he marched up to her, but when he went to take her hand she shook him off.

'You gave me the fright of my life. What were you thinking?'

What *had* he been thinking? Saying he'd done it for Max didn't sound very convincing. 'It seemed like a good idea at the time,' he said. 'Sorry I scared you but I couldn't lose face in front of the men.'

'Is that all you think about – how the other men think of you? They look up to you. You should be showing them a

248

good example, not casually throwing your life away over some ludicrous stunt.'

He knew she was right. The same thoughts had crossed his mind as he'd hung on to the branch for dear life. But his near miss had only heightened the adrenaline rush he was feeling, and he found himself snapping a retort before he could think of a sensible answer. 'No wonder Thea says you mollycoddle her too much. Is this how you treat all the people you love – like naughty children?'

'Who said anything about love? I didn't.' Pearl's eyes flashed. 'I was worried about you last night, but I accepted that you were doing your duty. I've spent the morning wondering if I could bear to carry on worrying each time you fly.' Her words were pouring out too fast for Greg to get a word in edgeways. All he could do was listen with a sense of growing shame.

'I even considered asking for a transfer,' Pearl raged, 'so I wouldn't know when you were flying ops and wouldn't spend every second of every hour terrified that something awful was happening and I didn't know. Then I decided there would be no point, because I would worry wherever I was, and at least being here I know as soon as you get back. And I accepted that I was going to have to live with the worry. Because it was the price I had to pay for... for... for caring.'

Loving. She had been about to say it was the price she had to pay for loving him, he was sure. She had paused for breath now, her face scarlet, but Greg was too stunned to speak. Anyway, what could he say in response? That he loved her too? The middle of a flaming row was hardly the best time to make that confession. All he could do was hug his aching ribs and wait for her to continue.

It didn't take long for her to recover her breath. 'And what do I get in return for caring, for worrying? You' – she stabbed his chest with a shaking index finger – 'you trying to break your neck. It's like you're deliberately putting yourself in danger. As though you *want* to be killed.'

He didn't even know what his response would be until it burst out. It was as though he stood outside himself, watching a stranger speak the words that poured from his mouth. He had no control over them, yet every word resonated like a death knell deep in his soul, and he knew them to be true. 'Maybe I do. Maybe I want to get it over with now so I don't have to dread it every single day. Maybe nothing in life is worth that.'

Pearl's shocked gasp acted like a slap to the face and brought him back to himself. All he could do was stand there, stunned, gazing at her white face. For a full ten seconds, neither uttered a word. Greg was too dazed to form a coherent sentence and he could see from her trembling lips that Pearl was struggling not to cry. She hugged her arms across her chest as though her ribs ached as much as his.

When she finally spoke, her voice was so quiet Greg had to strain to hear her over the hubbub of the station. 'Nothing? Not even me?'

This was where he should close the distance between them, take her in his arms and assure her that he cared for her. Loved her. But the words he had just spoken played in his mind on a continuous loop, rendering him speechless. *Maybe I do. Maybe I want to get it over with now so I don't have to dread it every single day. Maybe nothing in life is worth that. Maybe I do... maybe I do... maybe I do.*

Pearl couldn't tear her gaze from Greg. It felt as though a crushing weight was squeezing the air from her chest. Why didn't he answer? Did she mean nothing to him? She found she was clutching the fabric of her sleeve, and her fingers traced the outline of her propeller badge, feeling the scrape of each raised stitch. She was dimly aware of the sound of aero engines coming from the runway and the chatter of men and women as they strolled around the camp, but all the noise was muffled beneath a strange ringing in her ears.

Finally, when Greg's silence had stretched out to an unbearable degree, she had her answer. She drew a sobbing breath. 'I'm sorry. I can't go out with you any more if that's how you feel.'

The sound of her voice seemed to wake Greg from his daze. 'Pearl, I—'

But she cut across him in her need to get out the words before her throat became too tight to speak. 'No. Listen to me. I care for you and I hope we can stay friends. But I can't go out with you, not if you place so little value on your own life. It's bad enough seeing you fly off on a mission, but I won't stand by and watch you risk your neck needlessly. I deserve better than a man who has no regard for my feelings.'

Her voice cracked, and she turned away abruptly. Tears welled in her eyes, and she marched away on trembling legs. She mustn't let him see her cry, mustn't let him know how much she loved him. It was clear he didn't have deep feelings for her, and the last thing she wanted was his pity. The blood pounded in her ears. She thought he might be calling her name, but she couldn't afford to look back and let him see the pain it cost her to walk away.

She became aware that she was attracting concerned looks from the people she was storming past. It was only then that she felt the chill wetness of tears on her cheeks. Unable to face any questions, she hurried to the toilet block next door to the NAAFI. Once in the ladies', she rushed into a cubicle, slammed and bolted the door and then sank onto the seat.

To think she had nearly blurted out that she loved him. It was a good thing she had stopped herself, because she didn't want Greg to know how it broke her heart to finish with him. But as much as she loved him, she couldn't condone his reckless behaviour. Did he have so little regard for her heart? If he wouldn't take care for his own sake, she had hoped he would do it for her. By putting himself in unnecessary danger, he had proved he didn't love her at all.

Chapter Twenty-Four

'I still don't understand why you broke up with Greg,' Jenny said as they were walking to the Piebald Pony. 'You were so good together.'

It was a fortnight since Pearl had ended the relationship, and she missed Greg more than ever. That wasn't the point, though, and she tried explaining herself again. 'I told you why. He obviously didn't care enough for me if he could wilfully risk his life and put me through all that anxiety.'

'And I explained to you,' Thea said, 'that's how most of the aircrews react. He'd just got back from a mission where three of his crew were hurt. Don't you think he needed to let off steam? I saw the hole in *C-Charlie*'s fuselage, you know. If that shrapnel had hit a yard or two further back, it would have blown off the whole tail unit, and they'd all have been killed.'

'Don't tell me that! I don't want to know how close he came to death.'

'But you need to understand what it's like to go through that and come out the other side. I've been mixing with the bomber crews ever since I was posted to an operational unit, and I see the state the aircraft come back in. Yet if I ask them about it, they brush it off with a joke. Probably because they can't let themselves think about it too closely. These daredevil stunts are all about them proving to themselves that they're still alive.'

'Thea's got a point,' Jenny said. 'I read a psychology book a month or two back that I borrowed from Mr Haughton.' She pronounced the ch in psychology as in 'church', but Pearl let it pass. 'And from what I read, some of them might do mad dangerous stunts because they're not in control of what happens to them on a mission, so their high-jinks are all about doing something daring that they *do* have control over. Or even proving to themselves that they're brave enough to do something dangerous when they have a choice.'

'Maybe you're right.' Pearl could see the logic in what both Thea and Jenny were saying. 'But it doesn't make it any easier for me. I did the right thing.' Even if it did mean crying herself to sleep most nights.

'And do you feel any better now you're not seeing him any more?' Thea asked.

Pearl was saved from answering because they had arrived at the pub, and she pretended she hadn't heard over the noise from the public bar. Pausing before going through to the quieter snug, her heart twisted when her glance fell on Greg, in the crowded bar. He was with his crewmates, although she was relieved to see he was just talking and not balancing on anyone's shoulders this time. The answer to Thea's question was that no, she didn't feel better. She hadn't stopped worrying just because she was no longer seeing him. But the fact remained that she couldn't trust him with her heart. Not if he wouldn't take care of himself.

Thea stopped short when they entered the snug. 'The decorations are up. I'd forgotten it's nearly Christmas.'

Pearl looked around, admiring the effort Norah Brumby had taken to make the snug look festive. Colourful paper chains festooned the bar and the ceiling, and little foil stars dangled from the beams. 'How pretty. I'd forgotten too.' The continuing mild weather hadn't made her feel much like celebrating, meaning as it did that operations continued flying. 'You two find a table. I'll get the drinks.'

Norah was serving at the bar, and spoke before Pearl could give her order. 'Glad to see you here. There's a couple of women asking for Greg Tallis. I've been that busy, I haven't had a moment to slip into the public bar to let him know.' Norah pointed out two women sitting at a table by the fire. Neither were in uniform. One looked to be about Pearl's age and had brown, wavy hair. The other was younger and had reddened eyes, as though she had recently been crying.

Pearl's heart sank. Clearly Norah hadn't heard that she and Greg had split up. She couldn't imagine what the two women wanted with him, though, and her curiosity got the better of her. 'I'll have a quick word with them and tell Greg if it's anything important.'

Once she'd paid for her drinks, she took them over to where Thea and Jenny were waiting. 'I'll be back in a minute,' she said. 'Apparently those women over there have been asking for Greg. I'd better go and see what they want.'

'Absolutely,' Thea said. 'Stake your claim on Greg before they can get their claws into him. I knew you cared about him really.'

Ignoring her, Pearl went over to the fireside table. 'Excuse me, but the landlady said you were looking for Greg Tallis. I'm Pearl Cooper, a… a friend of his.'

The brown-haired woman glanced up. 'Pearl Cooper? Aren't you the one who helped Flight Sergeant Tallis recover my brother's watch?'

Pearl sat down on the nearest chair with a bump. 'Oh, are you Max Turner's sister? Yes, that was me.'

'I can't thank you enough for what you did. I'm Beatrice Little, by the way.'

'Is that why you're here – to thank Greg and me in person?' Pearl thought it a little odd. Beatrice had thanked them both by letter and, since people were being urged not to make unnecessary journeys, coming all this way to repeat thanks already sent by letter seemed over the top.

'No. It's something else.' Beatrice indicated the woman she was sitting with. She looked to be in her early twenties. Although she was dressed in a pretty frock, and from her neatly waved chestnut hair and carefully applied lipstick she evidently took care of her appearance, Pearl noticed that her finger-nails were ragged and her hands chapped and callused. 'This is Felicity Nugent. She's the sister of Harry Nugent, who was a gunner in *P-Peter*, one of the Lancasters in the same squadron as Greg.'

'*P-Peter*?' Pearl frowned. 'Didn't that—'

'It crashed, yes,' Felicity said. Her voice sounded a little hoarse, as though from crying.

'I'm so sorry. Did you come here to meet the people who knew him? I never met him myself, I'm afraid.'

It was Beatrice who answered. 'Felicity's got a story that will interest you. I can tell you most of it, though.'

Pearl glanced round to catch Thea and Jenny's eyes and signalled that she would be some time. It saddened her to see a space around Thea. Pearl distinctly saw one WAAF speak behind her hand to another, and they both moved a little farther away from Thea. Although the snug was busy, no one came to claim one of the empty seats at their table.

Pearl turned back to the two women at her table. 'Go on, then.' She had a feeling their tale would be to do with the theft of Max's watch, and, considering Thea was now a suspect in many people's eyes, it was best to keep her out of it.

Beatrice took up the story. 'First of all, I do want to thank you in person for going out of your way to find Max's watch. It means more than I can express to know I have something of his that I can give to my little boy. Oh. I nearly forgot.' She reached into her handbag and pulled out the jewelled pin. 'Greg Tallis sent this to me. It *was* Max's but he told me Max had given it to a girl he was keen on. I think she should have it back.'

'That was my sister, Thea.' Pearl concluded that Greg couldn't have told Beatrice of his suspicions, and she was grateful for that. It was reassuring to know that he had played no part in the general shunning of her sister. Ironic, too, that Beatrice and Greg now seemed to trust Thea more than Pearl did. For Pearl couldn't forget how she had been suspicious when

Thea had disappeared the night they had been waiting for the bombers to return. She was glad no one had reported anything missing from their lockers that night, or she would have been in a terrible quandary whether to report Thea's actions. As it was, she could keep silent with a clear conscience.

Beatrice handed the pin to Pearl. 'Will you give it back, please? Tell her I'm sorry for getting her into trouble.'

Pearl tucked the pin into her purse. 'Of course. What else did you want to say?'

'Well, Felicity here is a Land Girl, working on a farm not far from where I live. My local church held a memorial service last Sunday for all those who'd lost a loved one in the war, and that's where I met her.'

Felicity leaned forward. 'We got chatting after the service, you see, and it turned out that we both had brothers who had been at RAF Fenthorpe. The service was the first time I'd met Beatrice, or we might have discovered our connection earlier. Anyway, we got chatting about our brothers and—' Felicity's voice broke, and she signalled to Beatrice to carry on.

'It's like this,' Beatrice said. 'Felicity was upset because she'd just got her brother's belongings returned to her.'

Pearl could see where the tale was going. 'Don't tell me. There were some valuables missing.'

Felicity nodded, dabbing her eyes with a dainty lace-trimmed handkerchief.

'She had some leave coming up,' Beatrice carried on, 'so I persuaded her to come up to Lincoln with me for a few days so we could try to speak to Flight Sergeant Tallis. He was so helpful last time that I thought he ought to know.'

Pearl swallowed. 'What's missing?' This was the last thing she wanted to hear. Valuables going missing on a night when she had witnessed Thea emerge from somewhere near the locker rooms. Even as the thought crossed her mind, she hated herself for suspecting her sister.

Felicity, who was a little recovered, took over. 'There were a couple of items I missed. I know he had them because they were gifts from me and, as we only had each other after our parents died, he would never have given them away. There was a silver cigarette case and a fountain pen. Also I think there was some money stolen, although I couldn't swear to that, not knowing if he spent it, but he was saving up to buy a motorbike and I don't think he would have spent the money without good reason.'

'How awful,' Pearl said. She pulled a pencil and her note-book from her pocket. 'I don't think we'll be able to do anything about the money, but we can look out for the other items. Please can you describe them? Did they have any initials engraved? That would help us identify them.'

Felicity shook her head, dabbing her eyes again. 'No initials. I wish I'd thought of that now. But the cigarette case was engraved with a crescent moon and stars in one corner.' She sniffed. 'I chose it because I knew he flew mostly at night. The fountain pen was a Mentmore lever-filling pen in black and gold marble.'

Pearl jotted down the description with a heavy heart. There was nothing special about the pen apart from its sentimental value to Felicity. If she saw one, she would have no way of telling if it was the one that had belonged to Harry Nugent. 'Where did you get the cigarette case? I mean was it something that was unique, or were there other cases the same in the shop where you bought it?'

'From an antique shop in Cambridge. It was the only one of its kind in the shop, although I've no idea if there are others the same.'

'Still, it's a start,' Pearl said. 'We'll have more luck identifying that as Harry's than the fountain pen, although if we were to find both in the same place it would be very suspicious.'

Felicity tucked her hanky up her sleeve, looking recovered and determined. 'Will you help, then? To be honest, until I spoke to Beatrice I just thought that someone on the base had taken them as a keepsake, and I wasn't too upset. Neither the pen nor the cigarette case were valuable, and I thought one of

Harry's friends was welcome to them. But when I met Beatrice and heard her story, that's when I thought Harry's things might have been stolen too. And that made me angry, that some unscrupulous person is benefitting from Harry's death.'

Pearl patted Felicity's hand. 'I'll do what I can. You have my word.'

'What about Greg Tallis – will he help? He was so good to me last time, when the authorities had dismissed my complaint as hysterical nonsense,' Beatrice said.

Pearl hesitated. Part of her was tempted to keep this to herself. It would make a great story for the *Bombshell*, after all. But then the thought occurred that if she didn't involve Greg, he would be angry and disappointed when he found out what she had kept from him. What was more, she couldn't forget what Greg had said about feeling as responsible for his crew as she felt for Thea. If it turned out that Harry's things had been stolen, there was a good chance they had been taken by the same person who had stolen Max's watch. It would be wrong to exclude him.

She rose. 'I'm sure he would want to be involved. I saw him in the public bar as I came in, so I'll see if I can fetch him.'

It would be awkward and painful to be with him again, but that was no reason to keep him in the dark.

–

Greg stood watching the group who were writing yet more names on the ceiling. If Fenthorpe lost many more bomber crews, Norah Brumby would have to extend the public bar, because they were running out of space on the ceiling. He hadn't felt like joining in with the performance this time. It was enough to simply drink the health of the seven men who hadn't returned from last night's mission. The ironic thing was, it hadn't even been a bombing mission but a leaflet drop. These were usually done by crews in the operational training units, not fully fledged bomber crews, as leaflet drops were seen as routine and a good way of preparing for bombing runs. But the crew of S-*Stanley* was inexperienced, and, as there had been another lull in longer bombing missions, it had been felt that the crew needed more practice. It had been a routine run until the Lancaster had iced up. The pilot had dived to dislodge the ice, but S-*Stanley* had gone into a spin from which the pilot had been unable to recover. And now the young crew were nothing more than names on the ceiling. Greg couldn't even remember what any of them had looked like.

He sipped his pint, his thoughts inevitably turning to Pearl and her devastated expression when he had spoken those terrible words. He felt sick every time he remembered them, not because of their brutality but because he recognised their truth, that he could no longer bear the dread of waiting for death.

Maybe nothing in life is worth that.

Nothing? Not even me?

Her words had broken his heart, yet he had said nothing. He'd let her walk away. He had avoided her since the break-up, even to the extent of missing editorial meetings. He had still written a contribution for the next edition, but had sent it via Corporal Yates. He felt Pearl's absence keenly, missing her calming presence when he was off duty. It had always helped him avoid dwelling on hairy moments from his recent missions when she was with him.

A hand tapped his shoulder. He spun round, expecting to see one of his crew. Instead he came face to face with Pearl. Unprepared for the sudden pain of seeing her, he lashed out. 'Come to tell me off for encouraging dangerous behaviour? It must be bad if it makes you step foot in the public bar.' Already the presence of a woman was attracting attention, and there were one or two whistles.

She shook her head, flushing. 'Beatrice Little is here,' she said. 'She's brought a friend who's got news of more thefts.'

He forgot his hurt and confusion. If there was any chance of finding out who had stolen Max's watch, he would do all in his power to catch the culprit. 'Lead on.' He automatically reached out to take her hand, then recollected himself and let his hand fall to his side. Fighting down a fresh wave of pain, he followed Pearl into the snug.

The introductions to Felicity and Beatrice were quickly made, and he listened to Felicity's tale with a growing conviction that there was, indeed, a persistent thief in the station. 'I'm sorry this has happened to you,' he told Felicity. 'I will do everything I can to recover the cigarette case and pen, although the money will probably be gone for good.' He remembered Steve, then, and the lost money that should have gone to his fiancée, and wondered if the thief hadn't learned his lesson from the watch and was now stealing items that would be harder to trace. There were untold numbers of Mentmore pens around, and the cigarette case, although more unusual, probably wasn't unique. Even if they were found, would they be able to prove they were Harry's?

He questioned Felicity closely about the cigarette case and pen, hoping to uncover a detail that would help him identify them. The only possible identifying mark was a scratch on the back of the cigarette case, caused when Harry had been scrambling up a rocky hillside while on holiday and the case had dropped from his pocket.

'Do say you'll help us find his things.' Felicity turned pleading eyes upon him. 'Harry was my last close relative, and I would like to have something to remember him by.'

Greg couldn't refuse such a plea, even though it would mean working more closely with Pearl again, for he knew her too well to expect her to turn away from the investigation. She would want to be in on the story so she could write it up for the *Bombshell*. Anyway, he couldn't help hoping that spending time with her would give him the opportunity to show her he was the right man for her. 'I can't promise anything,' he told Felicity, 'but of course I'll look into it.'

Felicity and Beatrice thanked him profusely, then soon afterwards excused themselves, leaving Greg alone with Pearl. A long moment of silence stretched out between them, then Pearl said, 'Thank you for agreeing to help. That was kind.' She sounded stiff and formal, like a little girl thanking an elderly relative for inviting her to tea. Nothing like the Pearl who had spoken to him for hours, pouring out her heart about her ambitions and her worries about Thea.

'I'm glad you asked me,' he said. 'If there's any chance of finding the bastard who stole Max's watch, I want to be there when they catch him.' He wasn't surprised to see Pearl had her notebook open on the table. 'Did Beatrice or Felicity tell you anything they didn't mention to me?'

Pearl read through her notes, tapping her pencil against her lips. He wished she wouldn't do that; it reminded him all too strongly of how soft and kissable those lips were and sparked a line of thought that didn't help with the investigation at all. 'I don't think so,' she said finally. 'I didn't speak with them for long before coming to find you.' She flicked back through her notes. 'I suppose it's worth thinking about whether there *is* a connection between this theft and the theft of Max's watch.'

'And don't forget Steve Jonas's money.'

Pearl frowned. 'I remember you mentioning it but I don't think I wrote anything down about it. Maybe because it was money that went missing instead of a valuable item like a watch or a pen.'

Greg repeated what he remembered from that case. 'I only wondered if there was any connection with the other thefts because the money went missing from a locker.'

Pearl scribbled some notes about this other theft, then read them through. 'Funny how the thefts are confined to men who have been killed. In each case we've only found out because a relative has missed items from the returned belongings. Are you sure no one in your crew has ever mentioned having anything stolen?'

'I'm sure. You're right. It *is* strange. It could be the thief strikes when he hears about a death from the returning crews.'

He tapped his fingers on the table as he ran through a list of the people who would be the first to hear. 'There are the ambulance crews, of course, but they're too busy dealing with the injured and dying and they would notice if one of their number suddenly slipped away. The WAAF drivers would also be among the first to know.'

'But I was watching them the other night,' Pearl said, 'and they were too busy driving back and forth for one of them to slip into the locker room.'

Greg grimaced; he didn't want to make the next suggestion. 'There are the ground crews. They're generally there to meet their plane when it returns.' He hated to think any member of the ground crew was involved. They worked all hours of the day and night to keep the Lancasters in tip-top condition. Greg knew his life depended on them. He couldn't bear to think of any of them turning against the bomber crews for their own gain.

Pearl's face lost some of its colour. She looked as though she was about to say something, but stopped.

'What is it?' Greg asked.

She shook her head.

'Seriously, Pearl, anything you can think of would be helpful.'

'It's probably not relevant.' But her face said otherwise. Greg said nothing, but pinned her with his gaze and waited. Her hands were clasped over the notebook and she twisted them in a way that was most unlike her.

'Just spit it out, Pearl. Whatever it is can't be that bad.'

'But it might be.' Pearl's voice was barely above a whisper. 'You know I was volunteering with the WAAFs making tea the night *P-Peter* crashed? Well, Thea was there too, and she disappeared for a while.'

Greg listened while Pearl described the circumstances.

'I was so cross with you when you accused Thea of stealing Max's tiepin, but now I'm worried you were right,' she said at the end. 'What if I'm blinded to the signs because she's my sister?'

Greg knew what a big admission this was for Pearl. But even though he didn't know how to win back her heart, at least he could put her mind at rest. 'I know how difficult it must have been for you to have said that.' He glanced across the room to where Jenny and Thea were sitting. Alone. As though there was a quarantine zone around them. 'And I know I expressed my doubts about her before, but I really don't think Thea is involved. I'm sorry if I put any doubt in your mind.'

Pearl shook her head. 'It wasn't you. But Thea said she often waits up for the crews, and she's on the ground crew, after all. That's two groups of people who hear of any fatalities before most others.'

Greg wished he could take Pearl's hands between his own and still their fidgeting. But he did his best to reassure her. 'The night *P-Peter* was lost, we didn't have confirmation until some time after I got back. Yet you said she disappeared before the first crews returned. She couldn't have known then that Harry wasn't coming back.'

Pearl felt as though a lead weight had fallen from her chest. 'Of course. You're right. I wasn't thinking straight.' She had allowed her fear to get the better of her common sense. 'Although by your reasoning, I don't see how *anyone* had the opportunity to steal Harry's things. We only knew he wouldn't return after all the other Lancasters had returned, and by that time there would surely have been men in and out of the locker room. And I'm sure when you told me about Max, you said the Committee of Adjustment removed belongings from his locker very soon after he was reported dead.'

She saw the blaze of understanding flare in Greg's eyes. 'You're a genius. Of course.'

For the briefest of moments she thought he would lean across the table to kiss her. If she was being totally honest with herself, she wouldn't have pushed him away. Her treacherous body had even leaned towards him. She tried to disguise it by reaching for her notebook. 'Are you going to share your revelation with me?'

'It's the Committee of Adjustment. It explains everything. It explains why only dead crew members are having items stolen, and it explains why we never see anyone breaking into a locker. A member of the committee is stealing from dead crewmen. I saw one of them empty Max's locker not long after we got back from that mission. I'm a complete drongo for not thinking of it before.'

He was gabbling in his excitement, his Australian accent broader than ever. Pearl thought she could follow what he meant, though. 'Do you mean the person who officially empties the locker is the one who is stealing things?'

'Possibly. It would certainly be easy for that person to slip items into his pocket before taking them to be listed and packed up. But it's not necessarily that person. It's also possible that whoever's responsible for itemising everything is then leaving any item that strikes their fancy off the list and keeping it for themselves. The person who empties the locker probably wouldn't check the itemised list – and even if he did, who's to say if he'd remember everything he removed.' Greg grimaced. 'Not when they have so many other men's belongings to deal with.'

'I think you're right.' Pearl felt sick. 'How awful, though. The thief is benefitting from a man's death. He must be pleased when he hears of one of our Lancasters crashing. How vile is that?'

Greg's expression had gone rigid, and he barely seemed to be able to utter his next words. 'When I thought it was someone slipping into the locker room and breaking in… well, I thought that was bad enough. But this is so much worse. As you say, whoever it is must be actively *hoping* for one of us to be killed. It's despicable.'

'What do we do now?'

Greg turned his gaze on her, and his features softened. 'We?' There was no challenge in his tone. In fact there almost seemed to be a note of hope, and Pearl felt a flutter in her insides.

'I want to help in any way I can,' she replied. Then she hardened her heart. It would be cruel to let him believe there was a chance of winning her back. Although Greg had been the one to declare Thea innocent, there was still the matter of his reckless behaviour. Nothing had changed, even though she missed him terribly. She must be strong and remember that getting back together with him now wouldn't solve anything, not when he insisted on risking his neck needlessly. Although she hated herself for what she was about to say, she had to make it clear that she no longer had feelings for him. Even if that was a lie.

'This is huge news. Probably the biggest story we'll ever cover in Fenthorpe, and I want to publish it as soon as we've got the culprit. Don't you dare leave me out of this.'

Chapter Twenty-Five

The light went out of his eyes, and Pearl felt like the meanest being that had ever lived. The only thing that prevented her from throwing herself into his arms and begging forgiveness was the knowledge that she was being cruel to be kind. It was best for them both in the long run.

Then Greg pulled himself upright, straightening his shoulders. 'Don't worry. You'll get your story, and I could use your help.' Only someone who knew him as well as Pearl would have noticed that his cheerful tone sounded a little off. 'What about Jenny and Thea, do you want to include them too?'

Pearl considered it. 'Do you think we can handle it just the two of us? I'd like to keep Thea out of it if possible. She's being given a really hard time, and I don't want there to be any suspicion that she was involved. If she's part of the group that exposes the thief, people might say she covered up any evidence that implicated her.'

Greg gave a half-smile. 'Still protecting her, I see.'

'I don't think I'll ever stop, although I know I need to stop smothering her. But I think there's good reason to keep her out of this, don't you?'

'Yes, I think you're right.' Greg tapped his fingers on the table for a while, looking thoughtful. Yet some of the lines of stress around his mouth and eyes had eased, making him look more like the young, carefree man Pearl had got to know than the man burdened with responsibility that he had become over these past months. 'I think this has to be our course of action. First I must tell the police, even though they haven't listened in the past. If we don't say anything and then find definite evidence pointing to the criminal, they're going to want to know why we kept silent.'

'I suppose you're right. What next?'

'I don't know all the people who are on the Committee of Adjustment. Our next step has to be to find out exactly who is on it and who had access to the missing items.'

'I can do that.' Pearl felt a spark of excitement. Here at last was something she could investigate. 'We've been running a Day in the Life item in each edition of the *Bombshell*, so why not write about someone on the Committee of Adjustment?'

'Good idea. Flying Officer Sheldrick oversees the committee. You could ask him.' Greg's eyes twinkled. 'That'll be fun for you. He's so full of his own self-importance, he'll be falling over himself to tell you all about his vital work.'

'I didn't realise the adjutant did that, but it makes sense.' Pearl jotted down Sheldrick's name, then looked up. 'Actually, I should probably approach it by asking to interview him as station adjutant. Then I can mention his committee work in passing rather than focusing on it. You know how touchy the senior officers are about running articles that might lower station morale.'

'True. I don't suppose they'd be keen for us to dwell on a role that involves going through the personal possessions of dead people.'

'I'm jolly well writing about catching our thief once we find him, though. If anything's affecting morale, it's the knowledge that someone's making a profit from others' deaths.'

Greg nodded. 'I'll support you all the way if anyone kicks up a fuss. Right. So once we know who's on the committee, we need to keep an eye on them to see if any of them are acting suspicious.'

Was it wrong to be looking forward to that? Pearl had always thought of herself as cautious, but the prospect of spying on people didn't make her nervous. Instead it gave her a thrill.

She was starting to understand why Greg liked taking risks. Maybe she had spent so much of her time caring for Thea while growing up that she had squashed her fun-loving side. Maybe the reason she objected so much to Greg's daring nature was that it called to a side of her that frightened her. But perhaps it was time to embrace that aspect of her nature rather than flee from it.

There was no time like the present. The next morning Pearl had some free time so, notebook in hand, she marched into the administration block and knocked on the adjutant's door.

Flying Officer Sheldrick seemed absurdly pleased to be interviewed about his job. He puffed out his chest and waved Pearl into a seat. 'Everyone sings the praises of the Lancaster crews and the mechanics,' he told her, 'but no one realises the work that goes into the efficient running of the teams that get them into the air in the first place.'

Pearl bit back a smile and pretended to write something in her notebook. She sensed injured pride in Sheldrick, and knew she would have to flatter him if she wanted to get him to speak more openly about the Committee of Adjustment. As an opener, she decided to ask about his background. 'I know station adjutants are usually' – she sifted through appropriate descriptions in her mind, discarding 'older' and 'unfit for active service' before hitting on the right phrase – 'more experienced officers. Tell me about your service in the RAF. As a career officer, you must bring a wealth of experience to your job.'

Sheldrick settled back in his chair with an air of satisfaction. 'Yes, I joined the RAF in the early thirties. My father wasn't pleased at all – he'd wanted me to run the family business – but I wanted to serve my country. Do something more important with my life than rummaging around auction houses, you know?'

Because she knew he expected praise at this point, Pearl murmured, 'An admirable sentiment. What drew you to the administration side of the RAF?'

'Well, I didn't start out in admin. When I joined I wanted to be a pilot, and I was accepted into the pilot training programme. But I injured myself, riding a bicycle of all things, halfway into the course and hurt my back. The medical officer wouldn't pass me fit to fly after that, but I wanted to stay in the RAF, so I accepted an administrative role.'

'I'm sorry to hear about your accident.'

'It was a blow at the time, but I'm happy doing what I can to support our brave pilots.' Yet there was something in his expression that belied his words. A slight turning down of his mouth that told Pearl he wasn't at all happy with his lot in life. It probably explained why he was so officious and demanded respect from the NCOs, especially those who were members of the bomber crews, when the other officers seemed more relaxed.

'Tell me about the work you do. Our readers will want to know what a typical day is like for you, especially a day when we are flying operations.'

Sheldrick was clearly enjoying himself. He described how he was responsible for the administration side of the entire station. From the way he described it, the place would fall apart without him.

After letting him rattle on for some time, Pearl decided it was time to steer the conversation to his role on the Committee of Adjustment. 'It certainly sounds as though you do an excellent job supplying the teams taking care of all the Lancasters. It must be particularly painful when we lose one.' She chose her words carefully.

Sheldrick's features arranged into an expression of gloom. Pearl wasn't convinced it was genuine. 'It's very sad, of course. And it all makes more work for me. We have to bring in new crews, new Lancasters.'

'I suppose there must be a great deal of administration around the dead or missing crew members too,' Pearl prodded.

'Oh yes. We have to inform the correct people so that the families are notified. Then we have to make way for the incoming crews. I heard a story about new aircrews arriving on a Bomber Command station who found their billets were still full of dead men's kit. It was most upsetting for all concerned.'

Pearl seized the opening. 'I'd never thought of that. How do you stop that from happening?'

Sheldrick's chest swelled. 'It's one of our most important tasks, although no one involved likes to speak of it.'

'I'll be sure to give it a mention in the article,' Pearl assured him. 'This is the kind of background information that people want to read.'

Sheldrick looked pleased. 'Well, all the work involved around removing dead crewmen's belongings and returning everything to the families is undertaken by the Committee of Adjustment, which I head up. It's a very responsible task, which I take seriously. I make sure to remain contactable from the moment our Lancasters take to the skies so that, as soon as we learn of a loss, I can step into action.' He went on to outline the duties that Pearl already knew went on behind the scenes, describing how he oversaw the emptying of lockers and the clearing of billets, sifting through belongings to ensure nothing unsuitable was returned to families. Although he didn't specify what was meant by 'unsuitable', Pearl guessed it was things like pin-ups of scantily clad women or letters from a girlfriend being sent to a dead pilot's wife. Finally an inventory of all remaining items was drawn up and sent to the family together with the possessions. Pearl noted everything down in her rapid shorthand, then for the sake of appearances asked a few more general questions about Sheldrick's role, then some questions about his background, explaining that it was to give her article more depth.

Finally she thanked Sheldrick and left. One idea was forming in her mind, and she wanted to talk it over with someone.

Ideally she wanted to discuss it with Greg, and, as Fenthorpe currently lay under a blanket of fog, she had good reason to think he wouldn't be flying that day. In the event, she found him talking to Jenny in the NAAFI. It was something of a relief to see Jenny there as well, for she was finding it increasingly difficult to pretend that she didn't hurt every time she saw Greg. Spending time alone with him was an agonising reminder of the good times they had had together.

'Did you speak to Sheldrick?' Greg asked when she took a seat beside Jenny. She had opted to sit opposite him, not wishing to brush against him accidentally. Unfortunately, sitting opposite him meant she was looking directly at him, and that was equally uncomfortable.

All she could do was try to act as though she wasn't bothered and focus on her task. 'I did,' she replied. She had explained the situation to Jenny when they had been alone in Hut Three, so there was no need to fill her in.

'And did you find out exactly who's on the committee?'

'Yes, but while I was talking to Sheldrick I started to get the feeling the other committee members aren't important.'

'Why – do you think Sheldrick's the culprit?' Greg didn't look convinced.

'I know it sounds unlikely but hear me out.' She opened her notebook and consulted it to make sure she got her facts right. 'Sheldrick oversees the whole business of the Committee of Adjustments, so if someone else is stealing and he doesn't realise then he's not doing his job properly.'

'Look, Sheldrick's a pompous fool. No one likes him; but I don't seeing him stooping to theft.'

Pearl gave an impatient shake of the head. 'If I've understood him, he's not stealing because he needs the money but because he feels he's been cheated. He told me he had an accident when he was doing pilot training that meant he couldn't fly. He made a few comments about how the bomber crews are getting all the praise. I think he resents that when he's just seen as a laughing stock.'

'He's not a laughing stock because of the job he does but because of the way he acts.'

'I know that, but I doubt he does. Anyway, looking at how the committee works, he has by far the best opportunity to steal the goods. He often empties the lockers himself and, even if he doesn't, he's in a position to alter the inventory if necessary. And there's one other thing.'

'What?' Both Greg and Jenny had picked up Pearl's enthusiasm and their gazes were locked on her.

'At the beginning of the interview, he mentioned not wanting to work in his father's business because he wasn't interested in hanging around auction houses. That nagged at me all the way through the interview until I realised why right at the end. Before I left I asked what the family business was.'

Jenny had clearly seen the light, for she clapped her hands. 'Don't tell me – that antiques dealer in Lincoln?'

'Got it in one.'

Greg was looking grim. 'If I'd known, I'd have stuck *him* at the top of that tree, not just his cap.'

Jenny looked from one to the other. 'What do we do now? Should we tell the police?'

Greg shook his head. 'No way. We don't have any proof. Now we know he must be getting rid of the goods in Lincoln, we need to keep an eye on the shop and wait for him to go there.'

Jenny rose. 'I'll go and hover outside the admin hut. He doesn't know me. It would look odd if he saw you there now he knows you.' She hurried out.

–

Once she had finished reporting her discoveries, it hit Pearl like a physical pain to realise there was no reason to carry on sitting with Greg. When they were still seeing each other, they could have stayed in the NAAFI and talked of nothing in particular, simply enjoying being together. As matters stood between them, though, it would have been awkward to linger, so Pearl muttered an excuse and headed out. She had the day off but, as the fog didn't look like it was going to shift, she didn't feel like going anywhere.

She had just decided to return to Hut Three to check her kit and do any mending that needed to be done when she had to step off the road to allow a truck to pass. Glancing into the cab out of idle interest, she froze when she saw none other than Flying Officer Sheldrick in the passenger seat. She knew instantly that Sheldrick must have left his office before Jenny had taken up her station. She was probably still there, watching the door, not knowing he wasn't inside.

Pearl watched the truck as it pulled to a halt at the gate, waiting until the guard had raised the barrier, then lurched out onto the road outside, turning towards Lincoln.

Lincoln. And a rear gunner had been killed yesterday. If Sheldrick had stolen any of his valuables, he might be taking them to the shop. She had to follow him, and there was only one way of doing that.

She raced back into the NAAFI and tore up to Greg's table. 'Greg, you've got to come with me now.' She pulled his sleeve.

'But I was going to have another drink.'

'There's no time!' Seeing she was attracting attention, she lowered her voice. 'I just saw Sheldrick leave the station, heading towards Lincoln. We have to follow on your motorcycle.'

Understanding dawned in his eyes and he grabbed his coat. As they hurried outside, he said, 'Good thing I was planning to go into Lincoln later. I parked the bike behind the NAAFI.'

But when they got to the place where the bike stood, Pearl stopped in dismay. 'You took the sidecar off.'

'Yes, well I didn't think you'd want to come.' The bitterness in his voice was clear. 'I'll have to go alone. I promise to give you a full report.'

'I won't be left behind.'

'Be reasonable, Pearl. By the time I've driven to the huts where I keep the sidecar, fixed it on, then come back here to pick you up, we'll never get to Lincoln in time to catch Sheldrick in the act.'

'Forget the sidecar. I'll ride pillion.'

Greg raised his eyebrows and swung into the saddle, muttering something that sounded like, 'It's your funeral.'

She could only hope he didn't mean that literally as she climbed up behind him. Her skirt rode up her thighs but she pulled her coat over her legs, hoping it would keep her decently covered. After that there was no more time to worry about how she looked, not when Greg had already kicked the bike into action and was heading towards the gate. After a brief stop to sign out, he called, 'Hold on!' and powered up the lane to Lincoln. All Pearl could do was cling to his waist and thank her lucky stars that she was wearing her thick lisle stockings and blackouts. At least they kept her halfway warm. And decent.

As they approached a bend in the road, Greg shouted over his shoulder, 'Lean into the bend. Don't go against it or you'll have us over.'

That was all the warning she got before he took the bend at speed, and the bike banked sharply. Even though she was used to riding a bicycle and so knew better than to lean the other way, she couldn't suppress a gasp of shock as the road rose to meet her. Then the motorbike returned to the perpendicular as they came out of the bend and they shot down the long, straight road ahead. The wind roared in her ears. Looking over Greg's shoulder, she saw the needle of the speedometer pass fifty and then nudge towards sixty miles per hour. Pearl wanted to yell at him to slow down, to take care in the fog, but she held back, knowing that this could be their only chance to catch Sheldrick in possession of stolen items. Greg had a pair of goggles, but there were none for her. She turned her face to the side to protect her streaming eyes as much as possible, pressing her cheek against his shoulder blades. From this angle, she watched the hedges whiz past, no more than a brown blur. Her senses were overwhelmed with the roar and vibration of the engine, the rush of the wind, the blur of the scenery and the rough texture of Greg's coat against her face. This was… was…

Actually, it was fun. She wasn't afraid. She trusted Greg as a driver and knew he wouldn't take any unnecessary risks, and for the first time she was allowing herself to enjoy the moment. She had never understood before how exhilarating riding a motorcycle could be, flying through the air with the speed and ease of a hawk, skimming the contours of the land. She should be cold and frightened, but she felt secure and warm where she was pressed to Greg's back.

When they entered Lincoln and Greg reduced speed, Pearl felt a keen sense of loss. She was no longer a bird of prey, at one with the air currents, but Pearl, a sensible WAAF who was going to get a dressing-down from some passing WAAF officer if she didn't straighten her hair and smooth the creases from her skirt. Once Greg had parked in a side street, she scrambled off the bike, pulled her skirt down to a decent length and combed her fingers through her tangled hair. Then she pulled her cap from inside her coat, where, thankfully, she had had the presence of mind to stow it before Greg had sped off, and put it on, tucking stray locks into it to keep them from dangling over her collar.

'Any idea what we're going to do if we see Sheldrick?' she said, trotting up the hill beside Greg.

He shrugged. 'Play it by ear. Let's go straight to the shop. If we're right, that's where we'll find him.'

They jogged up the street to Keyes's Emporium. When they got there, Greg peered in cautiously through the window. 'I can't see anyone, but they could be behind the cabinets.'

He went to push the door open but Pearl stopped him with a hand on his wrist. She tried to ignore the flare of longing at the simple touch. 'Wait. They'll hear the bell. If there's any chance Sheldrick's got any stolen items, we don't want to warn him.' The door was ajar, and she peered up through the narrow opening to look at the bell above it. 'I think I should be able to squeeze inside without it ringing.' She shrugged off her coat and handed it to Greg. Luckily they were the only people in the street, or they would be attracting curious stares by now. Speaking in an undertone, she said, 'It's a simple bell. I can unhook it, then let you in.'

Greg didn't look happy, so she said, 'Look, do you want to catch him or not?'

'Fine. But don't do anything stupid. Make sure you let me in straight away.'

She nodded and eased the door open until the gap was just wide enough to squeeze through. For a horrible moment one of her buttons caught on the catch. Gritting her teeth, she pushed harder until the button tore free, tinkling on the pavement. Then she was through. It was only then that she realised her mistake. She couldn't reach high enough to unhook the bell, so there was no way to let Greg in without it chiming a warning.

Whispering to him, she explained the situation. 'I'll have to go in alone. I'll shout if I need you.'

'Wait!'

But she ignored him and crept away from the door. She could hear voices coming from the rear of the shop, so, after a glance at Greg, who was frantically waving at her through the glass, she turned her back on him and inched towards the noise, being careful to keep the high display cabinets between her and whoever was speaking.

When she got closer, she could hear what the people were saying. It was a man and a woman. She definitely recognised Sheldrick's voice, and thought the woman was Mrs Keyes.

'That's not going to make us much money,' the woman was saying.

'It's all right for you.' Sheldrick's voice came through clearly, and there was a distinct whine to his tone. 'It's not you who's risking a court martial.'

'Maybe not, but at least you get good food in the officers' mess. It's weeks since I've been able to afford a decent cut of beef.'

'What happened to the money I brought you?'

'I needed a new coat, didn't I? I've got appearances to keep up. Are you sure you didn't bring anything else?'

'I told you. We can't try and sell any new stuff yet. The police were digging around after Tallis found that pocket watch here, and now you've sacked Bright we can't use him as a scapegoat. Keep your head down for a while until the fuss dies down, then I can get some more.'

'You wouldn't let your sister walk around in rags, would you?'

Pearl, edging forward, feeling as though her heart was trying to crawl out of her throat, heard Sheldrick sigh. 'Fine. Sell the cigarette case, then. If you want my advice, you'll sell it in Grantham in case anyone's keeping an eye on the shop here.'

Peering around a high cabinet, Pearl saw Sheldrick and Mrs Keyes standing in the little storeroom where Greg had found Max's watch. The door opened outwards, and Pearl had a clear view through the gap. Sheldrick held out his hand to Mrs Keyes, and there was a glint of silver in the palm.

She had seen enough. It was high time she got back to Greg before he took matters in his own hands. Recalling a stool she had seen not far from the door, she decided to collect that to stand on so she could remove the bell from its bracket.

That was when her luck ran out. Turning, she caught her elbow on the display cabinet, rattling the stacks of china cups inside.

'Who's there?'

Pearl saw Mrs Keyes's and Sheldrick's faces turned towards her. Recognition dawned in both expressions, and Sheldrick's face set in a snarl. 'Why, you little sneak!'

He took a step towards her, swinging his clenched fist behind his shoulder, clearly intending to punch her. Pearl acted without thinking. She darted forward and, before Sheldrick could get out of the storeroom, she reached the open door and tried to slam the pair inside. Sheldrick's body was in the way and, as she flung her weight against it, an arm flew out, striking her on the mouth. She tasted coppery blood but didn't give up the struggle, her feet skidding on the polished wooden floor as she leaned against the door, trying to push it closed.

'Greg, help!' she cried.

Before she'd even finished speaking, she heard the jaunty jingle of the bell and pounding feet behind her. 'Where are you?' Greg shouted.

'Here, by the storeroom.' Then he was beside her. 'They've got stolen items in there,' she gasped. Every word made her wince in pain from her cut lip. 'We need to lock them in.'

With Greg's help, she had no difficulty slamming the door. The key was in the lock, so Pearl turned it and then slumped to the ground with her back to the door. She pulled out her handkerchief and dabbed her mouth.

Greg sat beside her and took the hanky off her. 'You're going to have one hell of a bruise.' He gently dabbed the handkerchief around her mouth, the white cotton coming away red. She wanted nothing more than to lean against him and revel in his touch this one last time. For nothing had changed. She couldn't deny she was attracted to him; but he was still a daredevil, and, although the motorbike ride might have revealed a hitherto unknown enjoyment of riding at speed, she still couldn't accept the way he gambled with his life and her heart.

Chapter Twenty-Six

Pearl thought more about Greg in the days that followed than about her success in preventing more thefts or even about the *Bombshell*. Greg was praised for his actions in uncovering Sheldrick's actions, and there was even talk of him being commissioned. Pearl got a stern talking-to for putting herself in danger and a warning to sew the button back on her tunic.

'That's life in the WAAF,' Thea remarked when Pearl told her and Jenny what Section Officer Blatchford had said. 'Still, now you've managed to get yourself into trouble, I'm proud to call you my sister.'

'I might get into even more trouble,' Pearl said.

'How so?'

'Blatchford didn't want me to publish my story about the thefts. It's ridiculous – everyone's talking about it. Sheldrick's getting court-martialled, for goodness' sake. Blatchford thinks it'll be bad for morale, but I think we need to know the facts, not rumour.'

Thea's eyes were dancing. 'You're going to publish it?'

'You bet I am. It's the biggest story we'll ever have. I'll wait until the court martial is over so I can't be accused of trying to affect the outcome, but then I'm releasing the story and putting it on the front page.'

Thea leapt up and slapped Pearl on the back. 'Attagirl! We'll make a rebel of you yet.'

Pearl looked at Jenny, worried that she would disapprove. But Jenny was smiling. 'Good. I think morale is far more damaged by rumour.' She looked at Thea. 'I hope when everyone reads the truth they'll apologise for the way they've treated you.'

Thea shrugged, although Pearl thought her attitude of unconcern was feigned. 'The people that matter believed in me, and that's all I care about.' She raised her eyebrows at Pearl. 'Anyway, talking of people we care about, what's going on with Greg? Isn't it time you two got back together?'

Now it was Pearl's turn to shrug. 'Nothing's changed. We're better off as friends.'

Thea snorted. 'Friends, my foot! If you really believed that, you wouldn't be wandering around the place with a face like a sour prune.'

Pearl choked. 'Like a what?'

'You know what I mean. I've never seen you look so miserable. Except when you're looking at Greg, and then you go all misty-eyed. It's time you swallowed your pride and told him you've made a mistake.'

–

'Letter for you, Gramps. Looks like a woman's handwriting. Got an admirer?'

Greg dropped the book he'd been reading, swung his legs off his bunk and snatched the envelope from Fitz. It only took a glance for his heart to sink – it wasn't Pearl's handwriting. For a wild moment he had thought she might have written to beg his forgiveness. He slumped back onto his bed and opened the letter. It was short, and a quick glance at the bottom of the page showed him it was from Beatrice Little.

> *Dear Flight Sergeant Tallis,*
>   *When I saw you in Fenthorpe I didn't thank you properly for all your help, so I thought I would write to let you know how much I appreciate everything you did for me and Max. Thanks to you I've had Max's watch*

*returned, and I will keep it for my son until he is old
enough.*

*As glad as I am to have his watch back, the thing I
really wanted to tell you was how thankful I am for the
way you took care of Max when he was still alive. He
always spoke very highly of you and said how proud he
was to serve in your crew.*

*I have one last favour to ask of you. Please tell Thea
Cooper that I will always be grateful that she made Max's
last days happy. Even though she always made it clear
she couldn't return his feelings, Max never gave up hope
that she would have a change of heart, and cherished
every moment they spent together.*

Yours sincerely,
Beatrice Little

Greg read and reread the last paragraph several times. He had
always thought Max was foolish for pursuing Thea when she
had told him repeatedly that she didn't return his feelings. Now
he wondered if Max hadn't been the wise one. He had been
happiest when he was with Thea and so he had treasured every
moment he could spend with her, knowing each time he saw
her that it could be his last. Inevitably, Greg's thoughts wandered
to his own behaviour, how he had become so fixated on the
probability of his death in action that he couldn't enjoy the
present.

If Max were still alive, no doubt he would be making the
most of his time with Thea, not agonising over his fate. He
would be angry with Greg for throwing away his chance of
love, for not appreciating what he had.

What a fool he had been. Now he had to ask himself if he was
too late, if there was any chance of winning Pearl back. Because
he knew that if he did, he would treasure every moment he
could have with her.

Then he remembered the letter he had written before the
mission to Mannheim. He had written it never intending it to

be sent, but it explained his feelings and why he had held back from saying he loved her. Maybe that, together with his latest piece for the *Bombshell*, would help her understand. Grabbing his writing case from his locker, he found the letter that was still tucked inside. Then he settled down to complete his article, this time giving enough clues to make his identity clear.

–

Pearl was still thinking of Thea's advice when she was sitting in the classroom putting together the new year edition of the *Bombshell*, ready to send to Mr Haughton the next day. The dummy sheets were proving to be a problem, for she had set aside a column for Greg's mysterious friend, as Greg had assured her there would be another one. However, time was ticking by and Greg hadn't appeared. She hoped his friend wasn't going to let them down.

She had a romantic story in reserve for the space. It was one she had been hoping to save for the February edition, in honour of Valentine's Day, but it looked like she was going to have to use it now. She had her pencil poised over the story, about to mark it up for the linotype operator, when the door opened and Greg walked in.

'Am I in time?' he asked, handing her some paper.

'I… yes, thank you.' *Well done, Pearl. That's probably the most you've said to him since you caught Sheldrick. Ask him to wait. Tell him you need help with the layout. Anything to stop him from walking out of here.*

But the words stuck in her throat and she watched in silence as Greg gave her an awkward nod and then left the classroom, closing the door behind him. She gazed at the shut door for some time, wishing he would open it again and come back inside, but it remained stubbornly closed. Eventually she picked up the paper and began to read.

There are times I feel as old as my nickname suggests when I'm with my crew. They are so young and should have years ahead of them, yet they willingly risk their futures for the sake of their countries.

We all take our missions seriously, but when we are not flying I feel it my duty to give them a taste of the life they've sacrificed. They need to have fun. If there was no war, some of them would be at university, while others would be just starting out in new trades or professions. All of them would be getting their first taste of freedom and celebrating the end of each working week with their friends.

Some people shake their heads when they see us acting the fool, but I say let them have their fun. Let them cram a lifetime of happiness into a few short weeks or months. Because most of us won't get to experience the really important things in life. We won't grow old with the women we love. We won't hold our firstborn in our arms and feel the joy as he or she grips our finger for the very first time. We won't achieve the great work we dreamed of since childhood. We won't do any of these things. So while hanging the station adjutant's cap on the highest branch of a tree might seem foolhardy, it's something we can do to bring some lightness and laughter into our lives. Please indulge us and let us have our fun.

Pearl read it with tears in her eyes, until finally the words were too blurred to read more.

Then she noticed another piece of paper slipped behind the article. Thinking it must be a continuation of what she had just read, or possibly a different article, she glanced at it; then her heart sped up, when she saw it was a letter addressed to her, although it was dated three weeks ago.

My dearest Pearl,

I once saw a movie in which, on the evening before her marriage, the heroine says to her fiancé, 'After tonight, there will be no more goodbyes.'

I wish that could be true of us, Pearl. Every time I say goodbye to you I feel something break inside because I know it could be our final goodbye. I would love to have the assurance that there will be many more tomorrows for us, that I could promise you my time. Because until I can, I can't promise you my heart. I dare not think past the end of each day, let alone of a future with you. Sometimes I find myself slipping. Only yesterday I said I'd like to meet your grandmother, and it hurt so much when I remembered that we can't make plans like a normal couple. I think the reason I feel this way is because, only a week after I arrived here, I met a pilot who was near the end of his tour. He was kind to me and gave me some good advice, then went on to tell me about his girlfriend and how they were planning a holiday in Scotland as soon as he had completed his last mission. I'm sure you can guess what happened – his Manchester was last seen in a ball of flame over Kiel. Ever since then I've refused to make plans. Even something as simple as going to the cinema – something normal couples should be able to do without thinking twice – I will only commit to once we hear we're not flying that day.

So, my darling Pearl, I can say it here because I know I'll never show this to you. I love you and I wish you knew. Maybe one day I'll be able to tell you but until then, I can only take one day at a time.

All my love,

Greg

Now she knew beyond doubt that Greg was the author of these anonymous articles. She had been so wrong. Greg wasn't thoughtless. He wasn't even heedless of her heart. Like her, he felt his responsibility keenly; but, unlike her, that responsibility was justified. Thea had proved that she was able to take care of herself, even if Pearl didn't agree with the way she went about things sometimes, yet Pearl had refused to treat her like a grown-up. Greg, on the other hand, was right to put his crew first and right to allow them to let off steam when circumstances allowed.

Thea was right. She needed to swallow her pride and ask Greg's forgiveness, because Greg didn't have time to waste on a woman who had made it clear she didn't trust him with her heart.

Flinging down the paper, she ran out of the door and looked around frantically for Greg. There he was, on the path that led to the sergeants' mess. She took off at high speed, desperate to reach him before he disappeared inside.

'Greg!' she shouted, heedless of the curious stares she was attracting. She tore past Section Officer Blatchford without pausing to salute, knowing she would get in trouble for it later but not caring. Some things were more important than rules. 'Greg, wait!'

By this time he was at the top of the steps, right by the door. He reached for the handle, then paused and turned. When he saw her, he walked to the bottom of the steps and waited but made no further move to meet her.

'I'm so sorry,' she gasped when she got there. 'It was you, wasn't it? You're the one who wrote those articles.'

He nodded, his expression wary, as well it might be.

'I've been such an idiot,' Pearl told him. 'When I told you I couldn't trust you with my heart, I was only considering myself. I forgot you had a crew to take care of as well. You're right to put them above me.'

'No.' Greg closed the distance between them and put his hands on her upper arms. 'They're important but so are you. I was wrong too because I was so consumed with my responsibility for the crew, I forgot that if I wanted a relationship with you, I needed to put you first.'

'Do you still—?' Then Pearl stopped. As she had been the one to break off the relationship, if she wanted them to get back together she needed to be brave and make the first move. Until that point she hadn't been able to look him in the face. Now she lifted her gaze to meet his and took a steadying breath. 'I love you,' she said, and was rewarded by the dawning of pure joy in Greg's expression. She didn't give him a chance to speak, though, needing to make a full confession before she could let herself believe that he might want to try again. 'I've been missing you terribly ever since I finished with you, but I was too scared to admit I was wrong. Too scared to risk entrusting my heart to you when you put yourself in danger all the time. I think I was looking for an excuse to break up with you because I was terrified of getting my heart broken. I'm so sorry for all the hurt I caused you.'

Greg shook his head, blinking, then pulled Pearl into an embrace. 'I couldn't blame you. You were right. It was wrong of me to be so reckless, and you helped me see how my mind had become twisted by despair. I couldn't promise you a future. I still can't. What I can do is promise I won't throw my life away carelessly.' His words poured out almost incoherently, but Pearl understood his meaning beneath the muddle and thought her heart might burst from joy. 'I do love you,' he said, 'and if you're prepared to risk it, then I'll take whatever time we can have together. You give me hope, a reason to strive for life.'

Pearl wound her arms round his neck, scarcely able to believe Greg had said the words she had dreamed of hearing for so long. 'I love you too. I'm done with caution. I just want to spend all the time we can together.' She stood on tiptoe and kissed him, and felt all her fears melt away when he returned the embrace.

When he broke the kiss, he said, 'Do you mean it about being done with caution? Because I've got a suggestion.'

'I meant it with all of my heart.'

'Well then.' And before Pearl realised what he was about to do, he'd dropped to one knee and taken her hand. 'Pearl Cooper, will you marry me? I love you with all of my heart, and whatever time I have left I want to spend it with you.'

The tears that had never been far away rolled down her cheeks. 'Yes!' she cried, 'Where's the fun in always being sensible?' And she pulled him down into another kiss.

Until: 'Cooper!' It was a scandalised cry from Section Officer Blatchford. 'Cease this exhibition at once!'

Chapter Twenty-Seven

'I still can't believe you're getting married. I thought it was the sort of thing I'd be more likely to do.' Thea turned Pearl's hand this way and that, letting the light catch the opal and diamond ring Greg had bought her that afternoon from Fortescue and Sons. Pearl still hadn't tired of the thrill of seeing it on her finger, and gazed at it, admiring the blue fire deep within the opal. Greg had been pleased she had liked it, telling her Australia was famous for its opals, but it also reminded him of the lustre of a pearl.

The whole editorial team was gathered at Mr Haughton's house. It was a party Mr Haughton had arranged some time before, to celebrate the new year and the continued success of the *Bombshell*. Now they had not only Pearl and Greg's engagement to celebrate as well but also the publication of Pearl's story about the thefts.

For Sheldrick's court martial was now over, and he had been dishonourably discharged. The investigation by the RAF and civilian police revealed that Sheldrick and Mrs Keyes were brother and sister, and, when wartime austerity had started to bite, Mrs Keyes had talked her brother into taking advantage of his position. The investigation had revealed many relatives had missed items from their loved ones' returned belongings, but most had assumed the items had been lost or given away. If Greg and Pearl hadn't continued with their investigation, Sheldrick might have continued to steal. Pearl had published her article, being careful to phrase it in a way that praised the investigation and reassured people that it was the sterling work of the police that ensured the recovery of many of the stolen items. It had even received grudging praise from Section Officer Blatchford.

'Have you set a date yet?' Jenny asked.

'As soon as we can arrange it,' Pearl replied. 'We need permission, of course, and then we need to get leave at the same time, so it could take a while to organise. But I won't wait a moment longer than we have to.'

'You're starting to sound positively reckless,' Thea said with a grin. 'Suddenly *I* feel like the sensible one.'

'It's high time you took your turn,' Pearl told her.

'You're not going to leave the WAAF, are you?' Jenny looked anxious.

'Absolutely not. I love what I do and I wouldn't give it up for the world.' Although the WAAF allowed married women in its ranks, she would be required to leave if she got pregnant. Pearl and Greg had discussed it and decided the times were too uncertain for bringing a baby into the world. Pearl was also fully aware that she might be a widow before the war finished. If the worst happened, she wanted a job to give her some purpose in life and to keep her occupied.

'Speaking of your job,' Mr Haughton said, 'I'm expecting a visitor who has a very interesting offer for you. She won't be much longer.' He would say no more, but looked very pleased with himself. Pearl didn't have to contain her curiosity for long, for soon there came a knock on the door. She was all agog to see who the mysterious visitor was, but nearly choked on her tea when Mrs Stockwell showed Section Officer Blatchford into the room.

Pearl sprang to her feet. 'Section Officer Blatchford,' she gasped when she'd stopped coughing.

'At ease, Cooper.' Blatchford acknowledged the others with a nod. 'No, thank you, I won't stay long,' she said to Mrs Stockwell, who was trying to hand her a cup of tea. 'I won't spoil your celebrations. However, I wanted to inform you of a change in post, Cooper.'

'Me?' Pearl was dismayed. Was she being sent away from Fenthorpe as a punishment for printing the article about Sheldrick? The WAAF could post her anywhere, and if she was posted far from Greg she couldn't bear it.

'Don't look so worried. I think you'll like it. You might not realise it, but officers from the other RAF stations nearby have seen your newspaper and have been so impressed they've considered setting up similar ones for their own stations.'

'A few of the officers approached me for advice,' Mr Haughton added. 'I told them they needed you.'

'But I can't run more than one paper.' Pearl had visions of dashing from one Bomber Command station to the next while still trying to carry out her duties.

'You misunderstand us,' Blatchford said with a ghost of a smile. 'Mr Haughton proposed expanding the *Bombshell* to cover the other bases in 5 Group. He will still print it and we would like you to be chief editor. Mr Haughton will provide you with an office in Lincoln, and you will work with teams in the various Bomber Command stations to collect news items from them all. Does that sound like something you would like to do?'

'Oh yes!' Pearl felt as though she had been offered the world.

Blatchford nodded at Greg. 'I gather a commission for your fiancé is in the works, so you'll stay at Fenthorpe until you're married, then move into married quarters with Tallis.'

'You'll be my neighbours,' Mr Haughton told them, his eyes twinkling.

'That's marvellous. I can't thank you enough.' Pearl looked between Blatchford and Mr Haughton with smiling eyes.

Greg looked as though he was about to kiss Blatchford on the cheek, but obviously thought better of it. Instead he seized Mr Haughton's hand and shook it enthusiastically. 'Who'd have guessed the day we came to see you in Lincoln we were at the start of such a remarkable journey? Thank you.'

'Don't thank me. If you and Miss Cooper here hadn't impressed me so much, I'd have never offered my help. I can't wait to see what heights the *Bombshell* will reach now it's expanding.'

Section Officer Blatchford left soon after she'd secured Pearl's amazed thanks and acceptance of the job. A job, she was stunned to discover, that came with a promotion to corporal. The party took off after that, with everyone slapping Pearl on the back, raising toasts to her, the *Bombshell* and to the happy couple.

'I can't thank you enough,' Pearl said to everyone as the evening drew to a close. 'If it wasn't for all your hard work on the paper, this would never have happened. When I joined the WAAF, I was disillusioned and dispirited and had no idea I would find love and friendship in such abundance. It seems appropriate that we're celebrating a new start at the new year. So here's wishing us all a happy new year.'

'Happy new year,' everyone chanted in reply.

Pearl looked at her friends with tears in her eyes and wished them the same joy she had found, a joy that would give them the strength to face whatever trials and sorrows the war might fling their way. As her gaze settled on Greg, Thea, Jenny and Mr Haughton, her heart harboured a silent prayer that their bonds of love and friendship would see them all safely through the war.

Author's Note

RAF Bomber Command had one of the highest casualty rates of any Allied unit during the Second World War. Around 125,000 men served as aircrew – all volunteers – and over 55,500 of them were killed over Europe. In fact, only 30 per cent of them made it through the war without being killed, injured or captured.[1] Although the men wouldn't have known of these statistics at the time, of course, they would have known that their chances of surviving a tour of duty unscathed were low. Learning about this made me hesitate to set a series of novels on a Bomber Command station, considering I like to write heartwarming romantic fiction! However, while reading accounts written by the men and women who served in Bomber Command, I was constantly struck by their determination not only to do their duty to the best of their ability but also to squeeze as much living as possible into their off-duty hours. I have done my best to reflect both these attitudes in the story.

The Committee of Adjustment was an all too necessary part of life in Bomber Command, and during my research I found several accounts of men only learning that their friends had failed to return from a mission when they discovered that their huts had been stripped of the possessions of their former hut-mates. Sadly, stealing valuables from dead crewmen also happened, and caused such outrage that the matter was actually addressed in the House of Commons.

---

[1] Statistics taken from the International Bomber Command Centre website.

Finally, to prove that no research goes unwasted, the inspiration for the newspaper thread of the story came when I was in Orkney, researching the Wrens series. Having read about a newspaper set up for the servicemen and women based in Orkney during the war, I spent a very happy day in the Orkney archives in Kirkwall, scrolling through all the back issues in search of snippets of information to include in the Wrens books. Very few items actually made it into the stories, but the idea of a newspaper for servicemen and women refused to leave me and, when I decided to set my next series in a fictional Bomber Command station in Lincolnshire, I knew I had to include my heroine starting up a newspaper. Calling it the *Bombshell* is a nod to the name of the Orkney newspaper – the *Orkney Blast*.

Acknowledgements

Thank you to all my friends and family who have encouraged me and kept me going in the months it has taken me to write and edit this book. I want to give an especial mention to all in the RNA Cariad Chapter for their warm welcome and the motivation I always get from our monthly Zoom get-togethers.

Researching a new subject can be daunting but, thanks to the very helpful staff at the Imperial War Museum research room, I found out far more than I'd thought possible about the life of an R/T operator in Bomber Command. The International Bomber Command Centre in Lincoln also proved invaluable and, thanks to their superb digital archive, I now have inspiration for about twenty books!

As ever, huge thanks to my agent, Lina Langlee, and to Emily Bedford, my editor at Canelo, for all their hard work and encouragement. Here's hoping we'll have many more celebrations like the one in March!